Feathered
Serpent
Press

In the Time of the Feathered Serpent

Published by Feathered Serpent Press
1812 Mayfair Dr.
Omaha, NE 68144

ISBN: 978-1-7345949-0-4

First Edition: May 2020

Printed in the United States of America

Thanks!

"In the Time of the Feathered Serpent" would not have been completed without the advice and assistance of many people. Foremost is Valerie, my wife of 40 years. Her intellect, encouragement, and ideas have always sustained me when I doubted myself. She labored tirelessly to ensure that each sentence and idea followed in logical sequence. Boys Town brothers John Mollison, Ed Flanagan, Larry Mulligan, and Raul Parra read the text and made helpful suggestions. John invested considerable time and I'm very grateful. Fellow Mensan, Jim Bunstock, designed the Feathered Serpent Logo, numerous book covers, and helped format the text. Jim is a wizard. Harriet Ottenheimer, Professor Emeritus of Anthropology at Kansas State University, proofed the original manuscript. Fellow author Hugh Reilly remains a pillar of support and advice. Manuscript readers Becky, Mariangela, Robin Tyler, Margaret Struble, and Mark Daniels provided good feedback and support at critical times.

Thanks, Thanks!

The Gonzalez - Corso family of Guadalajara, Mexico are special people. Thank you for your friendship and hospitality and for politely suffering my "gringo" ways and wretched Spanish on so many occasions. Your friendship is a treasure.

Thanks Especially

To those readers of mine who enjoy the unusual story set in exotic places and who have read one or more of my four early novels – thank you for your time and interest. Finding people that enjoy the uncommon story in unusual settings is always a blessing.

Special Acknowledgement

None of my books were possible without the enduring friendship of Jose Antonio Gonzalez Corzo of San Cristobal de las Casas, Chiapas. Tony is the rare companion whose interests, personal charisma, humor and life experiences complement your own. From the Yucatec and Lacandon Jungles of Mexico, to the highlands of Chiapas, and from the Valley of Mexico to the mountains of Oaxaca, Tony provided a personal connection and inspiration. He has been my teacher and informant on Mexican culture and history the last 45 years and has guided me through a menagerie of jungle-cloaked Mayan ruins throughout Chiapas and the Yucatan. He also got us out of some tough situations over the years. Thanks, Tony. We're 'Still Crazy After All These Years.'

Praise for the Feathered Serpent Series

"Struble does it again with unexpected new twists on a classic theme. Archaeology and ancient religion are intertwined with corruption and contemporary politics in this compelling page-turner."
— **Dr. Harriet Ottenheimer**, Professor of Anthropology, Kansas State University

"It's here…another Struble mystery! **Gospel of the Feathered Serpent** *is a whirlwind of excitement and an enticing mystery for those who don't like mysteries and religion. When Christianity's long-lost, sacred objects appear unexpectedly in the ruins of a Catholic church in southern Mexico, the great religions of the world contest to own them. Struble's page-turner and prose and plotting will keep you reading late into the night."*

—**Dr. Lew Hunter**, Chair Emeritus, UCLA Screenwriting School

"Struble's Feathered Serpent Trilogy transports you to an unknown time and place. You can feel sweat running down your neck and hear the jaguar roar. It is full of fascinating historical details, vivid descriptions, and enough plot twists to keep everyone satisfied. Stan Struble's new book, <u>In the Time of the Feathered Serpent</u> is a great addition to the niche of archaeological thrillers that he has carved out for himself."

—**Hugh Reilly**, Director UNO School of Communication and author of *Bound to Have Blood* and *Drinking with My Father's Ghost*

"Sr. Angelina's voice refreshes us like a Buenos Aires breeze at dawn. Her tenacious character and reflections on good and evil catapult her into an essential character in the novel. Through Angelina, Struble sheds light and pays homage to the enormous intellect and memory of Sister Juana Ines de la Cruz."

—Dr. Jose Badillo, Department of Languages, Metropolitan College, Omaha, NE

Online Book Club Review

Four Star Review!
(Abbreviated for length and space)

The author did an outstanding job at character development. Stanley Struble's ability to present each character's personal story whilst in the midst of almost 'fast and furious' type action astonished me. Each character's story was so rich that it felt like a different plot. The way the author fused it all together and managed to keep me not only engaged but biting my fingernails is simply astounding. I hated, rooted, cheered, giggled, felt terrified and anxious, felt relieved.

I was – still am – pleasantly overwhelmed with the author's ability to fuse together thrill and action. Viscerally, I was in that jungle, drinking magic mushroom brew, and feeling its effects. They were nothing like I had read before. I heard the rustling of the old papyrus rolls and crossed my fingers that they stay intact. I traced the outlines of the Feathered Serpent on the burial box. Struble did a grand job taking me to some magical places and getting me to feel connected with his characters.

This work contains several non-borderline profanities, so I advise caution. There are also some violent scenes that more sensitive readers should be aware of. Whilst these are not overly graphic, they may cause distress. I did not come across any erotic scenes. Questions of sexuality in Christianity are discussed, which may be found offensive or inappropriate by some readers.

There wasn't a single thing that I did not love about this book. I award Stanley Struble's *In the Time of the Feathered Serpent* 4 out of 4 stars. The book is brilliantly written and edited, and is incredibly engaging. I recommend it to all lovers of adventure, secrecy, thrill, history, and the controversy of Catholic teachings. You will not be disappointed.

Author Biography

Stanley Struble is a member of MENSA, the International High IQ Society. He holds an M.S. in Anthropology from Kansas State University, where he taught social anthropology. He is presently an Adjunct Professor of Social Sciences at Metropolitan Community College in Omaha, Nebraska.

Stan has published several mystery-suspense novels, including *Filth Eater, Sins of the Jaguar, Xibalba: In Search of the Lost Mayan Texts, Gospel of the Feathered Serpent, and In the Time of the Feathered Serpent. Xibalba* was translated into several languages.

Stan has worked offshore in the Gulf of Mexico, lived and worked in the Sierra Madres of Jalisco and the lowlands of Sinaloa on the Gulf of Baja. He is married, has three children, and lives in Omaha, Nebraska.

"It has served us well,

this myth of Christ."

Pope Leo X

This book is dedicated to Ted and Evelyn Neuburger.

In The Time of the Feathered Serpent

by

Stanley Struble

Prologue

The dreary molten sun hung low, bleeding red-orange and lavender into towering cumulus clouds, painting the western Mediterranean with subtle brush strokes. A quickening breeze carried the odor of salt sea, dead fish, and algae up and over the cliffs of southern Gaul, bringing a welcome coolness and lifting the spirits of those oppressed by the summer heat.

Joseph of Arimathea and his friend Thomas stood overlooking the rocky limestone cliffs bordering the small harbor. Below floated an unusual two-masted sloop on which Thomas had purchased passage west, beyond the Pillars of Hercules into unknown territory. The boat was Phoenician, and wider and more bulky than the swift, lean craft of Rome and Greece. The Phoenicians, renowned as sailors and traders, remained on the cutting edge of maritime technology. Thomas had first seen these Phoenician boats moored in Tyre, Lebanon. Talking with a trader, Thomas became first intrigued, then enthusiastic, and finally arranged passage. Stopping in Gaul, his hopes of meeting with Joseph and Mary

Magdalene were fulfilled. He had talked virtually non-stop for three days with his friend. The ship's captain, meanwhile, loaded water, food, and wine to ensure a successful voyage west of Iberia and beyond, anxious to set sail in the fine weather of the peak season.

Thomas was leaving tomorrow, much to Joseph's dismay, but the joy of their meeting and ideas exchanged had nourished and renewed their friendship. Thomas regaled his friend with tales of ancient Persia, the thousand-year old ruins of Susa and Babylon, and his long journey through the lands of the Moghul Emperors to India. He described his struggle to share Jesus' teachings with the poor or anyone else who would listen. In vain, he tried to explain the convoluted Hindu caste system to his bewildered colleague, and the challenges of teaching a people whose religion and civilization were already thousands of years old and sophisticated beyond comprehension by the unlearned.

Joseph, in turn, related how he had converted his properties to coin and fled Palestine and the heavy yoke of Rome and Vespasian. Evil times had visited the biblical Promised Land. Believing the situation would quickly worsen, with despair and fear the only future of Israel, Joseph decided to emigrate. His heart broken and spirit diminished, he convinced Marta and a six-month pregnant Mary Magdalene to accompany him to this near Eden in Southern Gaul. He detailed to his old friend Thomas their perilous trip and arrival here, and the years since carefully and resolutely building a life for themselves. He spoke of Mary Magdalene's beautiful child, Sarah, and how much he loved her, and how Mary had insisted that he write the story of her time with Jesus. Joseph described how she spent most days in meditation and prayer, in seclusion in a cave in the nearby foothills where she seemed to find an indescribable solace.

"She has written a book? A book about Jesus?" Thomas' eyes grew wide.

Joseph smiled. "I did the writing," he offered modestly. "You know Mary can't read or write. It took months," he added.

"And just now you tell me this? Am I not worthy to read her story? How can she...how does she know..."

"Please, please," Joseph smiled and held up a hand. "Calm yourself. I knew you would want to read it, but I didn't know how long you would stay with us. So...I spent a few moons making a copy on good papyrus to accompany you on your journey."

"It's written in Greek?"

"No...it's written in our language, Aramaic, the language of Judah." The old man paused, turned to watch the burning sky diminish as the tired, coral orb sank low into the sea. He looked back to his younger friend.

"I'm sure you already know this, but women really do see things differently than men."

"How so?"

"You'll see." Joseph cocked his wizened head and added, "All will become apparent once you've read it."

Thomas grunted, then caught Joseph's gaze. "Fascinating. Tell me, my friend, is it accurate? Is it *true*?"

"It's as true as anything. We both witnessed much of what she describes. You know as well as I that there are very strange stories, some being written as we speak. Have you heard about this Saul of Tarsus, who now calls himself Paul? The man never met Jesus, yet he travels the lands around the great sea claiming to know Jesus' mind." Joseph frowned and shook his head. He paused and took a deep breath.

"It's important that you write stories, and that you share them with us before it's too late, Thomas. You are the learned disciple. You are the teacher and scribe. You were the one with the questions."

Thomas nodded assent, smiled and gazed west into the magenta haze. Streaming from narrow kitchen chimneys in the village, black and gray smoke buckled and folded capriciously in the evening thermals. He turned, stroked a beard streaked with gray, and replied, "At one time I had twelve scrolls. I spent six months making my story as simple and short as possible, so that it doesn't require so much papyrus. Papyrus is so expensive."

Joseph of Arimathea rolled his eyes and threw up his hands, exasperated. "And I will not get to read your story? You will deprive us of your insight and knowledge of Jesus?"

"Please..." Thomas held up his hand to cut short his friend's protest. "In fact I plan to leave them with you."

"Leave what with me? Your new short version? I want the long one! The story with the detail. The story that tells Jesus' many years."

"Be at peace, my friend. I'm leaving the many scrolls, all that I can recall; all that was important to his ministry. I have become a near vagabond and have too much to carry. With the way I travel, everything risks being lost. I'm taking only the short version with me. I already know the story," he shrugged. "I entrust my work to you for safekeeping. I only hope that I live long enough to hear your voice again."

Chapter One

Pope Lucas made the sign of the cross and stood slowly, wincing at the pain in his knees and lower back, a nagging reminder of age and the need to move slowly. His suite at the Domus Sanctae Marthae Hotel on the edge of Vatican City was plain and suitable for a man who felt comfortable here, away from the ostentatious trappings of royalty, the distraction of affectations, and choreography of public ritual. Not that the Vatican hotel was a dump; far from it. Built in 1996, it boasted 105 two-room suites and 26 singles. The off-white walls were trimmed with mahogany. A beautiful parquet floor glistened in the light from a plain but large overhead fixture. His desk with its sitting room was large enough to accommodate a meeting of six people. The bedroom with clothes rack, night stand, and dresser were all he needed. A private bath and shower added a touch of comfort to the spartan furnishing.

The pontiff glanced at a wall clock and saw it was nearly time for the day's activities. He usually joined the hotel's employees in one of the building's four chapels for 7:00 a.m. daily mass, followed by breakfast in his room where he usually prepared his own food rather than eating in the common dining room downstairs. Preparing his own meals was a habit brought with him from Argentina. His breakfasts were simple; cereal, fruit, tea or coffee, and occasionally a piece of sweet bread if he managed to hide it from Sr. Angelina, his personal assistant and friend. Afterward time spent with his long-time friend and administrative assistant, Montoya, then, usually, a series of meetings, some unwelcome and a few distasteful. The difficult job of the pontiff was to provide leadership to the far-flung religious empire of Catholics. He had to organize and implement strategies of the various Vatican offices, College of Cardinals and gaggles of bishops. The pope's experience assured him the majority of the Vatican's cardinals and bishops were humble, spiritual men who could be trusted to discharge their duties as expected. However, hard-earned familiarity informed him of several ambitious and career oriented individuals whose values were anathema to the charitable goals of the Church. These men cause problems and created private fiefdoms to enhance their power and influence. A few, surprisingly, were as ethically challenged as anyone he had ever known.

And then there was the gay lobby, a group of long standing in the Vatican but little known by most outside the walls of the enclosed city. The article published by *La Repubblica,* reported at length on an influential "gay lobby" as a cohesive group of powerful homosexuals operating within the Vatican. The information supposedly came from the pope's butler, Paolo Gabriola, who had pilfered Pope Benedict's private papers, then leaked them. The 300-page report was compiled by several Cardinals Pope Benedict had tasked with investigating corruption within the curia. The news article speculated that these homosexual clerics were being blackmailed and that Pope Benedict had resigned because he felt incapable of undertaking the reforms required to repair the administrative apparatus of the Vatican.

Pope Lucas acquired and read the report, recognized it as an accurate description of the daily operations of the Vatican – and decided it was untenable. The largest church in the world must change, the ship righted and the corrupted leaders expelled. The Church was also a political entity and must interface with governments of countries rich and poor, powerful corporations, and many, many non-governmental organizations (NGO's). Here, too, was found the occasional careerist who abused rank and privilege for personal gain. The Vatican was not immune from thorny, secular issues such as money laundering, smuggling, and abuse of diplomatic privilege.

The Pope had arranged with Cardinal Montoya and Sr. Angelina, his two most trusted aides, to find other trustworthy souls to further investigate those Cardinals identified in the report as the most unethical, problematic, and resistant to correction, especially in such areas as canon law, banking, liturgy, and administration of diocesan offices. Efforts to complete the task quietly had proven impossible. Soon everyone knew their position, friends, and records were being examined and evaluated. Many, the pontiff was sure, did not wish him or his mission well. Those united against him believed that he had poisoned the water upon his arrival in Rome, and at least a few, he was certain, wished him dead.

Cardinal Alfredo Montoya, formerly of Guatemala, the pope's trusted assistant, had called at 6:00 a.m. to ensure that all was well with his boss. He had assured the pontiff that he would join him in his suite at 8:00 a.m. sharp with the day's itinerary, hinting at serious pending issues that could no longer be deferred without risking failure or public embarrassment. Pope Lucas glanced at the wall clock....7:55

a.m. He sighed, touched the cross that hung from a chain at his neck, and inclined head to chest for one last prayer, a request for assistance in his upcoming journey to the New World and the adventures that awaited.

The doorbell rang. The pope made the sign of the cross, groaned and pushed himself to his feet with effort. "Yes," he called, starting for the door. "Yes, I'm coming," then muttered to himself, "but where I'll end, only God knows." He walked to the door and opened it to his smiling friend and adjutant. Two Swiss Guards stood on either side of the entry in the hall.

"Father Montoya," he said smiling, holding the door wide.

"Holy Father."

The pontiff waved a dismissal at the title. "We've known each other for too long to use such names in private. I'm just a fisher of men, like Peter."

"Have you checked your blood sugar?"

"Yes."

"Morning insulin?"

"Yes, yes, of course."

"The press says that you are the Hope of the 21st Century Church and the Beacon on the Hill, but we both know that you are just an obsessive sugar addict with a bad pancreas and one kidney. Here...I brought you your fix." Cardinal Montoya removed a small sack of hard candy from within his robe.

"Don't tell anyone...it's no one's business but God's and myself." Pope Lucas smiled, eagerly reaching for the treasure bag. "There are worse sins than gluttony," he added.

"You are not committing an act of gluttony, my friend. You are damaging your diabetic body and shortening your time on this planet. You are committing slow suicide."

"It's my time and my body." Christ's Vicar groused, unrolling a cherry flavored piece, tossing it into his mouth, smacking his lips. "Don't tell Dr. Cabrini," he added.

"Lying is among my duties?" his friend smiled.

The pope shrugged. He pocketed the sack within his robe. "Hate to carry this on me," he added, "but nothing's safe from Angelina. She could find Satan's stash of souls in barren a womb."

Pope Lucas' trusted aide/housekeeper, a Dominican nun from a prominent Argentinian family, was as diligent as she was thorough. Her parents were old friends of his, and he had watched her grow from an inquisitive child into a woman of stunning, perplexing intellect. To the confusion of many, she had chosen to enter the vocations and by God's will had been assigned to the 60 - year-old bishop Lucas of Buenos Aires.

Her brusque manner and lack of patience had won her few friends. After a week of obsessive perfectionism, subliminal criticism and second guessing, he had thought to return her to the convent, but had grudgingly delayed rather than make excuses to her family. Again God's work. As weeks became months and he had engaged her in hundreds of hours of conversation, he found her insight and advice necessary to the completion of nearly any task he undertook.

Angelina's family connections were also valuable, especially her uncle, the General, a member of the ruling junta who had terrorized the general populace from 1975 to 1986 during the "Dirty War." The greatest challenge for the young bishop was the healing of the wounds caused by this junta. They had sought to extinguish all remnants of Isabella Peron's socialist supporters by abducting and "disappearing" hundreds of citizens and kidnapping 100's of children to be adopted by high class military families. Despite her faults she became irreplaceable, and there had been no question of her not accompanying him to the Vatican.

In Rome, one particularly thorny issue Pope Lucas shared with Sr. Angelina was the church's disastrous failure in Mexico under the previous pope. There was the matter of Father Sean Gregory a Vatican-trained priest-archaeologist, who had lost his life in the treacherous, wilderness state of southern Chiapas when recovering what appeared to be the lost body of St. Thomas, along with numerous 1st century books written in Aramaic. One of the texts appeared to be an early, if not original, copy of one of the apocryphal books, The Gospel of St. Thomas. The Vatican had received photocopies of three manuscripts from their late Papal Inquisitor in advance of his coming home, and had been told that there were as many as seven. But the tragic wreck on a mountainside that killed the Papal Inquisitor also lost the trove of manuscripts that was either incinerated or strewn throughout a steep, inaccessible jungle-clad mountainside. Perhaps by God's grace, some fell thousands of feet onto the dense jungle below the cliff face. None were recovered. Apart from Pope Lucas, no one knew of the documents' existence except his friend Cardinal Nizzi, Sr. Angelina, a Muslim academic from Beirut who first completed the translations, and Mexican archaeologist, David Wolf. The pope, himself an ancient language scholar, had studied the photocopies - in addition to reading the translations of short fragments provided to the Vatican's experts.

The pontiff had confided the secret story to his brilliant Argentine friend/assistant, Angelina, along with the translations. There was little of substance that she did not grasp immediately and he valued her opinion as much as, or more than, many who served under him. She had long been an advocate for change in the church, and in her own limited way insisted on parity among the sexes in the male-dominated arena of church politics, where female opinions were neither sought nor welcome. Pope Lucas knew that his secret was safe with her, but he remained cautious of her willingness and fervor to assist him in his great task of reforming the Catholic Church.

Pope Lucas frowned as the memories intertwined with the upcoming challenges. He shifted his weight to the other foot, sighed, and then looked to Montoya, his other principal advisor.

"Do you agree that the conversation with Bishop Gonzalez in Tuxtla Gutierrez went well?"

His friend hesitated, then said, "Yes...I suppose. I think the Skype connection was fine. The background clicking was annoying, but who knows what caused it?" He paused again, "Much depends on whether the bishop can locate that archaeologist, David Wolf, and convince him to find that Bone Man character that our poor, deceased Father Tom mentioned." Montoya frowned. "Frankly, I think there are too many variables. I know you mean well, Excellency, but we should not be surprised if this whole scheme of yours doesn't work. Those parts of Mexico and Guatemala are uncivilized. The Petén and Lacandon have dense jungle and mountains with few roads, no police, no hospitals, and more poor Indians than can be counted. The Zapatista Rebellion in southern Mexico continues, and the issues that caused it continue to fester. This is not a small thing. There's no guarantee that the archaeologist and this shaman, the Bone Man, will provide you the opportunity to talk with Father Salvador Lopez, this so called 'Holy Man'. If he really has the Holy Cup, which is preposterous, I can't think of one reason why he would willingly part with it. The stories – frankly - are getting crazier and...."

The pontiff waved off his objections, moving forward, "So, arrangements are complete for Monterrey and Mexico City also?"

"Yes. Except for your poorly designed and ill-advised intention to sneak away into the Lacandon Jungle in Chiapas State when we are in Southern Mexico and meet that renegade fool of a priest who is embarrassing us to death. Doctor Cabrini has been very specific in warning you about over-exertion. You must heed his advice and….."

"That discussion is over," the pope clicked his thumb against his middle finger.

"So you insist, but…"

"Please, please, Father Montoya." The pontiff extended the palm of his hand. "We were in seminary together. We have been friends for 40 years. I trust you implicitly. You must perform this one act of charity for me."

"Charity?"

"…with complete discretion," warned the pope. "I will not debate this with you anymore. With the exception of Sr. Angelina, no one knows of our venture."

Montoya tightened his lips and his head dipped momentarily. "As you wish, Holy Father."

Lucas' installation as Pope had surprised everyone and created unexpected challenges. The enormous amount of administrative work in unaccustomed areas left him exhausted. Discontent simmered due to a lack of time for his studies in history and ancient languages. Although 40 years removed from actual research, he subscribed to scholarly journals and found them fascinating. The three-year-old disaster in Chiapas, Mexico; the discovery and subsequent loss of St. Thomas' body, plus that of his putative books, set the pontiff's interest and imagination aflame. What a coup it would have been! What a joyous challenge or perhaps victory for Catholicism and Christianity the findings represented. But it was not to be - at least not yet - although the pontiff still held hope. He just couldn't let it go. Surely it was God's sense of humor that brought such gifts to a scholar of the ancients and then withdrew them! So close, yet so far.

Even more stunning, Lucas had read a report from his friend, Cardinal Nizzi, the Director of the Congregation for the Protection of the Faith, that claimed a renegade Catholic priest known as the 'Holy Man' supposedly possessed the Holy Grail. Incredible! Rumors of miraculous healings, some seemingly verified by local doctors and investigators, trickled out of the Lacandon and Petén Jungles of Mexico and Guatemala. Lucas heartily approved of the 'Holy Man' undertaking his mission among the poorest of the poor. He, too, had worked extensively among the poor his entire life and he believed that he understood this 'Holy Man's' motivation. But the Grail? The unresolved matter infected him with a discontent that could only be cured by action and effort. Pope Lucas simply couldn't sleep at night without knowing! He felt morally and spiritually compelled to escape the hostility engendered by his reforms, heavy schedule, and constant scrutiny to discover the truth that may lay within those documents. With so much at stake, and the current political climate in the Vatican inhibiting trust, he decided to intervene personally and had arranged a covert trip after arriving in the frontier state of Chiapas, Mexico. This would normally be impossible, as everything he did or said was heavily scrutinized and scheduled, but it was well known that the new pope was anything but traditional and that his administration was intent on a different path, altering the conventional and time-honored methods of the past. *Reform* was a hated word in most quarters, but now lurking in the minds, if not on the lips, of many who once thought such a thing was not possible.

The itinerary called for a final stop in the old town of San Cristobal de las Casas, located in the southernmost state of Mexico. He would steal away two days while in the colonial city under the guise of secluding himself and undergoing prayer and meditation. Because of the sensitivity of the matter and the possible repercussions of recovering artifacts that might shake the very foundations of Christianity, the pontiff had decided to undertake the task himself...or at least come to discover whether or not their recovery was as important as he believed it to be. Although many tracked his comings and goings, the pope reported to no one on earth and was ultimately responsible only to his own conscience. Unbeknownst to anyone in the Vatican (or Mexico), his trusted aides Father Montoya and Sr. Angelina had arranged for him to contact the archaeologist, Professor David Wolf, and attempt to organize a meeting with the Mayan shaman who controlled the Holy Man. He was arranging a side trip while in San Cristobal de las Casas. Nothing was set yet, but perhaps under the guise of attending a private tour at one of the local Mayan ruins, the pope would instead board a helicopter and fly to a different, obscure location near a Mayan ruin called Palenque. A venial lie, of course, but one directed at the welfare of the Church and Christianity itself. There, as arranged by Fr. Montoya and Sr. Angelina, he would meet Professor David Wolf - a trustworthy man he'd been told – the anthropologist who had discovered the 2,000-year-old corpse that appeared only recently deceased, along with papyrus scrolls in a Mayan-themed burial box under a church destroyed by an earthquake hundreds of years ago.

Unbeknownst to anyone, a shaman called the 'Bone Man' had apparently found in the box a cup some believed to be the

Holy Grail. The sarcophagus was made of crude mahogany and incised with a sinuous, red, Feathered Serpent that could only be the Mayan god, *Kulkulkan,* the southern version of the very old Feathered Serpent myth of *Quetzalcoatl* so prevalent in Mexican lore and religion. The body and books were all salvaged by the Papal Inquisitor.

Unfortunately, the loss of the recovered items, as well as their very own Inquisitor, Father Sean Gregory, occurred only hours before the Vatican representative was scheduled to depart Tuxtla Gutierrez, Chiapas for Rome. While making their way to the airport, he and his *federale* driver were killed descending Los Altos de Chiapas from the town of San Cristobal de las Casas in a violent thunderstorm. Strong, gusting winds had swept their automobile from a slickened, steep, winding road with treacherous curves.

Yet the cup, the "Holy Grail", was still out there, and perhaps Professor Wolf would guide Lucas to the Bone Man, an irascible and unfriendly shaman who did not like white people. With luck and God's blessing, perhaps this legendary leader in the Zapatista Rebellion would let Lucas meet the renegade priest who possessed the purported 'Holy Grail'. If, maybe, perhaps. Who would believe it? The pope had read good fiction less interesting and bizarre than this developing story; a renegade priest known as the Holy Man, a Mayan shaman called the 'Bone Man', and the Holy Grail.

The Cardinal had lingered patiently, but now cleared his throat. He waited for the pontiff to meet his eyes, opened his folder and glanced at the day's itinerary. He smiled at his friend. "You'll be happy to know that we begin with a 30-minute meeting with Cardinal Cardona."

The pope sagged and groaned. He scowled and his brow furrowed. Cardinal Cardona was no one's favorite. As head of the Vatican Bank he was hated, avoided, viewed with suspicion, and routinely pilloried. Under his guidance, the bank had been accused of mismanagement, fraud, money laundering, and even murder when one of his assistants was found hanging in a closet prior to an unscheduled audit upon Pope Lucas' ascension as head of the Catholic Church. Cardona was a difficult man with a prickly personality and defensive, impatient manner. During his 15 years as head of the bank he had acquired many enemies and behind his back was called Cardinal Machiavelli, the Vatican's Launderer, God's Representative in the Cosa Nostra, and the Devil's Purser. He could be obstinate, stoic, and calculating and was smart enough to know that he was high on the Pope's list of reforms.

"Cancel. Don't have time this morning." The pope waved dismissively.

"You have canceled two meetings already, Eminence. Word gets around. Some will see you as weak or intimidated by him."

The pope sighed. "Cut the meeting to 15 minutes, then interrupt with an emergency. That should show him where he stands with me. I'm going to deal with Cardona when I return - once and for all. He operates the bank like it belongs to him and is completely closed to suggestions or new ideas. We simply must have more accountability and transparency in the Vatican Bank."

A knock on the door stopped their conversation. "Yes," called Cardinal Montoya, "what is it?

"Sr. Angelina…I'm here for the Holy Father's laundry. And I brought the book he requested."

"Let her in," motioned the pope, dismissively. "She'll just be a moment." The door swung wide and the Dominican nun entered with a smile on her face. She handed him the book,

Aramaic in Ancient Judah, and eyed a coffee stain on the pope's robe.

"Off with it, Lucas, er...Holy Father," she insisted. She circled behind him. "We can't have you meeting heads of state in a stained robe. This will just take a moment." She reached for his collar.

The pope, used to being ordered about by his personal aide and long-time Argentine confidante, shed the gown into her waiting hands. "Forgot about it. Got a little clumsy this morning. Thanks...."

"And what's this? She pointed. "Is that what I think it is? Give me that. Did you bring this Cardinal Montoya?" She frowned, then snapped her fingers, waiting. "What's that in your mouth? It's candy isn't it?"

She stood, hand outstretched, while Cardinal Montoya guiltily fixed his gaze at a picture on the wall and Pope Lucas' eyes focused shamefully on his feet, then to her outstretched hand. *Caught again!* He reluctantly handed over the small sack of sweets, which she swiftly tucked away in her own robe.

"Don't tell Doctor Cabrini."

"What? Of course I will, Holy Father. Be assured that I will. If God wanted you to eat sweets he would have blessed you with a better pancreas and two kidneys." She marched into the bedroom and returned with a fresh garment. "Here," she held it aloft for him to place his arms. "Such a blessed day, isn't it Holy Father?" Her face beamed radiantly. When he finished adjusting the outer robe, she quickly went to the bathroom and retrieved the clothes hamper. "You boys do great things, okay? Get busy making our Mother Church better." She turned, opened the door, then hefted her load and disappeared down the hall.

"This day isn't getting any better," offered the Pope with a sigh.

Cardinal Montoya smiled. "But of course it will, Holy Father. God will bring you strength and joy to complete your tasks and to give you strength in your battle with diabetes. There will be more sweets and...."

"....and there's always my friend Sr. Angelina to ensure that God works in my best interest." He shifted weight from one foot to the other, adjusted his robe, sighed again and looked to his friend.

"Let's get on with it shall we, old friend? Bring in Satan's Purser and get it over with. We have much more important things to do than listen to the obfuscations of an ethically challenged banker."

Chapter Two

Foraging for medicine had become hard work. Squatting, once easy, had after 90-plus years, become painful for Balaam Reyes, a Mayan shaman and curandero. The Bone Man lifted his arm to shield his eyes from the late afternoon sunshine and glanced down at the flat limestone rock on which lay his harvest from Señor Medina's bull pasture. Psilocybin mushrooms, their dark heads, ivory trunks, and very thin, difficult to see Saturn-like rings on the upper stems distinguishing them from a look-a-like mushroom that caused soul sickness and bloody shits.

Señor Medina produced the finest bulls in Mexico for the corridas in Mexico City and Monterey. He fed them good grain and alfalfa and grazed them on thick, ample grass pastures that supported 10 to 20 bulls at any given time. The extra grain made their manure rich, and when the bulls evacuated their bowels it produced the perfect environment for the medicine to grow strong - powerful enough to launch the soul into the ether of the spirit world.

Balaam watched patiently as he had thousands of times before, while sun and hot stone cured the mushrooms. These mushrooms, wonderful medicine, were the best in all of Mexico. The sun shone strong, and it had rained yesterday. This was good - very good. Satisfied, he left them to darken to purple and moved into the shade of the Lacandon Jungle. He would rest, and in another hour gather his medicine and return to the Indian village of Lacanja, where one of his wives would prepare him a very good meal of chicken soup, tortillas, beans, and corn-on-the-cob. His stomach growled in response to imagined aroma.

For years, Balaam had walked to Medina's pasture after first traipsing through the ancient ruin of Palenque, a city built and inhabited during the Classic Period of Maya civilization, but abandoned five hundred years before the Conquest. There were no tourists in those days. He would saunter unmolested into the old city of lichen-blackened limestone to stare in awe at the massive 'Observatory' that fronted the southern edge of the ball court. Here, astronomic and religious studies had taken place for fifteen hundred years. Now it was a decrepit ruin. Splotches of faded red and blue paint clung to some of the friezes in the central courtyard. Mortared limestone lay fractured and strewn about the grounds. To the right rose the steep stairs of the well-preserved Temple Of Inscriptions. Deep inside this pyramid, Pakal, one of the great Jaguar Kings, lay interred in a subterranean sarcophagus. As a young man Balaam had climbed the stairs and felt the majesty of the ruin fill him with pride and purpose. But nowadays, not so much.

The Mexican government had strung power cables, straightened and widened the old forest paths created by the Indians, and built asphalt roads for big tourist buses. The dense, timeless jungle that once had protected the ruin from the dirty hands and heavy feet of tourists, was now strewn with hotels and restaurants. Eden had been perverted into a diesel-stinking, raucous playground.

The old Mayan leaned back onto his elbows, ignored the muted roar of diesels and the distant clamor of people, and gazed into the forest. Tall, old-growth ceiba and mahogany trees stretched toward blue skies. So dense was the forest that the sun peeked through the canopy only occasionally. Trees and lush tropical plants contested for every space; so many hues of green and leaf shapes! He heard, rather than saw animals scurrying in the bush. The relentless mosquitos were here, too. He relished being alone in the sacred forest.

Too often these days he was accompanied and guarded by a young retinue of rag-tag Zapatista soldiers earnest to demonstrate their devotion and readiness to protect the famous Mayan elder. Balaam was well-known as a curandero by the Indians, but the governments of Guatemala and Mexico knew him as an elusive and notorious planner/instigator of peasant revolutions. Having to live with body-guards was the price of being a man marked for capture or death.

He heard a shout and then a response to the call, and a tingle of apprehension stirred in his gut. Tourists sometimes wandered away from the ruins and into the forest. The trail grew wider as you approached the ruins, and the bush sparser as the path wound back north towards the old city. Ranchers had cleared this area of forest nearly a hundred years ago, and the forest was nowhere nearly as dense here as further south and west. Here sunlight leaked through the jungle canopy.

The Bone Man glanced again at his newly acquired pharmacopeia and saw that the stems had finally turned purple. Perhaps it was time to return to Lacanja. Unfortunately the Lacandon Indian village lay some 30 kilometers to the southwest off the highway. Even 10 years ago he would have set off on foot through the jungle, on well-worn, but well-known paths. But no more - age had had its way with him. He must do something he loathed – ride one of Mexico's easily recognizable commuter buses to arrive at his distant destination. He glanced up at the evening sun to verify the time of day, rose, and stacked his hallucinogens into a leather medicine sack. He paused to listen, and frowned as the sounds drew nearer. The last thing he wanted was to encounter people, especially young tourists. Even on a good day the old shaman cared little for people. He found them to be loud, other-focused, and ungrounded. And now, many were slaves, always playing with the electronic devices that had captured their souls. As if meaning and connection could be found in images on a flat, tiny, hand-held plastic box! He had heard that parents bought the boxes for their children! He did not believe it. Parents loved their children. Why would they deliberately afflict their loved ones? It just didn't make sense. Maybe it was the last, degraded stage before man succumbed to permanent, incurable soul-sickness. Sometimes Balaam thought he had lived too long; he no longer understood the world. Many times in the last 40 years he had been close to death, but had always been spared. Why?

The old curandero grasped his twisted mahogany cane and planted it firmly to lift himself erect. The cane, an affectation foreign to him 10-years ago, was now necessary. Old age required accommodation and respect, or the body rebelled. He sighed, broke wind, then turned to follow the fence line of Medina's pasture. He veered to the left onto a path known only to forest dwellers like himself. Brush and eroded landscape would replace trees as he made his way to the black highway where he must stand with other poor Indians, workers, and widows with their dirty, ragged children returning from business with the white man's world.

Balaam was anxious to try his new medicine. At night in his dreams his soul and its companion animal, a jaguar, were unhappy, hungry, and moving about the jungle without purpose. The jaguar never fed, but watched a large owl always perched some distance away that stared back unblinking. Owls were sacred animals, calm predators that fed without emotion and surveyed their domain with confidence and uncanny foresight. It was unnerving - two powerful spirits juxtaposed without purpose. Although white people denied it, the shaman knew that everyone had a companion soul, an animal that always accompanied their journeys at night into the spirit world. To whom did this owl belong and why was it stalking him? The Bone Man had come to believe that his place in the spirit world was out of harmony and he must enter the ether and see why his universe had become uneven and fractious. The new medicine, if it was good enough, would facilitate his entry. So be it. One more important task to be completed before moving on to others.

He checked that his sheathed machete was strapped to the back of his white *xikul* tunic, then held his leather satchel close as he repeatedly lifted and set the walking stick firmly onto the ground in rhythm with short, firm steps. The image of steaming chicken soup and a plate of black beans and warm tortillas called to him as he moved resolutely over root-laced trails until he disappeared into the forest.

Chapter Three

Meeting with the pope cancelled again! The bald, slightly built Vatican banker gripped the telephone tightly and groaned. Grimacing with frustration, Cardinal Cardona saddled the phone roughly, retrieved from his desktop a plain, yellow pencil and broke it. He tossed the pieces aside. This had to have been planned. This morning's meeting had come to an abrupt ending with no rescheduling, when that Argentine Plague, Sr. Angelina, had interrupted with news of some vague emergency regarding a Nigerian bishop and his wives (yes, a bishop with wives!) and American investigative reporters poking around. What was that woman's job description? Where in the curia was a document that defined her role in this irritating Pope's administration? She meddled in everything and offered uninvited opinions on anything. The pope and Cardinal Montoya said that she was Special Aide to the Holy See. "Special Aide"? What did that mean? A woman a "special aide" to the pope? Since when? She was an indecipherable aspect of Pope Lucas' Argentinian past that no one could explain or understand. Did she even have a college degree? Any experience outside the convent or working at a daycare center? She should confine herself to the pope's laundry or, maybe, be allowed to carry his briefcase.

Her clumsy arrival in the meeting was, obviously, to prevent Cardinal Cardona from presenting his plan of procedural changes that he hoped would mollify the Holy Father. The pope left in three days for his meaningless trip to Mexico. The cardinal's hope of getting another appointment in such a short window, he knew, was poor. The lack of interest on the part of the Holy Father was yet another signal that change was coming.

"Damn you, Montoya," he cursed silently, recalling his tepid conversation with the pope's chief assistant. The overly polite Montoya was a clever, gentle man whose soft voice and steady delivery revealed little of what he or the pontiff actually thought - and therein lay the problem. The banker's frustration changed to anger. It was an outrage, he decided - an obvious slight to put him in his place. Pope Lucas, Cardinal Cardona now realized, planned to replace him...perhaps after his return from the ill-advised trip to Mexico. Perhaps the pontiff did not want to face the unpleasant task and had already assigned the deed to Montoya or his staff? As the banker sat considering this possibility he conjured up an image of the soft-spoken Guatemalan Cardinal smiling kindly while thanking Cardona profusely for his labors on behalf of the Church, and subsequently reassigning him to a backwater position somewhere in the Vatican. Or worse, somewhere like Kinshasa, Zaire to minister to whores in the rows of bordellos that lined the streets. The thought sent a shiver down his spine.

His mind simmering, Cardona stood nervously, straightened the wrinkles in his gown, and moved to his office window overlooking the Piazza of the Pine Cone across from the Vatican Museum. It hummed with activity as tourists from the far reaches of Christianity chattered and laughed and pointed cameras at ancient Egyptian statuary placed strategically on the museum's portico. Arnaldo Pomodor's beautiful bronze, *Sphere within a Sphere*, beguiled rapt onlookers as the shining, cracked orb rotated to reveal yet another fractured orb within, symbolizing the fragility and complexity of the world. The beautiful globe, Cardona had long ago decided, was an unwritten allegory of life's complexity in the Vatican: faith; ambition, altruism, and wretched politics. Only the most promising minds were brought to the Eternal City to study. If you were lucky, or had made the right friends, you left the Vatican on completion of your training to be assigned somewhere commensurate with your abilities. Cardinal Cardona's old, Italian lineage included ancestors who had served the Vatican and Holy See over several centuries. An assignment in the Vatican was his birthright. It was in his blood. The banker was a legacy, a man from a family long dedicated to Christianity's past and future; a Christian soldier become lost in arcane bureaucracy and tradition encased in a modern world.

The official name of the Vatican bank was the Institute for the Works of Religion. Unknown to many, it was a privately held firm with a traditional CEO who reported only to a committee of cardinals and, of course, the Pope himself. It held about 30-50,000 accounts, and did business in well over 100 countries. It also had lots of money – about 10 billion Euro in assets – not a small sum. There is no record of the Vatican hierarchy ever taking a vow of poverty.

Banking completely changed in the 1990's. Gone were the casual, friendly relationships between individuals, trust freely given, and predictable outcomes. Computers and technology had ushered in a global economy with rapid changes, unrelenting cascades of data, and unprecedented daily challenges that simply had not existed before. The old standards and methods had changed in order to compete. Relationships and trust, although still important, must now be accompanied by a track record of success, unimpeachable support data, predictable outcomes, and the promise of lucre for all involved – lots of it, or the deal wasn't worth doing. Technocrats, computer nerds, inside knowledge and online bookkeeping were the new standards. Banking, even at the Vatican – a City State defined by history, tradition, and religion – had necessarily evolved to survive in the new global economy.

The new manner of doing business brought unexpected problems and, regrettably, unfortunate events. Cardinal Cardona, an old-style banker, had trusted his subordinates, and now accusations of money laundering and support for terrorism were leveled at the bank. At first disbelieving, then angry, he became impotently furious. His long-serving assistant, Monsignor Del Monico, hanged himself in a closet, leaving documents providing a trail to narco-traffickers attempting to launder profits through the Vatican Bank. Appalling! Cardinal Cardona had trusted those beneath him and had been deceived. Did money corrupt everything? Even the Vatican? Must every single thing in this new age be equated with or given a monetary value?

And now there was the problem of his own finances. An investigation had been initiated by Cardinal Montoya at the pope's insistence. In truth, Cardona had accumulated several hundred thousand dollars over the years. He was a banker, for Christ's sake! You earn a Euro or two when you know what's going on in the financial world unless you're incompetent, stupid, or worse – an ideological misfit who believes that privation is the key to redemption. Money fueled the clockwork of commerce. In a world controlled by multinationals and mega corporations, it was a commodity that needed little explanation. But Montoya's unexpected exploration of Iranian and Hezbollah money transfers had revealed a little skimmed from the top. Someone with inside knowledge of the bank's business had betrayed Cardona. It could have been any of five or six people. Maybe those damned Iranians for all he knew. Bunch of crazy zealots, that bunch.

It was unlikely he would ever see a courtroom, as he had not yet been judged a criminal by his peers. But his character and reputation were under fire and he felt he was losing a battle for which he had yet to muster either offense or defense. That must change - immediately. The Holy Father leaving for an extended stay in the Americas would provide the opportunity. He must secure evidence that proved the pope planned to institute intolerable changes in dogma and liturgy that most conservatives, priest and laity alike, would find appalling. The Cardinal must create a predictable outcome. He must arrange a coup. He would quietly and effectively argue for and lead a rebellion. He must stick his neck out. Cardinal Cardona must engage in the unthinkable – sedition. The rewards were great. And failure? Not really an option at this point. Africa was unthinkable, and the Balkans nearly as bad. He wouldn't let it happen. In order to prevent exile or being relegated to the financial oversight of some penurious convent in Albania, he must ensure that this new, radical, 21st – century pope was ushered out the door as unceremoniously as he waltzed in. Cardinal Cardona had voted against the Argentinian usurper, but the unsuspecting College of Cardinals had been fooled by the man's intelligence, quiet demeanor, and self-effacing manner. Now, reform (a dirty word if ever there was one) threatened orderly operation of the church. The banker was recipient of constant grumblings and accusations from the traditional stalwarts who actually ran things. Pope Lucas, the Great Reformer, loved by naïve simpletons, and the uninformed, needed to be returned to the isolation of the Pampas or to the political hotbed of Buenos Aires.

It was time to go to work. Cardona had heard rumors regarding mysterious "gospels" recovered by the now deceased Father Gregory in Mexico, but no one had seen or read them – at least no one he knew. Documents from Christianity's ancient past had sometimes appeared, but nothing important enough to merit significant changes that would alter the story line. The provenance of most were very questionable and thus empty vessels or food for conspiracy theories. If rumor was correct, these newly discovered documents were different. They were potentially damaging, as they might call into question important, fundamental aspects of Catholicism. The current Church had required two thousand years to construct. Cardinal Cardona and others were not simply going to sit by and allow this new 'reformer' to ruin God's church. If the documents existed, they probably lacked credibility, but could be easily manipulated by the unscrupulous – a person such as Pope Lucas.

The rebellion must be quiet, insidious, and effective. He returned to his desk, removed a Vatican phone directory from a drawer and began perusing the names of the various department heads, placing a check mark beside those he felt shared his pessimism and unhappiness with the new boss. Many were former classmates from 40 years ago that had moved upward into the Vatican hierarchy. Many owed him favors. Money was like glue, it created friends - and debt and favors.

He would have to be careful, of course. This was sedition, but the Cardinal knew that many old-timers like himself had much to lose under this new reformist pope. Those that were not forthcoming and did not agree with his message could pack their bags for Cape Town or Kinshasa, as far as he was concerned. There would be no place for them here after the coup was made permanent.

Chapter Four

Sr. Angelina removed a licorice candy from the bag she had confiscated from her friend, Pope Lucas, and tossed it into her mouth. *Delicious and undeserved*, she chastised herself. She rolled the sweet, syrupy rock around, caressing it with her tongue, then glanced down at the bag, and tossed it and its sweet treasures into a wastebasket near her desk.

Angelina looked about her small office, a broom closet in size as compared to others in the Vatican. In a man's world, office size and location were determinants of status and power. She heard the grumblings of "having a woman around" but smiled and remained cheerful, non-threatening, without rank; no power, no threat, and thus of little consequence. In truth, she was treated mostly as a curiosity, someone who would doubtless be out of sight and out of mind someday soon. She spent nights with her Dominican brethren in the Monastery of Mater Ecclesiae located on Vatican Hill near the Aquilone Fountain in Vatican City and days ushering about performing unknown activities unmonitored by anyone as far as the Vatican household could tell. She apparently only answered to the Pontiff. The history of women at the Vatican could be written on one page and it was very rare to see one assigned a regular task or position at the level of the pope's entourage.

A large gilded frame with the Virgin of Guadalupe graced the wall above her desk. The desk itself was small and old, but was made from fine hardwood. The Dell computer and printer sitting on it were not connected to the network. This raised no alarms. Why did a woman and a nun need to be connected to the Vatican Ethernet? The Argentine nun also had a laptop with a satellite connection and a cell phone that connected to the visitor's wi-fi instead of the in-house system required of all Vatican staff. She appeared to be more or less off the Vatican grid, although not completely isolated. The I.T. department and everyone else knew nothing about what she did, which was just the way she liked it.

Sr. Angelina was the youngest daughter of a wealthy Argentine family that included many businessmen and ranking military people. One, her uncle General Piccolo, had, along with others, committed many atrocities in the 1970's after a coup that deposed Isabel Peron and prosecuted the subsequent reign of terror and suppression against the socialist Peronists. Many thousands believed to be Peronist sympathizers were rounded up. Young and old, mothers separated from their children - all were interned in remote camps or soccer stadiums around the country. Thousands – the "Desaparecidos" - were executed by binding and flying them in helicopters out over the Atlantic, then tossing them out the doors to drown at sea.

Angelina stood apart as the odd duck in her family. Her three sisters married well, and two had children. Even as a child she had learned that her formidable intellect made others uncomfortable and that everyone preferred that she not share opinions. She was, after all, a female, and her destiny was to be fulfilled in the marriage bed or kitchen, not in the study of Marcus Aurelius or Kant. What good was a woman who quoted philosophy but remained unable to prepare a casserole or submit to the desires of her husband when called upon?

Even worse, Angelina, as the youngest daughter in the family, was never to marry, and instead care for her mother in old age. This old custom in well-to-do Latin American families left her few options or opportunities. A formal education would be denied to her. Angelina had decided early on that her only real alternative was the convent. This did not sit well with her family. However, the current Pope Lucas was a Cardinal at the time and a long-time family friend. He encouraged Angelina's decision, pointing out that her family had money to take care of themselves, so hiring domestic help was no burden. Although initially resistant to the idea, her parents had relented. Having a child in the Catholic vocations as a priest or nun was viewed as admirable and blessed and added prestige to the family credentials in a very Catholic nation.

Some might see her Dominican vocation as even more limiting and restrictive than spending the rest of her life as a household servant who was little more than a slave to her mother's meals, illnesses, and bowels. Sr. Angelina did not. She loved her mother but had cherished the opportunity to pursue her studies and interests and continue writing in the many areas in which she excelled – which were extensive. Then, even better, Angelina was posted as an aide to Bishop Lucas' home and office. Good luck, certainly, but Angelina's wide-ranging knowledge and outspokenness had been viewed as a problem by the abbess in the convent. Catholic Christianity is not a democracy, and outspoken men and women frequently find themselves silenced, regardless of good intentions. Even worse, 1700 years of tradition meant a woman was as likely to make a major contribution to Catholic dogma and practice as a house-broken, speaking chimpanzee. It would never happen.

Occasionally, she felt lonely and regressed into *"what if"*. *What if* she had been allowed to marry and have children? *What if* she had been allowed to go to college? When this happened, she shook off the self-pity, focused on the miracle of connecting viscerally and intellectually with her bishop. Most priests were the kind, traditional, unquestioning, dutiful, type. Easy to understand and predict, but a little disappointing – just as most men are, she had long ago decided. Lucas was genuine, kind, and smart, as were thousands in the Church. Yet this man was not threatened by her abilities and achievements. He valued her and what she could do. He even listened to her opinions on contentious issues such as birth control and homosexual priests.

Intelligence shone from his eyes and he had built a vitae of success with kindness and firmness, by being daring yet thoughtful. Always smiling, but remaining unwavering when under attack, he was respected. Complacency and ennui were strangers in his administration. He had proven himself a fearless reformer in the face of political opposition, working under the hardship of a murderous South American regime and a public looking to him for answers to difficult questions.

She checked the small clock on her desk and saw that it was 4:01 p.m. Prayers began at 6:26 at Rome's St. Cecilia Church and Convent, where she was housed. Its medieval Trastevere neighborhood was famous for Old World appearance and flavor. Although not a vowed member of the convent, she enjoyed the guest privileges accorded to a visiting nun. Being housed outside the Vatican also diminished oversight on her duties.

In spite of the Second Vatican Council asking the religious orders to modernize, the Dominicans led a semi-cloistered life, rarely leaving the convent. They restored liturgical documents or performed daily prayers at the altar of St. Cecilia, a woman martyred during the third century for sharing her Christian faith with others. They tended gardens inside the walled convent or prepared displays in the cathedral according to the church calendar. Her status and exactly what she did remained a subject of speculation among the Dominican sisters, but they had come to accept that she was a guest as well as a person who had a "special relationship" with the new Argentine pope. Sr. Angelina was free to come and go as she wished, but did try to pray regularly with her brethren. She had at least an hour before prayers began.

Her eight years in Buenos Aires with Lucas had been a gift from God, she knew. She now believed that he was the one; the only hope of changing a stagnant, traditional, male dominated institution that had become less relevant in a world of science, computers, and a rapacious global economy. And it had all been totally unexpected. When he had unexpectedly won the vote, Sr. Angelina had been ecstatic. They would all learn that this pope was different.

Her laptop pinged, indicating new mail. She checked the source and decided to wait. She knew the sender, and her reply would take some time, perhaps an hour or more. There was no urgency – it was an ongoing discussion.

The Dominican nun eyed the trashcan in which she had deposited the candy, but turned away and looked pensively at the virgin. Angelina then reached into her bottom desk drawer and withdrew a brown folder labeled "Old Arabic Recipes." She removed the paper-clipped files on top and reinserted them at the bottom, then removed the clip binding a group of 20 photocopied sheets of paper. She didn't read

35

Arabic, or in this case ancient Aramaic, but the photocopied pages were also accompanied by Spanish and English translations. Her friend Lucas had entrusted her with the documents after swearing her to secrecy. Like the man who had lent them to her, they brought great hope, but also a promise that might never be fulfilled if her friend was not successful in his reforms.

She stood, glanced again at the virgin and made the sign of the cross. She locked her door, turning off the overhead light in favor of a small desk lamp with its narrow beam in order to read and study the translations loaned her by Lucas. She never tired of the task, finding joy in the thought of their existence. She took a deep breath in anticipation and her heart skipped a beat. She turned to the first page of the documents inexplicably discovered somewhere in southern Mexico and began reading:

"My name is Thomas, and I and others were in the company of Jesus of Nazareth until the Pharisees condemned him and the Romans crucified him. To know Jesus is to know his teachers, and so I have done my best to travel the same roads that Jesus did as a young man.

I lived six months with the Essenes in the desert outside Jerusalem and studied the writings of the Teacher of Righteousness, as did Jesus. I traveled to ancient Susa near Babylon and to Damascus, then through the expanse of land controlled by the great khans, and east over the barren mountains into India, just as Jesus did. Now I know the man Jesus, and I want you to know him also."

Chapter Five

Archaeologist David Wolf used his dirty sleeve to wipe sweat from his brow. The late afternoon sun was faintly visible through the forest. His current archaeological site was just outside the Mayan Indian village, Lacanja, near the world famous Montes Azules Biosphere Reserve, the largest remnant of the untouched Lacandon jungle in Chiapas and now a national park of over 290,000 hectares north of the Bonampak Mayan ruin. Today was hot and humid and smelled of newly turned earth and composted vegetation mixed with occasional whiffs of diesel fuel, seasoned with raw sewage from three portable latrines. Large fruit bats darted in and out of the shadows, veering to avoid unseen obstacles. Although much of the brush and vegetation had been cleared before work began, the area was surrounded by the enormous trunks of towering ceiba trees as well as others with latin names like Terminalia Amazonia, Guatteria anomala, Swietenia macrophylla, Ulmus Mexican, and the Mammoth Guanacaste trees, all of them tangled with leafy vines and shrouded in red-flowered bromeliads. The Lacandon Jungle boasts 1,500 tree species, at least 25 percent of Mexico's animal species, 33 percent of all the country's Mexican bird species and an estimated 40 percent of Mexican butterflies. Jaguars, Mexico's largest and most dangerous jungle predator, stalk prey in the forests and along its many rivers. Swamp crocodiles, Red Macaw and tapirs still populate the forests as do eagles, howler monkeys and spider monkeys. Swarming ants can decimate a corpse in record time, and the vegetation can sting, poison, or entrap the unwary.

The professor glanced at his wristwatch and saw it was nearly 6:00 in the evening. His workers, most of them Indians from Lacanja village, were milling about. Some washed their hands and faces in broad water basins while others stood stoically in the shade, waiting to be told the workday was over. They were an eclectic group, many dressed as common Mexican laborers in cotton pants, light shirts, sandals, and a broad-brimmed hat. Others wore the distinctive traditional dress of the Lacandon Indian, a simple white cotton cloth thrown over the body with cutouts for arms and head.

David had been working at this site for three months with little to show for his labors. A once promising location, he now realized that the anomalous mounds and exposed, tumbled rock were quite probably nothing more than an administrative outpost, or garrison for the not-too-distant Classic Mayan Palenque ruin. He found little if any indication of religious ritual, burials, battles or even a residential community; trade and commerce, yes, but even this not so much. Just a site that would add little to the understanding of the Classic Era Maya – it was exactly the type of place he always tried to avoid. He had received a grant from private philanthropy and was afraid his results were going to disappoint his funders. Maybe it was best if he ceased operations sooner rather than later so as not to waste any more donor money. Funding was difficult to come by these days, and honesty was important.

The professor heard shouts and turned south toward the entry to the Lacanja trail to see what was happening. From the shadows a bent, older man with satchel and machete strapped over his back exited the shady trail and, leaning on a walking cane, stood in the sunlight. He smiled and nodded, acknowledged numerous greetings, spoke briefly to one man in particular, an older worker, Antonio, then turned and peered across the wheelbarrows, piles of earth, stone, and staked-out excavation areas to look at David. The old man frowned, lifted and thrust his cane forcefully into the earth as if annoyed, then began making his way across the site to the professor.

And so it begins, thought David, *or maybe not*. Who could say with certainty? He sighed and steeled himself. The unpredictability of the Bone Man, a Mayan shaman named Balaam, meaning jaguar in the Mayan language, was legendary. He referred to all non-Indians as Ladinos and seemed to despise them. However, he was much beloved and cherished by the Indians, and of Guatemala and Chiapas as a leader, healer, and very important person. The shaman's age was a point of speculation, and some believed he was more than 100 years old. His unwritten resume was known only to a few; shaman, curandero, mystic, Guatemalan terrorist, leader of the Zapatista Rebellion and, at times, rancorous malcontent. How many wives and children he had also remained a point of speculation. David had quit counting, wondering if perhaps the traditional Maya or even the shaman himself had a different definition of "wife" than most people did.

Balaam, coffee-skinned, short of stature, with a wrinkled Mayan face, prominent nose, and black eyes, stared up and into the professor's eyes. It was discomfiting. David knew the shaman better than many, yet found being around him unsettling. This time, though, it was unavoidable. David had sent a message two weeks ago, through the informal but reliable network of gossip and news flowing along the jungle paths throughout the Lacandon that he needed to see the Bone Man.

"*Ahua*," said Balaam, addressing the professor with the respectful Mayan term directed at important people. "You look, call me," he said in broken Spanish. "Me, I busy, but me come see you, *ahua*. What you want?" The Indian thumped the earth with his walking stick, frowning.

"Balaam, I have an important message, or I wouldn't have bothered you." David stared back at the old Indian. "A man in the Vatican, in Rome, Italy, called to say that Pope Lucas is coming to Chiapas and wants to meet you and Fr. Salvador. It's a secret. No one knows. He really wants to talk to Salvador, but I told him that this is not possible unless he talks to you first. Am I right?"

"You stupid like most white men, *ahua*, but I let go, okay this. No...no way black robes see talk *Hombre Sagrado*. Father Salvador belong Maya. He have Indian wife. He have baby. He have good cup heal medicine. Indian love Holy Man. Black robes want steal cup and hurt Holy Man. No, no, no!" the shaman cried, slamming his walking stick onto the earth repeatedly. Suddenly three Zapatista soldiers with rifles and bandoliers strapped over their chests charged into the open glade and moved to stand behind their leader.

David's heart skipped a beat and he took a step back, then took a deep breath, holding up his hand, palm outward toward Balaam. "I told them it wouldn't work. I told them the Pope was wasting his time."

"Who pope? The Big Potato come?" asked the curandero, badly skewering the Spanish word for pope and potato.

"Yes, Pope Lucas. That's what I said. Not black robe, white robe."

"Don't believe Big Potato come Lacandon Jungle. Why? Want cup, yes? Want kill Indian for white Jesus God, yes?" The old shaman seemed taken aback at the notion that the Catholic Pope himself was coming and wanted to meet him.

"Why me? Big Potato important man. Wear white robe. No. No more robe here. Tell Big Potato stay other side, big water...big ocean. He come here, Zapatista fight - all Indians fight robes and Ladinos."

"He wants to talk with you, Balaam," pleaded David. "He wants to see Salvador, but he wants to talk to you. Maybe about the books that were lost – you know – not just Salvador. I'm just delivering a message. It's a secret," David repeated.

"Books, *ahua*? Cylinders with old writing?" The shaman looked askance, then pointed his staff at the professor. "Secrets...what secret?"

"His visit, Balaam. No one must know he's coming."

"Secret visit Big Potato white robe? No Mexican soldier, no Ladino? No one but Balaam, Zapatista, and..." he left Fr. Salvador's name unsaid.

"Balaam, it's pronounced P*a*pa, not papa. It's disrespectful to say it wrong."

The curandero waved him off, looked at the ground a few moments, tapping his walking stick lightly on the earth. Finally he said, "Secreto, eh?" Then he caught David's eye and held it. "Maybe yes...maybe no *Hombre Sagrado*. Not decide now. Book...I have book, old book...maybe three-four book."

"What!" David blurted. "You recovered books? Why didn't you tell me, Balaam? Why didn't you..." then the old shaman lowered his walking stick and whacked David's knee. The soldiers took another menacing step forward, but Balaam held up a hand to stop them.

"Ow...what the...you grizzled old..." David reached for his leg.

"That nothing, *ahua*. Just reminder, you. Listen...tell friend Antonio," the shaman pointed to the older worker. "You say Antonio when meet Big Potato want come meet, ahua. Maybe I meet white robe. Maybe I give gift. Yes...you tell Big Potato I give gift," and he turned abruptly and lumbered across the work site, using his stick in rhythm. He stopped and smiled as he accepted everyone's best wishes. He listened to their stories and complaints for about 15 minutes, then waved and headed toward the shade of the Lacanja village trail.

Fetid piece of jaguar shit, groused David silently, watching the old man entertain his brethren near forest's edge. Why he put up with the cranky old man, he had never understood. The Bone Man did treat him a bit better than other "Ladinos", but David did not know why. Balaam knew everything there was to know about the forest and its animals. The shaman didn't speak Spanish as well as a small child, but probably was fluent in ten of the Mayan dialects spoken in Mexico and Guatemala. If there was anything that anyone still knew about the ancient Mayan way of life, religion, customs, healing, etc., it was because of Balaam. Unfortunately David had discovered that he had needed the curandero more than the old Indian needed him.

The professor's knee throbbed where the shaman had swatted him, but he didn't want to look at it with the workers milling about. He smiled, shouted a cheerful, "that's all for today!" and watched them turn and file south onto the trail toward the village or connecting road outside Lacanja that led to other Indian hamlets strewn through the forest. Alone at last, he sat, rolled up his pant leg and saw a lump near his shin. He touched it gingerly, ouch….new bone bruise. In all these years Balaam had never struck him, even a small glancing blow like this. What was this all about? Aging? Was it the sensitivity of the subject – Salvador and the cup, or the books? What had set him off? This is strange. And those darn Zapatista soldiers. They nearly always accompanied him. The professor knew that Balaam was important in the informal hierarchy of the Zapatista Rebellion, but now he was beginning to wonder just how high up the old man was.

Whatever – David needed to lock the tool sheds and make sure that the Honda generators were placed inside. After this day in the humidity and heat, he could use a brandy - better yet maybe a couple of cold Negra Modelo beers. It was time to walk the three kilometer trail to Lacanja and the highway where his car was parked. Although David had at first been skeptical, it appeared that this meeting was, in fact, going to occur. He would have to send an email to the address he had been given by the man at the Vatican. The name was easily recognizable to any student of Mexican history, and thus odd, thought the professor. *SorJuana@hotmail.com* was not a normal email address. Sor Juana (Sister Joan) had been one of the greatest writers of the Sixteenth Century. This, plus her genius and understanding of just about everything that had ever been written, had put her life in danger. She reluctantly agreed to enter a convent, under the control of the church, with the stipulation that she kept her books and could continue writing. It saved her from being burned at the stake. Women had no role, no education, no voice, and no nothing during her era. Even in the convent she and her work remained under constant scrutiny and criticism and continued to be viewed by some as heretical.

The professor really didn't want to get involved with anything having to do with that stupid cup or those damnable books again. He had hoped that horrible episode was over; tragic, ridiculous, and even incredulous. David had even spent a week in the San Cristobal jail after being entrapped in the machinations of the Bone Man and Papal Inquisitor. But now the Vatican had called – or at least some character who called herself Sor Juana had contacted him. He had first thought it was a crank call, but it was followed by several emails, and he had decided the whole mess was too involved to be the work of a nut or prankster.

David was a scientist and was intent on remaining a man of cause and effect in his understanding of the world. The Vatican held deep resources to illuminate the mysteries he had uncovered in the jungles of southern Mexico. He could have said no, but then he wouldn't know how all this worked out. David had been brought into this mess by a former student and priest, Salvador Lopez, now known as the *Holy Man*. Father Lopez had found a burial box with an uncorrupted, ancient body and papyrus books – really scrolls – beneath a ruined church and shared his discovery with David.

Balaam had discovered the "good cup heal medicine" in that same burial box when it was stolen by a thief and the body unceremoniously dumped. The Bone Man had taken the cup and given it to Fr. Lopez, and it seemed to be performing miracles of healing, resulting in his becoming known as the "Holy Man."

Could Salvador really possess Christendom's greatest treasure, the Holy Cup? And now that mean, little brown shit, Balaam, says he had recovered some of the books! Possibly some of Christianity's most important documents were in the hands of a disgruntled, disrespectful Mayan shaman. And what was that Big Potato crap? P*a*pa, as opposed to papa, or Pope as opposed to potato. The professor would bet a thousand pesos that the shaman spoke better Spanish than that. The big potato – what a jerk.

Ah Jeeez, he thought, limping deeper into the dappled shade of the Lacandon Jungle. He began to envision a sweating bottle of ice cold beer and his wife's welcoming smile. He picked up his pace and began to reflect on what he would say and how he would handle the email to ***SorJuana@hotmail.com***. His life was about to get complicated again.

Chapter Six

Pope Lucas, clad in pajamas and cotton robe, sat on the edge of his bed, watching Sr. Angelina head for the apartment's entry door. She had insisted on staying until he completed his insulin injection. The pope's health was a very serious issue to the nun. She was a whirlwind of energy, a friend, and one of very few women whose mere presence demanded notice. With the closing of the door, he relaxed in the dim room. A lamp with two bulbs shone brightly over his desk on the far side of the room. Light leaked through gaps in the curtains from the newly installed LED's illuminating various Vatican paths winding around buildings, residences, dormitories, and offices but did little to dispel the comfortable darkness. Just outside the world's smallest nation state, Rome, a bustling city that never really slept, rumbled on endlessly.

The pontiff was tired, and his shoulders sagged. The demands of the job weighed heavy, and his mind simmered, unable to sleep. So many thousands, or hundreds of thousands requiring guidance, love, or sometimes just a kind word and pat on the back. His least favorite chore? A stifling Vatican bureaucracy that was ever-present and tedious, and required constant attention. He glanced to his desk where a ceramic cup and pot of hot peppermint tea waited for him, but then his attention shifted to the small altar with kneeling bench in the corner near a window. The light from between his curtains illuminated the thorn - crowned head and sad face of Christ. Prayer and meditation were the only real salve for what ailed Lucas. Only in communing with the Holy Spirit would he find solace, the strength to endure, and any measure of peace. He rose to clear his mind with evening prayers, when he noticed the blinking light on his satellite fed laptop; mail from *SorJuana@hotmail.com*. He hesitated, so soon? Hadn't he answered her just last night? Unfortunately, only at this time of night when no one interrupted him could he sufficiently clear his mind to engage in the challenge and intellectual play that surely awaited in the emails. He enjoyed them, and the discussions were a treasured remnant of his former life in Argentina. *Maybe just a few paragraphs*, he assured himself. It was difficult to say "no" to Sor Juana, and he envisioned his intellectual nemesis and friend sitting at her own desk, waiting for his responses. He smiled, adjusted his robe, and tightened the belt, then sat at his desk to touch a couple of buttons and open his mail.

To my mentor Pope Lucas;

I want to thank you for the replies to my queries, although I must say that I found them inadequate and trite and very much what I would expect from someone steeped in canon law. I have tried mightily to remain interested in the misogynistic books that you ask me to read. Frankly, Augustine's Confessions seemed little more than a thinly-veiled mea culpa of a man with homosexual tendencies. St. Thomas Aquinas, I must confess, is an easier read, but his unsupported conclusions and assertions stretch even the most elastic of minds. As you will recall, Saint Thomas strongly inferred that women were little more than defective men, and that whereas man was created in the Glory of God, woman was created in the glory of man. What a bunch of nonsense. But much of Church law is derived from his SUMMA THEOLIGOCA and thus, Holy Father, it is canon law that remains a major culprit and impediment to reform as regards the status of women. I am working on the substantial list of books and essays you suggested, and I promise to focus how I address the issues I raise based on them.

If you will allow me to restate my basic premise in these discussions; tradition and laws written by men that place women socially, economically, and politically subservient to men in every sphere of life are simply unfounded in the Gospels – Augustine and Aquinas be damned. If one reads the Gospels, even today knowing they were heavily redacted to restrict female role and influence, it is still evident that Jesus almost always met with women, preached to women, and frequently spoke of helping women, children and the poor. Women disciples remained at the cross until Christ's death and they were the first at the empty tomb. It's obvious, even though much of it was edited out, Jesus was accompanied by Mary Magdalene until his death, perhaps as a wife. Although I have not seen them, I have read that there are paintings and drawings on the walls of the catacombs suggesting women played very significant roles in the early Church. This is not a small thing.

Furthermore, I find your constant references to St. Thomas Aquinas and St. Augustine, regarding the role of women and men to be very archaic and silly. Must we celebrate Aquinas and Augustine forever? Is there never to be anything new in the Church? Does the lens of the past blind us to the future? Is God so disgusted with His Creation that he has stopped speaking to us? You see, Holy Father, it really comes down to sex and babies, and male ignorance of both. During the Dark Ages when much of this ridiculous writing occurred, the only people who could read and write were monks, and most of them were truly unlearned and inexperienced as regards family, marriage and children. Many monasteries brewed beer and wine and were famous for their drunkenness, and most monks were into self-pleasuring and practiced "Onanism." In their ignorance of biology and cause and effect, countless theologians have forever wrapped female sexuality in a cloak of filth and superstition and condemned us to an endless existence of servitude to men. We are not truly people and need constantly to apologize for being born female.

There are a few Aquinas statements that are highly respected, yet prejudicial and ignorant beyond belief.

1. Men have a "noble role in the conjugal act."

What does that even mean? What's the role of the woman? How does passion and rutting with hedonistic fervor comprise noble behavior? Sex is a basic biological drive, not a "noble" act. Is Christian charity evident in the conjugal act? I think not.

2. Aquinas states that women are "more physical and carnal and insatiable than men." Really? Not the voice of experience, I suspect. He also rejected sexual intercourse "unless it led to spiritual, transcendent knowledge." I have no experience and am not a good authority, but I have learned that men engage in the "conjugal act" because it feels good while many women only do so because they are convinced they must. I fail to see how "feels good" equates with spiritual, transcendent knowledge. Other than making babies, an orgasm seems to be the only goal.

3. Early Church writings continue to influence us today even though these scribblings were unlearned and completely absent of science. Women, sex, birth, and especially menstruation were, and in many cases are, viewed with horror and sniggering jokes. We're filthy beasts, you see? Women's sexual organs are always portrayed as polluting and dangerous to men. Many medieval theologians believed that mother's milk was actually menstrual blood heated and transformed in the breast into milk to nourish the child. The vagina

has always been viewed as the filthiest place on the planet and a passageway to intercourse with Satan.

4. As regards the vagina, Melania the Younger (I guess there's an Older somewhere), a very well respected, but neglected woman writer, wrote that "no bodily part that God had created could be filthy because all the prophets and saints were born through one."

5. Melania's writings occurred early, around A.D. 414, but were ignored, as women's voices of reason were always rejected and overruled in the early Church, primarily because of the nonsense that the apostle Paul passed off as dogma that was nothing more than dysfunctional Jewish custom and tradition that has always favored males.

6. I understand that you are the Holy Father of our Church and I respect that. I also know that we are friends and that I can talk to you about things of which I cannot speak to others. You are destined to be the reformer. You have been chosen by peers to lead our Church in the 21st Century and beyond. No one but you has the power or respect required to initiate the sweeping changes required to even have an intelligent conversation based on science and reality rather than tradition and ignorance. What are the chances of this conversation occurring without your leadership? I think you know the answer. None.

Anyway, Lucas - on a different subject, the Mexican archaeologist, David Wolf, responded to my mail. It's difficult to gauge what's really going on over there. He is obviously harboring resentment over our Father Gregory placing him in jail three years ago in order to coerce his help. He feels wronged, embarrassed, and believes he was used badly. I have already reported this to you, and I responded to him with your apologies and kind offer of a paid trip here to Rome for him and his wife as well as access to the Vatican archives for his research – whether or not he decides to help us. I think your offer caught him by surprise and hopefully will have a beneficial result.

He reports he did see that Mayan shaman character, Balaam, and the meeting did not go well. Any meeting with the "Holy Man," the former Father Salvador Lopez of the Diocese of Tuxtla Gutierrez, will be difficult at best and most likely impossible. The good news is that this Indian shaman has agreed to meet you – sort of. The archaeologist also mentioned something about one of those old books like the one you loaned me on St. Thomas' travels that you said had been lost forever. Seems as though the shaman has a book or books and that there is a possibility that the he may give it to you, although why he would do so isn't mentioned. Do you have further instructions for me as regards this matter? Please advise:

Your Friend,
Angelina.

Books! All the ancient books were not destroyed? Extraordinary! Maybe. Pope Lucas smiled, logged off, and leaned back into his chair. Maybe a positive outcome in Chiapas was already in the works. These books, perhaps the writings of St. Thomas, haunted Lucas' thoughts. When copies of three of the manuscripts arrived, euphoria had captured the archivists and few individuals who knew of their existence. This had quickly turned to ashes with the wreck in the Chiapan Highlands that destroyed the originals and took the life of the Papal Inquisitor, Father Gregory. The possibility that even one of the books remained assured the pontiff he was correct to meet the professor, shaman and hopefully, former priest. If only he could see even one of these priceless, ancient treasures, or perhaps touch it! His mind conjured convincing images of this Balaam giving one or all of them to him. Rumors that the Holy Grail of ancient lore was performing miracles in southern Mexico were outlandish, but also must be investigated. The issue was not only one of religious piety, but also very political, and the man wielding it was a former Catholic priest. The right time to make the trip was now, and the professor's revelations about the book or books only made the trip more urgent. Although these issues were unknown to just about everyone, the importance of what the manuscripts might contain, as well as the cup itself, remained potential stumbling blocks to the Church's ability to maintain its credibility and govern a far-flung Catholic membership.

Pope Lucas set aside thoughts of treasures, real and imagined, that he might find in Mexico and returned to Sor Juana's arguments. What passion! And with Pope Lucas' guidance her ideas were framed by 2000 years of history and scholarship. Most of her analysis was correct, but ignored the truly formidable task of reform. Changing 1700 years of religious practice and dogma was a challenging, if not impossible, undertaking. History, tradition and scholarship were not easily tossed out the door. If it was simply a matter of issuing a Bull or edict of some sort, it would have already occurred if the previous pontiff had been willing to do so. Although the pope was, indeed, a powerful person in the Catholic Church, he too, had limitations under which he labored. Tradition was an onerous boss.

He glanced at the clock and saw that it was nearly 10:00. His altar beckoned, and the need to calm his will and center his mind tugged at him. Sor Juana would have to await his reply until tomorrow. There was no urgency. Angelina as Sor Juana was a brilliant advocate and difficult to debate. Under Pope Lucas' guidance, she had become more learned and well-read. Passion and advocacy were now supported with scholarship and logic.

Prayer and meditation were the only salve for a conflicted soul such as his. He studied the thorn-crowned Christ, made the sign of the cross, walked the few steps to the prayer bench and knelt heavily. He grasped a rosary that hung from the altar and began his first decade of prayer. As he moved through the Our Father's and Hail Mary's he felt his spirit calm and his mind focus as the ancient ritual provided solace and peace. Thirty minutes later he rose, turned off his desk lamp, and climbed into bed. His chest rose and fell briefly, as he took several large breaths. Then he relaxed and gave up the day's burdens. Within moments his breathing became shallow and he slept.

Chapter Seven

Father Salvador Lopez, the Holy Man, sat in the late afternoon shade of a Bejuco tree amidst a sweating warren of mud brick buildings with rusted, corrugated steel roofs. The village spread itself unevenly through hillsides riven with rutted, shady paths. His son sat nearby and played with a stick and string toy. He watched his spouse of two years, a tawny-skinned, raven haired Mayan Indian girl of about 20 years of age who wore a black cotton skirt and beautifully smocked blouse heavily embroidered with bright turquoise, red, and purple flowers. She squatted effortlessly on her haunches in the Indian fashion while cutting slivers of bark from a Bejuco tree limb, tossing them into a boiling pot of water. She glanced up at him, smiled, and returned to the task of making the Mayan Indian version of forest coffee from the tree's sap. She monitored the fluid's progress as it turned a sheer golden color and attained a thick consistency. The liquid was sweet without the bitterness of coffee, refreshing and welcome.

The Holy Man contemplated his situation, something he did often nowadays. He felt content – actually, more than content. He sometimes slept in squalid villages, other times in tents or shelters constructed from forest materials, depending on where they traveled, how important secrecy was, and if there were even any villages in the area. Almost daily he preached God's truths among those with dry, shriveled souls that were parched of emotion by life's hardships. These were some of the poorest people on the planet. The ceramic cup that he carried, in truth, was the glue that held everything together; the validation of his beliefs, the font and elixir of health, and the mysterious power that was a miracle. It was the chipped chalice and what it represented that provided him inspiration and cemented his commitment. Fr. Lopez used to wonder why he had been chosen for this task, but no longer. It didn't matter. He knew that he had been blessed beyond belief and that he was only a vessel, a purveyor of truth and spiritual enlightenment to the Maya of Guatemala and Mexico. They were unlearned and poor, but rich in faith, and drinking from the cup had, on many occasions, been the catalyst for healing physical ailments while restoring damaged souls and broken spirits.

Balaam, the Bone Man, had given him this cup recovered from the burial box of a previous "holy man" and charged him with undertaking this ministry. His unique life and the years of obsessive "truth-seeking" that had captured his mind and depressed his spirit had fallen away, giving him a clarity he had never known. Despite the constant moving to avoid authorities and government officials, as well as treasure seekers, cranks, and representatives of other Christian groups, he remained content and inexplicably happy. He had become part of a great work, as he had hoped and prayed as a young priest.

And now stories of miracles, healings, and tales of the "Holy Man" attracted those seeking to connect with the person and stories emanating from the jungles. Some, he knew, wanted the holy cup for themselves or their religious sect, but General Marcos and the Zapatistas were vigilant and secretive regarding his movements and schedule. Salvador had learned to trust and have faith in his Zapatista entourage. At this point he didn't know where he was going or how long he would be on any certain location after arriving. He had a wife, a child, and better food than most, and a mission which he simply could not and would not quit.

Salvador was a former priest from an upper middle class family in Mexico. Educated in Mexico, and then Rome, he had been "radicalized" by returning priests and monks from Central America who were active participants in the left-leaning political beliefs of Catholic Liberation Theology. These clergy actively pursued policies to better the lives of the wretchedly poor and disenfranchised of Meso-America. Five hundred years after Columbus mistakenly sailed onto the shores of these lands previously unknown to Europeans, the overwhelming majority of real estate in the southern hemisphere of the New World was inhabited by some of the poorest people on earth. Corruption in these countries remained endemic and virtually everyone was excluded from a social and economic mainstream dominated by rich families with genealogies stretching back to the Conquest. In the small country of El Salvador alone a group of families known as "Las Catorce" (the Fourteen) owned every piece of arable land in the country. These Liberation Theology priests and nuns based their work on the Gospels of the New Testament, believing that the truth of Christianity was readily understandable if only people read and studied what Jesus said and practiced when alive. They believed that our Savior didn't say anything difficult to understand – revolutionary perhaps – but not hard to grasp. He repeatedly stated that we must help the poor, women, and children and that the rich will have difficulty entering Heaven if they do not. But Christianity had been co-opted by the Industrial Revolution and Calvinist ideologies, which became ascendant and further diminished the role and importance of women. Christianity, as supported and promoted by USA's early industrialists, was mostly Protestant Calvinists who believed they had acquired God's favor and were preselected with a ticket to salvation and Heaven through the acquisition of money, property, and status. Their prosperity was proof that they were favored by God and destined to Heaven. These ideas in conjunction with the systemic corruption exported from the Old World to the New World resulted in the intractable, perhaps impossible situation that the poor of Latin America found themselves in today.

Catholic Liberation Theology, opposed by big money and existing power structures, became viewed as strictly political and Marxist, and a danger to the status quo. Religion, regardless of the variety practiced, must function smoothly within any society's framework, or it aids and abets social dysfunction and encourages revolution. Thus these priests and monks found themselves recalled to Rome by unhappy bishops to reassess their fitness for a priestly vocation, or to be reeducated and reassigned far away from the temptations of Latin American socialism. Salvador, however, listened and learned and became convinced of the inherent truths of Catholic Liberation Theology. When assigned to Mexico, he had been ripe for the picking by Zapatistas seeking a religious leader to focus on the spiritual needs of the Maya Indians. He agreed to join them, and thus willingly entered a lifetime of poverty and insecurity to practice what he believed to be basic truths imparted to mankind by Jesus in the Gospels. The fact that he unexpectedly acquired a holy cup that worked miracles and imbued followers with the Holy Spirit was quite simply an undeserved, but very welcome reward for his sacrifice.

The Holy Man had spent many years just going through the motions when celebrating mass and dispensing the sacraments. Even here, among the Indians to whom he administered the sacraments – especially communion – they approached the rite with dead eyes, their souls insulated from truly receiving Christ into their body. Robots. Some seemed to awaken with the miraculous cup and his ministry. Dormant beliefs turned to joy when partaking of communion by celebrating the ritual of mindfulness and renewal that communion provided spiritual seekers. His ministry created a new awareness and revival of spirit among the Indians. His obvious poverty, Indian wife, and much loved Zapatista brethren provided him instant credibility. Word always spread in advance of his coming, and nowadays he found himself in crowds of several hundred, if not a thousand or more seekers. He was the purveyor of good health and healing. He dispensed hope and spiritual joy. Unlike other priests in the Church, he went to the people, instead of the people having to come to the Church. He left his vows, the Church's doctrine, and its dogma behind.

With "miracles" occurring at each sermon among the needy, his reputation grew. Salvador found himself in a lifestyle similar to other famous religious vagabonds like Siddhartha, John the Baptist, Jesus, and Zoroaster; transcendent leaders teaching outside the framework of an established church and belief system; revolutionaries explaining man's place in the universe apart from religious orthodoxy and dogma. Although not his intention, he was becoming the catalyst for a bloodless coup. His revolution was spiritual in nature, but was infecting the poor in a land where opportunities existed only for the rich.

Thus he became a problem for the Catholic Church as well as the governments of Mexico and Guatemala. Some were starting to pay attention. Some worried. They had never faced a challenge like the Holy Man. His threat was not easily defined. He could be accused of heresy, but not sedition against the state. He could be labelled as a quack, except there were now too many testimonials to ignore. He could be pilloried as an extremist or religious nut, except his personal behavior and comportment was purportedly modest and normal. He could be attacked as a demagogue, but reportedly spoke sincerely and modestly, and asked for nothing – no money, no followers – and exhibited no extreme behavior. Simply stated, the Holy Man of the Lacandon and Petén jungles had become an unacknowledged problem for the state. He labored without supervision or control and with an agenda sure to conflict with theirs at some point. What would be the flashpoint? When would it occur and how would they handle it? This question and others stewed in a crucible of unshaped events sure to occur, but difficult to predict.

Unacknowledged at Los Pinos where the president lived, and out of sight and mind in the halls and offices of the Mexican Camera, was the Holy Man and his cup and his miracles. Many had met privately to discuss the issue and assess his ministry as a threat. This Holy Man was supported and protected by the Zapatistas, wasn't he? How and why was the Holy Man connected to the Zapatistas? This jungle evangelist and his ministry appeared as pure as the driven snow, but the Zapatistas...? The Mayan revolutionaries wanted to expel the white man and give all the land in Central America back to the filthy Indians. This "Holy Man" was just a tool, an unexpected political device employed by communist agitators using religion as their platform. The Zapatistas were socialist scum, but this Holy Man and his cup were different. How did a religious zealot and a bunch of dirty, illiterate Indians merit such good fortune? If the chalice was as reported, then it most assuredly should be taken from the former priest and his rag-tag Indian revolutionaries. Perhaps it was time to have a serious discussion with the pope. His avoidance, or ignorance of the issue was becoming a liability for the state. Control was the issue. Control was always the issue.

**

As Father Salvador sat on a stump sipping steaming bejuco, he heard the distant chatter and laughter of children from inside the Lacandon Jungle. The sounds drew near, then burst into the village from a shady path that wound through the dense forest. The children ran and jumped with excitement, exclaiming loudly, some pretending to be soldiers like the troop of Zapatista conscripts they had found and accompanied to the village. Midway down the line, somewhere in the middle, appeared a taller, broader man in heavy boots, dark long-sleeved shirt and blue jeans. He had acquired a beard and his hair now grew long, but his manner of walk and easy smile were familiar to all. He carried rifle and a leather bag hung from his neck and shoulder.

Accompanying him on his right was a raven haired, black-eyed, young woman in traditional Indian dress, sporting a wide smile with white teeth – also carrying a bag under her arm. Her belly was swollen and she appeared to be at least seven months pregnant, but walked with little effort, her gait graceful and light. As she entered the glade, Salvador's wife called out a greeting and gained her feet. She waved, dusted hands on her apron, and walked to her friend with outstretched arms. They had much in common these days;

young women, very pregnant and married to very important men living in mountainous jungles, commanding a very large following, yet having no real home of their own.

"Padre Salvador," called Marcos in greeting. He stopped momentarily to issue orders to the few soldiers accompanying him who listened keenly, then seemed to just wander away and merge into the village. His wife smiled and moved toward her friend's open arms. They embraced and kissed and began chattering at once. Tula, Salvador's wife, reached for her friend's hand, and then pulled her along, deeper into the village toward an adobe house in which they were currently staying.

"You have come far?" Salvador stood, hand extended in greeting. It had been a week since he last saw his friend and benefactor. It was Marcos and his men who were Salvador's guides and protector. Marcos was his only connection to the outside world, his link to the Bone Man, his sole source of news, and sometimes his only friend or confidant in this impenetrable jungle populated with poor Indians and myriad animals. It was Marcos who told him where they would next travel to hold services, and it was the Zapatista leader with whom he spent hours conversing about everything from politics and economics, to religion and wives and babies. They had been thrown together because of circumstances, but found that they genuinely enjoyed each other's company. The fact that they had both taken young wives, who themselves were friends, had created an even greater commonality.

Marcos accepted a mug of golden bejuco from his friend, reached and tousled the head of his godson who had lain down his string toy and come to stand nearby. He took a sip, paused to consider its flavor, and then looking to his friend, and said, "I have news."

"Ah… Let's hope it's good news. What have you brought us, Marco?" Salvador placed his own cup to his lips.

Marcos smiled slyly. "Nothing of consequence, but the pope is coming to Mexico."

Salvador's hand jerked, and liquid escaped his mug to dribble onto his shirt. "You're making a joke?" He flicked droplets from his shirt. "You're kidding, right?"

"In fact I'm not, my friend. Balaam asked me to share this information with you. As you know, my father cares little for priests and their rituals, except for you, er…you know…."

"I know. Tell me the rest." Fr. Lopez stared hungrily at his friend. The pope is coming from Italy and…?

"Apparently someone in the Vatican contacted David Wolf and he has spoken to my father. It seems the pope very much wants to meet you in person."

"Not possible. Not going to happen." The priest cast about momentarily, then caught his friend's eye. "What's going on, Marcos? You know this is a big deal for me. I can't get distracted with this…this Church stuff. When I left three years ago, it was forever. When I decided to leave, I didn't have the cup, or even know of its power. I was committed - I can't be tempted or drawn back into the old life. My decision is permanent. It's forever. I can't allow myself to be in the presence of someone like a pope or someone like a…."

"Balaam didn't say that you have to meet with him. He didn't agree to that. Father will know for sure how to handle it. Dr. Wolf is arranging the details. Balaam has a plan of sorts. I don't know what it is exactly, but I'm sure he has a strategy to deal with everything."

"I won't do it - can't do it. Meeting the pope? Do you have any idea how big a deal that would have been for me not so long ago? No," he said firmly. Not now that I have the cup. We have our mission. We have…"

"We have Balaam in our corner, my friend. My father would never compromise you or your mission. Believe me. The last thing he wants is for you to give up the cup. It's yours. No one else deserves it, or can even use it. It only works for you. It's…it's kind of your own thing that no one is going to mess with." Marcos shifted his weight to the other foot, paused, and then placed a hand on his friend's shoulder. "I wouldn't let him if he wanted to…trust me…but there are some issues here that haven't yet been dealt with…that Papal Inquisitor dying, and the books found in with the old Holy Man's burial box."

"I don't have the books - don't know anything about them."

"Neither do I, but I'm starting to think that maybe Balaam recovered one or two after the accident. No telling where he keeps them. Still, he's asking you to come to Lacanja in about a week or so. He's arranging a special gathering and service. Could be nearly a thousand people or so."

"Lacanja is very close to the highway, Marcos. Lots of tourist stuff; not too far from the Bonampak ruin. Palenque is just 40 kilometers up the road. Lots of traffic. Probably soldiers and federales around, you know that."

"Not in the jungle.

"I'm not leaving the jungle."

"No one is asking you. Only to come and serve maybe as a…er…consultant or something."

"Consultant? Don't patronize me. I'm not a political person. Balaam has forgotten more about manipulating people than I'll ever know. If I'm not supposed to meet the pope, what does he need me for? Why endanger the mission by getting so close to government people? The pope travels with a big entourage. Everything he does is publicized in advance. He's a very important man. What if someone informs on us and they know we're coming? It just doesn't make sense."

"I'm told that he's sneaking away to meet Balaam."

"What! The pope doesn't sneak. It would be impossible for him to be away and no one notice it."

"He lands up north in Monterrey tomorrow. He'll be there two days, then he leaves for Mexico City for 4-5 days. Then he's coming to San Cristobal."

"No! You jest! The pope is coming to Chiapas?"

"Two or three days, then he apparently has some sort of flex time where he's going to have a private tour of some ruins, go to one of the old convents, or something. No one knows which ones or when…it's all secret, but I suspect that that's when he'll meet with Balaam and talk about the books."

"And the cup," added Salvador.

"The cup and your mission will never, under any circumstances be compromised. You must believe me."

"My wife is pregnant."

"So is mine. It changes nothing. They wouldn't dream of letting us out of their sight."

The Holy Man hesitated, looked distantly toward the forested mountainsides, then back to his friend. "We're crazy to live like this."

"I never wanted to be like anyone else, and neither did you." Marcos patted his satchel. "I brought refreshments."

Fr. Lopez's face broke into a reluctant smile. "I wonder what the people would think if they knew I had an occasional tequila?"

"Most would be surprised if you didn't, considering your living conditions, others would just want to be invited to have a beverage with the Holy Man."

"You make fun of me?"

"Love you like a brother, my friend...believe it." Marcos extracted a bottle from his bag. "I know you'll want to pray about the pope, but all things in time. Let's have a drink. Let's talk some more. Tell me about the service at Chimaltenango and my friends the Tzotzil. Bunch of ornery troublemakers in that group. Anyway...you may be the Holy Man and me a general in the Zapatista army, but we still have wives to tell us what we're doing wrong." Marcos tossed the remaining bejuco from his cup and refilled it with tequila. Salvador sighed, did the same, and then offered a toast.

"To God and His revolution."

"To God and His revolution," repeated Marcos, tossing the liquid down his throat. "Jesus was a rebel. We're revolutionaries, my friend. I hear this new guy, this Argentine pope, is a progressive and is going to remake the Church."

The Holy Man emptied his cup and held it for refilling. "Unlikely," he said. The man that can reform the Catholic Church hasn't been born yet."

Chapter Eight

It was 9:30 p.m. and Pope Lucas, already fatigued from the day's activities, sat securely in the rear of the Boeing 777-200 Alitalia jet. Vatican City flags had been added to the crest on either side of the white plane's nose to identify it as the Pope's airplane. In actuality, the Vatican did not have an "Air Force One" or "Vatican One" available to the pope. The Holy See always rented a newer, well furbished airplane from Alitalia and paid for the rental by charging Business Class rates to the substantial press corps wishing to accompany the pope on his trips. It was a good solution to the dilemma of keeping costs down and enforcing frugality while improving image. A handful of Cardinals had been invited to accompany him on this trip, including Cardinal Montoya, his chief aide and spokesman. The ever-present Swiss Guard, who would not accompany him, stood at the plane's entry, and security personnel in plain clothes were stationed asymmetrically in the passenger seating and in each kitchenette on the plane to observe activities and preparation of refreshments and snacks.

The lights were turned off at 10:00 p.m. As always there would be insomniacs aboard, those who had difficulty sleeping on planes, others with uncooperative bladders and prostates, and some fraught with worry who roamed the aisles to the kitchenettes or toilets in the front and back. This made sleeping a challenge for everyone. Pope Lucas dreaded these trips. He knew many of the reporters and was on a first name basis with some. The press corps were well meaning, and most of them devout, but the pleasant greetings were quickly finished. Now the hard part began. Some wanted interviews on difficult subjects. Many wanted to ingratiate themselves or gain access to him for as-yet unknown reasons. Some were just pests that talked all the time when he desired nothing more than privacy so that he could read his mail, memos, and other documents vital to keeping his office afloat and crises averted. Around 10:00 p.m. his friend Cardinal Montoya would insist that he put everything aside and try to rest and, hopefully, sleep. When the plane landed in Monterrey, Mexico in the morning they would be met with a crush of excitement; hordes of reporters, thousands of Catholic well-wishers waiting for their once-in-a-lifetime personal view of the pope, a sea of bishops, clergy and Cardinals; plus an endless stream of government officials falling all over themselves trying to please. Although these visits were important, and probably essential in maintaining and invigorating the Catholic populace of the world, they took a toll. It took weeks to recover.

This particular trip included a week of whirlwind activities; visiting old basilicas from the Conquest, luncheons with bishops, daily Mass with thousands of faithful, interspersed with brief sojourns to visit the poor where he would wash the feet of the sick and wretched and bless more babies than could be counted. Ultimately he would leave Mexico City for the southern state of Chiapas and the old colonial town of San Cristobal de las Casas where he would do much the same. Except here he would take an unscheduled "few days" to visit the numerous Mayan ruins in the state as part of a private tour arranged by this Professor David Wolf, whom he had never met. Dr. Wolf, of course, was pivotal in the pope's plan (or scheme, as Cardinal Montoya called it) to meet with the Mayan Indian shaman and maybe former Catholic priest, Salvador Lopez, known in the southern jungles as the Holy Man, who supposedly possessed the holy cup from the last supper.

Although this trip was much needed and long planned, for Pope Lucas it was the last 3-4 days which he greatly anticipated. These meetings could determine much regarding the future of his plans for the Church in the 21st Century. The recovery of ancient writings, perhaps of St. Thomas, could inspire and support changes such as Lucas thought necessary for the health of the Church. Reform was a must, but he must have undisputable evidence and documentation that backed his ideas. He simply could not fail. And the Cup? The 'Holy Grail?' Difficult to believe, that.

***

Cardinal Cardona's robes billowed in the late afternoon breeze as he entered the Palace of Sixtus V, with its numerous offices, chapels, museum, and the exquisite Sistine Chapel. He ignored the priceless paintings, many from the Renaissance, that lined the walls and threatened to slow one's progress to a snail's crawl as people gawked at so many priceless treasures. Glancing at his wristwatch, he stepped into the hallway and briskly walked toward the office of an old acquaintance whom Cardona decided probably owed him favors. The banker had long supported Cardinal Nizzi's work as Director of the Congregation for the Protection of the Faith. Although he couldn't claim to be really "good friends" with the Cardinal, they were former classmates and colleagues and the banker had rarely opposed Nizzi's requests for personnel increases and expenses associated with his considerable outreach in the investigation of reports of "miracles" in some of the most remote places on the planet. Cardinal Cardona felt confident Cardinal Nizzi was the right person with whom to begin his outreach, his lobbying for support of the core values and mission of the Church, which this new pope obviously held in disdain. The banker remained optimistic that many shared his concerns, if not outright horror of what Pope Lucas' plans might be, even though the pope had not, as of yet, expounded on what they were. They would impact everyone – and most assuredly those of an office as conservative as the Congregation for the Protection of the Faith. He must move cautiously, yet firmly, after so many years of not engaging his former colleague. He needed this director as a foundation to Cardona's resistance to this false pope, this Argentine interloper whose inevitable demands for change would destroy the Church.

As he rounded the corner and moved east toward the Borgia apartments and Raphael rooms, he saw that infernal nun, Sr. Angelina, exiting the offices of the Congregation for the Protection of the Faith and head for the Vatican Archives. How did she get a key to the archives and what was she doing so far away from the **Domus Sanctae Marthae hotel where the pope spent his nights? He had heard she had an insignificant office, a broom closet really, somewhere in the building, but had no inclination to discover its location. Avoidance of the woman was the best policy. She was a joke – a nun pretending to be someone in the hierarchy of the Vatican, an institution long dominated by males. This new pope had really proven that he had no understanding of how the Vatican and its clockwork intricacies operated. Although Cardinal Cardona had never had a conversation with the nun, he felt sure that** she was as silly, superficial, and unimportant as all other nuns. Although she must be accommodated because of her relationship with the Argentine pope, she was absolutely no threat, little more than a bagatelle in the history of the Vatican.

He walked down the hallway, rehearsing in his mind the important points that he must deliver earnestly, concisely, and with great fervor to convince the director to join his cabal of powerful insiders who would resist this new pope and his ideas. A great deal was at stake, and much must be accomplished while this fake pope was away in the America's, sucking up to his Spanish - speaking brethren. God was on Cardinal Cardona's side. In the week that Pope Lucas was absent, Cardona would build an impenetrable wall of cooperation opposed to change. Orthodoxy would become supreme. He would construct an impassable barrier between tradition and New Age nonsense. This Argentine pope would fail miserably and Cardinal Cardona would be the puppet master, holding the reins to power, picking and choosing winners. He could assign this new pope to Kinshasa or Sao Paulo, or even the Balkans to share his ridiculous ideas.

The banker had much work to do. He took a deep breath, turned briefly to watch the retreating figure of Sr. Angelina stride purposely down the hallway, then turned the doorknob and entered the office of the Director of the Congregation for the Doctrine of the Faith (Inquisition). This was the beginning of something truly great. Cardona felt that it was inevitable that he assume the leadership of this group of powerful insiders to combat the Argentine fraud. Who knows? Maybe the burden of being pope might fall on more deserving shoulders: someone like him.

Chapter Nine

"Pull that stone away. Move it so I can get in," ordered the Bone Man in dialect, gesturing with his staff toward a rocky pile. Six Zapatista soldiers, most of them nineteen to twenty-five in age, hurried to follow his instructions and create an opening in the hillside that held they knew not what. A low, leaden ceiling of roiling thunderheads was sweeping the area, bringing lightning and blustering gusts of wind. Rain fell steadily through the lush, green canopy of *El Parque Natural de Montes Azules*, a national park and huge wildlife preserve in the heart of the Lacandon Jungle. Drizzling rivulets trickled through and over thick brush and leafy plants, creating a sodden, muddy, slippery surface in the jungle's clay soil. Brush, grass, and weeds had reclaimed the rubble strewn hillside since his last visit to the tomb three years ago. Tumbled stone and black lichen hid any edges that might suggest an entry, leaving a nondescript, virtually unidentifiable doorway into the mountainside.

"*Andale, andale!*" He switched to Spanish, pointing to the rubble strewn hillside. "*Mueva la roca, abra el hueco,*" he exclaimed (move the rock, open the hole). He waited impatiently, gesturing with his cane, encouraging while issuing orders. Finally a hole appeared. He lit a lantern and stooped to enter. "*Quédese aquí. Le llamaré si le necesito.*" (Stay here. I'll call if I need you.)

The Bone Man bent his aged back and ventured into the cavern, his lantern illuminating the walls and shadowing the objects within. He glanced backward to ensure that he was not followed. Lifting the lantern high, he slowly scanned the rugged room. A pile of grinning skulls, some missing jawbones, lay just as he had left them against the east wall. Old, rotted food, empty tequila bottles and the remnants of burnt candles were scattered on a makeshift rock-and-plank altar nearly as old as the skulls themselves. Ash from burnt copal incense heaped between the offerings, prayer to the great kings of old who sat inert and benign; now unable to pass judgment on the living.

The Bone Man was searching for a few items he had tossed into a corner behind the tomb's newest resident, *El Hombre Sagrado Viejo* (the old Holy Man). The corpse of the old Holy Man, thought by some to be St. Thomas, appeared as uncorrupted and lifelike as before when Balaam had placed him here three years ago. The body had not moved from its ledge near the altar. It was clothed as an Indian peasant and still wore the black armband of a Zapatista soldier placed on it while the Zapatista rebels had briefly held the body during negotiations with Professor Wolf and the Papal Inquisitor. The ancient Old World *Hombre Sagrado Viejo* was unnerving to look at. A 2,000-year-old body should be dust and bones by now, but the saint lay seemingly sleeping, its spirit hovering nearby, still seeking a final home in the spiritual ether.

The Bone Man had returned to the tomb just briefly to deposit for safe-keeping a few of the ancient scrolls found on the mountainside after a wreck in a thunderstorm claimed the life of the Papal Inquisitor who was traveling to the Tuxtla Gutierrez airport to return to Italy. The tragedy had left an unresolved issue: what to do with the body and books and cup recovered from the burial box by the deceased Inquisitor. The body and books were believed by the Vatican to have been lost. But Father Salvador Lopez, a disgruntled Mexican priest who had been recruited by Balaam and the Zapatistas to minister to the poor Mayans – millions of them in Guatemala and Mexico – had been given the cup which, unbeknownst to Balaam at the time, certainly seemed to be the Holy Grail of Christian lore. How and why the cup accompanied *El Hombre Sagrado* to the Americas was unknown and likely to remain so. Although most of Christendom was unaware of the body and books, stories regarding the healing power of a "magic" cup and a renegade Catholic priest had come to the attention of many people, some of them religious, some very political.

The aging shaman knew things could not remain as they are. Although Fr. Lopez had exceeded beyond hope in uniting the Indians in a common understanding and sense of purpose, Balaam knew that he could not ignore the pope's visit to Chiapas. The "situation" must be handled, but in a way that everyone would believe they had won, that they had not come away empty-handed. Therein lay the challenge. He must devise a strategy - implement a plan that would achieve his objectives.

Again he raised the lantern and scanned the room. He thought momentarily, then shuffled towards what appeared to be a fissure and rounding of the room, interrupted only by a dark passageway that ran east toward the mountainside that contained yet even more rooms. Light flickered and shadows revealed wood cylinders sealed with beeswax. A few had been opened by his sometime friend, David Wolf. The archaeologist said that there were seven in total, but only these were recovered and transported to Balaam by his followers. He hadn't known what to do with them, and so had given them back to the Old Saint. Now, he realized, they were valuable items – and potentially dangerous. They would attract the wrong kind of attention. How should he use them? He wasn't sure, but he was going to think about it – beginning tonight.

He dropped the leather satchel from his shoulder and, holding the lantern high, sought out the medicine he would need. He dug through the bag and found the plastic baggie with his most recent crop of cured mushrooms. He shook the bag, allowing three of the desiccated "magic mushrooms" to fall into his hand, hesitated, then added one more. He returned the medicine sack to his satchel, turned and called out to his soldiers. A head poked through the entry, then a couple more as the Zapatista youths hesitantly peered into the ancient tomb.

"Listen," Balaam spoke to them in dialect. "I must spend the night here with these ancient spirits. You set up camp, quietly and so that others do not know we are here. Understand? No one leaves. Maybe I need everyone tomorrow, yes? Bring me water and two torches, nothing more, no food. Then leave me for the night unless I call you. Okay? Understand? Get out now."

The soldiers listened and stared, respectful, but curious, at the skulls, ancient artifacts and brightly colored glyphs painted on the walls. They were not surprised at the shaman's odd orders. Nothing the old curandero did shocked them – rather they held him in awe. He had powerful medicine.

"*Si, senor*," the youngest replied.

"*Si, Comandante*," agreed a larger man with a bandolier of bullets strapped across his chest. He barked an order and the others disappeared, one returning quickly with a canteen of water and two unlit torches. He handed them one at a time to the shaman.

"*Gracias*," said the Bone Man, taking a long swig from the canteen. "Go now." He watched his adjutant exit the tomb, then set the lantern on the altar next to a grinning skull. He placed the desiccated, rubbery mushrooms in his mouth, purposely chewing them to ensure that he received maximum benefit from the psilocybin they contained. Balaam was a spiritual man and knew the answers to complex, difficult issues were found in the ether of the spirit world. He sat on the gravel floor and waited for the hard reality of now to be replaced with the elusive, ephemeral life-force of the universe. He must ride the ether currents and seek the streams of essence which led to knowledge and understanding while avoiding the *aluxes*, the Maya tricksters who wanted to lead seekers astray. They inhabited the netherworld and sought to distract all whom they encountered. You could get lost if you listened, or followed them. The Bone Man had seen them, even encountered them many times in the ether and in the forest itself throughout the Petén and Lacandon jungles. Tonight he would not be distracted. He must see if it was possible to understand this powerful white robe that was coming to Chiapas. Was he a good man, or was he like the other Ladinos, full of greed and avarice? Was he willing to destroy and hurt in order to realize his goal? This, Balaam realized, was the issue. Knowing the character and intent of the white robe would determine his strategy. He sighed, closed his eyes, and relaxed. Soon his breathing became slow and imperceptible as his soul fled the now.

In the tomb all remained quiet. The old *Hombre Sagrado* sat immobile and uncaring. The skulls next to the altar smiled, or looked askance at the dirt floor. Outside, young Zapatista soldiers sat complacently around a small fire, the woods and hills backlit in a golden aura of flickering flame, struggling to consume damp firewood gathered from the forest floor. Occasionally they heard a cry from inside the tomb, but the oldest soldier raised his hand and shook his head no. After a couple of hours, talk diminished and the young soldiers, tired from a day traipsing through the jungle, became bored and slept. The clouds cleared and the moon and stars unveiled. Finally, only the oldest soldier sat awake, looking upward through breaks in forest canopy, curious where Balaam was, wondering if the old shaman was looking down on him at this moment as the soldier stoked the fire, then raised his head to smile at the sky. He stirred the coals occasionally and listened to the night sounds of the jungle. If he stared into the misty gloom he could spot the fluorescent green eyes of a *Cocuyo* click beetle and hear its neck click when it moved its head. He dozed, but jerked awake when he thought that he heard the low, guttural bark of a jaguar stalking prey. Then he heard the muffled hoot of an owl, almost as if answering the cat. The soldier stoked the fire and listened carefully, but heard nothing more. Perhaps it was just a howler monkey high up in the trees? An hour later he decided he had just imagined it. His eyes grew heavy, then closed, and he dreamed of a young girl with big black eyes who had lived down the street from him when he was growing up. The memory of her bashful smile and white teeth accompanied him as his chest rose and fell rhythmically and he slid into a dream-filled slumber.

***

The Bone Man's soul drifted unfettered into the spirit world. The Maya believed in the concept of the dual soul. Every person had a corresponding totem animal spirit or soul with whom they were intricately connected, certainly spiritually and perhaps even physically. If your totem animal was sick, you were sick. The ether and spirit world was filled with these animals and spirits. Some of them wide-eyed and seeking a connection, others apparently sad or ill, but he didn't engage them. There was a curious coati, sniffing and investigating the area, and that caught his eye. It had a patient, expectant look, as if waiting for confirmation of something. Then he spotted an owl in the ether that he felt sure he had seen before. It lingered close by, as if not concerned that its curiosity be known, but never sought to engage him. And then he saw the Feathered Serpent – again. Balaam felt a little unnerved when he entered the ether and found the Feathered Serpent. It was a recent arrival in his drug-induced, spiritual journeys. He was familiar with Mayan religion and history and knew that it was a common theme in the abandoned, ruined cities throughout Mexico and Guatemala. But, as far as he knew, the Feathered Serpent was not a companion soul to any human. There was only one, and it was very ancient. The Feathered Serpent was called *Kulkulkan* in Mayan lore and *Quetzalcoatl* among the Toltec and Aztec peoples. Yet it had started appearing in the *Real Universe*, the ether, about three years ago. Its presence in and of itself wasn't threatening, just puzzling. He didn't know how to interpret this supernatural occurrence. It was significant, yet he was unable to connect it with the unresolved issues that had led him to the spirit world. Tonight, Balaam had traveled far in the *Real Universe*, seeking understanding of the pope and his visit. But to no avail. He found nothing.

Eventually, the shaman began to deviate from his path as the medicine left his body and the Real Universe, now murky and formless, slowly dissipated. Earthly perception returned and the tired immediacy of *now* slowly captured his attention as the psilocybin mushrooms wore off. Balaam reluctantly engaged the *now* of the hard reality. Disappointment hung heavy on his aged body and agitated his mind; no resolution, not even a hint! It was unexpected and unsatisfying. He rose stiffly, taking care to maintain his balance as he stood near the altar of skulls and the old world Holy Man whose eternal repose was his only offering to the living. The old shaman listened, hearing only the occasional bird chirp or animal scurrying about in the *madrugada*, the early morning hours before dawn. He walked to the tomb entrance, stooped and stepped out into the forest. His soldiers slept. Last night's coals flickered beneath a coating of gray dust and the air was still and moist. Drops of dew weighed heavily on leaves and drooping vines.

He thought to wake his men, but decided to wait. The darkness would allow him to focus and ponder and assess his visit into the ether. He sat silently a few more minutes, collecting his thoughts, recalling his less than revealing spiritual journey. He still carried the worn, leather satchel which contained his various medicines. Glancing within the satchel, he confirmed the damnable wooden cylinders with their ancient writings were still inside where he had placed them. He hefted the bag from his shoulder and lay it on the ground. With no gifts of insight from his spiritual journey, he must rely on his well-honed instincts as to the best way to handle the upcoming meeting with the white robe – this Big Potato.

The Bone Man and Zapatistas were in possession of valuable, highly sought-after items. Somehow, this must be leveraged to further the cause of prosperity for the poorest, the Indians of Southern Mexico and Guatemala. Some things were not to be part of the discussion. Some were simply not negotiable. Fr. Lopez, his new Holy Man, and the miraculous cup must stay where they are – here with the people who need them! When Balaam had rashly gifted Father Lopez with the cup, no one, especially the shaman, had any indication that it was a source of miraculous spiritual power. It only worked for the new Holy Man. Obviously, the ancient kings meant for him to hold and use it. It could never leave the Lacandon or Petén jungles, or the hands of Fr. Lopez.

The Bone Man decided that he could offer the wooden cylinders to the pope. If, and only if, after meeting the Catholic leader Balaam decided the pope was a good man, a person of his word like his sometime friend, *ahua* David. Maybe the gift of the cylinders could win the pope to the Zapatista's cause. Yes, he would gift the Big Potato with the books if he agreed to not pursue the Holy Man and cup that heals. It was right the ancient kings had brought Father Lopez and the Maya of the forests and mountains together in this way. They were very religious, very spiritual people best served by someone like them, a person who lived as they must and thus understood the reality of their physical poverty. The sermons, ministrations and miracles brought by the new Holy Man were also bringing a storm of change. A growing commonality of purpose would allow the Maya to state their demands with conviction and courage; to speak with one voice, determined in their mission. United, they would confront the governments of Mexico and Guatemala to gain sovereignty over the lands stolen during the Conquest and exploited for centuries by the Spanish and their ladino offspring.

The Bone Man must meet, discuss, bargain with, and ultimately send the Big Potato home to Italy while leaving Father Lopez and the cup to the Maya. Yes, this he would do. Too much was at stake to allow himself to be manipulated or bullied by heads of state or religious leaders. In the various Mayan dialects, *Balaam* meant jaguar. The Bone Man, Balaam

Reyes, was going to show them what being a jaguar was all about.

Chapter Ten

Finally, the day was done. Pope Lucas removed his *zucchetto*, his small skull cap, and slumped wearily into an overstuffed chair. He could hear the rustlings and voice of Cardinal Montoya diminish as he walked down the hallway. Vatican security personnel stood outside his door. Through the window facing him, framed by heavy, purple velour curtains, a coral sky streaked with blue backlit the modern skyline of Monterrey, Mexico. The baroque bell tower of Our Lady of Monterey rose majestically in front of the distant mountain skyline. The cathedral, begun in 1705, sat uncompleted until nearly 90 years later in 1791. It was magnificent. He loved the church, enchanted as much by its design and art as by its location on the arid plain fronting the distant Sierras.

The day's events had been exhausting. He took a deep breath and sat reflecting on the activities, faces, endless lines of clergy and nuns, and hordes of well-wishers and journalists. At the parade, police held throngs of people at bay, all of them wanting only a glimpse of him as he stood, waving from the Popemobile, occasionally making the sign of the cross, or imparting an acknowledging smile. He despised the Popemobile. It served its designed purpose, though, and riding was certainly easier than walking many miles along cobbled streets. He had quickly learned that his penchant for connecting personally with the faithful as he had in Argentina was a thing of the past. Security was paramount after the near assassination of Pope John Paul II by Mehmet Ali Agca in St. Peter's square in 1981. Even when the papal entourage had stopped at a local orphanage and drug treatment facility run by the Diocese of Linares, where he had washed the feet of a haggard, drug-addicted prostitute, he found himself continuously surrounded by security personnel and federal police. In many ways the event, in which he had hoped to display humility and self-effacement, was sadly transformed into theater and role-playing. Very unsatisfying to him and phony at best. When he complained to the ever-present and less-than-sympathetic Cardinal Montoya, his aide frowned and waved off his concerns, assuring him that there was absolutely no chance that the Bishop of Monterey or police would allow him to wander off into the dangerous streets and barrios of the city.

Pope Lucas swiveled in his armchair to better survey his new quarters. He spied a teapot and the one cup left for him on the small table. Yes - he could use a sip of tea. He rose and walked to the table and poured himself a draught of the steaming liquid. He carefully took a sip to test its temperature, then decided that it was just about perfect. Returning to his chair, he sat and sipped while looking out beyond the church steeple to the beautiful haze of the New World sunset.

The afternoon luncheon had featured wonderful ethnic foods, and surprisingly completely new to him. The pontiff had requested that the normal large meal with its inevitable important dignitaries take place over lunch rather than at dinner. He preferred this because of his age, but mostly because evenings were his private time; periods set aside for personal correspondence; careful analysis on pending issues that affected the Church; and reading, writing and study. With the fervor of a university student, he continued to stay abreast of discoveries, translations, and studies in his chosen field of ancient languages.

Vatican staff were educated and competent, but challenges in the new age of technology and a global economy required skills and an understanding that previous popes had never had to demonstrate. Who, one thousand years ago, could have foreseen the trials that science, computers, and quickly changing societies would create? The old Church, if it is to remain relevant, must become the new Church. No other options realistically presented themselves. It was simply unprecedented. The pope is the Church's ultimate servant, a near slave to 1700 years of tradition, dogma, and history. This was the challenge given him, and there were times, especially during evenings such as this, when he felt woefully inadequate to the task, yet determined to do what he could.

He had answered Sor Juana's email early this morning before the day's activities. The moods represented in her letters ranged from exhilaration to doom, dissatisfaction to prideful insistence, emotional, pleading diatribes and rants, to reliance on facts. Her well-developed and sharp intellect was intimidating to most people, not just the nearest unlucky male in her crosshairs. Whether she knew it or not, the Dominican nun had helped him many, many times by challenging his conventional thinking while insisting that he move forward now that the obvious presented itself. She was tireless. Whatever he asked, she always did, although Sor Juana didn't hesitated to chastise him or second-guess his intentions when she saw an opening. "The prerogative of the female," she once stated to him. "Get used to it if you want my help." And so he had, because there was no one else like her; no one who could accomplish what he needed and who flew under everyone's radar. Because she was a woman with a prickly personality, most men in the Vatican avoided her and just about everyone underestimated her. In many ways she was the perfect spy. The pontiff had requested that she 'keep an eye' on everything in his absence and report any unusual behavior. He knew that many were alarmed at his plans for reform and that some might join in common cause to thwart his efforts. He hoped that his friend was up to the task. He didn't need a revolt to deal with upon returning from the New World.

He glanced at the clock on the night stand, sat his teacup down, and retrieved his laptop, gently pushing the tea service aside. He placed it on the table, opened and plugged it in. After inserting a satellite USB from his suitcase, he pulled up a chair and opened his mail, then scrolled through several messages from his sister and a cousin in Argentina. He found his friend's reply to this morning's discussion, read the first line and smiled. Okay...he must concentrate. He took a deep breath and began.

***

Holy Father, as you know, I prefer the direct approach, but your obfuscations are better than nothing. I will reply to your queries at the end of this mail, but first I would like to proffer a few ideas for your examination. I am reluctant to leave the themes of last week's correspondence as I feel that it is important to further examine the root causes of prejudice and discrimination against women in the Catholic Church. I know these are not new and that they are apparent to many who have studied theology, but still remained unresolved. Unfortunately most writings are from men who, as far as I can tell, understand little about it, especially our friend St. Paul who may have condemned women to spiritual and social purgatory for eternity. Frankly stated, the Church's present views are an impediment to progress and reform.

Let's begin with female virginity, which, in my opinion, is greatly overrated. Much ink has been wasted putting prejudiced fantasy to paper and many women have been killed by men who have read those same pages. The Catholic encyclopedia has much to say about virginity and quotes everyone from St. Thomas to St. Jerome to lend credence and validity to the Church's position. What is surprising is that after all these years it remains inconsistent and illogical and is still associated with "purity."

Let's look at the gospels, shall we? The Bible, of course, is full of miracles. Let's focus on Mary's virginity for a moment. Yes - I know this is heretical, but if I can't talk with you about it, Holy Father, with whom is it possible? Anyway, the Bible clearly implies and the Church supports the idea that Mary was born without original sin, married an older man, Joseph, and that she miraculously became pregnant after being visited by an angel. You mean they got married and never had sex? Even the traitor Martin Luther agrees to this historical fantasy. This is certainly a miracle, no doubt about it. Anyone who can bypass the age-old method of man-on-top, hurry-up-and-get-it-over-with method is very special. I must admit, it does add to Mary's credentials. Historically, anyone who was anyone was born of a virgin. No one seems to be nearly as concerned about the "purity" of men. Probably because such a state isn't possible for males. Unfortunately, various ecumenical councils have placed a ridiculous burden on theologians and women forever by declaring Mary "ever virgin", a ridiculous concept if you possess a basic understanding of anatomy. If a penis doesn't take a woman's virginity, a baby certainly will. As I'm sure you know, the gospels of Matthew and Mark clearly state the existence of Jesus' brothers: James, Joseph, Simon and Judas and that there were also several sisters. This, of course, is a result of trying to defend a not-so-clear theology on Jesus being a man while being God at the same time.

The Church's outlook on virginity devalues and degrades women. I have no problem with sex being confined to marriage. It obviously requires a level of maturity and responsibility that is best exercised in marriage. To engage in sex outside of marriage only for the purpose of seeking pleasure is to court danger. There are no societies that allow it. You see...that's the problem with sex: pleasure. The ideal association of the sex act is love. The reality is that sex is an act of passion and closely associated with violence.

If the Church would journey further back to investigate historical models, and if we were to look in other fields for answers, we find that gender roles and expectations are entirely a function of culture, not religion, and that the sex act is innately NOT spiritual. St. Thomas is just flat-out wrong about that. The inherent problem seems to be that humans view themselves as being apart from nature and not subject to the same history and basic biological drives as other animals, or the selection pressures that govern the universe. Talk about hubris. Frankly, I'm of the opinion that the only good thing that came of the Protestant Reformation is that science was able to crawl out of the darkness into the sunlight so that it can deal with reality and explain the cause-and-effect of the universe.

Okay, Holy Father – here's a shoe for you to try on. Let's look at the field of anthropology for new ideas, okay? We now know that millions of years of physical evolution were accompanied by socio-cultural evolution - it's only natural that it would do so. Humankind attained its modern form about 300,000 years ago. Everyone was a hunter or gatherer and women actually contributed more food to the family than men who engaged in the "prestigious" occupation of hunting. The sexes held more-or-less equal status, and in many ways women carried higher esteem. We need only look at the 30,000 year-old Venus of Willendorf, the 17,000 year-old fertility *goddess from Serbia, or the 8,000 year-old mother goddess from Turkey to see this.*

According to archaeologists, the disparity between men and women's roles in societies, and the subsequent poor status of women began with the initiation of food production; mankind exerting control over nature by the domestication of animals and plants. This required that people settle down in villages and quit roaming around the countryside. Private property for food production became the norm. With the advent of agriculture, women also became a type of private property. Thus women's very poor status in all societies around the world stems from one thing: men exerting their control over property. As a person, I can state that being the private property of a man is galling. Most call that slavery.

Okay – let's approach this sex thing from another angle. Even today, in the animal world among the lower primates, with whom anthropologists insist we share a common ancestor about 5-7 million years ago, we find social arrangements that reflect gender and organize the behavior of troop members. If you look at gorillas you see that a dominant male silverback is the head of the troop which is composed of fertile females and their young and a few lesser male hanger's–on at the periphery. The dominant male has total sexual access to the females when they are in estrous. He's the tough guy, he owns all the women. He only shares when he's satiated. Occasionally a new male silverback arrives to challenge the dominance of the current silverback. If he wins, what does he do? He kills all the baby gorillas. Why? He's not invested in them. Those babies belong to the defeated rival. He knows they're not his.

Ever wonder why so many step-fathers sexually molest their step-daughters or kill their step-children? Don't have to look too far, do we? Why is this relevant? The sex act, "female purity," and the inheritance of private property are all the result of a male obsession to control every aspect of their environment and build wealth. This obviously extends to families and most assuredly to female sexuality.

You see, women almost always know who the father of their children are. Men, on the other hand, can never really be sure. It drives them crazy and has resulted in the oppressive control of women's sexuality and their terrible social status in every society in the world. In order to maintain control, male beliefs and insecurities have become institutionalized through a shared culture: society's beliefs and customs reflected most obviously in their religious doctrines. Let's face it – God is the ultimate authority, and if God is a male Who says that's the way it's supposed to be, who's going to argue? Pretty self-serving, but effective, wouldn't you agree?

So what's my thesis? The Church's view of sexuality and women, especially virginity as it relates to spirituality is, in essence, a summation of male insecurities that has been around for millions of years and continues today reinforced through scripture. You really should think about fixing this, Lucas.

Sor Juana

Okay, Lucas; on to your queries and the ridiculous machinations of males exercising power in the world.

1. According to his most recent mail, the archaeologist David Wolf now believes that that old Indian shaman he calls the Bone Man (talk about an odd name) is not only willing to meet with you, but has in his possession a wood cylinder containing one of the ancient books that was lost when our Father Sean Gregory was killed in a wreck in the storm on the mountainside many years ago. We can hope it's the original of the copy you loaned me. He still cannot confirm that our errant priest and "Holy Man," Father Salvador Lopez, who wanders the jungles and highlands of Mexico and Guatemala with a cup purported to be the Holy Grail will be present at the meeting. I have requested again, quite firmly, that he do

all in his power to have the priest present, even if only for a short time.

2. As you expected, Cardinal Cardona, bless his usurious soul, is making the rounds in your absence, stirring up trouble. I found him in the Vatican Archives yesterday where you have allowed me to volunteer and work. He has no reason to be in the archives as far as I know. While he engaged Cardinal Nizzi in conversation, an aide from the bank carefully perused the area and spent considerable time looking at the locked archives, taking surreptitious notes, and watching the actions of the few that have access (I do!) use their electronic keys to enter. As you know, all research must be done inside the 'cage' and nothing removed without Nizzi's permission. In that event, the borrower must fill out a form to state cause and necessity and agree to certain protocols of usage. Rumor of Father Gregory's Mexico 'books' is now common and is creating concern among the orthodox who can only speculate negatively what they may contain. My guess is that Cardona is scheming to gain access to these documents in order to discredit you. After leaving the archives, I followed him to the office of the Dicastery Laity, Family and Life where he met with Cardinal Ladaria. I also witnessed Cardinal Pazzio of the Congregation of the Clergy leave the meeting afterward. It's a trite phrase, but yes, while the cat's gone, the mice play. I have a plan, but for it to work you must email our friend Cardinal Nizzi to allow me to remove these documents and place them in my office. Frankly, it's just about the safest place in the Vatican. No one ever comes there, and no one would suspect me of having them. Please do this post-haste, Lucas, or I can't be responsible for what happens. Cardona cannot be trusted!

3. I can also report that I have made a friend in the Swiss Guard who I'm sure can be trusted. He has agreed to report

anything unusual in the normal gossip passed about quite freely at their communal dining table every night. I'm learning that an amazing amount of gossip is readily available for those seeking it. Because of their role, the Swiss Guard says little, but sees much. I have met a very remarkable man in the Guard with a calm sense of presence and easy smile, but I suspect he may have steel teeth, and that he has difficulty digesting some of the nonsense that goes on around here.

4. I would like to self-report that I didn't just deliver to you the book *Aramaic in Ancient Judah* that your friend forwarded to you. I kept it overnight and read it - all of it. I don't think I've done anything inherently dishonest and I don't know why I'm reporting this. I guess it made such a big impression on me that I needed to say something. You must be really bored to take a book like that with you to Mexico.

5. This leads me to the next item. I have read every book that you have suggested - a little over 150 at last count. No mean feat! I'm indeed grateful to have had you guiding my education and acting as a sounding board for my ideas. I must admit that proffering ideas and engaging in written conversation under the pseudonym of Sor Juana was a little awkward at first, but I am used to it now and believe that it has, as you predicted, allowed me more license to state clearly and without fear, my ideas just as she did. And it was all your idea!! It really is a shame that my family did not allow me to get an education. Anyway, I was hoping that you would allow me to take a look at the original photos or manuscripts of the old gnostic Gospel of Thomas that was translated by the Arab in Lebanon before all was lost in Father Gregory's accident. I'm very interested in how he might have converted some of the names and items as regards gender. I mean...let's face it. When males and females look at the same thing we sometimes or somehow manage to see different things.

6. Lucas, I want to reiterate again that your intention to sneak away from San Cristobal de las Casas to meet with the shaman is a stupid plan. How you think it's possible to avoid the eyes of hundreds of journalists, priests, nuns, government officials, and well-wishers to go play Indiana Jones in the jungle with a leader in the Zapatista Rebellion is the stuff of pulp novels. Your risk-taking behavior has always resulted in trouble. Maybe you need to be on medications, or something that will modify your occasional errant sense of judgement. Ever thought about that? A man with diabetes who has only one kidney that could easily fail, and your stubborn obsession with sweets has no business gallivanting around the Lacandon consorting with Mexican rebels. You risk your health, your reputation, the future of our Church, and my patience. You are my best friend. Please take care, Lucas. Some of us miss you desperately.

Sor Juana

Pope Lucas eased back into his chair and sighed. Medications? He chuckled. The woman always spoke her mind – something he had come to like about her. He used his mouse to scroll through Sor Juana's correspondence again, pausing initially at the paragraph on the events and players in the game of "palace intrigue" at the Vatican in his absence (nothing surprising there). Perhaps a cabal was in process? It wouldn't be surprising. He would send the requested email to Cardinal Nizzi this very night. He hoped she knew what she was doing. The woman was unusually competent most of the time.

Lucas stopped briefly to re-read the parts on gorillas and step-fathers killing children. Fascinating, and grim, but unfortunately her description had a ring of truth to it. He moved further down to item number one in her paragraphs and perused it again. A tingle of excitement rushed down his spine. Yes, there were books, or at least one, and it appeared that the old shaman might give it to him. Why? Why would he do such a thing? What was the quid-pro-quo? The pope wondered if there was more than one. Sor Juana's statement reiterated that a meeting with Fr. Lopez, the Lacandon Holy Man, was unlikely, but the tone had changed. No longer was anyone saying it absolutely wasn't going to happen. He would pray on this matter every single day. He would ask his friend and aide Cardinal Montoya to do the same. It was VERY important that he meet and talk in person with the errant and somewhat mysterious priest. The pontiff had developed a grudging respect for the renegade cleric. He was obviously totally dedicated to his work and willing to put up with more than a little personal discomfort in order to minister to the poor and live and work in such abominable conditions. Frankly, Lucas found himself admiring the man from afar. Misguided? Perhaps? But dedicated and modest and humble. *The Vatican could use a man like this*, he thought.

Pope Lucas glanced over his shoulder and saw that the sky had put on its night-time cloak. Gone were the cheerful coral and purple hues. A few stars appeared, and a half moon hung over the distant Sierras. On evenings like this he wished he were back in Buenos Aires in his own kitchen, preparing his own food. He could almost smell the Carbonada Criolla, simmering on his stove, the rich aroma of the meat and vegetables filling his senses with the thoughts of the warm stew soon to be had. Although his colleagues found it odd, he loved cooking and fending for himself. But he had been forced to give it all up upon becoming Christ's Vicar.

Enough, he thought. There was much to do before prayers and bed. He must take his evening insulin injection, give a quick reply to Sor Juana, encourage her to stay in contact with the archaeologist, and continue relaying information on the Vatican troublemakers.

What an awful job, he reflected, sneaking around and gathering intelligence on those who wished you ill or dead, whose primary goal in life was a career, comfort, and influence. The shakeup, like an earthquake, was coming – no doubt about that – he was going to lead it. His friend Cardinal Montoya reported that most of what would be needed to overhaul the Vatican bureaucracy was in place. Sor Juana had supporting information, factual details, including rationales for firing those deep into graft, theft, and unethical behavior. The restructuring would appear to be a major shakeup, but in actuality be relatively superficial. Changing basic Catholic dogma would be difficult at best and revolutionary. The culture of the Vatican, people's beliefs and values regarding their work in the Church, was entrenched in millennia of territorial wall-building and staking of positions on all matters. He likely did not have a lot of time, he was old and his health had not been good for over 20 years – and Father Montoya and Sr. Angelina and Dr. Cabrini seemed always to remind him.

What a tough job, this reform. Although many would hail his efforts, others would viciously condemn them. Most people were comfortable with the past and tradition. He, too, liked tradition and the comfort that accompanied it. Unfortunately, the world had changed so dramatically that everyone must change, or be lost. The new age of electronics, computers, video, and instant gratification had created unprecedented challenges that no one could have foreseen. *How it must have challenged the Pontiff when the printing press was invented. I wonder if there is something in the archives that might help*, he mused with a slight grin. The church must provide guidance and leadership to families in the new age. The new Church must meet the growing challenge of militant Islam, onerous and unwelcome, but necessary. The task required forward thinking people, not tradition bound, hidebound clerics who sought safety and comfort and personal gain.

The pontiff pricked his finger and dabbed a drop of blood on the gauge. Moments later the number appeared, and he frowned. He sauntered over to the refrigerator, extracted a small bottle of insulin and went through the process of giving himself an injection. He re-capped the syringe, tossed it into the trash, and returned the insulin to the refrigerator.

The pontiff returned to his computer, clicked the respond button, and began writing to his friend. He reminded himself not to get too far into the arguments where he was unprepared to respond with adequate scholarship. Sor Juana, unlike him and indeed most people, had perfect recall. She remembered everything she read or heard. This often affected her ability to maintain friendships. Lucas chuckled, he could encourage her even though others found her infuriating. Sor Juana didn't know it, but he had a surprise in store for her upon returning to Rome, and he was pretty sure that she was going to like it very much.

Chapter Eleven

Cardinal Cardona breezed through the doors of the Palace of Sixtus V, his cassock swishing with each step. There were so many buildings and offices in the Roman Curia, the administrative machine of the Holy See, that it was intimidating to neophytes or visitors. He remembered his own introduction to Vatican City 40 years ago as a young priest, and the memory brought a smile. Unlike first time visitors, Cardinal Cardona was from Rome and therefore familiar with it, first as a student, then as a freshly minted Monsignor assigned to the Tower of Nicholas, where the Vatican Bank was implemented in 1942. The city was like no other place on the planet. He had spent a couple of days since his last visit thinking further on the issue, and decided that there were at least two, possibly three more heads of state with whom he must have a conversation. These people and their offices, he had reasoned, were the most likely to experience significant change under the new pope – and it would not be pleasant for them.

The Cardinal was on his way to meet with Cardinal Tarcisio Parisi, a former Secretary of State who had been forced out of office and placed in charge of a children's hospital, a much lower but higher-profile position. Parisi, a former powerbroker and international figure, had over the years assumed what could only be described as a "the rules don't apply to me" attitude. Inevitably, this becomes a problem.

Cardona was planning to visit the building today when he had been approached by a young monsignor who had previously and unsuccessfully made application to move to the Vatican Bank from the State Accounting Administration where he had spent the last several years. Trafficking information was an age-old device to secure favor. The information acquired from the monsignor was that Cardinal Parisi had spent outrageous sums of money, lavishly refurbishing a couple of Vatican apartments for himself. That in and of itself wouldn't be so rare, except payment for work was billed and paid twice – and that the good cardinal knew all about it. This old way of doing business was not consistent with the new Argentine pope's often expressed dictum that austerity was to be the new normal – everyone's new normal. Parisi had been caught and demoted. Upon Lucas' arrival, the austerity pronouncement had been viewed with a big yawn and widely ignored until the pope arrived and he had unexpectedly eschewed the lavish quarters of Christ's Vicar to take up residence in a very spartan 750-square-foot apartment inside the Vatican's modest Santa Marthae guesthouse. Now everyone was paying attention. The pope wasn't just talking; he was clearly setting the example or "walking the walk" as our American brethren were wont to say - something not to be ignored if you had any sense of survival at all.

Cardinal Cardona didn't like lavish spenders and took a dim view of conspicuous consumption. He was a banker. In his vast experience, lavish spenders frequently had other problems as well, including some that demanded "creative banking or budgeting," that led to eventual and criminal collapse. Deep in thought, he arrived at the elevator, tapping his foot impatiently as he waited. Cardinal Parisi couldn't possibly be content with his removal from office. The man would have acquired many, many friends during his decade as Secretary of State. Maybe the good cardinal could use a new friend right now, maybe his old friends would like to come along. Cardona was sure that Parisi had collected enough markers in those ten years to sway his friends. The banker entered, selected the eighth floor, and pondered what he might say to Parisi as the old elevator whined and lurched in protest. The lift stopped, the doors hesitated, then opened. He stepped into the hallway, checked the office legend on the wall, and then pivoted to the right. Turning left, he spotted the children's hospital office at the end of the hall and marched resolutely toward it. The door exploded open. Out strode Sr. Angelina. Over her shoulder she tossed back:

"Thank you for taking the time to meet with me, Cardinal. I'll be so happy to relay your good wishes for health and success to the Holy Father." She nodded, "Buon Giorno," and smiled to the Vatican banker as she breezed past. He raised a hand in half-hearted acknowledgment, feeling awkward. How truly unexpected running into this busy-body of a woman again. What business could she possibly have with the head of the children's hospital?

"Well, Cardinal Cardona, it's been a day for unexpected guests." Parisi gestured Cardona through the door. "You know you're always welcome." Parisi wore wire-rimmed glasses with traces of grey hair peeking sparsely from beneath his red skull cap. He appeared older than Cardona recalled and fatigue hung on him like a damp frock. He offered a pained smile.

"Pleasure or business, my friend? Tell me, how I can be of assistance?"

***

David Wolf sat thoughtfully on a pile of tumbled stone in a broad clearing. He sipped coffee prepared by his wife from a thermos while viewing his work area – his dig. It was just after 7:00 a.m. and the Mayan workmen would not arrive for an hour. He loved early mornings in the forest. An early riser all his life, he used this peaceful time to collect his thoughts, organize his work day, and enjoy a few unencumbered moments with the spectacular display of nature that surrounded him. This morning promised to be one of those days. The sun peeked through a collision of distant thunderheads just above the eastern canopy, backlighting the sky with brushstrokes of pink and turquoise. A light breeze carrying the scent of wet stone and composted humus from last night's rain was tickled by lilting birdsong from a nearby copse of trees. If he concentrated, he could hear the occasional scurrying animal in the tall brush at the worksite's periphery. Howler monkeys barked or chattered in the distant forest covering. Whether or not the thunderheads would produce more rain, he didn't know, but as the sun rose, the sodden forest would grow thick and musty with humidity and everything would begin to perspire.

The professor took a few moments to sort out matters tugging at his consciousness. At his age and level of experience work, family, and professional matters had fallen into habit and comfort. The impending visit with the pope was most certainly not in that category. He hoped the whole affair collapsed quickly, easily, and quietly so that he could get on with his work and comfortable life. David still harbored vividly bad memories of when the Vatican's Papal Inquisitor,

98

Fr. Gregory, a pompous, overbearing ass aided by an overzealous federale had accused the professor of stealing Church property and summarily threw him in the dark and miserable San Cristobal jail for nearly a week. He had not been abused or roughed-up, and in fact had been treated much like a celebrity, but it had hurt his pride and damaged his family's reputation.

He had relayed his bitterness to Sor Juana. If she was to be believed, the new pope had been unaware of the event and claimed to be horrified by it. The pontiff had extended a heartfelt apology and an invitation for David and his wife, Alexandra, to visit Rome and the Vatican for two weeks, all expenses paid. Even better, Pope Lucas offered David access to the Vatican archives for anything associated with his archaeological work in Mexico, including information gathered by the Church during the Conquest. The Pope made it clear the proposition was not contingent on David aiding them to contact the Bone Man and Holy Man. The offer stood alone. David was impressed. Originally conflicted, he had decided to accept and to assist. In truth, he still saw himself as a central player in the events of three years ago even though the results were satisfactory to no one. Fr. Gregory's death in the thunderstorm descending the highlands from San Cristobal to the airport at Tuxtla Gutierrez had left the entire matter in flux and created a different set of problems - issues he fervently hoped would be resolved with this visit by the Pontiff.

A vacation to Rome would be welcome respite, and a chance to visit the world-famous Vatican Museum and peruse the Vatican Archives was a stunning offer. Alexandra, a devout Catholic, was even more excited than he was about the prospect. That was the easy part. The hard part was Balaam. The professor must still maneuver his way through a series of events, as yet unknown – involving that infernal shaman, Balaam Reyes – and the pope's schedule and entourage, which David imagined as being considerable. The real problem? David wasn't in charge. As far as he could tell, neither was the Vatican. Balaam Reyes was calling the shots and making arrangements and everyone else would have to have to make it work, possibly within very narrow windows of time. Although David's time was more or less flexible, he couldn't imagine how the pope would manage. His visit was the biggest thing happening since soccer's World Cup had landed in Mexico in 1986. A fever had seized the country and media coverage was simply non-stop.

The professor glanced at this wristwatch and saw that it was 7:20. His coffee had cooled, and he thought to refill it when he heard voices from within forest on the path leading from the village of Lacanja. Who might be coming so early? He stood and waited expectantly, listening to the chatter grow stronger. A bearded fellow in camo military apparel with a rifle strapped over his shoulder and accompanied by 5 or 6 comrades arrived in the clearing. *Marcos!* thought David, a little unnerved. He hadn't seen the Zapatista guerilla for well over a year. The Indian smiled and raised a hand in greeting. His followers slowed, and then held back as he approached the archaeologist. The Zapatista's face was a tawny brown and had a few light wrinkles tugging at the corner of his eyes. Grey streaked black hair clumped beneath a well-worn bush hat. Stocky, fit, he still wore his ever-present wan smile. David could still remember the young Marcos sitting in his classroom 30 years ago at UNAM in Mexico City. David suddenly felt very old.

"Professor Wolf, my friend!" the Zapatista extended a hand and his smile grew even wider, if that were possible.

The professor tossed the remnants of his coffee to the ground, and grasped the Indian's hand firmly. "Unexpected, but welcome, Marcos, truly," he added. What brings you to this area of the woods?"

It was an inoffensive intro into what might become a difficult conversation. The two were long time acquaintances whose paths had crossed more times that David could remember over the last 10 years, but not always pleasantly. Not because of Marcos, but because of his problematic father, the Bone Man. Marcos was frequently the bearer of bad tidings, as he usually arrived with the shaman's list of demands. This was not strictly a social call, David was sure.

"Just sharing information. Balaam asked me to stop by and give you some idea of what was going on."

"Big of him," said David sarcastically. What devious plan is he putting into play now? Is he going to kidnap the pope and his entourage and hold them hostage?"

"I sense some anger here," Marcos smiled wanly.

"The last time I got involved with your father, he placed several of those old cylinders in my shed without my knowledge and that damn Papal Inquisitor, Fr. Gregory, put me in jail for a week."

"If I recall correctly, *you* contacted *us* this time." Marcos stated the obvious. You're representing the Vatican in this, yes?"

"No…yes, I mean, I'm not sure." David shifted weight from one foot to the other. "I'm not sure why I'm involved. I don't hold enough curiosity to go looking for trouble again and I've expressed my displeasure at being drawn back into this matter. My devout Catholic wife doesn't understand how I could possibly not do as asked" he stated. I must admit that I have some curiosity regarding Salvador and his cup, the body and books, as they remain an unresolved issue, but not enough curiosity to go looking for trouble again."

"You're thinking of backing out?" Marcos stared directly at David.

The professor hesitated. "I was, believe me, I was, but have decided to go along and see how things unfold. I'm not interested in sticking my neck out again, and I can't imagine how, in God's name, the pope can disentangle himself from his entourage and the eyes of millions of adoring Mexican Catholics to meet with your crazy father. I don't think the pope has a clue what he's getting into. If they do have a meeting, Balaam will eat him alive."

"The pope will be treated with respect and his safety is paramount to us," Marcos stated simply.

"Really? Tell me, Marcos. How does Balaam meeting with the pope further the Zapatista agenda or aid Father Lopez with his mission?"

The Zapatista general shrugged. "I don't know all that father is thinking, but I can guess a few things. You already said much of it. The issue of the cup and the books are unresolved and the Catholic Church is not going to let go. They've had a taste of what could have been, or is, and they have to find answers, an ending, or a way to make it all go away. Losing the body of a man who may be a saint is a major issue to them. Those cylinders or books even more so. Having a former priest stir up trouble in the jungles of Mexico and Guatemala with a cup some think is the Holy Grail could start an uprising. I know for a fact that the governments of Guatemala and Mexico are becoming concerned. Everything is political, my friend." Marcos spread his hands wide as if offering his explanation as a gift.

David chewed his lower lip, crossed his arms and said, "Yes, I suppose you're right. I'm long past the time when I should be getting involved in miracles and revolutions. It's a young man's business. Marcos, you're my friend, but Balaam worries me to death. The man has a mind like a mouse trap and is as devious as a hungry jaguar."

Marcos chuckled at the statement. "I wouldn't disagree, David. So, are you in? Are you going to help us arrange the Holy Father's meeting with Balaam?"

"Do you think Salvador will show up for any of this?" David asked pointedly.

"I talked with him a couple of days ago and he is conflicted. I think that on the one hand, meeting the pope is every priest's dream. On the other hand, he fears it will distract him from his mission. The matter is not set. I imagine that Balaam and Fr. Lopez will reach an agreement."

David nodded, smiled, then seemed to relax somewhat. "Coffee?" He held up his cup and gestured toward a thermos sitting atop a large nearby boulder.

"Love some."

David poured a cup for the Zapatista, then stepped back to survey the entourage accompanying Marcos. "You guys ever go anywhere by yourselves?"

Marcos laughed. "I wish. Last I heard I still had a price on my head."

"I read that may be changing."

"In truth, I've heard the same. Now that we're not shooting at each other, El Presidente and the Camera are talking about a deal."

"Amnesty, or even a pardon?" asked David.

"Could be. Don't know. I'm suspicious. Our biggest concern is that we insist that the government stay out of our affairs in our towns and villages. We want to govern ourselves according to our own traditions and laws. We will no longer accept the Mexican government telling us what to do all the time. If they can agree to that, I think we may be close. We'll see." He took a sip from the cup. "Damn government," he added.

David leaned against the boulder, watching the shadows of the forest edge shorten upon the clearing floor. Humidity was starting rise and the forest was becoming active. "So, you have instructions for me?" he said finally. "Balaam has a plan?"

"Only an outline, no detail yet. The pope leaves Mexico City in two days for Chiapas. We would like for you to stay here in this area on this side of the mountains while the pope is in the highlands at San Cristobal. We want you to tell your contact, this Sor Juana character, that the pope needs to suddenly decide that he wants a private tour of the Mayan ruins at *Chiapa del Corso*. It's a small site and he must insist on not having his entourage accompany him: no reporters, no security personnel, and absolutely no one attached to the federal government. We have arranged for him to leave from San Cristobal airport in a helicopter that will transport him east over the mountains instead. If someone asks what's happening, he should say that he decided to see Palenque or Bonampak also. Everyone will be surprised, and equally angry, but what can they do? This pope has a reputation for being contrary and unorthodox. They'll write if off to his quirkiness. The trip should be announced as a day visit, but will most certainly take longer. We found a location nearby, a very nice tourist motel for families. It has patios, decks, walled backyards, and so forth where he can meet in private with Balaam."

David frowned. "I don't think Balaam appreciates how difficult it is for the pope to escape from his people. The Mexican government will be watching and monitoring every aspect of his trip. They don't want anything untoward to happen to him while he is in their country. I have a difficult time seeing how you can get away with this."

"Your misgivings aside, will you help us?"

"Perhaps," David hesitated, then said emphatically, "sure. If for no other reason than I'd like to see how your crazy father pulls this thing off. Does he have a backup plan if it all blows up on him?"

"I'm sure he does," replied Marcos.

"Yes, I'm sure he does, too," agreed David. He clapped his friend on the shoulder. "God bless his devious little Mayan heart."

Chapter Twelve

Sr. Angelina rounded the corner on the 4th floor of the Domus Sanctae Marthae Hotel and saw two men wearing maintenance uniforms in front of Pope Lucas' suite down the hall. She stopped in her tracks – she knew no work had been requested, after all, she would have been the one to order it. She watched as they fumbled with a small black box, attached with a cord to a key card inserted in the pope's door. The tall one jerked the door handle and frowned.

"Damn thing doesn't work. Supposed to override the code." He adjusted the keycard and cord again, but to no avail.

The shorter one cursed. "Shit. Gonna have to get a new one and try again."

"Don't want to. This place gets on my nerves."

What to do? They were attempting to burglarize Lucas' rooms! A ripple of apprehension stung her. She turned and walked to the handicapped, uni-sex, water closet at the end of the hall. Angelina pressed herself against the wall. Inside, she heard muffled, unintelligible conversation grow stronger, until they were just outside the door.

"I need to take a leak," said one of the burglars.

"Hurry up...Swiss Guard could show any second. I'll wait in the van."

Angelina bolted for the bathroom stall, locked the door, and climbed onto a toilet where she crouched, uncomfortable, holding her long skirts above her ankles. *How terribly awkward,* she thought.

The hallway door swung open and a man entered. "Anyone here?" he called. She heard him walking to the only urinal. Moments later she detected trickling urine and heard the burglar utter a satisfied sigh. Angelina held her breath, trying to not move. *How embarrassing! How ridiculous!* Finally, she heard him fumbling with his zipper and adjusting his clothing. Then, the toilet door jiggled against its lock and she saw his shadow stoop as he bent to look for legs beneath the door.

"Weird," he said, perplexed, but then turned and exited the toilet.

Angelina regathered her skirts and gingerly stepped from the toilet to the floor. She glanced through the hinged door crack. Satisfied the bathroom was empty, she exited the stall and placed her ear to the hallway door, but heard nothing. Sneaking around and espionage were not in her skill sets but Lucas had given her strict instructions to keep an eye on things - obviously, and unfortunately, necessary. Moments later, emboldened, she opened the door, looked both ways, and approached Pope Lucas' quarters. She stopped one door short of his entry, placed her keycard in the door lock, and entered a bedroom.

She turned on the light, checking that this attached, unused bedroom remained undisturbed in case it was needed by one of the pope's guests. But that was unlikely, as the wing on this level of the hotel was reserved for the pope, which left several rooms available. She opened the connecting door into the pope's apartment. She walked through his kitchen, dining area, and the living room that led to a balcony. All looked as it should, as did his bedroom that also served as an office. She sat on his desk chair. What had the fake maintenance men been doing? Why break into the pope's quarters? What did he have that anyone would want? She began opening desk drawers. Within a minute, she found it, two manila folders, containing copies of Father Gregory's Mexico files. Lucas had lent her the third. She removed a cloth bag from her habit, unrolled it, and placed the folders inside. She paused, took a deep breath, and continued searching, congratulating herself on instructing the desk clerk to remove the battery in the lock on the pope's door. No one could enter, regardless of electronic device.

In the bottom drawer Angelina discovered a small satchel and removed it. *Candy*! Just as she suspected. *That man,* she thought, frowning. She placed the sweets in her tote bag alongside the files. Angelina returned to the spare bedroom, closed the adjoining door, and quietly opened the door into the hallway. She looked both directions. All clear, so she walked briskly to the elevator. Moments later she was sauntering toward her office in the Palace of Sixtus V, the satchel with the files and contraband candy safe under her arm. Had she just thwarted a burglary? If so, by whom? She chuckled to herself, thinking, *Sr. Angelina, master of intrigue.* Should she tell Lucas the whole story, or just the part about the files? The bathroom part was a little embarrassing, but maybe he would see that he needed to head home post haste. Too much at stake here for him to be traipsing around Mexico!

***

Even with a dense, yellowish smog blanketing the valley, the pontiff decided that he liked Mexico City. He hadn't been sure upon flying in to the highland valley and seeing that

Lake Texcoco was now completely gone, an enormous lake once covering an entire valley was now replaced with a patchwork of houses and buildings, many of them hovels clambering precipitously up mountainsides, stretching wide and far like a plague of locusts devouring the earth. Over twenty million people crammed in such a confined space. It didn't seem appropriate, or safe, or good for anyone's health for so many to live so close together, but these resilient people were doing it and making it work. It was a miracle, really. It all seemed so fragile to Pope Lucas. What would happen if the water was turned off, or the electricity? But then he supposed it was the same in every large city in the world today from Tokyo to Sao Paolo. The world during his lifetime had experienced a complete demographic transition with the majority of people moving from rural areas to cities for jobs and opportunity. Places like Mexico City were becoming the new normal. In many ways civilization hung in the balance, teetering between chaos and a miracle supported by technology.

He had been dreading the three days here, but had come to enjoy his stay very much. The people were so joyful, so welcoming, and the excitement of his visit had rubbed off on him. He smiled so much his face hurt. Pope Lucas had journeyed down *Insurgentes* to the famous Mexico City *Zocalo* which was actually the heart of the old Aztec City, Tenochtitlan. At one time the entire valley floor had been covered by Lake Texcoco, with the Aztec capitol city established on an island in the lake with causeways and connecting bridges to protect them from enemies. The exact spot rumored to be the original location of the city's founding is now marked south of the plaza with a statue of an eagle and serpent.

Cortez with his ragtag army and Tlaxcalan Indian allies had conquered the city ruled by Moctezuma in 1521. Over the next four hundred years, the city of Tenochtitlan disappeared as its rock was stolen to build buildings and monuments. Mexico's National Palace and National Cathedral were built from the stone of razed pyramids. In 1978 a utility worker had uncovered the *Coyolxauhqui* stone near the reputed site of the old *Templo Mayor* of *Tenochtitlan*. Her discovery led archaeologists at UNAM (The National University in Mexico City) to excavate the remaining ruins of the old city. *Coyolxauhqui*, goddess of the moon and Milky Way, had been cut into sections by her blood thirsty brother and Aztec War god, Hummingbird on the Left, for her failure to support their promiscuous mother.

On the other side of this enormous zocalo is the Metropolitan Cathedral, National Palace, government offices, and more stores, shops, and local entertainment than can be imagined. It is named the *Plaza de la Constitucion* and is truly the heart of Mexico City. In the short time that the pontiff had been in the city, he had come to see that it was vibrant and exceptional in every way. The menagerie of colors, odors, and people was breathtaking and delightfully cheerful.

Today's mass at the Basilica of Our Lady of Guadalupe had been personally inspiring. Our Lady of Guadalupe is the patron saint of the Americas and revered from Canada to the tip of Tierra del Fuego. In the pope's own country of Argentina there were numerous churches named for her. She was the heart of Catholicism in the New World.

Tomorrow was the day his staff dreaded, as he would visit the dangerous and lawless barrio of Ecatepec. Ecatepec was wholly ridden with drug violence, gangland style killings and kidnappings. Here he would hold an outdoor mass for an estimated crowd of 400,000 people and try to bring them some semblance of hope and solidarity in face of the "evil one" who had cruelly taken up residence in their community.

His skittish handlers feared for his safety, but this church service, this visit, truly symbolized what he wanted his ministry to be known for. He was the pope for everyone - not just the middle-class and comfortable, but of the wretchedly poor and disenfranchised everywhere in the world. A population bomb of exponential proportions was going off around the planet, and with it came crippling poverty for millions of people. The Church must do everything in its power to provide spiritual leadership.

Pope Lucas retained a deep and abiding affinity for the poor. He had supported and promoted the destitute throughout his career and grown more firm and insistent in his demand that their needs be addressed as he aged. The pontiff never ceased to be amazed at the ingenuity and willingness of very poor people to work so hard, so long, and for so very little. No one chose to be born into poverty, yet they woke every day intent on bettering their situation, trying to create opportunities for their children and families. Poverty in its most pressing form was not caused by a lack of character or conscious choice, but rather the circumstance of birth. Hunger, poor health, lack of educational opportunities, discrimination, and capricious government faced them at every turn, but most displayed resilience and reliance on hope. And hope is what Lucas prayed he was bringing.

Jesus had been quite clear about the poor, women, and children. There is much to admire about the breadth and depth of the human spirit. But many Christians have fallen prey to their political ideologies and decided to "blame the poor" for their poverty. This, of course, is nonsense. Poverty and poor countries are caused by bad government, prejudice, discrimination, no education or health care, no access to birth control, being born female, and the lack of opportunity structures in society, not laziness. It wasn't something you had earned; it was what you were born to. The pope drew strength from people like those in Ecatepec. They provided solid inspiration for his beliefs, his work, and his desire to be part of the solution. He looked forward to spending time with them tomorrow.

The pope looked out his 14th story window into the night sky of the city. Distant mountainsides surrounding the highland valley were blanketed with the jaundiced light of hundreds of thousands of homes. Below, the city was a brilliant carpet of highways and roads lined with lampposts and filled with cars perilously chasing headlight beams haphazardly into the nightscape. Mexico City's *perifericos*, concrete ribbons that rimmed and webbed the city's skyline, allowed cars to traverse, overhead, huge portions of the city. The entire Valley of Mexico was lit, soft and luminous. Off to the south, offices rimmed the *zocalo*, and tall skyscrapers stood like sentinels guarding the millions below. The nearby Metropolitan Cathedral rose out of the city to tower over its center like a shepherd with his flock. It seemed eternal. The fountains in abundant plazas sparkle and gushed and bubbled like crystal treasures. It was 10:30 at night. As usual, the zocalo was crowded with thousands of people. Tourists, vendors, mariachis, and *policía* all contested for personal space. *Avenida Insurgentes*, the city's main thoroughfare, was lined for miles with all forms of motor vehicles; cars, taxi, vans, and trucks – all with headlights blazing and some with insistent horns. He saw little difference between traffic at night and during the day – too much and all of it chaotic. He imagined that he heard the cacophony in his suite and wished that he was outside mingling with the people, absorbing the joy of their spirit and goodwill. The city was alive, like an enormous slumbering creature come awake that must be tended, feted, and praised before being put to bed content and with a full stomach.

Pope Lucas reluctantly left the enchanting vista to sit at a small desk with lamp, telephone and electrical outlet placed near the bathroom entry. It was here he began his nightly ritual. Reading and answering correspondence was a tedious, but important part of his job. He had been so tired last night after that day's activities that he had skipped "booting up the beast," instead going directly to the peaceful sanctuary of prayer, then bed. He often wondered what the popes of time gone by had done before computers. More than likely they had waded through reams of documents, reading and parsing information, writing letters the old fashioned way – slowly, a great deal of thought given before each word was put to paper, or maybe just dictating them to ever present secretaries.

His laptop ready, he opened his mail and saw at least six messages that he should answer tonight, if only to tell the sender he would get back to them when he had more time. Of course, there was the inevitable mail from Sor Juana. Although she was always sincere and honest, he sometimes tired of reading her essays and diatribes. However, he must engage her regularly or fall behind. And it had all been his idea, which was inescapable. He was anxious about meeting the archaeologist, who he suspected was an atheist – a nice man maybe, but a non-believer and perhaps not someone who had the Church's best interests in mind. He was even more anxious about meeting the Mayan shaman, Balaam, and only God understood how deeply His servant desired to meet the new Holy Man, see the magic cup and perhaps acquire the ancient books. It would happen, or not, in three days and Sor Juana was the lynchpin. In two days he would be in Tuxtla

Gutierrez and three in San Cristobal de las Casas. Much of great import lay in the balance these final days. He was determined not to go home empty handed, and in order to succeed he must place trust in the hands of people of whom he had very little if any knowledge,

Perhaps it was best to begin with Sor Juana. Everyone else could wait. He clicked on her mail and began reading.

Sor Juana:

Holy Father many of us long for your return and hope that you are not overly tiring yourself. Perhaps we will see you by midweek and hopefully much will be resolved by that time. I have news from the archaeologist, David Wolf and I will relay it at the end of this mail. I have a few things that I wanted to toss into your oven to be baked or at least separated out and made singular from the whole.

Since we (or at least I) have been discussing numerous areas surrounding sex lately, my thoughts have turned to marriage, perhaps because I am not allowed to marry, or maybe because I constantly find myself in the company of men here at the Vatican. Imagine yourself only in the company of women and maybe you can see that much of the social interaction and communication that most of us take for granted, is in actuality, a challenge.

In particular, my thoughts have turned to the fact that women are prohibited from becoming priests. I'm not the only one with concerns, as you know. I will begin this discussion by stating that I find scriptural support for celibacy to be lame, contrived, non-scientific or overly philosophical. Much ink has been spilled justifying the practice and as far as I can tell, it's basically an archaic practice designed to prevent women from sharing wholeheartedly in the Christian experience and certainly the Church itself. Interpretation? Just another way to keep women at a disadvantage to men in all aspects of life.

I have discovered lots of information on the Internet! You should look for yourself, Holy Father! Experts from all over the world provide information that is readily available without having to go to the library. If you investigate you will see that the Church has been all over the map on sex and marriage as regards the priesthood. Here's a synopsis of what I have learned so far.

During the First Century the apostles were mostly married men and the New Testament implies that women presided at Eucharistic meals.

The Second century showed little concern for the issue. The Church was obsessed with Gnosticism during the Second and Third Centuries, then turned schizophrenic in the Fourth when it was declared that a priest would lose their job if they had sex with their wife the night before giving mass. The obvious implication is that sex creates a state of serious impurity.

At the Council of Nicea it was declared that a priest could not marry after ordination. By 385, however, Pope Siricius left his wife in order to become pope, and declared that priests could no longer sleep with their wives.

In the Fifth Century St. Augustine wrote that nothing draws the spirit of man down more than the caresses of a woman. What an idiot.

In the sixth Century Pope Gregory reportedly said that 'all sexual desire is sinful.' Really? Then why did God make us this way, and ensure this the only way to make more of us? In the Seventh Century the majority of French priests were married, and in the Eighth Century St. Boniface reported that there were no celibate bishops or priests.

In the Ninth Century at the Council of Aix-La-Chapelle it was stated that infanticide and abortion were commonplace at convents and monasteries to cover up for sexually exploitative priests. You guys have always been a bunch of dirty birds, Lucas.

In the Eleventh Century Pope Gregory VII said that "priests must escape the clutches of their wives." 'Clutches of their wives?' Who's the woman that potty-trained the Gregory child? Worse, in 1095 Pope Urban II ordered priest's wives sold into slavery, and the children abandoned. Lucas, if this man is in Heaven when I get there I'm going to hold you responsible!

Nothing remarkable in the Twelfth and Thirteenth Centuries, but in the Fourteenth Century, Bishop Pelagio complained that women were still ordained and hearing confessions. In the Fifteenth Century 50 percent of priests were married.

And then there's the Sixteenth Century when that constipated clown Martin Luther and randy Englishman, Henry VIII, gave the keys to our church to the money changers. If you fast-forward to 1980, married Anglican pastors were being ordained as Catholic priests in the United States, Canada, and England. That brings us to the present.

I think there were at least seven married popes, almost all of whom had children (Peter did not. Maybe he wasn't a guy-guy?), or at least there is no mention of children, only a mother-in-law. Eleven popes are listed who were the sons of other popes or clergy, and an additional six popes who sired illegitimate children. As you can see, the Church has never, ever spoken with a consistent voice. Frankly stated, God made us sexual beings. Men like sex a lot. So do some women. Everyone likes children and family and it is the perfect arena for all these activities to take place. Why priests should be excluded from marriage because of some sort of "higher calling," or view of "celibacy as a gift from God," or that being celibate allows one to be "closer to God" is a very poor use of philosophy and even worse practice. I think I understand now why the Lord's Prayer has the line in it "and lead us not into temptation." (Why would God do such a thing?) Why women would be excluded from the priesthood is obviously a function of men attempting to control all aspects of women's lives, especially their sexuality. If there are worse sins than those of the flesh, why has the Church been so obsessively insistent on getting it wrong for such a long time? Quite a history isn't it. Absolutely nothing coherent about it.

Eminence, with the Church's ridiculous record on married priests one would think that this might be one of the easier tasks for a serious reformer such as yourself to tackle. I think we can agree that there is no biblical justification for the practice and it can be argued that it's unnatural for men and women to NOT be married and having sex, just as it's not normal to excluded 50 percent of the population from becoming priests and being full participants in every aspect of the Church. What are you guys afraid of, anyway?

Okay, Lucas, enough Sor Juana. Let's talk shop. The Vatican Launderer, Cardona, continues to knock on doors to recruit and meet fellow schemers. I have so far foiled his two schemes: to rob our archives of the Fr. Sean Gregory Mexico files and search your office for what he sees as damning evidence of whatever extreme agenda you plan to pursue. What an idiot. Anyway, I requested the desk clerk at the hotel to remove the battery in your apartment door lock. This has been done. The battery will be replaced upon your return and I will have a new magnetic keycard for you. As regards Cardona and those he meets, I can report that I've met with some of the same people. I'm not convinced that he's bringing them into his cabal. Many appear to be humoring and engaging him out of courtesy. He *is* in charge of all the budgets, you know.

The very fascinating and charming Swiss Guard with whom I've made friends brought me an interesting story which I followed up on. It's simply amazing that such gossip is readily available around the Swiss Guard's communal dinner table. At any rate he reports that after you demoted Cardinal Parisi and assigned him to the children's hospital, the Cardinal subsequently charged well over $500,000 Euros remodeling an apartment for himself and three nuns, and that payment was made for the remodel twice, not just once and apparently with the approval of Cardinal Parisi. Can you imagine a nun doing such a thing? No, you can't, and neither can anyone else. Some of you guys have a sense of entitlement that is simply off the scale. It's like a sickness. Perhaps you will decide to remove Cardinal Parisi from his lofty perch and gilded cage and deposit him down on the floor with the detritus and spoor of dirt where the rest of us reside? Your call of course, but I think you know where I stand on this nonsense.

Lucas, you've proven to be a good friend and I really have no one else to share with. I'm having trouble sleeping. Some of it is your absence and my worry over your health, but I'm having odd dreams. Some of them are decidedly sexual in nature, which is very weird since I have no experience in that area. I'm wondering if this new young man I've met in the Swiss Guard is the cause. Have I mentioned him before? He's quite tall, about 6'4", but then all the Swiss Guard are large men. He has a wonderful smile, easy demeanor, and a five-year-old daughter. He speaks German, Spanish and Italian. Apparently his wife died two years ago of ovarian cancer. I haven't met the daughter yet, but he says that she is the most precious thing. I can only imagine. Anyway, we were having tea the other evening and he invited me to accompany him on a tour of the catacombs. Really! Can you imagine? I've been here three years and have never seen them. I've heard so many stories. Anyway, I accepted, but now I'm having second thoughts. Is this really appropriate, Lucas? I mean, what are his intentions? Is this a purely platonically inspired meeting? I think I came off as being too eager when I accepted. I'm out of my element. I'm a Dominican nun. Perhaps I should seek guidance from the Mother Superior, but then what does she know that I don't? I really do want to see the catacombs. Lucas, I fear I'm starting to behave erratically in your absence. Will you please come home?

Okay, sorry, sorry, enough self-pity. Business.

1. I have in my possession, hidden in my room at the convent, the three originals (the photographs) of Fr. Gregory's 'book' files from Mexico. I had planned to keep them in my office, but I believe the convent is safer. Although you secured me access to the archives, your email to Cardinal Nizzi did the job. He signed them out himself, then delivered them in a briefcase. This cloak and dagger stuff makes me very nervous. I think it would be much easier if you were here to provide support.

2. I received an email from the archaeologist, David Wolf. He says that this Bone Man character sent his son, Marcos, to set up plans for your side trip to eastern Chiapas and the Lacandon Jungle. This is soooo stupid, Lucas. It's times like this I wonder if you have a screw loose. You are NOT Allan Quartermaine searching for King Solomon's Mines.

3. Anyway, the plan is for Cardinal Montoya to direct the entourage and reporters west to a small archaeological site called *Chiapa del Corso* (I found it on a map), while you instead board a helicopter and fly east over the mountains to an area close to the Palenque archaeological site near the Lacandon forest where you will be met by the archaeologist and Zapatista characters who will take you to that shaman. The Zapatistas seem very, very averse to being anywhere near government people or the military. Will you see this *Holy* Man with whom you so desperately want to meet? The archaeologist says that's anyone's guess. Don't plan on it.

4. Lucas, Lucas, Lucas - what a ridiculous plan. It's times like this that I worry about the emotional wellbeing of men. Is

testosterone what makes you guys so crazy? So moody? So inclined to engage in desperate, aggressive, illogical behaviors? To take such risks? Are all men such slaves to their hormones? My father and brothers used to get stupid like this every once in a while. My mother would shake her head and go to her room and cry. Lucas, please reconsider. Don't do it! You're too old, you're diabetic, you only have one kidney, and I'm starting to wonder if you've taken leave of the one admirable asset that you possess, your brain. Please come home. Please?

Pope Lucas reread the entire email this time, not just the last paragraphs. Good! Nizzi had gotten the books to her as requested. They were probably safe in the archives, but why take chances? Most people would be surprised at the amount of intrigue and espionage that took place in the Vatican.

Some of the information on marriage and priests was familiar and had been openly discussed at different times. Married priests and the male priesthood were a sore point in both theology and philosophy, and Church history was rife with inconsistencies. In fact, it made little sense and caused much harm. Some suggested that the ban was promoted for centuries by a "homosexual cartel" that somehow managed to control Canon Law on the matter. Married priests would stand as a challenge to the authority of those who were not inclined to marry. Pope Lucas supposed that was possible, but unlikely – there had to be other causes as well. The church 1700 years ago made no more sense than the church of the twenty-first century. Few previous popes wished to deal with these issues. Unfortunately, Pope Lucas believed that his predecessors refused to deal with it in hopes that it would fall to someone else in another millennia - and it had - and now it was his obligation to do so. How? He hadn't decided, but something must be done, or the Church risked alienating nearly 50 percent of their membership.

The news from Chiapas was unsettling, to be sure. There was to be a meeting, but maybe not the kind for which he had hoped and prayed. But then maybe so. No one was saying that meeting this Fr. Salvador, this Holy Man, was impossible or not going to happen. He could only imagine what the shaman was like. Pope Lucas had the impression that Professor Wolf was not necessarily a big fan of the old Indian. But that didn't matter. The shaman was the door to the Holy Man. There was no choice but to accompany the Indian to that portal and see whether it was open or locked. Pope Lucas had no control at all over the matter and that really frustrated him. It must be God's challenge to him. His only solution was more prayer. Ask for guidance and strength and a bit of luck. This was a task that MUST be successfully completed because it potentially impacted the Church in so many ways. Sitting complacently was the old way and not an option if he wanted to look himself in the mirror every morning. It was important that he know for certain the truth; whether Fr. Salvador Lopez, the Holy Man and his magic cup were genuine or not. If they were not, the Church could move on. If they were 'real' they must be assessed and integrated into the modern Church. Pope Lucas was not interested in leading a religion based on lies or deception.

He suddenly felt overwhelmed. The pontiff grasped the cross that hung from his neck, muttered a few lines of prayer, and then looked to the small altar set against the wall. He mentally thanked his staff who so lovingly cared for him, making sure the picture of the Virgin and carving of the crucified Christ were with him wherever he went. If only prayer were so easy, providing solutions whenever and wherever he went. Sometimes prayer was hard work but it always brought solace and relief no matter what baggage of the mind encumbered him. Tonight the pope felt like he was carrying a lot of baggage. He lifted himself from the table and knelt at the altar. He glanced above at the crucified Jesus, kissed the cross in his hand and then clasped his hands together and bowed his head in prayer. Christ's Vicar knew he would not sleep well tonight without praying for clarity and strength, and in only two days he would more than likely be face-to-face with the Mayan shaman, and the thought unnerved him. He began with an 'Our Father' and then moved into the first decade of the rosary that hung from his waist. Soon he was in a comfortable rhythm and his breathing became slower and shallower. Anxiety dissipated and he felt his spirit focus. The pontiff prayed for another 30 minutes before making the sign of the cross, stood and walked to the bed where his night clothes were laid out. He undressed and dressed, then walked once more to view the beautiful lights and cars of the never sleeping city. He was tempted to sit and watch the coming and going of twenty million people, but the bed called. Tomorrow he must tour and give mass at Ecatepec, one of the worst places on the planet. He must be rested before undertaking such a challenge. Pope Lucas drew back the covers to his bed, sat, removed his slippers, and turned off the night lamp. As he lay down and closed his eyes, his mind filled with the memory of his mother standing next to his bed, smiling, encouraging, saying, *"Sleep well darling. Remember that God loves you and always helps those who believe in him."*

Chapter Thirteen

The Holy Man leaned forward in order to ease the stress on his back. He sat next to his wife and child on a tile floor of the four- hundred year old *San Juan Bautista Iglesia*, St. John the Baptist Church, among piles of aromatic flowers, pine needles, sage and grasses, all interspersed within rows of *posh* (a traditional alcoholic beverage) tequila, Pepsi, various foods, eggs, and dried fish. Women placed eggs in nests at the feet of the saints and behind them curanderos and shamans sacrificed chickens as part of ancient rituals and petitions directed at the proper saint to whom they issued appeals based on the illness that they wished to treat. Maya shamans focus on the balance between body and spirit, and most illnesses are viewed as being caused by an imbalance.

Flickering lights of innumerable candles danced capriciously around the room and reflected on the ceiling while he stared at the altar and images imbedded in the nave. Copal incense, an aromatic standard in Mayan rituals, wafted from piles of ashes while whimsical shadows danced sinuously on unseen thermals, creating odd designs and images of ancient specters in the gloom. There were no pews or altars in this church, which centered on a large statue of St. John the Baptist decorated with red and yellow ribbons. These Mayans worshiped traditional Catholic saints as images of their own gods. Pale-faced saints with Mayan noses stared from glass boxes. A mirror hung around the neck of each to reflect the sun god. Here, the Virgin Mary was largely absent. She has a place in ritual and observances, but not as the Mother of God, because the Indians consider the concept of a virgin birth ridiculous. The church sat in the village of Chamula, a Tzotzil Indian community in the Sierras above the highland colonial town of San Cristobal de las Casas. Today was the 25th of June, and it was a festival of Mayan and Catholic beliefs, blending in a unique way traditional Mayan animistic beliefs and their ancient cosmology with New World Christianity. The Tzotzil had maintained as many of their native beliefs as possible from the Conquest. All the saints had different duties and functions. Only one sacrament, baptism, was acknowledged, the other six were rejected. They revered St. John the Baptist above Jesus Christ. St. Peter, St. John and St. Sebastian represent the Catholic Trinity. The Christian cross represented the four directions of North, South, East and West and is used primarily to protect against evil spirits. Centered at the altar and draped with red and yellow ribbon was John the Baptist. To the left, St. John the Lessor, and above, Christ the Lessor, both of whom represent the Hero Twins of Mayan lore, representing the Sun and the Moon.

Fr. Lopez, the Holy Man, arrived three days ago with his friends and protectors Marcos and Balaam, the Bone Man, to witness the annual *Carnaval de San Juan Chamula*. He had watched as thousands of the faithful entered the church. Outside, in the central *zocalo* of the village, were more religious rites in addition to games, food, music and various forms of traditional entertainment. It was celebration unlike any he had ever witnessed, but today it ended. He would come again next year, he thought. It was fun and spiritually lifting, a good and wholesome combination.

Fr. Lopez had yet to sort out some of the symbolism in the events and short religious melodramas blending Christian and traditional belief, but he now understood many Mayan themes that had previously escaped him. Marrying a Mayan girl had helped, and he had spent the last three years learning the Lacandon language, a lowland Mayan dialect from Eastern Chiapas. His life had become so different in such a short time that he now found himself reflecting on those changes more than he did upon beginning his ministry.

Fr. Salvador Lopez had been a traditional parish priest, and now was a renegade in the Church – and content with his decision. His acceptance of Catholic Liberation Theology, in which he and his friends became immersed in Rome, was the beginning of his enlightenment and focus to help the poor of Latin America. Suddenly he had become excited and busy, and then he realized that he had given more masses in Guatemala and Mexico than he had in his entire former life. He had a young wife and a son. He was beginning to understand how Mayan themes blended into his simple, heartfelt homilies. His mindset for so long had been the ever-present jungle and small, sometimes nameless villages in which he stayed, as well as occasional hordes of people at the masses he led. Some of their expressions were indelibly printed in his mind. Their faces were summations of entire personal histories; brown dried skin, brow wrinkles, callused hands, and crow's feet radiating from eyes. You could envision their lifetime, a hard, mean existence with little or no hope of an improved life. And gratitude - he sensed that they were thankful for the sweet joys and spiritual and social rejuvenation they experienced when celebrating mass.

Some of the parishioners in his former life as an ordained priest had seemed nearly dead, as if they were toting around their own bodies, totally void of the Holy Spirit. It was his goal to resurrect these people with his heartfelt homilies and communion of spirit, reinforced by the hope and spiritual nourishment represented by the cup. It was the priest's responsibility to maintain the life of, or bring hope to, the community so that they still sought the Spiritual Kingdom and never lost hope. After watching the events of the last two days, the Holy Man now believed that he better understood Mayan beliefs and how they affected people's behavior at his masses.

Belief was perhaps the most powerful human trait ever developed. Whole nations, religions, wars, dynasties, and ideologies were predicated on the power of belief. With religion, belief was the engine and prayer the fuel. Fr. Lopez felt he was doing the most important, natural, honest thing in his life. This was his calling, and he had no reason to look another direction for meaning or purpose. Salvador had finally reached the stage where he was home all the time no matter where he was; comfortable in his present situation and content to know that he was doing and being who he wanted to be. Nothing else really mattered.

The Holy Man glanced upward at voluminous curtains hanging from the center beam of the church. They stretched to either side, attaching just above tall, stained-glass windows, occasionally wafting with a breeze from within the church or an opened door. He looked about him, smiled at his wife and beckoned his son to come closer. Tomorrow they would leave *Los Altos de Chiapas* and San Cristobal de las Casas for the eastern lowlands. They would stay temporarily at the village of Lacanja, a small Lacandon Indian village on the edge of the jungle near the archaeological ruin of Bonampak. It was also a place where his wife had many relatives. After a few days, instructions would inevitably arrive and he would be off to a new location, bible and cup in hand, intent on making a difference.

After talking with Marcos and Balaam the last couple of days, he realized that there was a remote possibility he might meet the pope - a pretty crazy idea at best. How many parish priests got to meet the pope? Very few, he knew, but a few surely. But how many persons like him, those considered on the fringe, nuts or near lunatics, people with serious mental issues, got to meet the pope? None, he was sure.

It really didn't matter to him if he met the pope or not. He didn't see how it could possibly influence his mission or work. God, not the pope, had given him the opportunity to do in life what he really wanted. He wasn't going to waste it on a, "What if?" Fr. Lopez felt his relationship with God to be strong and certain and that was the only thing that really mattered. If you didn't have that relationship, well, then you were little more than a charlatan.

Chapter Fourteen

The faithful lined the pope's motorcade route to the huge stadium where mass would take place. The people waited patiently to toss flower petals, cheer and wave yellow and white pom-poms, the color of the Vatican flag. Vendors sold T-shirts, plates with Lucas' image on them, pins, bandanas and cardboard-cutout figures of the pope.

Behind cheering crowds, storefronts gleamed with a new coat of paint. Trash, normally ever-present, was absent along the route, and the traffic lights had been freshly painted. If one glanced quickly down the concrete trails of side streets, one could see crowded borders of stained, cracked, plastered walls. Behind these distempered, fractured facades lived the people who were now happily cheering him. Each home was so similar that that it inferred the inhabitants were as indifferent or poor as their neighbor. Age, climate, and neglect were apparent. Maintenance and progress were expensive and beyond the means of the barrio's tenants. Tax monies were directed to where they were best needed – away from

Ecatepec. Building and maintaining infrastructure best served the rich. The residents of Ecatepec were poor.

Pope Lucas paused and surveyed the massive soccer stadium, looking over the bleachers and field of hundreds of thousands of people, all here to participate, to share the communion of mass with him and their neighbors. The view was amazing and humbling.

Ecatepec was perhaps the worst barrio in Mexico City - a place where young women were routinely kidnapped and ransomed or put into the sex trade, or just taken out and killed. For young men, the choices were little better; being sucked into the orbit of drugs, working to sell drugs, or fighting for territory to sell drugs. Drugs were money. Drugs were the common denominator. Without drugs, there was no money. Without money your country had no economy and thus no jobs. Pretty simple, really. That's why so many were involved in drugs in one way or another. In the face of government indifference, the 'Evil One' had taken control of this community and a life well-lived was too great a burden for most to bear.

The Pope's motorcade arrived at the stadium and he disembarked to say mass, blessing those that pressed close to him as he made his way. In a city like this, the Catholic Mass attended by numbers such as this was a protest against the crimes and meanness of a humanity that pursued nothing but money as well as a religious experience. Mass was proof of God's existence and proved that humans could and should congregate in large groups for common purpose without descending into barbaric behavior. It verified that God and socio-cultural evolution had allowed us to access and exercise judgement, and that we were indeed Homo sapiens (wise people). Otherwise we would be more similar to chimpanzees and gorillas, or maybe nothing at all that was aware of itself – just like most of nature. Cognitive low-lifes.

In a final prayer, Pope Francis urged Mexicans to remake their community and country into a place of opportunity "where there will be no need to leave your homes and family to emigrate in order to dream, no need to be exploited in order to work, no need to make the despair and poverty of many the opportunism of a few, a land that will not have to mourn men and women, young people and children who are destroyed at the hands of the dealers of death."

He looked out over hundreds of thousands of people. People dressed in every possible color, some with hands clasped in prayer, others waving and smiling, vied for his attention. All awaiting a sign or instruction, his leadership and authority unimpeachable, trust given and trust accepted. How could he help them? He wasn't sure. Although the pontiff experienced great joy when celebrating mass with his numberless followers, he often felt impotent to connect with them in a meaningful way. He was here because of their problems. They knew this. His homily had been short, but poignant, and filled with hope. Pope Lucas surveyed the crowd one more time before smiling, thanking everyone for coming, and reminding them to resist the Evil One that had taken up residence in their town. "Remember, there is no dialogue with the devil," he repeated, finally. He gestured and gave a final blessing to all, then turned and returned to his seat near the back and side of the altar. He waved, bowed his head to pay homage to their spirit, and with his entourage, headed toward the Popemobile and his hotel, feeling a malaise of spirit, considering that perhaps his efforts were not sufficient to make a difference.

Chiapas State and its challenges were very much on his mind as he waved to the throngs of the faithful. The tumult of cheers reached a near roar, and calls of approval rang out as he strode alongside his aides and security personnel as they approached the Popemobile. He suddenly felt tired, as if whatever had buoyed him was stolen in an instant, but perhaps it was just low blood sugar. He really wished he was home right now and not responsible for anything. It was then that he recalled his predecessor, St. Peter, asking for his burden to be taken away, not only did he ask once, he asked three times. If Peter could carry on, then so could he. Although sometimes the burden of office became so onerous that he wanted to turn and start walking in no particular direction and with no certain purpose, just saunter toward some semblance of peace, or resolution, or understanding, away from stress. Sometimes the pope needed prayers and understanding, also. Sometimes he was just like us.

Lucas had waited several years for this quest, an as-yet-unknown journey in an attempt to recover something meaningful from the southern natives: a cup, an ancient book, anything from the bonanza of artifacts discovered over three years ago in a coffin of a very ancient man found in tumbled rubble beneath a church with subterranean halls and catacombs decorated in various Mayan glyphs painted onto the walls and ceiling. The burial box itself sported a sinuous representation of *Kulkulkan*, the Mayan version of Mexico's famous Feathered Serpent of folklore and tradition. Were they even worth the effort? How would anyone know until they were recovered and their value assessed? Unfortunately, because of those with whom he must interact in Chiapas, this 'Bone Man' shaman, the aggrieved professor still hurting from his unfortunate jailing in San Cristobal by a Vatican representative and others as yet unknown, there really was no one whom he believed better qualified or capable of understanding the importance of recovering these items. And the journey towards answers begins tomorrow, after the parade and mass in San Cristobal. Tomorrow evening his adventure begins. Imbued with a sense of anticipation, he suddenly began to feel a bit younger.

He must quickly prepare for the evening flight to Tuxtla Gutierrez, the lowland capitol of mountainous Chiapas State. He would offer a late mass and spend the evening ingratiating local dignitaries before flying by helicopter the next morning to San Cristobal de las Casas in the southern highlands, an area of great poverty with at least six different Mayan Indian tribes. He would spend the day with Bishop Ruiz, celebrate with a short parade followed by an outdoor mass in El Centro at the Cathedral de San Cristobal, a spectacular church built in the late 1500's. Then he would travel and call on various tribal/village locations to visit the poor. An incipient tingle of anticipation raced down his spine. His big adventure in Southern Mexico was beginning. That evening, he would ditch his entourage and fly over the mountains to a location whose coordinates were given to Sor Juana by the archaeologist David Wolf this morning. This plan required a completely different mindset. He must be assertive with his staff and exercise control whenever possible. Although his aide Father Montoya was aware (and keenly disapproving) of his plan to steal away for a couple of days, his security had no idea and they were going to be very, very unhappy when he out-maneuvered them to keep his meeting with the Indian shaman and professor.

What would happen when he landed? He did not know. He hoped to meet with this "Bone Man." Maybe the shaman would give him one or more of the precious scrolls that had fired Lucas' mind for over two years. He prayed he would also meet the this intriguing and mysterious *Holy Man* and recover more of the reputed items from early Christendom found in catacombs beneath a Jesuit church destroyed by an earthquake 150 years ago. Really, it was all a little scary. But God would not have provided Lucas with opportunity if He did not want His faithful servant to embrace it. Going forward was the only option.

****

From: Sor Juana

Holy Father, much has occurred since my email two nights ago. Before beginning, I must confess that I am somewhat agitated. I continue to monitor the whereabouts of Cardinal Cardona, although there's nothing to report, really. This old city, I believe, is a cesspool of intrigue. Must everyone in this town engage in stratagems, trickery and deception in order to fulfill God's work? Is conspiracy and scheming natural to mankind? Aren't we a really odd creation? How petty and horrible we must appear to the Heavenly Host above us. People are so disappointing.

I admit that I'm suffering from personal discontent. Our arrangement (your idea) that I would assume the role of Sor Juana in order to feel more comfortable in expressing my ideas and pursue the readings you assigned is having mixed results. I thank you for the opportunity to convey my thoughts and perhaps better articulate my views on the archaic practices of the Church that harm women. I have no doubt that I would have been burned at the stake in previous centuries. After all the readings (some were better than others) I now have a better idea how the Church got to where it now is. For someone like me, of course, this causes unmitigated disgruntlement because of my inability to do anything about it. I curse you and bless you for this, Holy Father. I now see the world with open eyes, but they are jaundiced and I am aware that there is so much I will never know, or be able to fix. Is this the true fruit of Eden? The forbidden knowledge that resulted in our being expelled from Paradise? Did we learn that we will never, ever truly know the first cause-and-effect?

Or, that maybe God isn't as concerned about us as we are Him? That we are born, we suffer, and we die? Are we really so insecure? Maybe we're all Buddhists and don't know it? No wonder most academics are shy, retiring people with poor social skills. Studying the foibles of humans and learning all the disappointing things that they believe and do would destroy anyone's self-confidence.

Have I mentioned that I made a new friend in the Swiss Guard? Fascinating man, Gunther, and his 5-year-old daughter is precious beyond belief! After much reflection, I decided that it was okay and so I accompanied my friend on a foray into the catacombs last night. Yes, the catacombs! I've been aware, forever, that they are here, under Rome, and that they were somehow important to early Christianity, but I really had no idea. I'm still catching my breath. The bones were a little hard to deal with. How macabre. But the quality and array of art was stunning! So much history and reference to events that remain as yet, unclear, but obviously important.

I stopped briefly at the Visitors Center and picked up a book, Mothers of the Church, by Aquilino and Bailey. I read it last night. You are aware, I'm sure, Eminence, that the catacombs remain as indelible proof that women were very important in early Christianity. Women led mass. Should I repeat that? It's obvious from looking at the images that women and slaves were most assuredly the first leaders and proselytizers for Christianity, which began as a cult before becoming mainstream under Constantine. The images clearly demonstrate that women helped organize the early Church and that they routinely led Christian mass. It wasn't the attention-getting, self-important, repressed homosexual, Paul who created the Church - it was women. Women and slaves did all the hard work! I strongly suspect that you and many others know this. I also believe most men and some women feel comfortable with things the way they are because custom and belief are more comfortable for people than logic and proof and change. You don't have to think, just believe and do as you have always done. Having religion mirror society's gender roles is the best way to keep conflict at bay and men in power. Shame on you guys, Holy Father! A two-thousand-year-old scam.

Okay, enough Sor Juana. Let's talk shop shall we? Lucas, I'm miserable, and I'm starting to suspect there's nothing I can do about it. This young man I've met was totally unexpected. I'm relatively new in the Dominican vocation and my reasons for joining are already known to you. Suffice it to say that I am starting to wonder if I did the right thing. My mother is deceased and my father is in a facility somewhere in Buenos Aires dealing with Alzheimer's. My three brothers and two sisters are all married, have children, and are doing well. It's like I'm a person apart, bereft from any social mooring, and the convent has not been able to provide one.

Can I tell you something in confidence? I think Gunther smells good. I don't know what this means or why it's important, it's just that it's on my mind of late. It's not like he smells like cologne, or a pasta and tomato sauce carbonara, or a cheeseburger, it's that he smells…interesting, I guess. I looked up pheromones in Wikipedia (You should try it. Great site!). Basically it says that although many suspect their presence, there's no evidence that they exist in humans. As you know, not being able to understand or define important matters is very frustrating for me. Frustration can lead to acting out. I find myself daydreaming and thinking thoughts I previously suppressed. Now I don't even care. God must be crazy or a sadist to have orchestrated this mess. Maybe he really does hate women (like so many church fathers seem to). Anyway, I don't believe that this would be happening if you were around to help me organize my life and focus on what's important, Lucas. Some friend you are, running off to Mexico without me.

This brings us to the final matter – your stupid plan to run away from everyone who loves you into the arms of some Indian shaman and atheist archaeologist. The more I consider this situation, the more I wonder if I really ever knew you, Lucas. You know, you can be a bit of a nut sometimes. Think about it. You are the Pope – the head of the largest Christian Church in the world and charged with responsibilities far beyond the capabilities of almost any man. You are Solomon incarnate, yet here you are: an old diabetic with one kidney insistent on putting himself at the mercy of unknown, perhaps malevolent forces in the wilderness of southern Mexico. Interpretation? You're acting like a dumb ass. This is not hyperbole! Frankly, I sometimes wonder if you have two brain cells in your whole head. If in fact you do, I and others, including Fr. Montoya, would like for you to call off this ridiculous escapade and come home as fast as you can. This little town is seething with sedition in your absence and some of us need you desperately, Lucas. Everything is falling apart! I've become a discontented nun with a boyfriend who hasn't kissed me yet, and you think you're Admiral Perry or Pizzaro. What is happening to us? How did we get to this point? I'm very concerned that this is going to take a lot more than prayer to fix.

I will be sending at least one more mail your way. The archaeologist, who claims to know nothing at this point (this is very concerning), says that he will have more information and GPS coordinates tonight regarding your San Cristobal exit. By tomorrow morning I promise to have any and all information and instructions mailed to you. My God, Lucas! You're supposed to be a grown man. Please start making better decisions...please?

Chapter Fifteen

Luis Cruz, a *sicario*, a drug soldier for the Sinaloa Cartel, found himself in church once again. The Cathedral of St. Joseph in Tapachula, a city on the Pan American Highway just next to the Guatemalan border, was one of his favorites, and the priests didn't bother him even though they knew he was a *sicario*. Perhaps they were afraid to confront him, or maybe they liked the money he placed in an envelope and deposited in the Mites Box at each visit. It's quite possible that they believed Luis really, really needed to be in church. Who knows? Still…it was a little alarming to see him.

He drove a Ford Expedition with windows so darkly tinted that it was nearly impossible to see inside. He was a very large man with bull shoulders, jet black hair, and facial scars from numerous fights that projected an aura of malice and intimidation. For a man in his business, his nose was uncharacteristically straight. Luis had been a pretty good boxer when he was young. He always carried a large pistol which he tried to hide, with little effectiveness, behind his back tucked into his pants' waistband and covered by a light and loose fitting jacket. Luis sometimes appeared to be agitated or have problems concentrating in church. Whether from guilt or shame, or fear of being discovered, he glanced about frequently, looking furtively over his shoulder, occasionally startled upon hearing a noise. It was a sense of his surroundings and "situational awareness" that had, no doubt, kept him alive so far. The *sicario* had tattoos adorning each forearm. *La Santa Muerte*, a narco saint in the image of a crowned, robed skeleton with a scythe, much like the Grim Reaper of western literature, was inked onto his right forearm. *Jesus Malverde*, the debonair, mustachioed narco saint from Northwestern Sinaloa State was tattooed on his left forearm. One shouldn't take chances or offend, thus he paid obeisance to both. Luis had an unnerving habit, bordering on superstition, of seeking solace by stroking these tattoos, and it served to ratchet chills along the spines of the area priests. The clerics knew what the tattoos represented, and they were very disapproving. They also agreed that it was probably not a good idea to make an issue of it. It was better to let guilt punish a man like him and best to retrieve his ill-gotten pesos from the Mites Box and use them to help the area poor.

In a Catholic Church, each pew has a small bench for kneeling as is required at various times during the mass. It has two settings – up or down. Luis was kneeling, filled with discontent, ruminating on his family and work situation. Tapachula was the last town of any size in Mexico located on the Pan American Highway before crossing into Guatemala. Tapachula was as bad a place as you could find. In short – it sucked; no jobs, military and federales everywhere, no opportunity for young people. Everyone hustled for a living here. *Maras*, gangs of unemployed males with large and intimidating facial tattoos and arms inked with 'sleeves' dominated the underworld – day and night; and nights were an especially bad time to be out. Drugs, violence, assault, and every type of thievery was the norm.

Church and home were the only places he found respite these days. The narco stroked the tattoo of *Jesus Malverde* on his left arm fondly, then glanced around the church. Impressive pillars supported a vaulted blue ceiling. A golden eastern sunlight illuminated the stained glass windows with images of saints and various biblical scenes. Flickering votive candles created darting shadows against a smoke-stained wall next to a row of saints, all short in stature with Mayan noses and broad foreheads. He found comfort in the familiar images and stroked both forearms yet again.

The cathedral was one of the few places he could ruminate on his delicate situation. He had been a *sicario* now for nearly 18 years, an unheard degree of longevity in a heartless, brutal business. Luis had quit going to church for many years, but returned about 10 years ago. Many of his fellow *sicarios* that survived did the same, reasoning that something more than luck kept them alive. They, too, had trouble sleeping or were guilt ridden and unable to reconcile violent behavior with their traditional family upbringings. Besides, everyone was aware that an unexpected vicious death could visit you at any moment. It was the nature of their work, being a soldier in a drug cartel. If there was a more insane job in the world, Luis was unaware of it. Sometimes you were whoring and drinking, or just spending time with your family – if you still had any. The next day you were in a wild chase at high speeds, or on the run, hiding, fighting, and killing and sometimes having to commit barbaric acts like cutting people's heads off. He and his men had once decapitated and tossed 12 heads of a competitor cartel onto the courthouse lawn in Acapulco – the group had been vying to operate in their area and just had to be stopped. That was a very bad day, Luis remembered, wracked by a shiver.

The *sicario* had long avoided hard drugs - the cocaine, meth, and fentanyl that was shipped north. He had restricted himself to pot and booze, having seen too many of his fellow soldiers lose their lives, ingesting drugs to keep their rampaging psyches under control or out-of-control, depending on the state of mind required to do the job. Luis didn't need to get all ramped up. That came naturally. He was ready – always ready. He could turn on the violence and rock 'n roll in an instant. Luis had decided he needed something different: good medicine prescribed by a doctor to smooth the edges and allow him to step back from the abyss without muddying his thinking. He had started taking Xanax and it had proved itself a miracle drug for him. When his anxieties began to peak, a few of the pills helped tremendously and didn't seem to alter his ability to react. He was never without them now. He reached to pat his shirt pocket to reassure himself that he had brought them along. Their presence and touch caused him to smile.

He had spent the last five years picking up loads of meth from contractors in Guatemala and shipping it north to those stupid, sick-in-the-head Americans who apparently couldn't get enough of it. This was becoming increasingly more difficult. The problem was these damn Zapatistas. The Mayan Indians controlled the jungles and forested mountains and they knew every cave, trail, stream, and nook in the wilderness state. They hated drugs, but they did like guns – and that was how the Sinaloa Cartel secured a toehold in the area and encouraged them to look the other way while they did business. Now the Zapatistas had plenty of guns, but the politics of rebellion seemed to be changing. There wasn't much fighting going on anymore. The Mexican government was talking more, threatening less, or simply ignoring the demands and provocations of the upstart Indians. The Zapatistas still didn't like drugs, but they had acquired all the guns that they needed. Meanwhile a crazy religious zealot was roaming the jungles of Guatemala and Mexico performing miracles with a "magic cup" and this somehow seemed to be unifying the Indians of both countries. This in turn created a different kind of unwanted attention, and made Luis very uneasy. It was difficult to predict a rapidly changing political climate.

He had accumulated enough bad karma for a hundred lifetimes and wasn't happy about it. In fact, he was thinking very, very seriously about leaving the business – if such a thing was even possible. At age forty-four the chances of his luck holding were just about zero, he had decided. If he was ever to leave, he must do it soon. The Sinaloa Cartel was under stress from the newly arrived Zetas, a violent cartel that had originated in the northeast and spread along the gulf coast. Luis knew he would not survive the upcoming war.

His wife had been killed ten years ago by the rival New Generation Cartel, and he had struggled mightily to maintain a relationship with his daughter since that time. She was a very talented singer and entertainer but was now living with a boyfriend, with whom she had a son, and was pregnant again. Her man, a very good musician, wanted in the cartel, but Luis had said no…absolutely not. The *sicario* had a better plan. His daughter and grandchildren were going to have a better life than he had, and that was why he was in church today. Thinking and planning, reflecting on his limited options, but Luis had learned a thing or two working for the Sinaloa Cartel. Bosses had come and gone and now he was a boss. He stroked *Jesus Malverde* lightly and then glanced at the crucified Jesus hanging from the rafters above the altar.

Time to go. He needed to check his Yahoo account to get instructions for a pickup in a couple of days, meanwhile he had a grandson that he thought about constantly. God help him, the *sicario* loved that child. He loved him so much it hurt. The thought of the child sometimes brought tears to his eyes. If there was any tangible, identifiable reason why Luis had decided to change his life, it was his grandson. He had decided that his grandchild was the most important person on the planet and Luis was determined to set him up for success.

The sicario gently stroked a tattoo on each forearm, made the sign of the cross, and then glanced over his shoulder to see who, if anyone, lurked in the shadows in the back of the church. He rose from his pew and strode toward the doors, stopping to drop an envelope with a thousand peso note inside the Mite Box. He hesitated at the entry, placed his hand on the pistol grip in his waist band, and stuck his head out the door to view the area. All appeared to be well. He stepped outside, quickly moved the gun to the front waistband inside his light jacket, and sauntered toward his Ford Expedition, thinking he really needed to stop being so predictable. Everyone, including the opposing Zetas, knew he drove this car. Stupid. Maybe those pills were messing with his head more than he suspected. He looked around again, circled the vehicle to see if anything was obviously amiss, climbed in and fired the ignition. He checked his mirrors, pulled into traffic and headed for his daughter's house.

The *sicario* needed to finalize his meth "business" plans, but wanted to see his grandson first. He wished his daughter was as easy to deal with as her baby son and husband, but such was not the case. She needed to lay off the pot, but she didn't want any of his advice. Luis knew he must keep his mouth shut. He loved her more than he could express, but unfortunately, self-expression was not his long suit. These were the only family he had and he would somehow create a better life for them. It was the one remaining good act of which he felt capable. Luis took a deep breath to calm himself, checked his rearview mirror again, then reached and removed a couple of Xanax from the bottle in his shirt pocket. He felt a shit-storm blowing in and must ensure that his family was safe and far away if and when it arrived. They might have to depart on an unscheduled vacation in the next couple of weeks, but didn't know it yet. They must trust him. They could do this. He had the money, lots of it, and everyone had the motivation to save their lives. He stroked Jesus Malverde on his forearm, then turned right onto Calle Revolucion. Luis could deal with his own anxieties, it was handling the fear of others that messed everything up. That, he decided, was not going to happen this time. Too much at stake.

***

Professor Wolf stood with coffee cup in hand on his patio enjoying the delicious morning air and flighty, fussy birds. He looked west into verdant foothills buttressing the pine-clad mountains. The sun was weak at his back, mottling the hills and sierras with blue-gray shade. His wife, Ali, joined him and put an arm around his waist.

"You're not excavating?"

"No digging today…maybe not tomorrow either. I'll just be puttering around the site." He raised the cup to his mouth and sipped. "Don't know why exactly. I'll be waiting for Marcos to contact me later today at Lacanja. This big meeting I've been telling you about is on. Didn't believe it, but it seems to be happening. I'm going to meet the pope and be involved in another of Balaam Reyes' schemes. This one is pretty high profile. Maybe I shouldn't be trusting him?"

"You say that your contact in Rome, this Sor Juana, she's reliable?"

David hesitated, considered, then nodded and said, "Yes, she seems to be authentic. Very bright lady. Straight to the point on everything. Asks lots of questions. I guess I'm still surprised that the pope would actually do anything like this, but then if you think about it from his perspective, this could be big for the Vatican, or dangerous. He's a brave man, I'll tell you that. I swear this will be the last time I get involved with that grizzled forest gnome. He looks like he's a hundred years old. Do Indians live longer than white people?"

She smiled, "No dear, usually they don't. Only the ones who want to remain your nemesis until you die."

"Funny."

"Not so much it appears. You're unusually cranky this morning."

The professor paused, took another sip, and then turned to his wife. "Yeah....I seem to have a knack for letting that old shaman get to me. Lots of history. Sorry. I hope to be back by evening sometime, but maybe not. I'm taking the cell phone, but I don't know if I can get a signal down there with the mountains. Don't worry about me."

"I'll worry if I want. I'm very fond of you and to be honest, you must live long enough to take me to Rome."

"You really want to do that?"

"We haven't been anywhere in ages, David."

"What?"

"Think about it. When's the last time you took off longer than a four-day weekend? When's the last time we didn't have to be somewhere, or readying ourselves to go on one of your digs or something?"

The professor turned to her, sighed, and then smiled. "Yeah, sure, you're right as usual. And there was no hurry most of the time...only in my head." He paused briefly, then said, "This excavation close to Lacanja? It's pretty meaningless. I intend to shut it down. Really hasn't panned out as I hoped…squandered a year. Nothing to publish, really. Just been a waste of hard-to-find research money. Maybe in a week or two we can back off, set down, and put a plan together. Actually, Rome doesn't sound so bad. The Eternal City," he mused. David reached to put an arm around her waist. "So does the Vatican archives – I'd love to spend a few years in the Church archives."

"Not with me," she warned him. "I'm not traveling to Rome to be a research widow. You can go once, maybe twice to the archives. You belong to me on this trip, *señor*. We're talking Rome, get it? You come with me and I promise you a very good time." She smiled and winked.

Did his pretty, but conservative Catholic wife just smile and wink at him? Yes – no doubt about it. She'd done this before and things had worked out well. He returned her smile, then said. "Yes, well, I'm sure there's so much to see. I've never taken the time…"

"We'll see it all, David, anything we want. We'll do anything we want. Meanwhile, you get the pope, Marcos, and Balaam taken care of, okay? She hesitated and turned, then started to say something.

"Don't ask, please." David held up a hand to deflect her request.

"It really would be great to meet the pope." She said anyway, lowering her head, demurely.

"Please don't do that. No – at least not on this. Too much at stake. This is almost like cloak and dagger stuff. Maybe we can get an audience when we get to Rome. It isn't like the pope and I won't know each other after tomorrow and the next day. Of course - if things don't go well…" His sentence trailed into an indefinite ending. "He may never want to see me again." he added, finally.

"True," she agreed with a grin. "You're so smart." She hugged him, then took his cup to refill. "I trust you, David. You have pretty good sense for a man with so much mileage. Just stay in touch, agreed? Keep trying on the phone until you raise me."

"Agreed, Ali. I wish it was two days from now. I'm getting too old for this nonsense."

****

Marcos, Fr. Lopez, and their wives sat in the back of a blue and green panel van that boasted the name *El Sendero Jaguar* (The Jaguar Path). The vehicle belonged to a large travel company that arranged tours for European and American tourists. The company provided services throughout most of Chiapas State and just happened to have an owner who was half Indian and a Zapatista sympathizer. The loan of a van was a small thing to the owner. He trusted the Zapatistas, unlike the Mexican government or police or military. He knew the Indians wouldn't mess things up. They wouldn't ask unless they really needed it. Besides, if things did go bad, they might not get the loan of another vehicle.

While the women chatted and held their sleepy children, the two men spoke quietly of the next two days. Father Lopez thought the van ride to be a delightful change. During the last three years he had been constantly on foot, walking paths known only to the Indians as his ministry moved back and forth across the Usumacinta River, up and down through Mexican and Guatemalan jungles, always avoiding roads and the federales.

A collision of thunderheads swirled ominously above. It was the rainy season, but had not rained for over a week. This appeared to be at an end as foreboding, mountain-sized clouds moved in from the west coast and encircled the highlands. The storm turned black and gray with roiling shadows and jags of lightning backlighting the huge mass. The van was descending *Los Altos de Chiapas*, the mountain range in which San Cristobal de las Casas sat, moving east toward the Lacandon Jungle and various classic Mayan ruins that dotted the eastern landscape.

As they talked, speculated, and told jokes, both seemed nervous but neither wished to destroy the calm. Not knowing how the events of the next two days would unfold was the biggest downside to the moment. The Holy Man would spend a few days in Lacanja in preparation for a mass planned three days from today. It would take people a while to arrive. Notice of the event had been issued two weeks previously, and word-of-mouth would spread more effectively than any electronic message. The Indians would walk endless miles through forest and jungle, intent on seeing the Holy Man.

Marcos and the professor would meet the pope, and using this very same van, drive him to an isolated, but nice, hotel near the Palenque ruin located about ten miles from the site. The hotel was surrounded by heavy forest, and abundant wildlife. It had separate bedrooms, a swimming pool, and patios and backyards fenced for privacy. Ten miles from the ruins and expensive, it was never more than half-full at any time during the year. At this time in June, the low season, it was virtually empty.

The storm was fast moving and threatening and began to overtake them as mottled towers grew more sinister by the minute. The road was winding, steep, and treacherous, and guardrails were absent in places where steep drops would spell certain doom for anyone going over the edge. A wrong turn would send the van thousands of feet down sheer cliffs. They were supposed to be on the outside lane, but Marcos insisted they drive on the inside at all times if possible.

Moving over only when other vehicles approached. Lots of weaving in-and-out required.

As they moved east, the storm arrived with a fury. Gusts of wind whipped the road and sheets of driving rain arrived. Still, they continued cautiously onward and downward, the driver slumped forward with white knuckles gripping the steering wheel, peering ahead intently. Marcos encouraged him to pull over if the winds became too strong. Lightening cracked loudly, unexpectedly close, and the women stopped talking and looked to their husbands. All was fine, Marcos assured them, but Fr. Lopez rose and extended his head out the side window to better see the tempest.

"Maybe we ought to pull over," Fr. Lopez suggested, seeing the expressions of concern on the faces of the women.

"We will if it gets worse, my friend. Just a few gusts right now, but we are nearly down the mountain. We can stop in Ocosingo near the base of the mountains and sit this one out. Still plenty of time to get to Lacanja and meet David."

Marcos would meet with Professor David Wolf later this afternoon and give him the GPS coordinates that should be relayed to the pope's people in order for the helicopter to transport the pontiff and a few of his entourage to eastern Chiapas to a remote and privately owned site near the Bonampak archaeological site.

"And Balaam?"

"Later. He's in the area, I'm sure. He'll probably meet me at the hotel when David and I arrive with Pope Lucas. You will stay with the ladies in Lacanja, yes?"

"Yes, it would be fantastic to see the pope, but probably not best right now. Need to concentrate on what's important. Big mass with lots of people arriving in a few days. I must say something worthy to them."

Marcos grinned. "You will, Fr. Lopez. You always find a way."

Thirty minutes later they sat incognito, two unknowns (they hoped) with wives and children outside a highway restaurant under a roof of billowing tarps in Ocosingo. The Holy Man felt uneasy. He couldn't remember the last time he had sat in comfort outside at a restaurant. He remembered with fondness the visit to San Cristobal and the Carnaval in the Indian village of Chamula. Hopefully he could do it again one of these years. His ability to speak the Mayan language would be even better, and he would have an easier time connecting with the people. The past week had essentially been a vacation for him, but it would not be good to get acclimated to comfort, convenience, and the entertainment of towns and festivals. Maybe again one of these years, but for now he must pursue his mission.

Lightning cracked and roared, shaking the heavens, creating an odor of ozone in the air. Ocosingo sat at about two thousand feet and the clouds that had pummeled them rolled down the mountainsides, raging at the lowlands below. Marcos walked to the crest of the hill and viewed the layers of clouds above, and then into the gap, down into the lowlands where the very bowels of the tempest were evacuating its water on the complacent, eternal forest and foothills. He could see it all – a relatively calm field of clouds, and a fury of a downpour below. He doubted if anyone below could see anything. Visibility would be zero. He glanced at his watch. One more hour and they would follow the departing downpour to Lacanja where they would be welcomed with open arms.

Marcos still must talk with the professor, and everyone would more than likely meet the pope the next day. He had experienced life's highs and lows, the sublime and the ridiculous, festive celebrations, and ceremonies of sadness. He had fought in battles, experienced euphoria and despair – but he had never met a pope, and the thought of doing so somehow filled him with hope and anticipation. He glanced at his friend, whom he admired greatly, and wondered what he was thinking. The man was a Catholic priest, or used to be. Wouldn't meeting the pope be a "red letter day" if you were a priest? But, obviously, the Holy Man thought his work more important.

Fr. Salvador had proven his worth many times over and Marcos was proud to call him a friend. He was selfless, always putting others first. The Holy Man even did house calls when relatives of the sick sent word. The Holy Man traipsed miles through the jungle in sometimes horrible conditions of heat and mosquitos, and over root-bound trails with clinging brambles and sting weed to pray with the sick. In many ways, Salvador wasn't anything at all like Marcos – just the opposite. But that's why Marcos loved him. His friend might be the only truly, genuine, selfless person he had ever met. Everyone should know at least one person whom they admired. Even a rebel general needed someone he recognized as better than himself. Everyone needs a role-model – and a trusted friend.

Chapter Sixteen

Pope Lucas' soul soared with the helicopter as it lifted away from Tuxtla Gutierrez and toward the distant mountain range and colonial town of San Cristobal de las Casas, which lay in a highland valley at 8,000 feet. It was 6:30 a.m., a lethargic morning, and a red-orange corona in the east struggled to rise above distant, sentinel *barrancas* awaiting the quickening rays of sunlight to give them life. The mountainsides were a blanket of ancient forest interspersed with occasional fields of bare red soil, winding roads, and trails that disappeared into the canopy and sudden valleys.

The pope's heart pounded, and he took a deep breath and exhaled slowly. He must remember to pace himself. He was worn down from repeated meetings, constant going-and-coming, meeting and interfacing with endless crowds of well-wishers, maintaining a pace that alternated between torrid activity and impatient waiting. He greatly missed his own bed in the Marthae Sanctae Hotel in Vatican City. His books and studies called to him from across the Atlantic, but they must wait. He touched the GPS coordinates and instructions written on a sheet of paper and tucked into an inner pocket of his robe. He would follow the plan.

Today included a short parade around the *zocalo* and Cathedral, mass with thousands and a series of short visits to various Indian villages in the area. Then, he would escape from Bishop Ruiz and his entourage and execute the plan given to him by Professor David Wolf and that shaman fellow. *Bone Man. What an odd name,* mused the pope. Perhaps this was unwise. Perhaps he was following the gentle nudges of God. Who Knew? Uncertainty flooded him.

Twice he had woken in the night to re-read the instructions in Sor Juana's email. This morning he woke wishing his mind was one with Christ in heaven. Instead his psyche floated aimlessly in limbo while his body remained bound to this terrestrial hell of uncertainty and trepidation. Today and tomorrow required whatever determination and strength he held in reserve. He had insisted that these uncertain events occur. It was his time and his show. Sor Juana was correct; no – he wasn't Indiana Jones, but he was near important events fundamentally important to the future of Christianity and his beloved Church. He must investigate. He was the pivot and focal point of the entire process for the next two days, and apprehension was visible in his face. Still, a curious smile sat resolutely on his face. The ruse would hurt no one. Those around him must either help or get out of the way. No one would be injured in any manner; feelings might be hurt, but nothing more.

He had met last night, then again early this morning to explain his plan to his horrified security staff. Other than Cardinal Montoya, they were the only ones in his entourage aware of his ambitious plan. He had forbidden anyone to speak to the press or the bishop's staff, or to contact their superiors in Rome regarding the matter. Sor Juana's mail last night had firmed everything up and set it all in motion. The pope had met with them again this morning and clearly spelled out their duties, their role in his plan, and his explicit expectations. He was serious about this and they were going to do it his way. He was the pope, remember? They didn't like it. In fact they were aghast. All protested, but had grudgingly acquiesced once they saw the passion with which he directed them and explained his purpose. They were told that arrangements were made over a month ago, but kept secret so as not to expose the plan and unintentionally invite the eyes of the public. He asked if he could trust them – right now at this moment and for the next few days. Could they promise fealty and follow his directions? If not, they must to stay behind in Tuxtla and keep their mouths shut. Any leaks would cause complications, perhaps danger to the Pope and demonstrate the leaker was not supportive of the pope and his very, very important task. He, God's Shepherd on Earth, needed their help.

The pontiff was visiting, privately and after hours, the spectacular archaeological ruin of Palenque. He wished to visit the ancient Mayan city of pyramids and tumbled stone like a normal tourist without the complications and constant hordes of press and well-wishers. Afterwards, he planned to meet friends with whom he would spend the night in a nearby luxury hotel. The name of the hotel would not be released, to ensure privacy. All would be fine. The following day Pope Lucas would either return to Tuxtla Gutierrez before flying to Mexico City and subsequently on to Rome, or he might make an unscheduled, but important visit to a missionary priest in the area who was in need of the pope's special pastoral attention. If so, this would delay leaving by one day. All would be fine. He was sure of it.

The pontiff touched a small satchel of personal items resting against his foot. The bag contained his small laptop computer, satellite USB, a change of clothes, insulin and needles, a few hard candies slipped to him by Fr. Montoya. He clutched a leather-bound bible, its cover soft with use and wear. The holy book had belonged to his mother and her mother, and it gave him comfort just to hold it. He never traveled without it.

The helicopter rose like the Phoenix above the dusky red hills, up over the shady forest that cloaked the mountainside and finally, he could see the old colonial town of San Cristobal. As they entered the highland valley and sped toward the zocalo and distant cathedral, he saw gaping wounds on the hillsides where forest was being felled. The town had grown from 40,000 to a city of 200,000 after the Zapatista Rebellion in 1994 when the Mexican government had established a permanent presence, and federal pesos rained onto the city and surrounding area. A military fort was built in the Lacandon Jungle, and many sleepy towns along the asphalt snake that wound through the mountains and down into the eastern lowlands had experienced unprecedented growth. Much of frontier Mexico was disappearing to developers, loggers, miners, and others seeking to access to natural resources.

The Pope was aware that the Maya were suffering unprecedented stress in their communities, and that their land and natural resources were being stolen at a rate not seen since the Conquest. Young people were leaving traditional Indian communities in droves, ashamed of their poverty and families, lured by the promise of the Internet, jobs, cell phones, and lifestyles only seen in video. The lives of millions of poor Indians in Guatemala and Mexico were in flux as the rich and powerful disenfranchised them of their land, minerals, and basic human rights. This same sordid scenario played out over all the world as indigenous communities fought local developers and multi-national corporations. This made the Pope feel powerless. So far prayer had accomplished little to counteract it.

The pontiff was only one man, but a person of influence whose opinion was sought by presidents and prime ministers. Unfortunately, this seemed to be lip service only, as too few of those who asked actually followed given advice. Money comes with its own explanations, rationales, and counsel and is more-or-less morally neutral. Money has no conscience. Wealth acquisition had remained a tough competitor ever since the Protestant Reformation. Once an egregious offense in Christianity, the sin of usury existed only in Islam and Buddhism now. During today's mass he would offer a message of hope and resiliency to the poor while lecturing the rich and powerful about the sins of greed and wanton pursuit of wealth for no purpose other than enriching oneself. Yet money, unfortunately, persisted as the easiest means to corrupt just about anyone on the planet. Sometimes the pope wondered if money wasn't the invention of the *Evil One*. The societies of history, while not perfect, were rich in tradition of family and spirituality. Modern society, sadly, possessed none of these traits. Families were weak, often beyond repair, religion optional, technology the new god, and tradition an impediment to the accumulation of wealth. Sometimes Pope Lucas was absolutely certain that he was born in the wrong century.

Chapter Seventeen

Luis felt the Xanax calm him as he logged onto his computer. He took a deep breath, refreshed and imbued. He must be in the right state of mind to get his plan together. If he was anxious or in a hurry he might make mistakes. Errors were fatal in his business.

From his chair and through the doorway, he could see down the hall to his home's interior where sunlight reflected off the polished, white, terrazzo floor. A gentle breeze wafted from the open courtyard where bountiful, aggressive blooms of red and purple bougainvillea webbed tall trellises and reached for the sun before cascading over stuccoed walls. He loved his home. It was his castle, his place of refuge in a mean and dangerous world. Luis had watched this neighborhood for a couple of years and paid cash when he spotted a realtor putting up a new sign. His home was off the main streets, away from prying eyes. It was a relatively new, traditional house no more than 100 years old, and had been well maintained by an old widow who had finally passed.

His daughter didn't know it yet, but she owned the house. It was purchased in her name. Luis, because of his vocation, never knew if he would be alive from one day to the next. He wished his daughter, son-in-law, and grandson could live with him, as he had plenty of room. But they could too easily end up as collateral damage, much like his deceased wife, so he rented them a smaller unit in a not-so-bad area of Tapachula where Emilio, her boyfriend, could go to tech school during the day and blow his trombone evenings in nightclubs. Luis' daughter was a very, very good Tejano singer and had sung in area clubs for several years. But a bar was no place for a woman to make a living and Luis had finally convinced her to stay at home with her son. Luis would pay the rent. Did she want her son to grow up like she did? No – of course not. He knew that she still harbored resentment, but she took his money. She did her best to make a home for her son and boyfriend.

She was also pregnant again. When Luis mentioned that perhaps marriage might be a good idea at this late date, she had screamed him out of the house. Luis didn't understand it. When he was a young man, all the girls wanted to get married, especially if they were pregnant. Women were so independent nowadays. Being a single mother just didn't seem to have the same stigma. He didn't know what the younger generation was thinking. He was only forty-four. How could he have gotten out of touch so quickly?

With his computer booted and ready, he opened his internet connection and went to Yahoo, his home page. He checked his mail, which was mostly advertisements. One of his old *sicario* buddies from up in Sinaloa sent him a short porn video, as well as pictures of his new girlfriend and her kid. *Guys never change do they?* he asked himself rhetorically.

He signed out, then clicked the **Sign In** button to open a different account and typed in a different email address and password. He closed accounts and changed passwords regularly, and only the latest contractor or soldiers with whom he must communicate knew the latest account name and new password. This had proven invaluable in terms of safety. Luis would type an email but never send it. It would go into the **Drafts** section of the menu, as it avoided sending emails through servers or hubs where the high-tech shitheads in the United States used sophisticated algorithms to spot key words and identify cartel correspondence. Mail was never sent. Those who needed to know simply opened up the account, went to the **Drafts** tab and read the information and instructions needed for the job. The contractors never sent an email either. If they had a response or message to send, they followed the same procedure. Prepare a message, then save it in **Drafts**. <u>Never Send It!</u> The system wasn't perfect, but worked pretty well. Its simplicity was the best part. The downside was that some of his soldiers had never learned to read or write, or didn't do it so well. These people had absolutely no business around a computer and Luis wisely refused to share information with them that could be inadvertently disclosed or that they had no need to know.

Luis wasn't a good writer, but he read just fine and scribbled well enough to provide simple instructions. He provided his final updates in **Drafts**: writing where he would be, on what day, at what time, and where the meth should be so that he could pick it up. He signed off as 'The Big Enchilada.' They didn't need to know his real name. The product was already paid for. He wanted in and out, traveling another thirty minutes back to the small town where his soldiers waited to do their part in the complex chain that would carry the product to the United States.

Luis walked with purpose to his bedroom chest of drawers and removed the middle drawer. He lay it carefully on the bed, removed the underwear and socks, and with a familiar move, lifted the false bottom. Three passports, Guatemalan, Mexican, and Belizean were wrapped in a rubber band. Thick rolls of fresh U.S. hundred dollar bills, several boxes of ammo and pistol, a Glock knife, and other odds and ends rolled around inside his "toolbox." He would need his Mexican passport today. He removed it, along with a wad of bills to change to pesos at the bank, and then replaced the bottom and clothing. He packed a travel bag with enough for four days. He wouldn't need more because anything longer probably meant that he was dead or in jail. He must stop by his new attorney's office to ensure that his Last Will & Testament was completed as instructed. He would then go by his daughter's to see his grandson and leave information and telephone numbers that she might need if she didn't hear from him for a while – or ever again.

Luis tossed down two more Xanax and drove to his attorney's office. He had long ago decided that they were all smiling, obfuscating crooks – opportunists and parasites – but just try ignoring or not paying one and see what happened. Javier Gonzalez-Hernandez greeted him with a great smile, white teeth, and hearty handshake. The mayor didn't like Javier, the police didn't like him and the *federales* had been preparing a case against him for years that had never made it to court. He was well connected and virtually untouchable. A well-known criminal lawyer, he had represented more people in Sinaloa Cartel than Luis could recall. Sometimes Gonzalez-Hernandez occasionally did pro bono work for the area gangs, mostly to keep them away from his own neighborhood, but a few were relatively prosperous at times and could afford to pay when receiving subcontractor work from the cartel. While *sicarios* didn't need lawyers, as they frequently ended up dead, their families sometimes did. Javier was probably the closest thing you could find to an honest lawyer, although he didn't hesitate to lean on a widow or pretty daughter for a little something extra when he thought he could leverage them.

Luis indicated that he was pressed for time and would like to finalize his Last Will & Testament. Gonzalez-Hernandez was expecting him and retrieved a file folder from his desktop. Luis held it in his hand momentarily and reflected: twenty years ago who would have thought that he would have enough assets to need an attorney? He didn't take the time to read the document. He had told Javier what he wanted - everything to his grandkid and daughter; and $10,000.00 to Javier if Luis was killed or turned up missing to get Luis' daughter out of town. Retribution or blowback were very real possibilities in Luis' world. Revenge was mindless and didn't make a lot of sense. Luis himself had committed unnecessary, punitive collateral damage when told to do so by bosses. Shit job. He wasn't proud of it, but it happened. All the Xanax in the world wasn't going to fix that. Just one more reason to start looking for an out.

Luis took a copy of his Last Will and Testament and left his daughter's cell number in addition to his own with the attorney, then headed to Cuca's two-bedroom, stained stucco, near the train tracks.

He drove through the Niño's Heroes barrio. The area was filthy, littered with trash, and empty buildings with broken windows were the norm. The sidewalks were cracked and ruptured, and the area so neglected and ruined that it appeared to have been condemned by God. Indeed, the barrio was controlled by the violent *Salvatrucha* (MS13) gang, and if there was a more violent gang in Latin America, Luis certainly didn't want to know them. They routinely shook down, robbed, raped, and killed desperate refugees from El Salvador, Guatemala, and Panama moving through Mexico on their journey north to the United States. He agreed with a news article he had read that speculated the *Salvatrucha* members must have been raised without mothers or by wolves. Such was the nature of their reputation. Very few immigrants made it across the Guatemala-Mexican border through Tapachula untouched. He needed to find a place closer to his neighborhood for his daughter and grandchild. Cuca, he knew, had already put up with unimaginable bullshit and he believed that she was a miracle to have coped as well as she had. No reason to ruin the grandchild's life in addition. He hoped this would be his last job. He had tempted fate for years and now wanted to be done with it.

When she let him in, she frowned and pretended to pout. She was tired, her baby had a runny nose, and her new pregnancy was beginning to show. She was fat and was ugly, she said, and her boyfriend Emilio spent all his time jamming with friends at their houses while she stayed home and cleaned dirty diapers. Not too happy today.

The rhythmic beat of Tejano singer Selena's, *Dreaming of You*, lilted in from the back bedroom. He went into the bedroom and watched his sleeping grandson. His chest expanded with pride and he was tempted to wake him, but knew Cuca would throw a fit if he did. She joined him in the bedroom and Luis told her she was beautiful, she was doing everything right, and that, yes, her boyfriend was a lay about and stoner, but she had gone with worse, and knew it. If she spent less time smoking weed and more singing, she would feel better, he told her – as long as she wasn't doing it in nightclubs. Under protest, she allowed him to leave a roll of U.S. hundred dollar bills with her "in case of emergency," both pretending his return was a forgone conclusion. He hugged Cuca tightly, then jabbered nonsense to his sleeping grandson, telling him how strong he was and how proud Luis was and what a perfect child he was, then gave his daughter a peck on the head and exited the small one-bedroom house. Next stop – the Tapachula Alamo Rent-a-Car.

Thirty minutes later, Luis held the keys to a two-year-old Chevrolet Cabriola: a non-descript car that worked great, but looked forgettable. Luis had parked his Ford Expedition away from prying eyes, under an awning at the rent-a-car. The business sat recessed from the street thirty yards, creating a partial occlusion for those looking down the street. The Expedition, although not hidden, was not obvious. For the next two days, no one would pay much attention – he hoped. It's just the way things worked out at these places. Not hidden, but not obvious. He would return when this job was over. He'd done this a time or two. Fidelity to what had proven to work was the only way anyone stayed alive in this business - even then you were sometimes surprised. Luis had a few "surprises," but had somehow managed to survive, even thrive through the years. He was personable and dependable, something the bosses liked a lot. He had no time for B.S. and expected those about him to be competent. No excuses. Otherwise they were not going to be on his team. Luis' groups were relatively small. He learned many years ago that the fewer people involved, the better things fared. Less mouths to compromise his work. The chance that events might not go well in a drug interaction were high. Everyone on your team needed to be on the same page.

He opened the door of the Cabriola and tossed in his laptop computer, gun and bullets, clothes and toiletries in the overnight bag, his passport, a fat roll of dollars and pesos, and a bottle of Cuervo Tequila. Yes, he was ready, he decided. He paused and reflected. He would drive to San Cristobal de las Casas, exit the highland valley, cross over the cordillera, and then drive southeast toward the lush Lacandon forest to a small tourist hotel south of the Bonampak ruins. He had discovered the inn during his last trip through and decided he like the non-descript location with quality rooms, restaurant, pool, and bar. The Lacandon jungle loomed tall and dense on three sides, providing privacy and security.

Tomorrow, from the hotel, he would drive south on Highway 307 along the Usumacinta River, to arrive at the river border town of *El Planchon*. El *Planchon* wasn't really a town as far has he was concerned, but he could rent an eighteen-foot boat with outboard motor and pilot up and down the Usumacinta River that divided Guatemala and Mexico. He would pass the famous Yaxchilan ruin that sat covered in jungle forty-five minutes north of Benemerito. Every thirty to forty-five minutes on a busy day, he might see a tourist boat rented by the young or daring to take them to the ruin.

The whole area was a lawless hotbed of smuggling; cattle from El Salvador, and drugs from Honduras, Guatemala, and Nicaragua were moved illegally, mostly into Mexico despite attempts by the authorities to stop it. Destitute immigrants wanting to avoid the rape and pillage awaiting them in towns like Tapachula opted to pay a coyote exorbitant fees to guide them through the Petén and Lacandon Jungles to cross the river. The Usumacinta is the major boundary between Guatemala and Mexico, and was characterized by loops and oxbows which made it difficult to monitor activity, illicit or otherwise. A benefit to the work that Luis performed. Jungle encroached on either side of the river bank and virtually no roads allowed access where smugglers could be apprehended. No one entered the forbidding jungle as there were no roads and few paths, and more danger than could be imagined. Only the locals knew the crossing points, invisible and life-threatening dangers of the river, or where people unfriendly to commerce might attempt to highjack them. There were few, if any, *federales,* in the area and the military maintained a stronger presence up near the popular ruins of Paleneque, Bonampak, and Piedras Negras where the tourists played and felt safer in the presence of uniformed men. Thus the forest and jungle along both sides was largely ignored, creating an ideal, but little monitored location for illegal activities.

Luis was going to a very small ruin, an outpost really, located on the Guatemalan side of the river that had never been promoted to tourists as it was not significant enough to merit development. He had discovered it three years ago and used it twice to receive meth from mules carrying product from his contractors in Guatemala. From there he would motor downstream back to the small community of *El Planchon* on the Mexican side of the Usumacinta where he planned to hand over his load, about eighty kilos of it, to three of his soldiers. They would transport it on the *La Trinitaria – Palenque* road before turning northeast into the lowland marshes where the Usumacinta flowed into the Gulf of Mexico. His soldiers would travel by night on selected roads deemed "safe" by *federale* officials and local mayors on the cartel's payroll, to the Gulf of Campeche. There they would load their product onto small tugs or freighters which transported the illicit cargo north to the waiting masses in the United States, who apparently couldn't get enough of it.

He slid behind the Cabriola's steering wheel and fired the engine, looked in his rearview mirror, and slowly pulled away from the curb. He maneuvered through a couple of barrios and more topes – speed bumps – until arriving at the Pan American Highway. He followed the road to Huixtla, then turned right and drove highway 211 east, then north to San Cristobal de las Casas. From there he would descend the *cordillera* and take Highway 199 to Palenque. He planned to stay at a very nice hotel, *Palenque Classica* that had Internet access. He had spotted it during his last visit. It was rustic, but new and expensive with quality rooms, restaurant and pool and bar. It was worth the rate, and almost hidden from prying eyes, which was very important.

He took a deep breath and exhaled loudly, tapped his shirt pocket to ensure that he had brought his Xanax, then pulled out onto the highway. If he made good time he would arrive at the hotel this evening. Into the player, he slid a CD of Selena songs that his daughter had recorded in a studio in Tuxtla a couple of years back into the player. Relaxing, he put the car on cruise control, and began to listen intently. Cuca had the smoothest and most beautiful voice. Within moments he was singing along; a few of the songs brought smiles or made his eyes a little misty.

Life was tough, but you had to do whatever was required to be successful. Luis had been born into abject poverty, but had always done his best. He was worried a bit that his luck might be running out, but right now he felt pretty good, so he just leaned back into the seat and drove the speed limit. The drug deal, always fraught with anxiety, was out there, but he would worry about that when it was time.

Chapter Eighteen

Pope Lucas mustered a tired smile as he held up a hand in salute to the Indians of San Lorenzo de Zinacantán. Unlike the church of San Juan Bautista in the Indian village of Chamula which he had visited earlier this morning, the church of San Lorenzo was four hundred years old and built in traditional fashion with a glorious nave featuring Jesus Christ surrounded by other saints and symbols of Christianity. The glory, however, was the flowers. The town of Zinacantán's primary export was flowers. In fact, most of the blossoms and blooms exported in Mexico came from this highland Indian village. The colors were visually stunning. The pope had never been in a church with so many flowers! The walls, nave, statues of saints, and floor were completely cloaked with brilliance the likes of which he had never seen. The inhabitants of the town wore these same brilliant colors and designs. The Tzotzil Indian women of Zinacantán were renowned for creating this marvel of color and design. In the open-air market in the zocalo that surrounded the church, Indian women wove beautiful flowers onto smocked blouses, table cloths, backpacks, handkerchiefs, handbags, wall hangings, and just about anything utilizing cloth. Stunning. You simply couldn't take in the vista without smiling.

A very satisfying ending to a fascinating, eventful day – at least here in the highlands. Bishop Ruiz, with whom he had corresponded prior to coming to Mexico, had proven himself an excellent host. The bishop was a Liberation Theologist and believed that anything and everything should be done to improve the plight of the Indians. He spoke at least four of the Mayan dialects and was frequently found visiting village elders in surrounding communities. His outspoken support and patience with Mayan elements in worship services, especially those in Chamula, were a point of contention that created resentment in the Catholic hierarchy. It was also obvious that the Indians loved him.

But now it was time to leave the village of San Lorenzo de Zinacantán and begin his adventure. His entourage slowly retraced their steps to a motorcade outside the church, the pope waving and calling out good wishes and thanks for the tremendous reception he had received. As he ducked to seat himself in the expansive Mercury Marquis, the door thunked to a quiet close and he was surrounded by silence. A tremor raced down his spine as the pope realized that the time to execute his plan was nearly upon him. A thirty minute car ride back to the rectory in San Cristobal would be followed by a flurry of activity.

No events were planned for the evening, as was usual. Cardinal Montoya would kindly deflect Bishop Ruiz and his staff with idle conversation while Lucas quickly changed into the civilian garb. He would grab his tote bag of essentials with laptop computer, diabetes kit, and family bible and exit from the back gate of the expansive, walled patio of the church rectory. There two of his security men waited outside the fence and gate with a car to take him to the non-descript, local airfield. He would board the same helicopter that had transported him from Tuxtla Gutierrez this morning and fly east to his destination over the mountains and to a future that only God knew. His security staff had already given the GPS coordinates to the pilot, who had looked them up and found nothing unusual about them. Helicopters landed just about anywhere with level ground, not just in airports. A quick look at Google Maps revealed the location to be a relatively open field near a small Indian community called Lacanja near the bio-reserve of Montes Azules, a large area of primeval jungle with no roads or amenities. No cause for alarm. The pilot wouldn't even know that it was the pope he was transporting over the *barrancas* and down to the lowlands until perhaps recognizing him during the flight.

In the car, across from the pope, sat Cardinal Montoya, taciturn and disapproving. Montoya had made his views on this venture known and was obviously upset. They had argued again this morning. Right now he was not speaking to his friend. He seemed lost in his own thoughts and circumstances, quite probably how he would handle the next few hours, then days. Pope Lucas had insisted that he use the special after-hours guided tour of the archaeological ruin of Palenque as the official story. It was really the only viable tale he believed the press, well-wishers, and diocesan staff would buy into. Their previous plan to travel to the nearby *Chiapa del Corso* ruin would have allowed too many strap-hangers and journalists to ferret around and seek photographs.

Thirty minutes later, as they entered San Cristobal, Pope Lucas simmered in a stew of misgivings and anxiety. Where WAS he going after the helicopter ride? Unknown - and that murky scenario was more than a little worrying. Still, he must trust in the Lord, he decided. He must do this. There was no backing out now. He grasped a small tin cross that hung inside his gown and squeezed it, uttering a silent, fervent prayer for assistance. If he ever needed the guidance and help of God before, he certainly did now. He exited the Mercury Marquis, walked to thank his host, Bishop Ruiz for the wonderful tour, and then requested that a light dinner be brought to his room later. Fr. Montoya would be there to receive it. The pope was "Very, very tired after such a successful day, and needed to rest." He turned to face flashing cameras and cheers, waved and smiled, and then turned and headed into the rectory. He quickly changed clothes in his room, then knelt at the altar near the wall for a final, fervent prayer before leaving.

While the remainder of the entourage and Bishop Ruiz's staff were attending to duties, Cardinal Montoya walked out to the patio and knocked on the back gate. It cracked slightly, and he asked, "Ready?"

"Yes, we're ready," came the sour reply of the two security personnel. "Stupid damn plan if you ask me."

Montoya nodded agreement, then shut the gate and returned to the pope's bedroom. Pope Lucas knelt at his altar, but had changed into civilian clothing, including a wool jacket to keep him warm at this high altitude. Montoya waited respectfully.

"Ready," said the pontiff. Let's do it." He stood, smiled at this friend. "Please don't judge me, my friend. You know I must do this."

"I'm not judging you, I'm terrified that this will go badly." He choked up, looked away, then used the back of his hand to wipe away a tear. "You have my phone, the rectory's number, my email and everything?"

"Yes, of course. Please, let's go. I must leave now or I might not take the first step later." Pope Lucas retrieved his travel bag. "We're here, we've been planning to do this, and nothing has changed. Please lead the way, my friend."

The two priests walked through the walled patio over red inter-locking bricks past a gurgling fountain of St. Francis Assisi feeding birds, to the back gate surrounded on both sides by gushing, exuberant purple bougainvillea. Montoya knocked twice and the gate quickly opened.

Cardinal Montoya held out his hand, but the pontiff reached and hugged him instead. "Thank you, my friend. Take cheer. See you in a few days, okay?" But Montoya was overtaken with grief, and turned his head momentarily, before catching the pope's eyes and returning a smile.

"God go with you, Holy Father."

"Yes, we can only hope so." The pontiff turned and entered the car his staff had secretly secured. In five minutes they were out of town and had arrived at the rugged local airstrip. There were no commercial flights into San Cristobal. Mostly only rich locals or an occasional bigwig would fly a one-or two-engine plane into the airstrip.

The helicopter waited, and the pontiff saw the rotors starting to spin as the car approached. Pope Lucas exited the car and turned to his two security men. He grasped one's hands then the other. "Thank you, boys."

"This is just plain nuts," said the tall one.

"Yeah…" agreed the other.

"God will reward you," said the Pope. "If he doesn't, be assured that I will. Please help me get in this noisy contraption."

The pilot held up a hand in greeting and announced that the flight would take about one hour or so. Not so far as the crow flies. By automobile it would take nearly four hours to cross the mountains and descend into the eastern forests and plain.

"You by yourself, *señor*?" asked the pilot, looking into his mirror. He stared as if his passenger looked familiar.

"Yes, I'm meeting new friends who have offered me a special tour of the archaeological ruins."

The pilot throttled up the engine and the rotors created a tornado of dust and noise outside while he checked his gauges. "Man...you're really going to like that. Been there a couple times. Absolutely spectacular." He fiddled with a couple of knobs, tested the tail rotor pedals, the collective pitch control, and then cyclic pitch control that comprised the flight controls of the helicopter. "Belt tightened? We're taking off."

The pope felt his stomach waffle and sink to the mild "G" forces as the helicopter rose to clear the surrounding pine and oak clad mountainsides. And then they were off and over the *barrancas*, flying above several *cordilleras* of peaks, before descending somewhat, but still high above foothills, and distant fields that extended for miles in every direction until they ran up against slopes or mountains. Pope Lucas felt his heart beat rapidly, and so he took several deep breaths to calm himself. Actually, he didn't feel so good right now. This was much different than flying in the jetliner that brought him to Mexico. His old joints ached and his wool jacket felt a little too warm. Could be a diabetic reaction he thought, but then decided it wasn't. This felt different, and he had taken a shot just before leaving. He should be good until tomorrow morning. Probably just excitement, anxiety, or altitude, but he would be really glad to get out of this rattling machine and get back on solid ground.

Pope Lucas hoped the meeting with David Wolf and the Balaam character would bring him some or all of the ancient papyrus texts. In essence, he realized, he was merely a beggar. He might receive nothing for his efforts but a curt dismissal.

There was no reason to expect that this Balaam character would give him anything. He certainly was under no obligation to do so. This shaman, unfortunately held all the cards.

Pope Lucas fervently wished to talk to Father Salvador Lopez. This was very important. The Mexican priest's file had been shipped to him two years ago and Pope Lucas had spent many late hours perusing it, examining it in detail, searching to understand why a priest would leave the Church under the circumstances that Father Salvador did to undertake such a life-changing, perilous mission in the jungle. The priest had left a comfortable life to pursue a most unusual and difficult ministry. Most priests lived relatively comfortable lives and were paid a monthly stipend. Although duties sometimes became onerous, depending on where they were stationed, priests had comfortable beds to which they returned at night and sometimes more well-wishers and friends than could be accommodated. To do what Salvador Lopez did required a very powerful combination of commitment and belief or an extraordinarily strong belief that his church had failed him. Belief was powerful stuff, this the pope knew. Some of the best and most horrific decisions in the history of mankind were made based on "belief." Commitment, however, was easy to talk about, but difficult to implement. This is where reality became abundantly clear; where living your faith and principles were more than just talk. You must have the conviction to stay the course. In the pontiff's experience very few people were capable of serious lifestyle changes. A man didn't just jettison his family and friends, or his status in the Catholic Church, without serious ideological conflicts. It took serious motivation to do so. To reject the beliefs and values that guided his perceptions of the world, Father Lopez must have reached catastrophic realizations that altered his perception of society and shook him to his core. He had demonstrated a clear appreciation of these new insights by sacrificing comfort and choosing hardship. Father Lopez was either a true servant of God or a man fractured by delusion.

If events played out as Pope Lucas hoped, this Holy Man of the southern tropical jungles, would become a man for the ages, a person whose life would be examined in detail by historians in order to understand his motivations and life. He might have a profound effect on the Church. Meanwhile, the pope knew his role. His duty was to understand, to engage the unknown, to risk his own life if necessary, to meet with this Holy Man. And he must investigate this "healing cup." Unfortunately no one else could do this, and Pope Lucas was an old man of poor health. But he was also a man of conviction and faith and determined to do the right thing, just like the Holy Man. If this quest would were to take his life, then it would all be worth it.

We all have our roles to play in life. Lucas' belonged to a Power greater than himself and a communion of people, the Holy Catholic Church, that promoted and celebrated the person, or gradually wore him down and cast him aside like others in a long line of men who had aspired to make a difference. God requested, but the Church demanded.

****

David and Marcos walked, talked, and scanned the sky, anxiously awaiting the Pope's helicopter. Both had arrived early, meeting on the northern outskirts of the Lacandon Indian village of Lacanja. The pope was scheduled to land in a field cleared from the forest, once farmed for potatoes and peppers, but that now lay fallow and neglected, covered in weeds and grass. The pontiff was flying incognito – if such a thing was truly possible. The coordinates were correct, Marcos had seen to it.

The time at which the prelate would arrive was unknown, although 8:00 p.m. had been suggested as a nebulous, but good-as-any, projection. It was now at least 7:30 by the professor's calculation, and he was tired, nervous, and still trying to decide what he might say to Pope Lucas upon his arrival. It wasn't every day that you met the pope, especially if you were an indifferent, uncaring atheist, or at least close to one. David's dilemma, of course, was the result of Balaam's machinations. The archaeologist hoped that when the Bone Man died that he went straight to whatever version of Mayan Hell was appropriate for political schemers, manipulators, and pain-in-the-asses. He swore to himself that this was the last time he would ever become involved with Balaam Reyes. He was getting too old for this crap. Intrigue and adventure were for the young and bored.

David was long in the tooth and comfortable with habit. He was even thinking of retirement, a subject that he had refused to consider the last 10-15 years. For some reason this potential trip to Italy, offered by the pontiff and eagerly promoted by his wife, was starting to look good. Maybe it *was* time to see more of the world. He had read a lot, envisioned a lot, but never been to most of these places other than attending professional conferences. Reading about them simply wasn't the same, and David knew it. After years of teaching at UNAM (Universidad Autonomo de Mexico), countless years in the field and publishing over a sixty articles in scholarly journals, there was little left to prove. The most difficult aspect of becoming educated was realizing that the more you learn, the more you realize you don't know and thus must learn. It's an academic abyss. He had been there close to forty years now. Maybe he should give it a rest.

"Excited?" asked Marcos, turning to David. He added. "I am. Never thought I'd ever meet the pope."

"Me neither," the professor quickly agreed, "especially not under these circumstances."

Marcos chuckled affirmatively, then gestured toward the western sky where the sun was fleeing and falling rapidly behind the distant *cordilleras*, preparing to battle the demons of the underworld. As it sank behind rocky, resolute sentinels, the sky blushed a quicksilver pool of turquoise and coral that brush-stroked the western horizon in brilliant hues, which bled and slowly expired as night struggled to slay the sun god.

"What will Balaam give him, Marcos? Is he going to give the pope one of those books lost in the wreck?" David turned and faced the Zapatista general, his former student. "Will he allow him to talk to Salvador? What's he thinking?"

Marcos shrugged. "Your guess is as good as mine. The man is my father, but he drives me to distraction. He thinks keeping his own counsel is a virtue when, in fact, it becomes a problem because no one knows what to do when he doesn't share thoughts or plans. It's all very confusing at times." He sighed, as if the familiarity of the circumstances did little to provide him with optimism.

"I think I hear it."

"The helicopter?"

Marcos searched the sky. "Don't hear anything. Wait a minute – could be." He peered into the western sky, searching for a flickering black dot against the mottled, dark mountains. As he searched, he saw nothing, but believed he heard it – a faint whop, whop, whop, as helicopter rotor blades chewed the air. Then he saw a small black dot, flying lower than he would have suspected, but here it was. The helicopter grew steadily larger, backlit by the watercolor sunset.

Their eyes met and David frowned. "Sure hope this goes well. I'm too old for this nonsense. Thinking maybe I should retire."

"Use your natural charm, David. Like in the classroom in the old days."

"I was younger then and not smart enough to be self-conscious." His mouth was drawn tight with worry.

His friend retorted, "Huh...not enough experience, yet to have learned that everything is worse than you had imagined. It's humbling."

And then it arrived and it became too loud to talk. The bird hovered, adjusted to face them, and landed. The blades slackened, and the door opened. A gray-haired, late-seventyish man bent low at the knees clambered to the ground. He held a night bag in one hand and waved with the other. He ducked instinctively, then walked toward Marcos and David. He spoke loudly in Spanish over the clamor of the blades.

"*Como está*, my friend. And which one are you? You're young to be a professor." The pontiff motioned for David to come closer. Marcos shouted a greeting over the noise, then circled around to the pilot's side to speak through the small cockpit window. He gave instructions, asked a couple of questions, and then grabbed his cell phone to check something. He nodded an affirmative, then held up his index finger and said, "One moment."

Marcos circled back to the others and extended his hand. "We are very grateful you are here, Holy Father."

"I am hopeful the pleasure will be mine if we truly have the time to talk and get to know each other."

Marcos smiled, "I think that's what's planned." He walked to the copter door and surveyed the interior, then walked back to the pope.

"You have everything? That all you brought?"

The pope hefted his meager luggage. "This is it. Everything essential, except food and water. I had hoped I might be staying somewhere where both were available."

"Be assured," David laughed, as Marcos waved off the pilot and shut the helicopter door. David extended his arm in assistance to Pope Lucas, who accepted it gratefully.

"Thank you, professor. It's been a long day with many, many events and activities."

The pontiff gripped the professor's arm, looked at him with a smile and added, "And then I had to sneak away. I may have made a few enemies with that, but I hope not." They walked a few seconds more and the pope continued, "I'm actually feeling a little tired. At my age fatigue is a reality that one must accommodate each moment."

"I understand, let me get you to our transportation. We have a very good hotel about fifteen minutes away called the *Palenque Classica*. It's comfortable, quiet, and has excellent food. You can meet Marcos' father, Balaam, there."

"Balaam is the father of this man," Pope Lucas pointed with a smile. "Such a big strapping boy." He hesitated, then asked, "Are you *the* Marcos, the General Marcos of the Zapatistas who I have read about in the newspapers for several years?"

"I'm pretty sure I am," admitted David's former student. He hesitated a moment then said, "...and you are the famous Pope Lucas, are you not? I didn't recognize you at first without your robes."

"There are many who would agree with you that I am the pope. There are some who wish I were not, and there are a few, including myself and my friend, Angelina, who believe that this is all really an accident of unenviable fate." The pope hesitated then asked, "Tell me General Marcos, is your father an agreeable man?"

"No," interjected David. "He's very...er...sorry, Marcos. Sorry." His arms moved as if to defer and deflect criticism.

Marcos tossed his head and smiled. The young revolutionary didn't think his father was an agreeable person either. "You'll have to judge for yourself, Holy Father," replied Marcos diplomatically. "He's pretty old and has become a little more...how do you say - cantankerous."

"Yes," said the pope. "Old age is the last stage of life where you can't lie to yourself and practice deceptions. You know your failings too well, and can only hope that those around you are more lenient in their evaluation of you than your own honest, introspective assessment."

Marcos winked at David who nodded assent. This old fellow was the real deal: intelligent, humble and self-effacing - a powerful man, but with little ego to wade through. A reassuring sign, because the Bone Man tolerated none of the opposite traits when dealing with white men or authority figures. Hopefully the pontiff would be able to deal with the irascible shaman, and these nebulous, as-yet-undefined series of events would move toward an amicable solution. It wasn't wise to underestimate the Bone Man's penchant for misunderstanding or over-planning. The shaman was a Mayan Machiavelli, and a good way to ruin a perfectly fine day was to try and predict what Balaam would say or do.

Trundling down the trail, into the forest, over a shallow arroyo, and they arrived. Their borrowed tourist van with *El Sendero Jaguar* painted on its side waited with slide door open. Two Zapatista soldiers waited. One was in the driver's seat, the other wide-eyed and holding the door. David went first, extended a hand to the pope, then Marcos entered.

"Go," ordered Marcos to the driver. "You," he said to the other, "get in the car with the others and follow about 400 meters back, okay? Don't get too close. It's supposed to be clear, but if it isn't, you know what to do. When we get to the hotel just wait for me to give you the sign, and you can return, okay?"

"*Si, señor*," saluted the diminutive Mayan. He took another look at the pope, then trotted down the trail to where his friends waited in another *El Sendero Jaguar* van.

"*Vaya!*" ordered Marcos, and they were off, slowly bouncing over the rutted road, swerving around potholes, until finally arriving at the highway. As they headed north, the conversation began to pick up.

"My father doesn't speak very Spanish well."

"No? He's speaks dialect? Unfortunately the only dialect I ever learned as a young man was that of wine and rich foods. Now I'm a diabetic and have discovered that I don't speak the language as well as I should."

"You'll do fine if you're patient. He can be...er...a little challenging sometimes," added Marcos, disingenuously.

David guffawed, and the pope sighed as if he knew others who fit the description. Well, he would just have to manage the best he could. He wasn't here to pick a fight, just to prostrate himself and beg favors. If the pope was holding any high cards, he didn't know what they were. He had essentially put himself at the complete mercy of an old, irascible, Mayan shaman. At this point, there weren't any decisions to make, he just needed to say, '*Yes, sir*,' and dance when told. For two days, he reasoned, he could do anything - anything. Especially if the rewards were so great.

Chapter Nineteen

The *El Sendero Jaguar* van turned east at the small *Palenque Classica* sign at the road's edge. A 'Vacancy' sign hung from a post. They entered a heavily wooded frontage near the highway, and then followed a winding trail of dark, dense vegetation. Suddenly they entered a well-groomed airy clearing, revealing a large stucco building with red-tiled roof. The building looked fairly new, and the hotel's facade was clean and freshly painted. More cleared land lay behind the building, belying more than could be seen from the front, and this was where the rooms, amenities and swimming pool were located. No cars were present in the parking lot.

"It would seem we are alone at the *Palenque Classica*," offered the pope, glancing at the empty lot. "I insisted those around me lie as a pretense for my absence, saying I left for a private tour of the Palenque ruin." The pope seemed to reflect on this a moment, then added as an afterthought, "I hope that my coming didn't scare anyone off. I prefer remain invisible for this venture, but of course that isn't possible. Today, however, appears to be promising."

David felt comfortable with the old fellow. It was beyond his imagination that the pope seemed more like grandpa than the grandiose Holy Father of the entire Catholic world. David supposed this charming, gentle old man had dealt with many a difficult person in his time. He had yet to introduce the pope to his disagreeable shaman friend, but David considered that just maybe these two very different personalities might find common ground. It might just all work out, but then again, maybe not. He was, after all, dealing with Balaam Reyes. The pope would do what the pope would do, and so would Balaam.

****

Casual waves and welcomes from the hotel staff greeted the Zapatista/Pontiff Entourage as they walked through a traditional, stucco-walled, terrazzo floored building. To the left was a bar/restaurant and to the right stood the entrance to a small museum that would be open upon personal arrangement for guests. They emerged into the rear courtyard. No one recognized a pope without the signature robes, hat, draping cords and rosaries that adorned him in full regalia. They walked around the outdoor swimming pool and toward the hotel's west end; a bank of upscale, upper class suites. Not many rooms for such a big place. They arrived at the end suite. Marcos knocked once, exchanged passwords and the door swung wide into a spacious room of filtered light, two king beds, an over-sized television, mini kitchen, and spa/whirlpool on the back deck that overlooked the green, lush jungle. Much better, really, than the Domus Sanctae Marthae in Vatican City.

Two rag-tag, fiercely alert Zapatista soldiers stood as the pope's entourage entered the room. An elder, diminutive Indian stood in silhouette, backlit by the sunset. He leaned on a cane, and his nostrils flared as the group entered.

"Ah, you are "Big Potato," Balaam half-smiled and gestured a welcome. "Please," he pointed to a curvature of divans, "down, relax back, yes? You, me, same old men, you think?" Balaam barked an instruction and one of the soldiers moved smartly into the kitchen to heat a pot of water on the mini-stove.

The weary pope nearly collapsed onto the sofa. He looked to his diminutive Indian host, shrugged off the "potato" insult, and said, "I want to thank you for allowing me to come. I know you didn't have to. I am grateful." The pontiff gestured toward the Bone Man. "My assistants and my new friends here all tell me that you are a notable person of good character and that you can be trusted."

Balaam looked to his son, and then over to the professor. "He this all time?"

"I think so," David offered.

"Yeah, me too. He's okay, father. Be gentle, okay?"

The shaman fired off a rebuke in dialect, and Marcos winced.

Balaam turned to the pontiff and said, "No much time. Me have know, trust and medicine are be truth. You me drink tea, you me talk, okay? We know see friends, maybe?"

"I'm absolutely positive," replied Pope Lucas. "Tea and talk. I'd love a cup. Been a long day. But my time here is very short. I'm hoping tomorrow I can meet Fr. Salvador also."

Balaam walked to the couch and sat next to the pope. He stared momentarily, then asked, "What? Why have big meeting? Why you talk, *Hombre Sagrado*? Fr. Salvador is Maya. No is Ladino now. Is total be Maya. He have Indian wife and baby. He not harm Big Potato. He help Maya. You leave Holy Man. No touch Fr. Salvador, or big, big problem you. Fr. Lopez belong Maya."

"I agree. I know that," smiled the pontiff, reassuringly. "Couldn't happen any other way. Fr. Lopez is special. Why I come, my new friend, is to ask that you follow the charity in your heart to give me the ancient texts you recovered after the death of our very special Inquisitor, Father Gregory. You know - the wooden cylinders of papyrus. These books do not belong here. They should be on the other side of the ocean, in my library in the Vatican."

"Catholic town?"

"Yes, a city of priests and religious people very much like your Father Lopez."

The Bone Man considered, reflected, and then looked to the kitchen. "Tea…me, guest. Hot?"

"Very," came the reply.

Balaam looked over to his son, the professor, and young Zapatista followers. "You, go all. You go. Papa have tea with Balaam. Soon be brothers in spirit. Go…" He waved them off.

The soldiers moved quickly, and after a quick glance at Marcos, the professor followed suit. *Rude, cranky, bastard,* thought David. Now what? Hang around? *Might be two days of this crap left,* he reminded himself as he exited Balaam's suite. Maybe drive all the way home to Alexandra, or just hit the bar? He glanced at his watch, then looked around, but Marcos had disappeared. Shit. This could mean more waiting. The tourist van was still parked. Maybe he could use a cold beer before deciding. Maybe he would spend the night here. Maybe he should just give it up for the day and breathe, forget all about this nonsense for a few hours.

David entered the bar. Nice place with nobody present but the bartender, a young woman of about thirty with little visible history in her face. He ordered a cold *Tecate* and stared blankly into the mirror. What was all that 'tea' nonsense about, he wondered. Something odd about the way the shaman said it. He considered a few more moments, then startled and said aloud, "You don't suppose that he would...?"

****

Pope Lucas knew something was wrong when the lines of the room started to slowly waffle – and smile. It was unnerving. The pontiff blinked his eyes...no that wasn't right. He reached to touch something, but it really wasn't there. He gasped.

"Here, *ahua*. Tea with Balaam," the shaman lifted the pot and poured more into the pontiff's cup. Pretty good stuff the pope decided, feeling less afraid, but he really didn't recall this particular variety. A good, but funky tasting, earthy stuff. That was the best thing about going to other countries - you saw what the people actually ate, drank, and listened too.

After a short while, the pope realized that he had been daydreaming. He felt a little uncomfortable alone with the shaman, not knowing where this whole experience was going. The Bone Man stared at him expectantly, as if waiting for something. He decided to relax. This was actually the ideal situation - a neutral setting; no pressure, no one watching, and no expectations at this particular moment. He finally relaxed, leaned back into the sofa pillow, and glanced across the room at his new acquaintance. And then after the third sip of tea with no conversation, everything changed. Pope Lucas found himself transported out into the jungle and somehow understood that he was in the body of a coati, a South American mammal similar to a raccoon/possum mix and, even more astounding, it didn't bother him.

As the *now* and earthly perception fled, Pope Lucas recognized that he was not in his right mind – yet he did not become alarmed. He decided to engage the colorful visions and reality in which he was immersed. He had no idea where he was, as he had never been here before. He seemed to be sitting in a tree, observing all that paraded before him, which should have been distressing but for some reason was not. Moments later he realized that he was, in fact, hallucinating.

The sudden appearance of a shaggy old, sad-eyed jaguar startled him. Jaguars killed and ate people didn't they? But this cat seemed content to watch him as the pope/coati explored its perimeter. He sniffed the air and gazed around him. He was in the woods behind the hotel, he realized, and the forest contained a myriad of wildlife; animals that had taken ephemeral form that appeared to be aware of other phantoms navigating the ether. The old cat again. What was it up to? It seemed to be observing. It climbed the tree and sniffed him, then removed to a distant limb and blinked at him. This was a little unnerving, but when the pope coati thought about it, it wasn't any worse than the joint ache and intense fatigue he had begun to experience earlier. He must have entered into some sort of spiritual ether where prayer and meditation had never taken him. It was new. It was enthralling. He decided that he was going to do everything he could to savor and enjoy this other-worldly event.

****

Balaam Reyes had boosted his soul into the spirit world again – probably for at least the thousandth time. As a curandero you must know the spirit world as intimately as your own, or you would fail. Human physical health was dependent on the duality of the universe. Everyone had a major or minor self, an alternate spirit animal that traveled the ether and did it's best to make good decisions and enjoy good health. Sometimes this wasn't possible and one became sick. Spirit sickness was the primary cause of human illness. You could learn the essence of someone's soul by observing them in the spirit world, and this is why Balaam had decided that he and the pope would share a pot of his special magic mushroom tea. The Bone Man would only allow the pope to talk with the Holy Man after watching how the pope behaved in the transcendent ether. His time, his rules, his Holy Man…if *ahua* potato wanted to get into Balaam's sphere, he would have to earn it.

The Bone Man wondered what it would be like to be the pope; a religious man somewhat similar to himself - yet very, very different. This Big Potato was a very educated ladino, a leader who operated in a complicated world of money, power, and politics – very unlike the world of a shaman. Balaam was very religious also, but eschewed power and money. He pursued and connected with the supernatural, within the framework of his beliefs. From this tradition came healing – of the body and spirit. Like the pope, he believed all people had a soul. But in his tradition the soul had a mirror image in the spirit world and ether. Balance between the two spheres, the reality of 'now' and the spirit world, determined health, happiness, and good or evil. The pope was an important man, but was he honest? Could he be part of the tradition of healing? Who was he when stripped of all earthly pretense and forced to expose the true character of his soul in the ether? This was why the Bone Man had decided to have a 'tea party' with the pontiff. The jaguar stalked the pope/coati from a distance, observing, remembering, and judging. The owl was back, sitting on a low branch, serenely observing, non-threatening, but curious. Balaam's gaze returned to the pope/coati and found that it stood quietly, looking up into the bough of a tree of a fearsome snake. Not just any snake. The Feathered Serpent had returned and lay passively coiled, watching the pope/coati also. Why, the old shaman didn't know. Again – very curious, but he still did not understand the significance of the Feathered Serpent in the ether. The shaman, too, focused on the pope/coati. It was many hours until dawn, but so far the jaguar/shaman liked what he saw.

****

It was five hours later when the pope realized he had not slept the whole night. No longer trapped in an unsure reality, he sought to connect with earthly perception. As the reality of *now* came into focus, the pontiff realized he was nude, with scratches on parts of his lower body. He was wet, but drying, and sitting on the sofa in the hotel room. His clothes lay in a pile at his feet. *Uh oh,* he thought. *Oh my!* What had happened!!? Why was he naked? Mortified, he quickly reached for his clothing and began dressing, looking about the room to see if anyone noticed. For an old man, loss of dignity and face is only an excruciatingly unfortunate moment away. He tried to remember, but the fog in his mind was only now beginning to lift.

Suddenly he realized he wasn't sitting where he had been when he had blanked out. The spot on which he sat was wet. Fleeting recollections of surreal images from the forest, animals and plants, ran through his mind. The creatures seemed personified, almost human-like in their qualities or personalities. Jaguars, ocelots, birds, and a very curious and sinister creature, a snake with feathers. Bizarre. Many had peered at him, or given knowing looks, but did not engage him; none had spoken or touched him or others. As the pope/coati watched them, the jaguar had observed him. Where in the world had he been?

Hunger gnawed at him and he could use a glass of water, but he felt more embarrassed than anything. He still felt achy and fatigued, but that was only natural at his age. Donning his clothing helped him regain a sense of poise, and he searched the room for something to anchor him in the present. He spotted the microwave clock: 5:00 a.m. He had been somewhere for nearly seven or eight hours – and apparently without his clothing, a mortifying thought anyway you considered it.

On a couch across the room, his host sat glassy-eyed and staring. *Oh, Lord!* The pontiff realized. The old shaman had given him hallucinatory drugs. The tea had contained drugs! Should he leave? It was still dark, was there anyone to talk to? His anxiety rocketed, then backed off gradually and he took calming breaths, assessing that except for the body aches and scratches, he was fine. There seemed to be no danger. Whatever he had ingested had run its course and seemed to be over – he hoped. What and why? What had he gotten himself into? He looked again to the shaman and saw him begin to stir.

The pope suddenly fell into prayer, the most logical and predictable action he could think of, seeking any solace he could find. He prayed silently, gathering his wits, and felt himself easing into the present. He thought about his comfortable bed at the Sanctae Marthae Hotel in Vatican City, and then recalled his compelling reason for being here, why he had ditched his entourage and ridden the helicopter east over the mountains to meet with this grizzled, almost scary shaman and Zapatista rabble rouser. He quickly reminded himself he wasn't in control, an unenviable situation, considering what he had just been through, and that this old Indian didn't like people who looked like him. The pope wasn't calling the shots. Rather he was an open-handed beggar, and must be calm and out-wait the old shaman.

"*Ahua* Potato…you have thirst? You want water?"

Pope Lucas saw Balaam Reyes had risen and was standing in the kitchenette.

"Love a glass of water, my friend. Wouldn't mind a piece of bread either if such a thing is available."

"No bread, only water," was Balaam's curt reply, then caught himself and said with more understanding: "yeah, is late, early. Maybe need food." He looked at the clock on the microwave and considered. "No here. Restaurant close. Maybe in hour."

The shaman carried a glass of water to Pope Lucas, watched him drink deeply, pause and drink again. The pontiff sighed, sat his glass on the end table and looked to where Balaam had seated himself close by.

Balaam began the conversation. "You not like..." the shaman waved his hand, looking for a word, "not like other ladino." The shaman looked pleased with himself and choice of words. "You, me, surprise, you be...okay man." The shaman smiled, an uncommon occurrence.

"Your tea is very powerful. A local variety?" asked the pope diplomatically, but tinged with sarcasm. "I seem to have lost most of the night as well as my clothing."

"Yes. You drink good Balaam tea. Best mushroom Chiapas, lose clothes and climb tree. See spirit world. Good, good see spirit with Balaam. You, me, be good spirit world." The shaman seemed refreshed and enthusiastic.

Pope Lucas wasn't exactly sure what the shaman meant, except the word "mushroom" explained a lot. Psilocybin mushrooms, he had read, were a hallucinogen widely used by traditional healers. This Bone Man character seemed happy and satisfied with the outcome – as if he had been worried, as if Lucas had passed some sort of test. What, the pontiff couldn't imagine. If the shaman was to be believed, he claimed that the Holy Father, the Pope of the Catholic Church, had removed his clothes and sat in a tree most of the night. Pope Lucas could only hope it wasn't true, but he strongly suspected that it was. That would certainly account for the scratches on his legs, bottom and arms. The issue was no longer one of losing his dignity, it might very well be that he had lost his mind – at least temporarily – and the old, short Indian with yellow teeth sitting next to him had planned the whole thing. He made the sign of the cross and silently thanked God for seeing him through the night.

"Yes, you good prayer man like Indian prayer man, *Hombre Sagrado*, Fr. Lopez." The shaman hesitated a moment, as if distracted, then added, "You go wrong end water. Balaam call Zapatista to help ahua potato. Dangerous, but all okay."

What? He had jumped in the swimming pool? The deep end, also. No wonder he was wet when he gained consciousness. Pope Lucas wasn't sure he wanted to hear any more about last night's adventures. What a fanciful story, and he was afraid his adventure was just beginning. The pope put a hand to his forehead a leaned forward, resting while re-gaining his wits.

"*Ahua* potato okay?" asked a concerned Balaam. "Need food? Cup tequila?"

The pontiff chuckled. "No tequila, thank you. I'm pretty sure I need to eat some food. I'm a diabetic. I need to check my blood sugar, then eat. I'm on a strict regimen."

"What? No understand. Sugar blood? What mean?" The shaman looked confused then smiled and said, "I think have, sausage, blood sausage here...restaurant. You like, we get soon soon."

Pope Lucas stood, located his very important bag, extracted his family bible, glucose meter and injection needles to show Balaam, who initially appeared befuddled, but then understood.

"Ah, yes, yes! Ladino sugar sickness. Eat bad food sick blood. Understand. Jaguar smelled. We go restaurant soon. Promise me you. You wait, Balaam fix. Okay?"

"Agreed," smiled the pope, tired and uncommonly achy. His joints seemed to have thickened and felt sore and reluctant to articulate. The pope touched the back of his hand to his forehead and wondered if he had a fever. The aching joints made sense, although he felt stiffer than usual. No wonder, he thought, considering he was seventy-four years old and was out climbing trees last night. If that had been what really happened. The joints made sense. A fever? He didn't think so. Probably just needed sleep.

"Okay, *ahua*. We talk book, Holy Man, okay? We talk. What want Papa? Why come see Balaam?"

Pope Lucas turned to his diminutive host and took a shaky breath. "You know I am the pope, the leader of the Catholic Church?"

The shaman nodded. "Yes…Big potato…understand."

The Big Potato, thought Pope Lucas, wryly, but decided not to take offense, remembering that the Indian spoke Spanish very poorly.

"This old Holy Man, the first one discovered three years ago? I sent a priest, Fr. Gregory, to come to Chiapas to investigate to see if this Holy Man was a very important person who became lost and ended up here in this country." The pope squeezed his eyes shut to clear his vision and search the shaman's face for signs of understanding. He saw none.

The pope continued. "Fr. Gregory discovered that you and your friend, Professor Wolf took many old books, the wooden cylinders from a funeral box. These books are very, very important to me and my church, Balaam. So very important that I am here with you, at your mercy, drinking mushroom tea, and running through the forest naked. I really wish I could make you understand how important these books are..."

"What *Hombre Sagrado*, Fr. Lopez?" interrupted the shaman. "You steal *Hombre Sagrado*, cup for church?"

"No!" the pope held up a hand. "No. The Holy Man, the new Holy Man, makes his own decisions. I would never try to influence him. I think he is a great man."

"He Indian man now!" the shaman stomped a foot. "He belong Maya. Have Maya baby. *Ahua* Potato leave *Hombre Sagrado* Chiapas. Ladino no have everything!"

"No...yes...er...I agree," the pope extended his hand in acquiescence. "I want the books. The books from the old Holy Man. I really, really want the books." The pontiff hung his head, sure that he was messing up an appeal that he had rehearsed many times in his head.

"And *Hombre Sagrado*? Why want see Fr. Lopez? He no not have boss. He religion boss. Have cup. No need Ladino religion boss." The shaman leaned forward, waiting for the pope to challenge him.

The pope grasped his mother's bible, stood, walked to the Bone Man and went down on one knee. "I swear on this Holy Bible, Balaam, that I am not here to steal the cup or Fr. Lopez. He belongs to you, to the Indian people. I swear it." The pope held the bible to his heart, then looked into the shaman's eyes. "Please believe me."

The shaman unexpectedly switched frames. "Your spirit soul be coati, *ahua*. Good medicine. Good animal jungle. He...how you say? He wise animal, good soul."

What the...thought the pope. *I'm missing something here?*

"Okay. Yes...okay. I bring book, many book, Big Potato." The Bone Man walked into the kitchen, pulled opened the oven door and revealed five wooden cylinders as the pontiff stared, astounded. "I believe *ahua* Potato. You man be honest.

You go *ahua* David tomorrow. Go Yaxchilan. *Hombre Sagrado* religion with Indian in morning. Must safe be all time, military, and federale. Later, travel *Hombre Sagrado* to jungle and Yaxchilan. I bring *Hombre Sagrado*. Fr. Lopez go Yaxchilan meet Big Potato. Yes," the shaman agreed with himself. "*Ahua* David and *ahua* Potato go Yaxchilan." The shaman carefully collected the cylinders in his arms and brought them to the pope. Balaam placed them on the coffee table. Pope Lucas wobbled to his feet, stared wide-eyed and disbelieving at this unlikely turn of events. Five cylinders? Five!!? Just like that. Just like that the grumpy old shaman had acquiesced. In front of Pope Lucas sat the ancient books that contained only God knows what. Overcome with emotion, the pope teared up and grasped the hand of his host.

"Thank you, thank you, my friend. Thank you, Balaam," he repeated, then wiped a tear from his cheek. I am so...I'm just so..." the pope, a man rarely at a loss of words, suddenly found himself speechless.

The shaman waved him off. "Just trouble...big trouble this book." He pointed to the cylinders. "No have meaning Father Lopez. No need..." he said finally.

"You say I'm going to meet Father Lopez today?"

The shaman hesitated, then said, "Yes. *Hombre Sagrado* have meet religion to people in morning. Must be careful. Government, military look see find *Hombre Sagrado*. Be safe. When sun up, after second eat, Zapatista bring Fr. Lopez Yaxchilan meet *ahua* Potato." The shaman looked to see if the pope was following his instructions, then added. "Then *friend* Potato go...go very fast. Go across water, home. Lacandon Jungle not place *ahua* Potato. Jungle dangerous for *ahua* Potato. Big Potato die in jungle."

Let's hope not, thought Pope Lucas. He again smiled his gratitude at the Bone Man. Then returned to the bonanza in front of him. He moved the cylinders around on the table, saw that the wax seals on two were broken. He was so tempted to open one of them, but decided not to. *This is so unexpected.*

"I thought, maybe one book, my aides told me. I heard that there seven originally."

"Yes, be seven before crash wreck you man priest. My friend - Zapatista look find bring me." The shaman shrugged. "But I no want. Just trouble."

"Yes," agreed the pope. He had an inkling of how much trouble these documents would create. His startled brain could barely begin to assess the disruption they would bring to the existing order.

"*Ahua* Potato – friend Potato, have hunger now. Want tortilla. Coffee?"

"Yes, thank you. I'm very hungry." The pope hesitated, then began gingerly placing the cylinders inside his tote bag. "But listen, Balaam, no more tea, okay? I've had enough tea."

The shaman burst out laughing. "You different Ladino, *ahua*. No…no tea. Good medicine, mushroom. Maybe bean, tortilla. Maybe coffee, egg. I see." The shaman walked to the hotel room door, summoned his soldiers, issued orders, and returned.

"You know, that thing Papa – friend Papa. You know – maybe think know – Balaam and Friend Potato maybe little same, eh? I see understand you in spirit world and I see you me watch also. I think you good man. I think maybe Papa and Balaam same."

"Yesterday I would have not have thought so. Today…today I agree with you. You are much different than I expected. You are a good man - a very smart man who wants to do the right thing."

The shaman's face skewed quizzically, and he asked. "You think say Balaam okay *hombre*, okay man? Think Balaam and Big Papa same of all world same?"

"Yes."

"You agree Balaam, you smart ladino," the shaman stated firmly. Balaam waved his arm. "Up. Time *desayunar*. Time eat morning food." The door opened and three Zapatista soldiers brought in a heaping tray of tortillas, warm beans, freshly scrambled eggs, and steaming coffee. Outside the *madrugada*, the early morning, waned. Growing light in the eastern sky promised a glorious, risen sun to bless the day's events. It was the rainy season and a late afternoon storm would likely bluster in, behave badly, and move on.

The pope, achy, tired and battered, managed to sigh with satisfaction. He had been victorious. If he could just get through this day, all would be well. He was sure of it. His stomach growled and his clothes were damp. What an adventure! Where was Yaxchilan? This wasn't going to be difficult was it? *Oh bother*, he thought. A tingle of trepidation rippled down his spine. Although fatigued, he felt anxious and in need of sleep - even a little nauseous, but stopping now was out of the question. So much at stake. A chance to talk with Fr. Lopez and perhaps see the "healing" cup was powerful motivation to shrug off his ailments. Too bad this hadn't happened twenty years ago when he was a younger man of fifty. But God would give him strength. He certainly had so far.

Chapter Twenty

Luis, stiff and tired, piloted the little Chevy between the sheer cliff wall on his left and the sheer drop to oblivion on his right. Allowing a tire to slide off the edge of the asphalt would hurtle him thousands of feet to his death. A couple of Xanax taken earlier helped him drive slowly, taking a little time to enjoy the spectacular view. Safer, but still nerve wracking. No hurry. He groaned and stretched. Riding in cars was no one's favorite task, especially a dinky, pregnant bathtub like this Cabriola, but it was unobtrusive and drew little attention, and that was absolutely essential to his goal today. He had driven many miles over the rocky sierras around San Cristobal, descending downward toward the lowlands for several hours on perilous, winding mountain roads, long expanses with no guard rails. Very stressful. *Must have taken a hundred years to pave this thing*, he thought.

Today's journey reminded him of a terrible event, an accident three years ago in a violent thunderstorm as he drove up a narrow, asphalt highway towards San Cristobal de las Casas. Being on time was important in this business. With a hot load of meth stashed under a false floorboard in his Ford

Expedition, he found that he had no time to spare and was moving crisply. His car was large, the tires were new, and he could slow upon seeing headlights. Still, he must focus. It had been purple/gray that evening; jagged streaks of lightning, sheets of pouring rain, and powerful, gusting winds made it nearly impossible to keep your lane. Luis had the inside track on the mountainside as he rounded a tight corner at about 5,000 feet. He was startled by headlights, and found a small pickup truck in his lane, attempting to navigate the storm safely by avoiding the perilous outer lane with no shoulder or protective railing.

Luis had swerved toward the wall, sideswiping and sending the small truck skidding across slippery asphalt to cliff's edge. Stunned, but aware, Luis cursed and watched helplessly as the truck sat momentarily, as if in balance, then slowly tilted and slipped from the cliff's edge. It crashed and tumbled and struck the mountain walls for several thousand feet, until finally lying in flames, raindrops sizzling and turning to steam, attempting to douse the small inferno.

Terrible night, remembered Luis, his mind relaxed and recalling the events. Luis had been responsible for lots of mayhem in his life, but swore this one wasn't his fault. He was driving in his lane. The other car's lights were unseen behind the cliff wall just before Luis made a tight turn around the curve, toward the wall, and found a car in his lane. How could he have avoided it? Unfortunate, but inevitable. Everyone knew it was a dangerous road. Most people didn't drive this highway unless familiar with its sheer drops and hairpin curves.

But today was another day and Luis believed that all would go well. There were always intangibles, but, through experience, he had a good idea what to expect and knew how to react when things didn't go well. He stroked the *Santa*

Muerte on his forearm. He'd completed a hundred deals like this in different parts of Chiapas and Guatemala the last three years. Luis would pick up a load of crystal meth rock today at a very small ruin on the Guatemala side of the Usumacinta River. He had tried to call ahead a couple of hours before leaving San Cristobal to reserve a boat and motor, but no one had answered his call. Sometimes it was difficult to get a signal in the lowlands. Checking his Yahoo account had revealed no new, unsent drafts, so it was a go. He had given them the password of, "Big Enchilada," silly but unlikely to be stolen. The gig was on. His heart beat faster. Just thinking about the drug deal changed things, you know?

Once before, the *sicario* had used this contractor to cook a fifty-kilo load. He'd retrieved it near Las Lagunas de Montebello (The Beautiful Mountain Lakes) off highway 190, just on the Guatemalan border near a sparsely populated span of isolated, rocky land unfit for farming. Luis was not impressed. The product, he'd later learned, was mediocre and prone to powder easily. Unacceptable. Quality was important in the business, as the competition did their best to maintain high standards. The Sinaloa Cartel purchased the chemicals themselves and distributed it to contractors - and expected a worthy product. It was easier and more profitable to sell good dope than mediocre stuff. If these idiots didn't get it right this time, Luis was going to find another contractor who took pride in their work. Moving dope was dangerous and difficult, and no one wanted to deliver or accept shit product after taking such chances.

A couple of interminable hours brought Luis to a wide turn on the mountain road and he could see down the mountainside to the town of Ocosingo, a prosperous community hugging the foothills of the mountain; the last staging ground of trucks, tourist busses, and automobiles before the serious trek upward into the pines and oaks of the Sierra Madres toward San Cristobal de las Casas. He needed to stretch his legs, and a hot coffee and bowl of chicken-vegetable soup, his favorite, sounded tasty right now. Normally he would have put away a couple of tequila shots by now, but Luis didn't drink on work days. Xanax was better than booze, anyway. His work required a clear head and good measure of intestinal fortitude. He kissed the fingertips of his left hand and stroked the *Santa Muerte* on his right forearm. He wondered if maybe there was a small chapel somewhere along the road. Wouldn't hurt to pause a moment and give thanks for his good run of luck. He'd keep his eyes open.

Luis reached under the seat to ensure that his 9mm Browning was ready and in place. It was, and his thoughts moved ahead to the meet and the deal. What if the product was no good? What would he say? How would he react? Nervous, he kissed the fingertips on his right hand and stroked the tattooed image of *Jesus Malverde* on the other arm. He entered the outskirts of Ocosingo, turned left at the stoplight, and guided his unobtrusive little car uphill into town. He stopped six blocks later at a restaurant with a sign promising *Pollo Sinaloense*, Chicken Sinaloa Style. After gassing up and a meal, maybe he would call his daughter. Probably Cuca would be in a better mood today, and he needed to check up on his grandson to make sure that he was okay. That boy was everyone's future.

****

After receiving a cheerful, early morning call from Marcos, David showered, dressed, and exited his house, slowly navigating the thirty-minute, winding asphalt snake to the *Palenque Classica*. The archaeologist recalled how fifteen years ago the road was a perilous gravel strip, barely wide enough to accommodate two cars squeezed abreast. Now it was half again as wide, although with no shoulder, but still much, much safer. Unless interrupted by a weed-choked ravine, or dense foliage, towering trees, like sentinels, were still the norm. The professor sighed. This drive might be the best and easiest part of his day. He was not optimistic that the day's affairs would be any better than they were at this moment.

Marcos reported that Balaam would allow the pope to meet Fr. Lopez. This was surprising and out of character for the shaman, David believed. The professor was certain that an interesting story or convoluted logic lay behind the decision. The news accompanied an instruction from the high and mighty (irritating and demanding) Bone Man: giving orders and expecting them to be followed, even by those who had no real affiliation or loyalty to him. Balaam says David must transport the pope downstream to the old classic Mayan ruin of Yaxchilan today...and *could he be sure to pick him up this morning before 9:00 a.m.*

'Maybe I can't,' bitched David. Maybe you need to say 'please,' *you cantankerous, disagreeable piece of crocodile shit.* Perhaps he was being unreasonable, but his patience was eroding with this affair. He resolved that today was the last he would take orders from this dwarf, Zapatista revolutionary. Affiliation with the shaman had proven over the years to be unhealthy, personally and professionally, for the archaeologist. Marcos could start doing some or all of this stuff. After all, the Zapatista General's primary assignment now was to protect, transport, and take care of the Holy Man. Fr. Salvador Lopez required a retinue that had taken the form of soldiers, a few workers and their wives, and wait staff. Half his wife's family had come to join them a year ago. The Holy Man's entourage, though small and unskilled, required planning and handling in order to organize religious services

for the poor Indians living in various locations on both sides of the Usumacinta.

Although Fr. Lopez lived and worked in the jungle, he knew nothing about it. He was a dependent. His wife, a young Lacandon Indian girl, had forgotten more jungle lore than Fr. Lopez would ever acquire. Most important, of course, was to protect Fr. Lopez from *federales*, military personnel, or anyone who wanted what he had or was threatened by what he possessed. Thus they moved secretly, usually slowly, with a deliberate, low-tech plan. It was a full-time job taking care of him.

David agreed, reluctantly, that there really wasn't anyone else to transport the pope to Yaxchilan. They were meeting at the ruin because government officials didn't frequent the vicinity, only a few adventurous tourists. There were no roads in or out. The ruin was surrounded by dense jungle and full of wildlife. The Usumacinta River was the highway and border of eastern Chiapas. It was a safe location for a meeting, and a spectacular Mayan archaeological site – something Balaam thought likely to impress the pontiff. Sneaky and effective – as usual. The old Mayan shaman would remain a tough adversary until the day he died for those who contested him.

Within minutes David found himself at the wooded entry into *Palenque Classica*. He drove slowly through the shaded overgrowth. An occasional flash of light stabbed through an opening in the canopy as the morning sun fought for supremacy. He turned the corner, and was there. The facade on the administration building was constructed in the style of a Mayan temple complete with a large, thatched, Mayan style roof as a watershed. Unusual location, he decided. In a few years, this place could be filled with tourists, but right now it was heavily wooded, isolated, and relatively unknown. David stopped, put the car in park, turned off the key and reflected.

He wondered what Balaam's connection to this place might be; there had to be one. In spite of that, it was possible today could be a special. He was going to have the pope all to himself for several hours. How often did that happen to anyone? Plus, there were worse tasks than boating up and down the wild Usumacinta through untamed jungle to a classic Mayan ruin. Yaxchilan could only be reached by boat and thus remained more intact and less weathered by the feet of tourists. Likely, this would be much more fun than wasting his time at that worthless archaeological site he had been working all year. Maybe today would be a great day - a day to remember. He smiled, took a deep breath and opened his car door, ready for a battle of wits with the Bone Man.

****

Pope Lucas thought he should be feeling better by now. The coffee was good. The *Huevos Mexicanos* tasty, as were the beans, but the tortillas disappointing – rubbery and not nearly hot enough. But he continued to feel very achy, probably the result of his drug-addled, branch-swinging, simian journey through a hallucinogenic jungle last night. *How many popes had done that?* he asked himself. *Not funny, Lucas,* he told himself. Was it the 'tea' or was something else going on?

But God was great! Christianity had been gifted with five of the ancient books that could shake or deepen the Church's understanding of its deep past. Stupendous!

The old shaman had proven to be pretty good with the carrot. Was there a stick? The pope must remain alert and calm during another big travel day. He must be deft and present, not focusing on his aching body when meeting the famous and beloved spiritual leader of some of the poorest people in the world – the Mayan Holy Man. This might be one of the most important events of his life. He did not, as he suspected, want to become sick from one of those tropical bugs he had been warned about before traveling. Surely Fr. Cabrini had vaccinated him with every known vaccine! At this point, his health was in God's hands as he did God's work.

Meanwhile his new friend Professor Wolf had arrived. The archaeologist was smiling! Apparently he didn't have any tea last night. The pontiff, who was starting to believe he might be in need of assistance, decided he would follow this man anywhere – Shangri La, Eden, or Yaxchilan. Maybe Walden's Pond in a pinch if there were no mosquitos. Lucas, having commenced his 'awakening journey' with the mushroom tea, was ready to get on with it. What were a few aches and sniffles in the face of meeting the Holy Man? Nothing. He would persevere, just as he would expect of others when so much was at stake.

Chapter Twenty One

Sr. Angelina replayed the voice message from the Mother Superior at St. Cecilia's Church and Convent: *"Be sure and stop by and visit. Just a tea…just a visit to get caught up,"* she'd said. Sr. Angelina did not believe that she would be at an advantage in that meeting. This felt like a problem, and she wiped her palms on her pant legs as she considered why she had quit wearing her habit. It wasn't strictly required, and she was rarely at the convent since being installed at the Vatican. Did Mother Superior know about Gunther? Her new friend, her very good friend, who was coming to her office tonight to visit. And that was a problem – maybe. She felt her heart flutter and wiped her palms again. She had gone with him on brief outings, such as the catacombs. Delightful! And his daughter, Elsa? What a precious, precocious child. And the girl no longer had a mother, such a tragedy. But she was so fortunate to have a strong, friendly father who doted on her. Sr. Angelina felt as if she wanted to just sweep the little girl into her arms and love her to death.

Her new male friend was a distraction, one she had thought she was beyond. She had been warned not to place herself in circumstances like this. She knew they could result in the loss of her vocation. Her position and vows were so hard won. And her feelings – feelings! –about Gunther threatened her confidence in the path she had chosen for herself. The result was awkward situations that encouraged emotional conflict – as they resurrected old issues of family pressure, commitment, absence of love and marriage, and ruing past decisions after one's life had fast-forwarded ten years. Hindsight was crystal clear wasn't it? Maybe when Lucas returned from that hopeless trip to Mexico he would make time for her, and maybe even Gunther.

Lucas. She was very concerned about her friend, the pope. Three nights ago he'd emailed that he was executing his ridiculous strategy to meet with that professor and Bone Man character, Balaam Reyes. Why and how did someone get the name, 'Bone Man?'

She felt morose, and any day without word from Lucas created a sense of trepidation. Everyone had warned him against his plan to recover the 1st Century documents, fascinating as they appeared to be. This supposed Holy Man operating in the tropical jungles, stirring up the Indians? That was a problem for the Mexican and Guatemalan governments, not the Vatican – even if it was one of their priests – and Sr. Angelina had tried to frame it in that manner, but her friend disagreed. The issues were one and the same to him and required resolution in his mind. Lucas insisted that failing to act would be an *abdication of his duties.* Stupid men. Even when they're seventy-four years of age, diabetic, and have only one kidney they believe they must demonstrate the health and vitality of a young man and go somewhere to sprint up a pyramid. Stupid men. What? No, wait, wasn't there a famous saying? She shook her head. 'Foolish Men.' Wasn't that the title of a famous Sor Juana poem? She remembered it to this day - *Foolish Men.* She was going to send a copy to the Holy Father just as soon as she could boot up her computer. She would do it right now! Maybe he had responded to her earlier mail?

Emboldened, feeling much more like Sor Juana than basket case Sr. Angelina, the Dominican nun checked her desk clock, reopened her laptop, and inserted the special USB drive for a satellite connection. She waited a moment, then opened her Hot Mail account. *Shoot!* No mail from Lucas. Guatemalan natives, she speculated, had made him the guest of honor and placed him in a tribal stew pot by now. Lucas was so old that he couldn't escape a three-legged sloth. Darn that man! Anyway...where was that poem? She went to Google, typed in a couple of key words, and it came up quickly. She read it again, nodding as she did so. *You Foolish Men.* Yes, she would copy and send it to him. Just the poem – not one of her lengthy essays tonight. She had things on her mind other than the gender inequities of the Catholic Church. *Chew on this a while, Holy Father*, she thought. *Consider the words of the world's wisest woman.* She highlighted the text, copied and pasted, and then clicked **Send**.

Holy Father, could the issue and fault be any clearer than Sor Juana so eloquently states? Her voice is as relevant now as then – perhaps more so. Why isn't this sort of literature required reading for those preparing to be priests? If it's true, why is it not mandatory in every school in the world? Why do males insist on institutionalized stupidity? There are so many 'why's' that I find myself perpetually perplexed at the aggressive ignorance of males. Foolish men.

Maybe it's genetic? Maybe you guys really are the inferior half? You do know that female is the default form in-utero? Prior to having their cells tainted with testosterone, and messing up the effects of a perfectly fine chromosome, the default is female. Everything is fine, and then testosterone rewires the brain circuitry, along with everything else. Female as the default form makes perfect sense. It's not surprising. I mean, it's possible that males are simply an aberration, an unfortunate mutation which Nature never took the time to discard until it became too late and the XY took over the world. Foolish men.

Although it may sound like a long time ago, women and men were perfectly equal for hundreds of thousands of years as hunters and gatherers until people domesticated animals and cereal grains 10,000 years ago. That's when men asserted ascendancy and women became property just like goats and grain. Foolish men.

And you guys have done such a terrible job, Holy Father. Look back to the earliest civilizations on the Tigris and Euphrates, the Sumerians and Akkadians, the Egyptians on the Nile, and others: the Persians, Greeks, and Romans. It's been one war after another, stealing someone else's property, women, and resources. I think it's entirely possible that men are behaviorally disordered, genetically stupid, and that nothing can be done to fix them. If not for your abilities to kill Simba the lion, no one would have ever tolerated such creatures. Foolish men.

Sincerely,
Your Sor Juana

Someone knocked and Sr. Angelina twitched. She hit **Send** and glanced quickly around. She was awaiting her guest, Gunther. There was little to show in her small, spare cubicle – certainly nothing suggesting she worked for the pontiff. This is where she did most of her work, unbeknownst to just about everyone in the building, but it revealed little of her inquisitive personality or prodigious intellect. She didn't see how anyone's view would change after spending all of one-minute in her office. Was that a problem, too? *Holy Father,* she thought, *come home and help me sort out of this stuff.*

Sr. Angelina opened her office door and there stood a Swiss Guard, a tall and very handsome man. Standing in front of him, coming up to his waist, was his smiling daughter. A pleasant tingle rippled across Angelina's skin. Why had she ever imagined that there would be a problem?

Chapter Twenty Two

David and Pope Lucas sat in opposite seats facing each other in the tourist van, *El Sendero Jaguar (The Jaguar Path)*, as it carefully navigated the asphalt south toward the jungle. Upon reaching the Usumacinta River and small community of *Benemerito de las Americas* that supported the staging area, David would rent one of the tourist vessels – a fourteen-foot river boat with planked seating on each side and a tin sun roof over the middle half of the boat. There was always a launch available, especially this early in the day. Few tourists visited, as the Yaxchilan ruin was lightly attended. Most people were not adventuresome enough to ride a small craft downstream on a major river in the jungle to an archaeological site. Medical help, police, car mechanics, grocery stores, pharmacies, and the other amenities of civilization were some distance away, and this made many folks uncomfortable.

Really big day for the pope, surmised David. Balaam allowing the pontiff to meet Fr. Lopez had surprised everyone. David had no idea that the Bone Man had recovered so many of the ancient books, but he felt content that the shaman had given them to Pope Lucas. It would be a tragedy if they were lost from humanity's treasure of early literature. So, the issue was resolved – more or less.

The archaeologist glanced at the pope, who seemed really out of sorts. He'd been interested and friendly yesterday, but this morning had seemed an effort. He slumped and appeared to withdraw within himself, not seeking conversation. David watched more closely. The pontiff's complexion was flushed, and scratches had appeared on his hands and face since last night. What was that all about? Was David watching a tired old man, or was something else going on?

David asked, "Holy Father, did you get much sleep last night? How are you feeling?"

The pope hesitated, then looked up and across to David. He gave a wan smile, then said, "No, no sleep last night, my friend. Your friend the Bone Man decided that it was important to get to know me better and insisted that I take a cup of tea with him. Really, I don't remember much about it."

Tea? He doesn't remember much about it? The professor recalled his premonition from last night while in the bar at the *Palenque Classica*. Oh my, gawwd, he thought.

"Er, Pope Lucas?" David appealed.

"Yes. Yes, what is it?" responded the pope, distracted.

"Did Balaam give you his, er, "special" tea last night? The mushroom-flavored variety?"

"You're so polite in your questioning, my friend." The pope mustered a smile. "Yes, I'm afraid it was, as you imply, of a religious/spiritual variety, or that's what Balaam said."

"That lowlife spoor of the jungle gave you magic mushrooms? Balaam gave the Pope of the Catholic Church hallucinogenic mushrooms? I can't believe that man. I just can't believe…"

The pope held up a hand. "I'd do it again if I must. The reward has been so great…" he meandered off. "The books…

It's just that I don't feel as well as I usually do. It's been a very, very busy week and I'm not sure my body is up to it anymore."

David was relieved the shaman had given the recovered books to Pope Lucas. This is where they belonged. Who knew what thorny issues the papyrus scrolls from the 1st Century might raise? But that wasn't David's problem either. The surprise of the pontiff's meeting with Father Lopez, was, however, and the professor hoped the pope was up to it.

"Are you feeling sick, Pope Lucas? Your face is a little rosy and I see you scratching yourself."

"Oh no, it's just the achy stuff in my joints right now that really bothers me. I'll be fine. Don't concern yourself, my friend. All is well." The pope straightened some and rewarded David with a broad smile. This lasted only a few moments, and then with a soft groan he leaned back into the padded seating against the van wall.

****

Pope Lucas knew he would start to feel better once he was out of the van, breathing good air, soaking up a little sun. It appeared that there was going to be a lot of it today. But right now all was shadows. A monotonous run of dappled shade from the forest canopy capriciously sprinkled light all along the highway like a camouflaged cloth. It was starting to heat up outside and he felt overly warm himself. Did this van have an air conditioner?

The pope glanced again at his new friend and found him watching. David quickly looked away, but then resumed again when he thought the pontiff unaware. The pope surmised that he was a very lucky man to have so many who cared about him so much, especially in a world where so many had so little. It was just about the best thing that could happen to anyone. Everyone seemed to be concerned about him nowadays. Perhaps he really was starting to look old. He was sure he was not deserving, but how could he possibly complain of the attention?

****

Time seemed slow and interminable for a while, but then the vegetation changed, denser – encroaching all along the highway – and the trees were thicker and taller. They had stopped twice already to allow small herds of cattle with watchful herdsmen move across the highway into unseen fields. It was impossible to see into the jungle for more than six feet or so, and the air was thick with moisture and the odor of composting vegetation. Around 11:00 a.m., just as the sun was arriving overhead, the van pulled into an unused asphalt parking lot rife with weeds, limbs, and jungle detritus. The Visitors Center that guarded it been closed for years. David exited first, then turned and helped the pope down from the van.

"Wait here a moment, please." David crossed the front of the van to talk with their Zapatista driver.

"Just call," answered the driver to his query. "Call my number. You have it. Do you have Marcos' phone?" he asked.

"Yes," replied the professor. He was having trouble imagining the young man in a uniform of any type, even the ragged ones of the Zapatistas.

"We're good," the young man waved him off. "Someone will pick you up when you're ready. That's the way it works," he stated optimistically. The driver put the van in gear, slowly circled and exited the parking lot, waving at the unknown old man who had ridden with them, and set out on the road to return to wherever he was instructed.

The pope walked and stood under the shade of an oak tree and then shivered, feeling a chill. There was a sense of finality about today, an awareness that choices were even

212

more limited. They were now required to get in a boat and go downstream to a ruin to meet Father Lopez. *What was that all about*, he wondered? Why meet at an archaeological ruin in the middle of the Lacandon Jungle? He felt his forehead. He was warm, no doubt about it. Hard to tell in this humid jungle and bright sun. Heat waves shimmered from the asphalt parking lot as it absorbed, then radiated heat.

David motioned that he was walking down to the river. The pope sat heavily on a bench to wait. He saw a rickety shed down by the water, eight to ten boats, and drivers young and old—all along the shore. No doubt the archaeologist would rent the one that appeared most worthy. The pope knew nothing of boats and could only hope that the professor was an expert.

A scabrous, yellow dog with bowed neck and cowed tail between its legs shot covetous glances at his tote bag. The pope had packed a sweet roll and a few tortillas in a napkin inside his bag before leaving the restaurant. He didn't feel hungry at all. He opened his bag and began to break off pieces of tortilla and cast them toward the dog, whose head and tail suddenly shot upward. The dog yipped a time or two, then approached sideways with caution. By the time the pope was crumbling the last tortilla, the dog stood at his side, head up and expectant, tail wagging. The pope cast the last piece aside to encourage the dog to move away from him. He felt great sympathy for the beast, but the animal was obviously infected with some sort of skin ailment and the pope didn't want to contract it.

David waved and called out from below. He beckoned for the pope to come down and meet him by the river. The prelate sighed and took a deep breath. It was time to for the adventure to begin; a boat ride through the jungle on the mighty Usumacinta. The pope wished he felt alive and energized, keenly anticipating a meeting with Fr. Lopez, but instead a chill wracked him and he could focus on little else. Lucas didn't know if he was up to this or not. It just wasn't getting better. But, there was no option but to keep moving. He put on a good face, clutched the tote bag under his arm and inclined forward, tottering unsteadily down to river's edge where David stood talking to their boat driver. The helmsman was a youth of no more than sixteen years of age, which the pope found surprising, but then he surmised that the youngster had probably grown up in the jungle and around the river or he wouldn't be doing this for a living. Didn't matter. Right now he just wanted to find a seat in the shade and get out on the cool water. He suddenly felt flush and nauseous, then a chill wracked him as if he had a fever, and here he was standing in the sun. The heat and odor of sunbaked detritus; dead fish, dog manure, and stink bait entrails, composting along the riverbank was strong and sickening. He wanted to be away from here ASAP.

****

David gave the young boat captain forty dollars, a substantial amount for only two people on a boat meant for twelve, to take them downstream and wait four to six hours while they visited the ruins and met with the Zapatista entourage of Fr. Salvador Lopez, the Bone Man, almost assuredly Marcos, and who knew how many soldiers, wives, and camp hangers-on.

"Here," said David, standing on the bank, extending a hand to help the pope board. The youthful helmsman stood in the boat while extending a hand from the other side, and together they successfully boarded the old fellow, who promptly sat heavily, then lifted a hand to shield his eyes from the sun. The pontiff surveyed the boat from bow to stern, and then seeing shade beneath the corrugated roof near the boat's center, sat with a grunt, and then scooted further out of direct sunlight. The old cleric rested his weight against the back support of the bench. David hopped inside to join the other two, giving a thumbs-up to the young mariner, who revved the engine and backed the long boat slowly out into the heavy current. He adjusted the prop and then lightly twisted the accelerator control on the handle as they idled away from the bank and out into the slipstream. And then they were off, the boat engine whined and the bow inclined slightly up as they moved quickly with the current downriver, skirting bends of forest, giant fallen ceiba trees, whitened sandbars with sunning crocodiles, and myriad collections of water fowl.

What a day this promised to be. The boat would speed them downriver for about an hour before they actually docked at the decrepit boat landing below the ruin. At this time of year it was unlikely that more than two or three tourist groups would make the journey. They would essentially have the large, spectacular, jungle-cloaked ruin to themselves, far from the prying eyes of *federales* and military personnel.

It had been seven or eight years since David last took a boat to Yaxchilan. He loved the area, lots of good memories, and the academic started relating to Pope Lucas what he knew of the river, the jungle, how many times he had toured the ruins and what he hoped the pope would see today. They had been on the river nearly forty minutes and when he received no response other than an occasional wan smile from the old man, he asked the boy how much further before arriving. The archaeologist glanced at the pope, whose head turned south, to look upstream from where they had come, and David saw that the man was very ill, and the realization alarmed him.

"Holy Father you look sick," accused David.

"I fear that I am, my friend," mumbled, the pontiff, sighing. "I'm so hot and miserable, and I'm getting chills. I can't move without pain. I'm very itchy. Maybe it's these clothes. I'm wondering if maybe I have one of your tropical bugs infecting me – one of those mosquito diseases I read about sometimes."

'*Mosquito diseases?*' thought David. He stooped beneath the roof shade and made his way to the pope, placing his hand against the pontiff's forehead. The man was burning up – and sweaty. This old fellow was the leader of hundreds of millions of Catholics worldwide, and he was sick with who knows what and…dying? David hoped that was a little over-dramatic. Still, the pope had gone from being a tired old man to a sick old man and this was David's problem. They were in a boat on the Usumacinta River in the middle of the Lacandon Jungle, at least 4-5 hours or more from a physician. What had the pope contracted? Did he bring this with him, or was this because of Balaam's damn magic tea?

The boat's young skipper called out in a panicked voice, and David followed his pointing hand. A boat had left from the Guatemala side of the river was speeding toward them, its bow tilted high and the rear exhaust ejecting a rooster tail of spume as the boat, at high speed, screamed aggressively to intersect them. The boy yelled toward the boat and shook a fist. He took evasive action, waving the boat away, threatening, but they followed. One man stood at the stern with the outboard motor while another stood resolutely with a rifle in his hands. As they chased and drew near, David saw the man with the rifle had an evil look to him, a wild look; big eyes, big body, in a sleeveless shirt. *Bandits*! he cursed silently, then looked to the pope who seemed alarmed, befuddled, and very ill. They were being hijacked - robbed by thieves who preyed on tourists moving up and down the river on their vacation to Yaxchilan. Just when he thought the Bone Man's plans couldn't get any crazier, they were being hijacked. The primary goal was now to stay alive.

Fortunately, the young man driving their boat knew how to pilot his watercraft. He outmaneuvered the menacing robbers for nearly five minutes, ignoring their demands, enduring their threats. The pope, his eyes wide and mouth gaped with fear, grasped the aluminum supports of the sun roof to keep from being ejected as the boat made sudden turns and abruptly changed speed.

David called encouragement to their pilot, but the robbers maneuvered a smaller, newer, faster model, finally corralled them when the young driver hit a submerged sandbar. The prop kicked up from the water and heaved the boat sideways, nearly capsizing before righting itself. The pope held onto the sunshade for support, stunned, his face bloodied in the crash. David stood to fight, or talk, or do whatever. The standing robber fired several times, hitting the boy and then David, who tumbled onto the sandbar, shocked and in pain, reaching for his upper arm. David lay face down on the sandbar, struggling to rise, but then a booted foot caught the side of his head and he collapsed. The robber roughly searched, then discarded his wallet. Then he heard cries, shouts, orders given, and then they were gone.

He lay on the sand, trying to gain his senses. His shoulder was on fire and seeping blood, but the wound appeared superficial – he hoped. He used his other arm to sit up. The bandits had disappeared and the professor was alone. His boat drifted aimlessly near the sandbar. David stood, tested his balance and walked cautiously to the sandbar's edge. He waded about a foot into shallow water, but the empty boat lost purchase and drifted out into the river where it rode the strong current downstream.

Where was the boat driver? Where was Pope Lucas??? There was no sign of the young man, or the pope. The archaeologist remembered the boy skipper folding and falling forward when shot. David looked around, trembling and near panic. He dropped to his knees in pain and despair. He had to get his act together, he had to do something. Staying here and bleeding to death was not an option. He took several deep breaths and looked around, really looked. He spotted the raider's boat downstream on the Guatemala side of the river. Suddenly, he recognized the area. He hadn't been there in twenty years, but there was an old, very small, 1000-year-old Mayan guard post on the opposite side of the river. In the heyday of the Classic Mayan Civilization, it was built to observe activities and forestall the enemies of Yaxchilan. There was no reason for anyone to go there, as little remained. He wasted a minute wishing it was still an active guard post. But it wasn't, and very bad things could happen in a lawless place like that. The thought made him choke. The pope had been captured and taken to that lookout. Kidnapped! They needed help fast - but how? The Yaxchilan ruin was probably only about five minutes further by boat, maybe hours by foot, if anyone could even manage to walk through the nearly impenetrable Lacandon Jungle to get there.

He groaned. What a horrible day. For a breath or two he let himself blame it all on that shithead Mayan shaman. If he ever saw him again he would strangle him – guaranteed. But now he must get off this sandbar and over to the Mexico side. It appeared quite close, but was a good thirty yards west of the main current in the middle of the river. He just hoped the water between this sandbar and riverbank wasn't too deep or too swift. He also hoped that there were no crocodiles nearby to sniff the blood oozing from his arm. David found himself in the least enviable position of his life. Somehow, he had to find the Zapatistas – or there was a good chance the pope would die at the hands of bandits – or succumb to his illness, and David had to do so without going into shock himself. Time to get moving.

Chapter Twenty Three

Luis was almost enjoying himself. He had gotten a good night's sleep for a change at the Palenque Classica; no nightmares or anxiety filled dreams – which too often was the norm. With the exception of some early morning shouting and excitement out by the swimming pool that had quickly abated, he had risen feeling fresh and eager to commence today's challenges. Tooling south through the emerald green, jungle-clad hills and breasting sudden ravines was fun. There was little traffic on the road, which he loved, and even better – he had yet to encounter a single military roadblock. That in itself might be a record of sorts. He lowered his window and allowed in a jet stream of moist air smelling of humus and rot with the occasional repulsive stench of an open sewer. A merciless sun rose in a cloudless sky. As it warmed up, he closed the window and turned on his air conditioner. It would be hot in about an hour, and he was not looking forward to the sweat and humidity, or the task awaiting him. The radio reported a thunderstorm moving east over the Sierras Madres, but as yet he saw no sign of it. This time of year they appeared suddenly and could be violent. He didn't want to be out on the river in a huge downpour. Best to stay organized - stay alert - and keep moving.

The *sicario* finally arrived at the small town of *El Planchon*, clinging tenuously to a patch of intermediate jungle between the Usumacinta and the highway. There was little commerce in the village. Most inhabitants made earned a meager living selling goods or services to each other, or the occasional tourist who inexplicably found themselves there. Several small places sold soda pop, chips, and other sundries, but there were no drugstores, no gas stations, no grocery stores, and certainly no police or doctors. He turned onto a rutted, pocked street and moved slowly east toward the river. He stopped a few blocks from what appeared to be a very poor excuse for a zocalo. A few stained adobe houses sat to the north next to a shack that was a bundle of mismatched boards nailed onto an uncertain frame and topped with rusted, corrugated steel held in place by old tires to protect it from the wind.

He needed a cold bottle of Sidral before driving down to the river and boat rental, and so walked to a small shed with a protruding counter that had a Coca Cola sign nailed to its front. A young Indian woman wearing a beautifully embroidered blouse stood inside, attending the small store. An old man with a hiccup and swollen eyelids sat on an upside down bucket next to the counter. His lips were frothed with saliva and he stared vacantly and unfocused out the door toward the broken cobblestone street. Luis ignored him. Towns like *El Planchon* had a ready supply of bent and crippled people scarred from life's battles. He purchased a Sidral, which unfortunately was tepid, but still refreshingly fruity. He checked his wristwatch and saw that it was noon. Terrible hour to be doing this, but the least likely time to encounter authorities. People moved toward the shade at this time of day in the tropics.

Luis gulped the last few swallows, returned the bottle and tossed a bit of change onto the counter for the girl. He returned to his Chevy. Time to rock and roll. He drove gingerly over badly cracked and rutted roads to the riverside and the only real business in the town – *Alquiler de Botes, Jose* (Jose's boat rentals). Luis had tried to call ahead, but there was no published phone number and certainly no Internet site. He had, however, used this place before. The *sicario* wasn't concerned about boat availability, rather that no one would be here to rent him one. This time of the year business was so slow, you couldn't predict if a place would be open for business.

El Planchon was downstream from Yaxchilan as well as the much smaller ruin of rock residue on the Guatemala side to which Luis traveled today. His two men would meet him here in about three hours. They would arrive early and sit in one of the cold beer bungalows on the hill watching the area for suspicious activity. When Luis arrived with the dope, they would quickly shift the load from his boat and depart north toward Tenosique and eventually Villahermosa and the Gulf of Mexico. Although optimism was not his default mindset, he felt that things would go well today. He kissed his fingertips and stroked the patron saints on each forearm.

Luis entered what passed for the office of the boat rental, a shack devoid of paint, decrepit and bleached raw by the sun. He greeted the owner and inquired about renting a boat. In particular he wanted a skiff with a reliable engine and sun roof. There was only one with a sunroof he was told, a tourist fishing rig, but it was expensive. *How surprising*, Luis thought sarcastically.

"How much?"

"A thousand pesos."

"You're kidding? For a 4-hour rental you want a thousand pesos?" The price angered him.

"*Señor* Luis," he pleaded with as much sincerity as he could muster, "it is my only boat with a roof and motor that is working. It is much in demand."

"Really?" said Luis, looking around the room and then out the window to the river. Not a soul around. *Fucking thief.*

"I'll take it," he agreed, disgusted. He pulled a roll of bills from a pocket. Not the time to be arguing over penny – ante crap. He must get out on the water and upstream. The *sicario* was starting to feel nervous and anxious again. Damn it all! While the owner went outside to ready the boat, Luis opened his pill bottle and swallowed a couple of Xanax, then thought better of it and added a third. It wasn't possible to be too calm in these situations. He locked his car, grabbed a liter water bottle, and then checked to see that his 9mm Browning automatic pistol was still in the back waistline of his jeans.

He stepped from the dock onto the boat. After listening to operating instructions, and while the owner watched, Luis pulled the starter rope twice and it fired. He backed away from the dock, then turned and goosed it out into the middle of the river. He was going upstream into the current, so it would take a little longer, but he had time. He just hoped that the mules awaiting him at the ruin were the calm type and weren't too stupid. These low-level "grunts" were fine if they just followed orders. When they started trying to think or innovate, something always went wrong. In drug deals, it was best to avoid dumb people. They would get you killed or jailed.

Jeez, it's hot. Luis stopped and pulled his shirt off, took a swig from his water bottle and checked his watch. Another thirty minutes he estimated. A few dark clouds gathered over the hilly, forested skyline. Rain was on the way. The *sicario* continued up river for about fifteen minutes and then saw another boat coming downstream. *Very odd*, he thought. Looked like one of those long tourist models with a sun roof and benches on each side, but no one seemed to be in the boat. As it drew closer, he saw that it was unmanned and adrift in the river. *Whoa*, he thought, *someone's going to be in deep shit over that*. He slowed to watch it drift by, considered tying on to tow it, but decided that was a move of incalculable stupidity. *What would I do with it?* Someone else could save the boat. He needed to get his product, pass it on, and go home to see his grandson. *Odd*, though. He directed his boat back to the center and accelerated. Another thirty minutes, he reminded himself. If all went well, he would be in one of those beer cantinas overlooking the river in a few hours, a cold one in hand, and his cargo intact and safely on its way to the dope heads in the United States. Luis lightly touched each forearm in succession, silently thanking La *Santa Muerte* and *Jesus Malverde* for providing him such good luck. All would be well, he was certain.

****

A dark, foreboding cloud floated high above the jungle, seemed to hesitate and check out the area, and then moved resolutely east on westerly thermals. David shaded his eyes with a hand and glanced toward the sun, a relentless fiery corona that would bleach his bones given the opportunity. He thought it was supposed to rain today. Disappointing, but time to go. He would die here, as would the pope, if he didn't begin now.

The archaeologist reached and touched the side of his head that had been impacted by the boot of the robber. Scraped and swelling, but no cut. His neck and head ached continuously, but he no longer received jolts of protest when he moved it. He inspected the wound on his upper arm and decided he would treat it after his swim. It appeared superficial as far as gunshot wounds went. Seemed to be a flesh wound. No hole, just a chunk of skin blown away. Hurt like hell, though. He raised his arm and rotated his shoulder joint to ensure all worked properly. It sounded a bit stupid to think that the professor was lucky, but he had fared very well considering events and circumstances. He glanced once more across the water to where the boat that had accosted them was beached. Nothing good going on over there. He would think about that later, too. He must hurry.

What was important right now were the crocodiles. Parts of the river had a few of the ugly beasts, other sections, especially where illegal cattle from El Salvador and Nicaragua were smuggled across, were infested with them. He looked up and down the river, slowly, in an attempt to spot partially submerged lurkers. Nothing. He chose the narrowest part of the channel and waded carefully from the sandbar into the water, testing the current as he went. One step at a time, careful to maintain traction. Suddenly he was up to his waist in swift water, still a good twenty meters from the riverbank. He hadn't swum in years, and certainly not in jeans and boots. He pushed off into the stream, stroking as hard as he could with his good arm, until he arrived at river's edge. He pulled himself out, gasping and trembling. More excitement than he wanted! He rolled onto his back to catch his breath. He sat up and attempted to bind his seeping wound with a bandana from his pocket. He worried, briefly, about infection from the river water. Best thing for it was to get out of here. But the bandana kept slipping, and he resorted to ripping strips from the bottom of his shirt to hold it in place and shield the wound from jungle insects seeking a bloody lunch.

Time to go. He glanced across the river one more time to the boat on the Guatemalan side, then rose to navigate the jungle and its vegetation. He walked about ten-fifteen feet west into the forest, the jungle canopy blocking out the sun. The archaeologist's legs quickly became tangled in bindweed and he decided that he should move north, parallel with the river, not away from it. He stopped and took a deep breath. *Gawwd, this is awful,* he thought. The professor realized that he was making a lot of noise and perhaps attracting unwanted attention. He hoped there weren't any hungry jaguars in the area. There were a million ways to die in the jungle. He remembered Yaxchilan being only half mile away, but it was entirely possible he might not make it. He felt very fatigued and was growing weak from loss of blood.

David took a deep breath, and resolutely trudged towards an area of bright light, a break through the jungle canopy. He hadn't worked this area in twenty years, but remembered that Lacandon Indians lived nearby and that they were friends with the jungle. They traversed many routes on a daily basis, some known only to them, but trails nonetheless. Moments later he found a path. *My gawwd!* he exulted. But it went two directions. Which should he take? He turned right, back towards the river and began to follow the footpath – if that's what it was. *Could be an animal trail,* he reminded himself. *Big animals like jaguars and ocelots.* Whatever it was, he must take a chance. He could make better time on this trail – if it led to the ruins. Otherwise he would be helpless and lost in the middle of the green hell of the Lacandon Jungle – devoid of water, webbed with clinging vines – and unable to recover the pope or have the pleasure of strangling Balaam Reyes. The thought of his hands around the Bone Man's neck energized him. *Time to walk it out, David,* he told himself. *Move it.*

****

The kidnappers lashed the old man's arms spread-eagled to a scraggly tree, as if crucifying him. A loop of rope held his legs together. His captors were disappointed. The kid boat driver, shot in the chest, was likely dead and being eaten by crocodiles or alligator gar. The other guy, shot in the arm and kicked unconscious, had yielded a wallet with a few thousand pesos and two credit cards - a slim haul for taking such a big chance. Tourists were so stupid. Why didn't they just allow themselves to be robbed and everything would be fine?

Fernando and Mariano were always open to picking up a few extra pesos in addition to what they earned by transporting meth. Rich tourists were usually easy to rob. This one hadn't gone so well. That damn kid, the boat driver, had messed up everything. Now they had this old guy, who was either nuts or sick, or both. He didn't look prosperous. Snatching him didn't seem as good an idea as it had before. Would anyone even bother to pay money to get him back? And the timing was not the best. They couldn't hang out here much longer, not with an empty boat floating down the river. Someone would come searching eventually, probably sooner than later. It was time for the Big Enchilada to get here so they could load the meth and split. They had done their job. Didn't know yet what they would do with the wimpy old man – maybe nothing. Although he hadn't thought it out yet, Mariano was starting to suspect that the old guy might have to be disposed of – permanently.

Mariano took another swig from the tequila bottle, then checked the GPS coordinates on his cell phone again. This was definitely the place. The numbers were right. Couldn't be any others like it for miles around. No foot traffic, no roads in or out, and the jungle canopy provided great cover. No law enforcement. This weird-named Enchilada guy had obviously moved a lot of dope and knew what he was doing. Where was he, anyway? The dope mule, already nervous from the day's activities, was more than a little inebriated and starting to worry about his companion, Fernando, who was proving to have less than full mentally stability. His accomplice-in-crime kept badgering the old guy; had punched him in the head and gut several times, and once threatened him with a knife. Right now the old man was out of it; bloody face, hanging from the ropes that secured him to a tree, looking as if someone had crucified him. What would they do with him? Maybe nothing; maybe they would have to feed the crocodiles again.

Sympathy was not a characteristic anyone would use to describe Mariano. He was a well-known thug from Las Pozas, Guatemala who had spent his early life in orphanages, then graduated to life on the streets, finally engaging in petty crime and running dope around and through the highland forests of Guatemala's remote Indian communities. Sometimes he made good money, other times he was stealing and robbing to keep himself in tequila and pussy. Tequila was cheap, women were not – even the easy ones. Mariano had barely known Fernando, but he was eager to help when the thug had approached him with the task of transporting meth to the Usumacinta. Mariano knew the tropics - especially the river area. Every two months he had a steady gig with guys who rustled cattle in El Salvador and transported them across the river to Mexico. It probably violated about a hundred international treaties, but no one gave a shit, least of all the Mexican government. Unfortunately it was less than steady work, and so when Fernando had asked for help to mule-in a load of meth, he had jumped at the chance. Didn't know it was going to turn out like this, though. Sure wished that Enchilada character would arrive so he could get back to town for a glass of mescal and a warm, young female that would get horizontal with him for a few bucks. Maybe he would walk back down to the river bank and take a look?

****

Pope Lucas, bleeding and burning with fever, barely conscious, arched his back in agony when the kidnapper viciously punched him in the kidneys once again – on the side of the one remaining organ. The pain was beyond belief. He had descended into hell. The Evil One had been trolling his speeches and sermons and decided to take action. The worst headache of his life pounded, his throat was burnt dry, and his skin prickled with heat as icy chills raced up his spine. Any movement disturbed the painful, sharp needles in his joints.

He had been seized by very bad men – men with a conditional moral code. They wanted to ransom him. Their shriveled souls were parched of emotion. These men must have been raised without mothers. The ransom would never happen. He would not survive the day, of this he was sure. Sr. Angelina, as usual, had been correct. In a moment of lucidity he had tried to explain to the short crazy one with the bad teeth and worse breath that Lucas had no family and that he was a priest. He was rewarded with a good beating and realized he had seriously jeopardized his life by being honest. Now the demon incarnate waved a knife in the pope's face. He should have lied; told them he was rich and that many would pay to have him back. Lucas didn't believe he would live another fifteen minutes – wasn't sure he wanted to – and then felt himself gratefully slipping into unconsciousness.

Fernando emptied the old man's tote bag on the ground, finding only a small laptop, a diabetes kit, a sweet roll, a bible, and the five wood cylinders. This angered him even further, and he stomped the items in frustration, doing little damage to the ancient wood book cylinders, but completely destroying the glucose meter and syringes. The narco mule grabbed the bible and threw it at his captive's head.

"Stupid old man!" he shouted. Stupid fucking tourist!" He mumbled to himself with secret cruelty, fists doubled and chest heaving. Fernando turned away, frustrated, and walked to where Mariano sat nursing a bottle.

"Gimme me that," demanded Fernando, reaching for the Cuervo tequila bottle.

Mariano handed it to his accomplice, rose from his perch, belched, and then sauntered toward the hill overlooking the river. The mid-afternoon sun blazed onto clear river water and erupted in an explosion of twinkling silver lights. Looking up river, he saw acrobatic, cavorting birds swoop and threaten smaller, unseen creatures in the tall grass and river. When he glanced north, down river, he spied a black dot. He stared intently, the sound of an outboard motor growing. He assumed it was the Big Enchilada come to pick up his dope. A dart of trepidation stung him and adrenaline pulsed through his veins, riding the tequila toward an uncertain climax. He glanced back at the old man hanging limply from the tree limbs and his jaw clenched. *Time to do the deed, take care of this problem,* he told himself.

Maybe they shouldn't have attacked the boat of tourists? Tourists were supposed to be carrying a lot of money, but this venture sure as hell hadn't turned up much of anything, and now they had a sick old man, who no one would probably pay for, to contend with. Neither had experience hiding hostages, and as far as he knew his companion had never actually pulled off a kidnapping for ransom. Pretty stupid in retrospect. Now they were going to have to make a decision about the old fellow.

Mariano called out to Fernando that a boat approached, and motioned him away from the spread-eagled pontiff, hanging unconscious from the tree. Mariano assumed that the Big Enchilada was not going to be happy when he arrived.

"What we do with the old man?"

"Don't know. Maybe eat him, or give him to the crocs. He said he doesn't have any money, and I believe him...should have shot him instead of the kid. The boy had at least forty dollars from renting the boat. This decrepit asshole doesn't have a centavo. Can you believe it? No wallet and no money at all!"

Mariano stood calmly and reflected. "We have to decide. This Big Enchilada character is due any time and he won't be happy to see a hostage crucified on a tree when he gets here."

Mariano turned to watch the boat draw near. "It was your idea and your deed," he continued. "You figure it out, but I ain't draggin' him back to town," Mariano added with finality. He took the bottle from Fernando's hand and took a long swig. He looked at the near empty bottle, reflected, then said. "We're going to need more tequila."

****

Luis slowed his approach and held up a hand to shield the sun as he searched the nearly impenetrable wall of jungle on the Guatemala side of the river, looking for the spot where he would meet his mules. He glanced at the GPS on his telephone. *Very* close. He had passed the classic ruin of Yaxchilan ten minutes earlier and knew he was in the vicinity of the landing. There – he recognized the old giant ceiba tree to the south on the river bank, only now it tilted toward the river, nearly parallel to the formless currents below, a forest giant stricken and felled by a wrathful God. Towards the shore and on the sandbar, a small skiff sat next to the steep river bank. Yes, the mules were here. No one else would possibly stop at a remote, meaningless place like this in the jungle. He glanced about, up and down the river, then tilted

231

his head to survey the dense, verdant forest line above. There! He spotted the old, broken stairway leading up to the ruin and thick, Guatemalan Petén Jungle. He steered his boat to the riverbank. Two crocodiles, one a large bull, the other a juvenile, complacently baked their armored hides in the sun at the far north end of the sandbar. He hated those damn things. Never had a problem with one, but didn't want to either.

The *sicario* beached his boat, hopped out and drug it further onto the sandbar and out of the current for safety. He eyed the distant crocodiles again, perused the broken steps of tumbled stone and weeds that led up to the ancient Maya lookout site, then stepped up, off the sandbar onto the river bank and walked toward the cracked and broken stairway. Two men with pistols, one holding a liquor bottle, stood above, watching. *Assholes,* thought Luis. Drinking during the day in the middle of a drug deal. *Unprofessional rabble.* He reached to his back waistband to ensure that his pistol was in place, then called out, "I'm the Big Enchilada. You guys hungry?"

"Si, *señor*," returned the tall one. "Come on up," he gestured with the bottle in hand. "We're friendly. Lots to talk about."

Probably not, frowned Luis as he carefully began to tread the broken, lichen blackened stairway, occasionally stopping where the aged stairs had collapsed, then jumping to gain solid footing. He wasn't here for conversation. *Get the meth and get out,* he reminded himself. He hoped these guys weren't a bunch of doped-up pinheads.

Upon reaching the top, he stopped and looked around to familiarize himself. Hadn't been here for a year, but seemed to be the same neglected ruin of tumbled stone, weeds, scraggly trees, and clinging vines - an encampment of the damned with pocked walls and graffiti. The sweet smell of composted leaves and rotting detritus mingled with stale cigarette smoke. A few small structures, all in bad repair, sat in a semi-circle. He knew there were more, further back into the woods, but had no reason to investigate them. Towering trees created a canopy to shield the sun, and it took a moment for his eyes to discern shape within the shadows forest.

"I'm Mariano, this is Fernando," said the tall one with the tequila bottle, appearing hesitant to talk. "The Ruiz brothers sent us with your stuff."

"You have it? You brought the dope?"

"Si, *señor*. All packaged and ready to load. Fernando and I were just waiting, or kind of waiting. We…er…had a little distraction earlier, but…."

"What the fuck is that?" asked Luis sternly. He pointed toward the edge of the clearing toward the forest wall. "Is that what it looks like?"

"I don't know," sniggered Fernando, the smaller one.

"What's it look like, *cabron*?" He smiled impishly, inebriated and unable to control his mouth.

Stupid, fucking idiots, thought Luis. He took a deep breath for calm, but a slow burn flickered. *Easy, easy*, he told himself. He reached and retrieved his pistol. "Put your guns on the ground, now, both of you.

"No need," spouted Mariano. "We can explain."

"Now," said Luis, pointing his gun at Mariano, then Fernando.

"Amigo, take it easy," pleaded Mariano. "He's just a tourist."

"A poor tourist, added Fernando. "A sick tourist."

Luis groaned. "Don't tell me." Then he asked anyway, "You robbed some tourists, right?" Then, "Last time hombres. Guns on the ground, now! I'm in charge here, understand?

Do as I say or I start shooting." He pointed his gun at the little mouthy one, Fernando. "You first, dickhead."

The mule hesitated, looked at Mariano, then reached slowly to his waistband and removed his pistol. "No need for this, Enchilada. No problem. Just a tourist. We have the meth."

"Now you," Luis gestured with his pistol.

"I don't carry a gun."

"Bullshit." Luis fired at Mariano's feet.

"Yes, okay, *si, señor*." Mariano extracted a pistol from his rear waistband and lay it on the ground.

"Bunch of fucking amateurs. Where's the product? Where is it!" he demanded.

"Not to worry, *señor*. It's there, behind the tourist." He pointed to the old man, hanging unconscious from a scraggly tree. We can load it, *senor*. Now, let us…"

Luis was seething - the slow burn now a barely controlled fire. He gripped his pistol, set for action. Ready for someone to fuck up and pay the price. Stupid *hijos de puta* (sons-of-whores).

"Now," he motioned with his pistol. "Get the shit and put it in my boat. Let's go, *andale, andale*, move it."

Luis bent and recovered their firearms, then followed as they walked to retrieve the dope. "*Pronto!*" (hurry up!) "No time for this shit."

Luis stopped and took a good look at the battered old man tied to the tree. *Fucking pitiful*, he decided. *Bunch of assholes*. Luis was a *sicario* and knew that it was a bad life full of bad deeds, but as far as he was concerned those who kidnapped for ransom and casually killed people under the guise of business were all lowlifes. All of them. Fucking scum. Even the criminal world was stratified and had unwritten codes of behavior. Although he was sending product north to rich, bored idiots who played too many video games, kidnappers ruined perfectly innocent lives, everyone's lives. *Cunts. Every fucking one of them.*

Fernando and Mariano hastily toted sisal bound packages to the stairway, then down to Luis' boat. He accompanied them the first two trips, then gave in to his curiosity and went to check out the old guy hanging from the tree. Luis was a hard man, some would judge totally void of sensitivity or kindness, but he had moments of melancholy and introspection when compassion leaked through the chinks of his emotional armor. It was very difficult to look at this sad fellow man. It bothered him. He unconsciously stroked the tattoos on his forearm. Luis circled the tree and looked around to the area where the meth had been stacked. *What was that?* he wondered, eyeing an object in the shadows behind the tree trunk. He stooped to retrieved it.

Oh my God! thought Luis, his hands shaking. A bible! Here? What the fuck? He turned and saw the short one, Fernando, after having scaled the broken steps. The drug mule hesitated a moment, then walked toward Luis. His chest heaved from exertion of several trips up and down the fractured stairs.

"What the fuck is this?" Luis shook the bible at the mule. "Where did this come from?"

"Easy, *amigo*," Fernando raise a calming hand. "The tourist had it in a bag. It's just a bible. The old man claimed he was a priest." Fernando wiped sweat from his forehead. "These guys will say anything when they get nabbed."

Luis's alarms began to scream. *A priest? The man might be a priest? And these drunken lowlifes were torturing him? A priest? No...no...can't be,* he thought, stroking his left forearm with the barrel of his Browning 9mm.

Mariano joined them, panting also. "All loaded," he said. "We're gone, Enchilada. Don't want any trouble, señor. Can we have our guns?"

The *sicario* trembled as he stared at the old guy strung to the tree. They were torturing a priest? *Sorry motherfuckers.* Suddenly Luis amped out. He wheeled around. "A gun? You want a gun? *Si, señor.* Take this." He fired twice into Fernando's chest, then three shots into the back of the fleeing Mariano. Luis kicked Fernando in the head until he nearly slipped and lost footing. He heard Mariano groan, so walked and shot him again. A priest? They were torturing a priest?

Luis pulled out his Glock knife as walked toward the aged captive. He quickly cut the legs free, then each arm. The old man collapsed on the ground, either dead or nearly so. Luis panicked. What to do? *What could he do? Water!* he remembered. The *sicario* scrambled for the stairway, taking them two at a time down to the river to retrieve his half full bottle of water. He returned, panting, and put it to the old man's mouth and talked to him. "Water, *señor.* Here, I have water. Please drink *señor.* Are you a priest, *señor?* Please come back." He placed his hand on the pontiff's forehead and felt a high fever. He poured a dab of liquid on the old fellow's forehead, then put the bottle to his lips again, pouring water into the gaping mouth, which caused a reflexive, choking action and the pope woke, but still near death.

"Are you a priest, *señor?* Talk to me." Luis begged, barely able to control himself. He roughly slapped the old man. "Talk to me," he demanded. "Are you a priest?"

The man seemed to focus momentarily, looked into the *sicario's* face seeking recognition, but found none. "Yes," he mumbled. "I'm Lucas," he said, "Pope Lucas."

"What? What did you say? Tell me," he shook the pope. "Are you a priest?"

"Yes, I'm a priest. I'm…"

Luis groaned and laid the old man down. A righteous rage enveloped him. It was true. He could tell. Those stupid sons-of-bitches had kidnapped a priest vacationing with friends on their way to the Yaxchilan ruin. Luis was glad the bastards were dead. They were bad men. Really bad men. *Fucking kidnappers!* But the *sicario* had a problem. He had a load of meth growing hot in his boat. He had to move fast, practically fly down the Usumacinta without drawing attention to himself. The priest looked so bad that he might die at any time. Luis did NOT need a dead man in his vessel, especially a priest. No way could that be explained. What to do? There was a second boat that belonged to the mules. Maybe he would just leave the guy this bottle of water and tell him to get to the craft below. "*Chingada*," he cursed. "Shit! Shit! Shit!" he screamed in frustration.

Luis placed the bottle in the pope's hands, rose, and looked toward the river. What a terrible day. His narco saints had not intervened for him. Everything was planned to go so well. "I'm so sorry, Fr. Lucas. That's your name right? Lucas? I have to go. I'm so sorry. I'm not a good man…have to go." The *sicario* turned and slumped, walking unsteadily toward the steps. He turned again, glanced at the dead bodies and priest, who had one eye open, staring at him. Luis made the sign of the cross and said, "Forgive me father for I have sinned," and he turned and leaped down, taking the steps two at a time.

The crocodiles seemed to have awakened from their lethargy and the bull was making slow progress toward the boats. Luis growled fiercely at the beast, jumped into his boat, fired the engine with a couple of yanks, and maxed out the accelerator. He was in the river, the boat bow high as the motor propelled him forward, the raging sound of the overwrought engine a reflection of his inner being. He kept the throttled on full for five minutes, just past the Yaxchilan ruin, before backing off. Finally, he stopped and drifted, reached in his shirt pocket and extracted his bottle of Xanax. He popped three into his mouth, then realized he had no water. His throat was dry and they stuck in his esophagus, but eventually made their way down. He took a deep breath and reflected momentarily. *This is it*, he decided. *The last one.* The storm was on its way and the western sky above the jungle-clad hills was dark with menacing thunderheads, some laced with flickers of lightning, as they drifted east toward Belize and the Yucatan Peninsula. *Shit!* he thought. *Now I get caught out on the water in a thunderstorm? Damn it all!* Luis glanced first at the distant boat dock on the Mexico side that sat below the Yaxchilan ruin in the jungle, then cranked the engine again, and he was off. Going downstream, with the current, he made much better time. With his right hand guiding the tiller, he stroked his forearm with the other hand, mumbling promises to the *La Santa Muerte*. Calming, he returned to the business of the river, glancing nervously at the gathering storm. Luis' anger was in abeyance now. He would just make it, he decided. He was going to win again. What he was going to win, though, really wasn't that clear anymore. Luis would never forget this day as long as he lived.

****

Sweat and filth caked David's face and hands, and his river-soaked clothing tugged and inhibited his every movement. Blood from a throbbing shoulder oozed through his makeshift bandages. He was so hot he felt he might faint. He braced his good hand on his knee and, panting, considered the paths that deviated from this main trail. Thunder rumbled and the burden of losing the pope lay on his shoulders like a death shroud. He felt totally alone and helpless.

The jungle was the enemy of those who didn't know it or respect its authority. Mosquitos swarmed him, slime covered pools of forest detritus encumbered the path, and howler monkeys screamed and threw leaves, feces, and sticks. He'd only been walking for about fifteen minutes and had kept the river nearby. It would invite death to wander from the jungle corridor. One could walk for hours through stricken forest, void of water, webbed in thorny vines. The Lacandon Indians who inhabited this area were remarkable. He would love to see one right now – see anyone for that matter. Yaxchilan couldn't be that far away. He must keep close to the river or he could easily traipse unknowingly past the ruin in this dense wilderness. Lost in the jungle likely meant death. This thought caused his adrenaline to surge and he picked up his pace, desperate to encounter the old city. It had to be here. It must be close. He was sure. The professor must find Marcos and get across the river to where the pope was being held. If he didn't, well, he guessed he just have to settle for strangling the Bone Man.

****

"They should have arrived by now," stated Marcos, looking at his wristwatch. His father, Balaam Reyes, grunted assent. "Did you hear the gunshots earlier?" asked Marcos. Sounded as if they were coming from across the river."

"Maybe hunters," replied the shaman, laconically. He sat on a log, tired, from the three - hour march through the jungle from the Lacandon village of Lacanja. Balaam was born in the Petén Jungle in Guatemala and had spent his entire life traversing the forested mountains and lowlands of Meso-America. Now, at ninety-plus years of age, he was still moving, but had grown long in the tooth. Finally, about six years ago, his incredible vigor had begun to wane. He now allowed extra time when planning a trip, and there were fewer journeys. He could no longer maintain the torrid pace of his youth.

Balaam was thinking about his Holy Man, Father Lopez. Earlier this morning, the priest had performed mass in a clearing in the jungle two miles southeast of Lacanja near the river of the same name. Even Balaam, an animist and a man with deep-seated antipathies for Christianity, had been moved by the ceremony. The trust, mood, and dedication of the poor Indians who sought solace and connection with the renegade Catholic priest and his ministry was simply striking. The Maya were a religious people, more so than any Ladinos or Europeans, he was sure. People in the United States, he knew, had no religion except money. They were raised that way. The Bone Man, however, had once met a group of traveling Buddhist monks from Thailand visiting Guatemala and they had impressed him greatly. It was a religion for the people, he had learned, not the state, not the rich and powerful and not just for show. It was a way of life, as all religions should be.

The distant chatter of children and pleasant laughter of women drifted from the forest where they camped on the outskirts of Yaxchilan, so as not to disturb the boat of rare tourists who journeyed to the old city during low-season. Fr. Lopez, his family, and a dozen Zapatistas and their families had arrived earlier in the day. Marcos had told him only one boat had come earlier in the day and that they would probably leave soon, as it was after 3:00 and a seasonal thunderstorm was threatening the area.

The long walk had taken a physical toll on the shaman. He closed his eyes to rest, but found himself caught up in unresolved issues. Fatigue was taking him – it was time to act. At his age and in view of present events, the Bone Man believed he had to finish with these issues very soon. For most of his life he had ranged through the Petén and Lacandon in various roles. As an eleven-year-old he had fled the abject poverty of his home in the small community near the spectacular highland lake of Chichicastenango in Guatemala to follow a traditional Indian curandero and learn the trade. A spiritual child by nature, Balaam had been attracted to the obvious truths of traditional medicine. He had experienced much of it personally, then learned to apply it to others. In the process, as part of that apprenticeship, he had acquired beliefs consistent with spiritual healing, the two-soul existence of man and a spirit animal, as well as the pharmacopeia to make it all work.

The shaman stood and raised his arm. An attendant with gun in hand, raggedy clothes and a black armband bent his head to listen closely, nodded, and hurried off. He returned with the Bone Man's friend from Lacanja, Antonio, who also worked for *ahua* David. Balaam greeted him as the old friend that he was – almost family. A fifteen-minute discussion ensued with Antonio listening, then asking questions. Finally, both nodded in agreement. They embraced and Antonio turned to call out several names. The chatter ceased, and four Zapatistas exited the gathering and moved toward the jungle, awaiting his instructions. Moments later they separated to make personal arrangements. Soon, the five men headed back into the jungle in the direction of Lacanja. Balaam watched them go, then sat with eyes closed to relax and conserve energy, this time achieving a light doze. But then he startled awake at the sound of Marco's voice. His son was shouting and running toward the path from Lacanja.

"What is it?" he asked of anyone. What's going on?"

Balaam saw Antonio and a comrade struggling up the Lacanja trail, supporting *ahua* David between them. *Pig shit,* he thought. *Bad, pig shit luck. Stinky luck.*

The shaman called out and gestured to bring the archaeologist to him. *Where was his new friend, the Big Potato? Why was ahua David in such bad shape? What had happened?* They were very late. Obviously, something had gone very wrong. *Pig shit...*he cursed again, silently. As they approached, Balaam saw that the professor was injured in the shoulder. It looked ugly. The man appeared dehydrated, stumbled frequently, and barely kept his feet; he was near collapse. Antonio put him down gingerly, with his back against the trunk of a tree, and Marcos gave him water to drink. He began to gasp out his story.

Balaam stood and issued orders to make ready to leave immediately. A Zapatista soldier stationed at the docks below the ruin materialized, saying the tourist boat was preparing to leave. And, the boat driver was taking a second unmanned craft with him. He'd pursued and pulled this derelict craft from the water, securing it to his own boat. Earlier in the afternoon, sitting in the shade by the river, awaiting his tourists to return, he had spotted the boat, just like his, adrift in the river. He thought he recognized it as a boat docked with his and eight others just upstream about an hour. The boat driver had quickly untied and pursued the derelict, secured it to his boat, and then returned back to the landing. He would tow it with him upon leaving with his group to return from the day's activities.

When Balaam heard the story, he cried out, "No! Stop him. We must have that boat! Tell him it's our boat. Get that boat," he insisted, alarmed. He gestured and then slammed his walking stick to the ground twice for emphasis, speaking rapidly in dialect. Two other men charged after the soldier as he headed back down to the docks. All chatter and activity stopped. Everyone paid attention when Balaam raised his voice. He knew they had to get across the river – immediately.

Chapter Twenty Four

The engine pinged in protest as the tourist boat fought the current, transporting ten people upstream to an old ruin on the Guatemala side of the river. David had insisted on coming after catching his breath and drinking his fill of water. The pope had been lost on his watch and the ache of responsibility was almost greater than the pain in his arm. The sky darkened and jets of wind gusted, tossing spray in preamble to the coming torment. Lightning flashed, backlit in blue, black, and gray as clouds roiled inexorably eastward. They must locate the old ruin on the Guatemala side and get off the water, quickly.

"There!" shouted Marcos, pointing. The boat adjusted its vector. David and eight others, including Father Lopez and Balaam gripped the sides of the boat, willing it toward the forested river bank. A small motorboat was beached on the sand, and two crocodiles, a bull and juvenile, had paused in their climb up an old, corrupted staircase of broken stone and mortar.

Marcos placed his rifle to his shoulder and fired three shots into the juvenile leading the assault on the stairs. He aimed again and fired twice more, hitting the bull crocodile just approaching the lower the steps.

"There," he shouted, jubilantly. "I see someone!"

A person lay crunched and sideways at the top step, collapsed from exertion. His valiant effort had not led him to the boat below. It had, however, captured the attention of the two crocodiles. They were now dead or dying.

The boat beached, Marcos jumped out and raced up the broken limestone steps. He frantically, but gently turned the person over. "It's Lucas!" Father Lopez followed, struggling up the stairs.

The Bone Man, excited and cranky, shouted orders and swung his walking cane at anyone nearby. Most had long ago learned to avoid the cane's arc and impact as well as the one employing it. The Zapatistas ducked and clambered from the boat, then pulled it securely on to the sandbank. The sky opened, gushing a torrent of large drops, and thunder pealed loudly, rolling and ending in violent explosions.

"Is he alive?" called the shaman. "Marcos! Is he alive?" *Damn boat. Probably built by drunk Ladino.* The Bone Man struggled to exit the river craft, and a Zapatista reached to carefully help him out. Balaam began the onerous trek up the sheer, ruined stairs and his helper moved to assist when needed. Balaam turned to berate him, even whack him with his stick, but tripped over the larger crocodile. The soldier caught the old man, setting him on his feet. The Bone Man cursed in dialect, then turned to the stairs again and used his walking stick for support, eyeing the unmoving crocodiles. He moved slowly and deliberately, bent and slow, muttering maliciously, clearly unhappy at the turn of events.

At the top step Balaam looked down at the swollen, red face of his new friend. "What happening," he demanded. "Is alive?" Blood caked on the pontiff's face from a large gash above his eye. The shaman squatted to put a hand to the pontiff's face, then frowned and released the top two buttons of the pope's shirt. A feverish, cherry red rash stared back.

"Humph," grunted the Bone Man. He reached for Pope Lucas' leg to articulate a knee, but the pontiff unexpectedly cried out. Balaam rocked back on his feet to survey the situation.

"What is it?" asked David, last out of the boat and holding his arm steady, clearly the worse for wear. "What's happened? Is he okay?"

"Maybe no," frowned the shaman. "Maybe in spirit world. Look good soul friend. Sad. Bad. Give water. Give much water. He have…" the shaman waved a hand, looking for the right words. "He have break-the-bone sickness."

Eh…thought David, trying to interpret the shaman's wretched Spanish. *"Break-the-bone sickness?"* Break Bone Disease! The pope had contracted Dengue Fever. *Aw Jeez*, thought, the archaeologist. Very bad news, and someone had clearly beaten the old man. His face was swollen and mottled and sported a black eye with numerous facial abrasions. A deep cut still oozed from above his left eye.

"Oh my God," whispered the professor. The pope lay limp and unconscious, nearly dead – and they were hours away from medical intervention. The leader of the Catholic world lay dying on the edge of a river, wracked with Dengue, beaten by robbers, and left for dead. He might die and David would likely be caught up in a major blowback, trying to explain to hundreds of millions of Catholics how the pope had died in his charge in the middle of a jungle. How things could have changed so quickly and so badly, and with no apparent cause other than robbers, was baffling. What were the chances?

"Go away," commanded Father Lopez. He gently pushed the archaeologist aside and touched Balaam, and then Marcos on the shoulder. "Go away. Everyone. Just me and the pope. Please," he repeated kindly with a smile. "Leave us."

Everyone looked to Father Lopez, then to each other, and finally the Bone Man. The shaman pushed himself to his feet with the help of his cane and trudged upward, over the top step, and out of sight into the shade of the old ruin. Marcos gave David the "look," and they followed, shooing the rest of the rescue party before them.

****

Father Lopez placed his canteen to the pope's cracked lips, jiggling it to get his attention. "Drink, drink," he urged, stroking the pontiff's face and neck. "The Holy Spirit is strong with you, Holy Father. Drink and come back to us. Come back to my voice." The Holy Man coaxed, continuing to lightly touch the pontiff's head and neck. He poured water on his hand to loosen and washed away the clotted blood. For a moment he sat quietly and offered a brief prayer, then returned to his task, soothingly encouraging the pope to take water.

Thinking this might be the only time he might ever talk to the pope, Father Lopez began to talk to the pontiff as if they were close friends. He began with his fears that he really was different from everyone else in the world. He had been offered a mission that led him silently traipsing jungle trails with too much time and nothing to do but live with himself, in his own mind. He had accepted the challenge, but understood it as if God or Nature had said – 'I'll give you this, but not that. It's your job to figure out how to make it work.'

Father Lopez, unaware if the pope listened or not, spoke of his regret that he had not seen nor communicated with his family since before he disappeared into the Lacandon Jungle with the Zapatistas three years previous. He missed them terribly. He loved them and was worried that they were ashamed of him, regretful that he had not trusted and contacted them before his draconian decision.

Of course, a woman had been involved. His beautiful archaeologist, lover muse, and catalyst that opened him to the reality of poverty, want, and despair that afflicted billions around the world. Who in their right mind would seek out such a thing? Probably only someone like him, Salvador ruminated. He didn't see anyone else in this line of work. The pay and benefits were just about the worst thing on the planet.

****

"You could introduce yourself," whispered a voice in his lap.

Father Lopez jerked with surprise, then smiled. "Welcome back, Holy Father!" then he added:

"I am Salvador Lopez, formerly of the Tuxtla Gutierrez Diocese of Chiapas."

The pope blinked, his parched lips twitched, then parted with a quick intake of breath. A bit of white teeth shone through. He closed his eyes and a painful smile tugged his face as he became aware of where and with whom he spoke. A look of contentment in the form of a faint smile lay easily on his swollen face. He felt better already. It wasn't possible to have felt any worse.

"Actually, nowadays, I'm not sure who I am," continued the priest. "My friend Marcos tells me that I have acquired many names, not all of them good, in the last several years. Mostly, I think I'm just a servant of God, a vessel that carries the good things of God to the deserving. How this came to me is still a mystery."

The pope opened his eyes and hung on every word from this Holy Man. He said, "Help me sit up, Father Lopez, please. I want to sit up."

Father Lopez helped the pontiff to do so.

"Please, may I hold your hand, Fr. Lopez?" Pope Lucas reached for the younger man's hand and squeezed it tightly. "I am one of your admirers, from afar," offered the pope. "I want you to know that I believe in you – believe in your mission, and I know in my heart that you are the most remarkable person I've ever met. You may be the most extraordinary man to walk the earth since Christ, two-thousand years ago."

"Holy Father, please..."

"No. No, listen to me, Father Lopez. You *are* a holy man. Your good works are already a matter of legend. For those in our Church who doubt, those who scheme, those engaged in Byzantine machinations who promote themselves or their careers, you are a threat. Societies and religions everywhere have become jaded, indifferent bureaucracies. You are what no one believes in anymore. You are the Word of God on Earth and you are here, in the Lacandon Jungle, ministering to those who need it the most. You came to correct injustices just as Christ did when he appeared in Palestine to minister to the poor and women and children, and to correct the wrong thinking of his friends, the Jews. He was crucified for his efforts. You should understand that the same fate awaits you if you ever leave this jungle to return to civilization, Father Lopez. You will be accused as a charlatan and manipulator and will likely be jailed by the state, who sees you as a threat to their authority."

The pope hesitated a moment, the said, "Excuse me, I really must stand. My joints have been absolutely killing me all day."

He stood with help from Fr. Lopez, teetered precipitously on the top step, and then one-by-one, articulated his knees and elbows. The pope rested his eyes on the broad, gleaming Usumacinta River, then smiled, and looked to Fr. Lopez. "Another one of your miracles, no doubt."

"Really, Holy Father, it has nothing to do with me. I'm just a vessel..."

"Oh I understand, believe me, but it's still a miracle. What ailed me?"

"My good friend Balaam says that you contracted Dengue Fever."

"Really!" said the pope, excited. "Doesn't that last days and days? Isn't it often fatal?"

Fr. Lopez's eyes twinkled and he laughed. "Yes, yes, Holy Father. It's quite awful and some do die."

Consternation clouded the pontiff's face. "Where's your cup, Fr. Lopez? I hear you have an ancient cup taken from the burial box of the old Holy Man, the corpse discovered by our Fr. Gregory three years ago."

The Holy Man hesitated, "Well, I was in a hurry and forgot to bring it. Actually, I discovered early on that I really didn't need the cup. The Holy Spirit seemed to bless my work and answer my prayers regardless of whether or not I had the cup. I guess it's..."

The pope nodded, smiling, as he interrupted. "I'm not surprised. God works through *His* creation, not the creations of man." The pontiff hesitated, "You do realize the significance of this?"

"Most of the time I'm scared to death, Holy Father. I don't understand why this was given to me, of all people. I'm not deserving. I was comfortable growing up in a middle class family. And yet I've always found fault, with the Church, my family, with my country, and with Christianity in general. I often feel despair. As strange as it may sound, I doubt what I'm doing. Sometimes I think I'm crazy."

"Of course you do!" said the pope, with emphasis, a broad smile on his face. "That's part of it. What you describe is identical to the trials of hundreds of other saints and holy people through the ages who doubted themselves and their faith. My goodness, Father Lopez, please never doubt yourself or the God that has gifted you. He has placed a very heavy burden on you, but you have performed beautifully. I will sing your praises until the day I die."

The pope stretched. "I feel quite refreshed. Actually, I feel hungry. Haven't felt like eating in days." The pontiff turned toward the ruins. The Zapatistas milled about, some sitting in the shade of the forest umbrella or the area of fallen, tumbled stone and black, lichen-covered rocks. The two men who had captured and tormented him lay dead on the ground. The pontiff could not recall how they died. He knew he should pray for them, and he would, but not yet. He vaguely remembered a large, dark-haired man cutting him down, giving him water, and trying to talk to him. Maybe it was a hallucination, he didn't know, but he wished that man well wherever he was, because he had helped save Pope Lucas' life.

****

Balaam, Marcos, and David Wolf gathered around the pontiff, touching him, apologizing and expressing amazement. This man had been near death only minutes before, but now was walking, talking, and smiling. And, of course, it made no sense whatsoever.

David, a confirmed atheist, was baffled. Totally incongruent. It looked like a miracle, and in the professor's world, miracles did not occur. Cause and effect, reason and logic, and common sense had long been his operating system.

Magic cups, virgin births, and miraculous healing were nothing more than fairy-tales passed down to validate magic and myth. All religions required belief, the acceptance of a "reality" not supported by facts. He had never been able to fathom why so many people were eager to do so. And yet here stood Lucas, hale and hearty.

Balaam planted his cane into the earth. "Is go time. Is rain soon come," he said in his broken Spanish. "Father Lopez, *ahua* Papa go Yaxchilan. Leave soldier bring wife. Go Lacanja. Leave Big Papa. All is over, end," he stated with finality, thumping his staff in emphasis. "You have book...you see Holy Man. Over. All thing." David nodded agreement. It was time get the pope back to Lacanja, on a helicopter, and out of Chiapas.

"You call airplane. He gestured to Marcos. The helicopter would be summoned to the same location to pick up the pope and transport him back to San Cristobal de las Casas.

"You have telephone? Call fly man?" asked Balaam.

Marcos nodded an affirmative and reached for his phone to see if he had enough bars up to call.

Balaam continued. "Meet Big Papa same later."

"I no walk now," said the Bone Man. "Tired, take boat. Ride stupid van Lacanja." And he turned to descend the steps down to the sandbar and river. He moved stiffly, paused briefly to look at the crocodiles, poked the big bull with his cane and harrumphed. Marcos rushed down the stairs to help the old man onto the sandbar and into the tourist boat that carried them across the river from Yaxchilan.

A half hour later, all were aboard and moving upstream. Spectacular wheels of light incandesced across the water. Cavorting birds trailed the boat, hoping for a bit of refuse or food to fall into their hungry beaks. The rain had come and gone, lasting only ten minutes, but bringing cool air from the mountains. The smell of ozone generated by lightning remained strong, and the jungle was coming to life again.

David cradled the priceless cylinders in his arms. Holding the muddy, stepped-upon, relics hurt his shoulder, but the pain did not matter. These miraculous survivors of the 1st Century were the impetus for all the disasters of the past day and he was not going to let them go. Meanwhile, as they had climbed into the boat, the pope had gravely thanked David for gathering the cylinders. Now, all the pope's attention was on Father Salvador Lopez. Perhaps, that was as it should be, but David, still the doubter, preferred materials to miracles. Perhaps he should ask the young priest to heal his shoulder and see what happened. David brushed some mud from what was likely the most important find of his career. *Almost over*, he said to himself. He hadn't lost the spiritual leader of millions of people. Rather, the kind, likable old man was right up front, under David's eye. The pope was saved, the Holy Man doing very well, and Marcos was on the phone making everything right as they rode up the river. At present, David felt as good as anyone might in his situation. Such incredible drama, and now resolution and return to normalcy – he hoped. The professor smiled. Things could be – and had been – much worse. He guessed that he would just have to wait and strangle Balaam Reyes on another day.

Chapter Twenty Five

David watched Balaam wearily collapse onto a stool in the shade of a giant ceiba tree near forest's edge outside the village of Lacanja. The Bone Man grimaced and slumped with fatigue, impatient and looking as if he wished he was somewhere else. This was not the vigorous, indomitable shaman David remembered. Balaam remained intimidating, issuing instructions, making demands and sending people scurrying. The old man glanced about impatiently and barked at Marcos. He maintained an ongoing conversation in dialect with his son regarding orders given earlier that did not appear to have been fulfilled. Marcos glanced at his watch and explained that the helicopter was not due for thirty minutes. Balaam seemed even more upset that a troop of Zapatistas led by Antonio had not yet arrived. Why was the shaman upset at their absence? David decided this was the shaman's puzzle and he was determined not to involve himself in another Bone Man intrigue.

The storm had passed and the warming air released the odor of compost from the damp jungle soil. The tranquil hours just before sunset crept upon them and a red-orange corona struggled impotently behind the distant sierras. Soon it would succumb and enter the nightly void to do battle with demons.

David had called Alexandra. After a few short moments of panic, she quickly agreed to pick up and take him into the nearby town of Palenque, named after the famous classic ruin, to see a physician. The pope would be safely on the helicopter, returning to his worried entourage, and continue with his international obligations. Or, perhaps if she hurried, Alexandra could meet him. She would like that. David wasn't looking forward to having his arm doctored. It was scabbing over, but was swollen, red and furious. He hoped antibiotics and a few stitches would set him right.

A cry from the forest, back up the trail toward Lacanja village, caught his attention. Balaam, smiling, stood and slammed his walking stick onto the ground, a sign of approval. He issued a directive and two Zapatistas ran toward the shout. They assisted Antonio and his men to carry a long, rectangular mahogany box into the clearing. They set it gently down, and Balaam called out to his friend. The others remained protectively around the box while the tired Antonio walked to receive a hearty embrace.

Oh, no, thought David. *Can't be. Isn't possible. Is that what I think it is?* He listened intently to their conversation, but most of it was in dialect. The clearing buzzed with curiosity. Balaam ordered the lid removed and waved for Fr. Lopez and the pope to come near. Father Lopez, aghast, watched the pope approach the box.

"Last *regalo,* last gift, friend *ahua* Papa." The shaman thumped his stick.

Antonio's men easily removed the lid. David drew closer, pretty sure what he would see. He recognized him immediately - the old Holy Man - the one discovered by Fr. Lopez three years previous beneath an old Jesuit church, and it still looked as if he had died only two hours ago, if such a circumstance was possible. Some, including the pope, thought the body to be St. Thomas, the inquiring apostle who had disappeared from the written record many years after Christ's death. This was the body and original funeral box lost in Fr. Gregory's tragic wreck three years ago. David recognized the well-built mahogany structure with its spectacularly engraved Mayan *Kulkulkan*, the Feathered Serpent, sinuously encircling the chest. This was the box that held seven wooden cylinders, containing papyrus writings and the famous cup that Balaam Reyes had given Father Lopez. This burial chest had caused all the trouble of the past few days and everyone, except obviously Balaam Reyes, had thought it lost for all time. But against so many odds, the Bone Man and his people had searched the sheer, nearly unscalable mountainsides to recover these artifacts – an almost impossible feat.

A gift? The shaman had said. *What a gift!* How had the shaman pulled this off? The body still resisted rot and putrification, something that greatly disturbed the professor. Unknown methods of body preservation? If so the archaeologist knew of no other example. And, the Maya religion was not obsessed with living forever. When you were dead, you were dead and moved on into the spirit world. Kindly creatures or demons awaited you.

This was the ancient man that the archaeologist believed was celebrated in the Xibalba cave where his friend and colleague (and Marcos' former lover), Karen, still excavated. The old Holy Man was painted on the walls in the Xibalba cave. Shown in Maya regalia, this east European, his features recognizable as the body in front of David, was the obvious focus of attention in a limestone cavern filled with ancient paintings and glyphs commemorating historical events of nearly two thousand years ago.

If this was the body of St. Thomas, it was two thousand years old. Absolutely stunning. What had given this old Holy Man such a very long life and even more incredible after life? David would love to run a Carbon 14 dating analysis on it or the wood of the box to determine its age.

The pope grasped the cross hanging at his neck, looked to Marcos and then to Father Lopez. "What have we here?" he inquired. "Is this…" the pontiff hesitated, seeing the perfectly preserved human form. He swallowed and tried again. "Is this the…er, corpse, the body lost by Father Gregory?"

"It is," confirmed, Salvador, and both Marcos and David nodded assent. "I'm the one who discovered it," offered Fr. Lopez.

"Of course you did," agreed the pope. "You are the man who succeeded him, who assumed his mission of bringing the Word to these people. You were supposed to discover him."

Father Lopez's face went blank, then skewed with consternation as he contemplated the pontiff's words. His discovering the old Holy Man's body in the catacombs beneath the ruined Jesuit church might not have been an accident? The Mexican priest had avoided considering it, but the pope asserted it as an obvious truth.

The shaman interjected. "Balaam understand." His long cane pounded the earth. "Balaam see know snake with feathers Dream World. See old Holy Man, see new Holy man. Look see snake on box." The Bone Man pointed to the embossed *Kulkulkan*, the Feathered Serpent of Mexico's ancient civilizations. The serpent wrapped gracefully around the burial box. "Is same all feathers snake," he gestured toward Fr. Lopez, then paused to remember the correct term. "Feathered Serpent is spirit animal Father Lopez, old Holy Man. Balaam understand."

"Is gift," the shaman continued, motioning expansively with his walking cane. "Balaam to amigo ahua Papa. I no want. Zapatista no want. Is problem all time. Old *Hombre Sagrado* bring Ladinos and shit Mexican soldier. Go home Papa Jesus town. *Ahua* Papa now have book. Have body. Have friend Father Lopez. Time go…now soon soon." His cane thumped the ground yet again.

The pontiff stood mesmerized, looking into the mahogany casket. Tears streaked his face and David turned from the pontiff to consider the "saint" in the box. The archeologist saw a man who appeared to be of Middle Eastern ancestry: long black hair, prominent nose, not unlike that of many Mayans. He was dressed in typical Mexican *campesino* clothing, and David chuckled – a black armband, the sign of the Zapatista Rebellion - was tied to his left forearm. *I guess he's been recruited?* The absurd concept nearly made David bark with laughter and he stepped back to control himself.

The pope, overcome with emotion, turned to Father Lopez, Marcos, and finally Balaam and gave heartfelt embraces to all. When he turned to do the same with David, the professor held up a hand and pointed to his shoulder, offering a hand instead and the pontiff grasped it with both of his, muttering earnest thanks.

"Is come fly man? I hear plane?" the Bone Man inquired.

"No," said Marcos. Looking up and listening intently. He scanned the horizon.

"I go," said Balaam to the pope. "You be friend Zapatista. Leave Zapatista. No problem now ever, yes?"

"I will do everything in my power to ensure that you are not bothered, my friend. I will speak to Bishop Ruiz in San Cristobal, I have already agreed to talk with Father Lopez's family in Guadalajara."

"*Ahua* Ruiz good man. Zapatista friend. Not stupid Ladino." The shaman turned and barked orders to the few soldiers attending him. He thumped his stick, and then said with finality, "All good, you, I go."

David sighed with relief. The shaman was a walking apocalypse, consumed with Machiavellian schemes. Because of the shaman's misadventures and plans gone astray over the years, David had been stabbed in the Xibalba Cave, thrown in jail for a week, and now shot by robbers on the Usumacinta. Getting away from him was the best outcome David could imagine. In this time of miracles, perhaps the old shaman would develop a bad case of constipation, or least a case of severe, agonizing gout for all the misery he had caused the professor. This last thought made the archaeologist giggle, again. He felt goofy. What was wrong with him? Must be the loss of blood combined with all the excitement.

The Bone Man turned to leave, but took only a few steps before turning back. He thumped his cane on the ground twice, seemingly agitated, then pointed his walking stick at the archaeologist. "*Ahua* David. More *regalo*...more gift. I know cave. Many great Maya king. *Parque Nacional de Montes Azules*. You want, you have." He thumped his cane twice more, impatient for an answer.

WTF, thought David. The shaman was offering him an old Mayan tomb with several bodies? With Mayan kings? *Not possible,* he thought. *Another Bone Man trick? A ruse to use him in another of the shaman's scheme?*

"No want? Okay. You lose." The Bone Man abruptly turned to leave.

"Wait!" called out the professor. He moved a few steps toward the cantankerous shaman. "Listen...Balaam. Why? Why now? Why would you show me after all these years?"

"Loggers come, *ahua*," he spun his staff in frustration. "Ladinos, roads, Mexican government, shit soldier. No safe. Nothing safe. Everything be lost. Is good place...is *sagrado*, you know? *Sagrado* Maya. Is reason give old *Hombre Sagrado*, amigo papa. No safe. Only problem." He sighed, looked to the professor and pointed with his staff. "You fix arm. You talk friend Antonio, you tell...say you ready old cave, okay?" And he turned and walked away, bent with age and fatigue, and as much an enigma to the professor as he had ever been.

Well crap, thought the professor. *Maybe I'll wait until tomorrow to strangle him and see if he actually shows me this tomb of his.* David had spent little time in *El Parque Nacional de Montes Azules,* as any development or archaeology was discouraged and even prohibited. It was basically what remained of the pristine, ancient Lacandon Jungle, now reduced to several hundred square miles. Maybe he could change that? Maybe he could make one more discovery before retiring?

"Awck, I hear it," called Marcos. He searched the sky. "There," he pointed. The distinctive rapid chop of blades grew loud as the helicopter flew closer, appearing in silhouette and backlit by a blue-coral haze streaking the sierras. In two minutes it landed, very near to the previous location of two days ago. The blades slowed and the side door opened. Marcos extended his hand to the pontiff, but the pontiff pulled the Zapatista into an embrace. The pope reached out and took David's hand. The pontiff's grip was strong, too strong for an elderly, diabetic man who had suffered the abuses of the past 24 hours. Miracles? David clenched his jaw to push down a rising light-headedness.

The noise and wind of the helicopter blades buffeted them all as the pope reached with both arms to embrace Father Lopez.

"I brought you something," David thought he overheard. "I'm sure you would like to have it, and I really don't need it." Father Lopez placed an old, gray, chipped cup into the pope's extended hands.

"Is that the...is this what I think it is?" He gently cradled the gift.

"I can only say for sure that it was removed from the burial casket of my predecessor here, in the box," he pointed to the old Holy Man. "Balaam Reyes recovered both. When he offered it, I had no idea what it was or its significance. The...er...uh, miracles started occurring right away, when I first used it. I thought it was the cup. The thought that the healer was me was too scary to consider. Actually, the thought never even occurred to me until later when I forgot the cup and used something else. I don't know its true worth other than reflecting the fruits of the faith to those wishing to see their beliefs mirrored back to them."

The pope took a deep breath, then smiled. He said, "Thank you, thank you, thank you Salvador! You are so wise for such a young man. You are indeed a holy man. Be assured that I will support your work and tell your story until the day I die." Using as much care as he would with a newborn infant, the pope gently placed the cup inside his tote bag beside his bible. The wooden cylinders nested on the other side of the Holy Bible.

Father Lopez laughed. "You know, that's great. I'll probably never know, and it's probably best that way – it's just a distraction." He paused, then said, "Er...is it okay to remind you about my parents? You know, have someone talk with them?"

"I will do it personally, Father Lopez. Be assured, my friend. I promise. It's the least that I can do." The pope kissed his index and middle fingers and touched them to Salvador

Lopez's forehead. "Bless you, Father Lopez, although I feel a blessing from you would carry infinitely more value. Your mission has afforded me great adventure, tremendous insight, and more knowledge of myself and the workings of God than I thought possible at this age." The pontiff chuckled, "Being in charge of the Vatican will be a piece of cake after this."

****

Antonio and his men finished wrestling the burial box into the helicopter. The pope and Father Lopez walked under the blades and the young priest helped the old one into the craft. The door slid shut as Marcos finished his conversation with the Indian pilot. The blades revved and picked up speed.

The navigator turned and looked into the back until he caught pope's eye. "You didn't tell me you were the pope last time," accused the smiling aviator.

"I'm so sorry," grinned the pope. "I apologize. Are you Catholic?"

"Uh no...not at all Pope, er...sir...er...your majesty. I'm Protestant."

"All good. It's been suggested to me by my friend, Angelina that I need to broaden my mind away from orthodoxy and dogma if I want to be a deep and true thinker. I'm attempting to do so."

"Yeah," agreed the pilot, philosophically. "I've had couple of women like that too." He studied his dashboard and revved the engine, then waved to the archaeologist and his Zapatista friends before hauling on the collective to begin lifting the huge, ungainly machine into the air. "We're off," he cried loudly.

They were up, then off, rapidly over the corrugated roofs and warren of huts that was Lacanja. The pope waved farewell to some of the finest people he had ever met as the helicopter flew resolutely toward the distant cordillera through a sky that changed from coral, to dark blue, returning to its nightly battle.

Pope Lucas, overcome by the past two days, fell into fervent prayer. Well into the flight, he began to consider what awaited him in San Cristobal, then Mexico City and finally on his flight home the next day. Had his good friend Sor Juana written again? He was anxious for news of her personal adventures as well as detail on the normal plotting and scheming that consumed the Vatican.

Before leaving, he must have what he believed was a 'meaningful' conversation with Bishop Ruiz of the San Cristobal Archdiocese. He had promised the Bone Man that the bishop would not make changes at the Chamula "Catholic" Church, or send new priests without the Indian's permission. They like the ones they have. It took a while to break them in to the Mayan version of Christianity. The pope rested his hand on the rough sarcophagus, the wonder of its incredible contents, and the contents of his tote bag, filling his mind. Much remained to do. This would be a difficult conversation, but with God's help and the fact that he was the pope, he would convince the bishop that the Indians liked the priests they had. If God didn't help him with the conversation, Pope Lucas would have to make it an order. This trip, Father Lopez and the miracles, including the Pope's own healing, had convinced him to leave the Mayan version of Catholicism alone, at least for now.

About forty-five minutes later the pope crouched forward and craned his neck to better see out the window into the distance. He felt restless and moved about in his seat. An immense relief cloaked him as he realized that he was nearly back to his temporary home and the safety of his entourage and friend Cardinal Montoya. As the evening gray fled to be replaced by a darkness sprinkled with stars, the helicopter topped the eastern edge of the Sierra Madre *cordillera* and descended into the highland valley that contained the colonial town of San Cristobal de las Casas with its red tile roofs and white stucco colonial homes.

The whole city was lit up, and street lights from the four main roads leading to the zocalo and cathedral shone brightly and were lined with people. People sat in sidewalk cafes, eating and drinking, greeting friends and acquaintances parading through the streets. They took pictures and laughed and kissed and sometimes went to dance the samba in corner bars. Mayan matrons in beautifully smocked blouses, herded their children, encouraging them to help sell their homemade products. They approached dining tables and pestered tourists, hawking beautifully embroidered textiles to anyone who would listen or suffer their sales spiel. Life returned to normal, or at least some semblance thereof.

The helicopter hovered briefly, then sat lightly onto the red soil. "We're here, your majesty. Hope you had a great trip!" intoned the pilot.

Chapter Twenty Six

Sor Juana

Holy Father, your email since leaving for Mexico has been too brief and spotty at best. Are you okay? Of course not. You're out dashing around Mexico like Pizzaro after Atahualpa, pursuing Conquistador gold like a charade of Don Quixote tilting at windmills, challenging anyone who impedes your way. Okay, enough metaphors, but a tired aphorism is in order. All that glitters is not gold, Lucas. Although many doubt you are still alive, I have enough faith to write what I've been thinking the last couple of weeks, and then maybe end with a short note regarding my affection for Gunther, which is something I've learned I'm not terribly good at.

Actually, Holy Father, I feel that I have been denied affection for much of my life. I know there are many types of affection, but we all have to find those forms most satisfying to us. Although I cherish our correspondence, it will never replace the satisfaction humans feel from the physical presence and touching of those we care about when being hugged or intimate. Even lower primates spend hours each day grooming others and being groomed, maintaining feelings of tenderness and belonging. This may sound self-indulgent, but in hindsight I'm pretty sure that the choices presented to me as a young girl were not the only ones available.

You know, Lucas, I'm tired tonight after visiting so late with Gunther. I had planned an in-depth rant to upset your carefully constructed, but fragile psychic constructs regarding sex, the bible, the Catholic Church, as opposed to sex as it actually occurs in real life. But I'm not really in the mood. Why? I don't know anything about sex other than what I've read in a book or what I overheard my sniggering brothers laughing about when they didn't know I was listening. Sex isn't pretty, but it's fascinating in a clever sort of way. It's fueled by hormones and very primal and uncontrollable – and natural. An itch that feels good that must be scratched – sometimes again and again. Lucas, every time I see Gunther I want to be close to him, have his arms wrapped around me. I feel an urgency that I really should be doing something. It isn't clear what that is. But I have suspicions, and I've decided I'm going to do it a lot when my suspicions are confirmed.

Anyway, here's the situation, Lucas. I took vows. It's a serious thing, I know. I feel as if I was coerced and manipulated. I'm sure everyone in the family viewed me as a problem; the troublesome, irritating little sister that wanted to know everything and thought too logically. Get her out of sight and out of mind. 'That girl is difficult to be around. She'll have a tough time finding a husband.' Lucas, if I wasn't so filled with Christian charity and courtesy, I'd tell you what those people can go do to themselves. But now I guess I'm judgmental. I'm being a bitch. Isn't what men say when women feel out of sorts, or have an opinion? She's being a bitch?

So, I've made a decision. I have decided to renounce my vows with the Dominicans. I know you'll believe that it's because of Gunther, but the reasons I've discovered are deeper and very personal. I'm going to do this whether or not Gunther decides to be there for me. He doesn't even know at this point. I've lived in the world of men as a submissive female that is beholden to men for everything I have. I'm a second class citizen, and I don't like it. I don't know how to fix it, or if I should, but I'm taking some time off to think about it. Unfortunately, I'll likely be living at the Salvation Army Shelter in Rome very soon. Although there were times I thought you were just trying to show me how smart you were, Lucas, insisting that I read those hundred fifty books. I know now that you saw something in me that my family never did, and I thank you for that. You are the definition of a good friend. If you're still alive, my friend, I hope that you will stay in contact with me during this big adventure in my life. You've always been there for me before.

Your friend and kindred spirit,
Sor Juana

P.S.

I just learned that Cardinal Cardona had a brainstem stroke last night while visiting a male friend over near the Palatine Hill. He was moved to hospice today. His family was notified and the place is buzzing with speculation regarding his replacement. You won't be surprised that I have some ideas myself. There will be a state level funeral in St. Peter Basilica as Satan's Purser was an important man here. I will send condolences on your behalf, since it appears you're never coming home. No doubt the Iranians and drug cartels will do the same. I wonder what they will do now that Cardona isn't available to launder their dirty money through our Vatican Bank. Everyone has problems and challenges, don't they?

****

Six security men surrounded the pope as he climbed out of the helicopter. As Cardinal Montoya reached for both of the pontiff's hands, he smiled. The cardinal led the pope out of the wash of the helicopter.

"Are you well?"

"Better than I should be," assured Lucas, "and do I have a story to tell!"

The sarcophagus and body were totally unexpected. Lucas directed his alarmed security detail to unload the casket and carry it through the same back gate from which the pontiff had departed, and quickly and quietly place it in his bedroom. The pontiff had no qualms at all about sharing a room with a man who might be St. Thomas.

Upon returning (also through the back gate), Montoya and Lucas, moving with an alacrity at odds with everyone's expectations, followed the mahogany box with its winding, feathered serpent into his room. Lucas thanked his security detail, waved them off and firmly shut the door, then presented the unimaginable to Montoya, who seemed like a child in a candy store. The cardinal reacted with emotions ranging from awe and disbelief to gleeful chortling as the pope displayed his Christian treasures. Montoya could not refrain from touching the cylinders, the cup, and especially the uncorrupted body. A stunning haul and completely unexpected.

Montoya's eyes glistened with affection and relief. "Lucas, I have always known you are a very unusual man and I always believed you were the only person who could lead our Church into the 21st Century. But this...." He gently touched the dead saint's cheek, "...is beyond expectation, even fantasy. I will never doubt you again, or at least try not to. I just can't believe it." He looked at this friend and smiled, then frowned. "Is that a scar over your left eye? It's quite noticeable. I don't recall ever seeing a scar on your face."

The pope sighed. "Look, I must call on Bishop Ruiz to apologize for my disappearance. I also have a promise to keep before I forget, or lose my courage." The pope stood and walked to his friend and put an arm around his shoulders.

"Montoya, when I get back from meeting Bishop Ruiz, I'm going to tell you a story. You can't tell anyone else, okay? Not without my permission. Frankly, no one will believe it anyway." Pope Lucas saw his friend's eyebrows arch in anticipation, then he moved toward the door.

"One more thing, my friend. Are we still flying to Mexico City tomorrow morning, then leaving for Rome tomorrow night?"

"All is arranged, Holy Father. I assumed that you were as good as your word and that you would return to us intact."

"It seems that everyone has more faith in me than I have in myself, except for Angelina, of course. God bless her."

Cardinal Montoya scooted from the room to set up a meeting with the bishop. Pope Lucas walked to the small altar against the wall, knelt and gave thanks for the wonders in his life; the challenges, the work still to be done, the friends, and the hardships he had endured that brought lessons. He prayed his heartfelt thanks that the horrors and joys of the past few days were behind him. It was enough. At the end of his life, he would be able to say he had lived a complete life, tried to make the world a better place, and given his best effort. If you can do that, he mused, your conscience is clear.

****

Luis had driven into the night, straight home without stopping – an exhausting 8 hours. It had taken at least six more Xanax to calm him. The events of the day had upset his equilibrium and depleted his macho persona. He didn't feel tough today – he felt guilty, he felt dirty, and he was tired. Old heartfelt values from childhood, long suppressed, had reasserted themselves.

He stood in his doorway looking to the street and sidewalks as people came and went, scurrying about in a desperate effort to keep food on the table, clothes on their children, and a roof over their heads. Tapachula always looked the same: skeletal, mangy yellow dogs, scrounging for a morsel, dirty cracked stucco homes, dead cars mounted on concrete blocks, gang members with tattooed faces and distant stares, and the ever-present odor of rotting meat and diesel exhaust. Enough was enough. Tomorrow morning he would go to Cuca's and they were going to have a very serious talk. His grandson was not going to grow up in a place like this. It wasn't going to happen. Luis had saved or stolen plenty of money and he had decided that the only thing worthy to spend it on was family. He wasn't happy…hadn't been in twenty years, but this last escapade had pushed him over the edge. That old priest in the jungle, that Father Lucas at the ruin on the Usumacinta River had totally blown his socks off. Luis had done a lot of really bad things in his life, but leaving that old priest, possibly to die, flooded the *sicario* with guilt like never before. '*Guilt is good*,' a priest had once told him. '*If you feel guilt, you're not a sociopath.*' So, maybe he wasn't a sociopath. But he had to get right with God and his small family – whether either liked it or not.

This afternoon he would visit a travel agency and make plans for a family vacation to Costa Rica. Everyone - Cuca, his grandson, and the silly-assed musician who kept impregnating his daughter were going on a trip for a couple of weeks. If all went well, they would stay. The *sicario* was calling it quits before a bullet with his name on it retired him.

Luis knew deep in his bones that it was time to quit the life - to get his family and get out. It was the only real option, but anxiety gnawed at his soul. The sicario was troubled and in need of solace. He would stop by the church this morning.

He could think without interruption there and plan what he must say to his daughter. The church was one of the few places he felt respite and safety. He stroked each narco saint in sequence. *Help me out guys*, he pleaded, silently. *I've never needed you as much as I do now.*

Chapter Twenty Seven

(Two Weeks Later)

"How's the shoulder, David?" inquired Marcos. "You seem to be doing okay."

"All is well," asserted the professor. "Really stiff and sore for about a week, but the stitches are out and I have full mobility. I'm a very lucky man."

"Yes...very lucky. Crazy time. I still don't know what to think of it."

For two hours they had walked shady Indian paths, crossed tangles of bramble, and listened to unseen animals scurry in the underbrush. Above, velvet shadows of gray-black stretched long and eerie as the remnants of a morning thunderstorm dissipated and blew east toward the Yucatan. Humidity made the air heavy. In the forest canopy, a horde of Howler monkeys had pursued them the last hour, screaming simian curses and throwing sticks and leaves. *El Parque Nacional de Montes Azules* was some of the last remaining pristine jungle in existence, as any development was prohibited. It remained in stasis, a reminder to those who cared of the world where the ancient Maya must had worked, played, made love, and built incredible stone cities, all the while engaged in hundreds of years of near-constant warfare.

An entourage of Zapatistas rhythmically swung machetes to clear trails, toted supplies of food and water, and served as grips to move stone and forest when called upon. They would spend the day and night, and then return tomorrow to civilization after the professor had viewed the contents of the ancient tomb promised by the Bone Man. Balaam couldn't make it. He had sent word that he was ill, but ordered Marcos to attend. This seemed to please the young Zapatista, as he was a former student of David's at UNAM, the national university in Mexico City, and like his teacher, treasured his country's deep history.

"I don't know if you can talk about it, but I heard on the news this morning that El Presidente declared a truce of sorts with the Zapatistas. He said they will give you some of what you ask for: more autonomy, make your own rules in the Indian villages without interference, a little more development money to teach how to grow cash crops – a very "hands-off" approach."

"Yeah, but the fort in the middle of the Lacandon stays. Pisses me off," replied Marcos.

"I also hear that there's no longer a price on your head. That's no small thing?"

The Zapatista smiled, "That's a good thing, professor. It's been a lot of years since I could move about freely."

"What are you planning to do? What will happen to the Zapatistas? Will they go away?"

"Never...not as long as I'm involved," Marcos stated firmly. "Tons of work yet to do. I'm thinking about taking a walk."

"A walk. What kind of walk?"

"Around the country – all of Mexico, David. See everything, everyone and try to stir up interest in the condition of the Indians here and around the world. I suspect there are many people who would join our movement if we can bring it out of the jungle into the mainstream. We plan to go global, if we can find the resources. Indigenous communities all over the world are being abused and robbed of their heritage and natural resources by big corporations and corrupt governments. They're just like the Maya here in the highlands."

"I support you one hundred percent, Marcos, you know that."

"Yes, and I am grateful. There may be others who will involve themselves, too. I hope."

David stopped again to take water and wipe the sweat from his brow. He was in good condition for a 65-year-old man, but the jungle was hot and the walk long. David took a deep breath and glanced around, it all looked the same to him. Jungle. The Zapatista general stopped a moment, looked around, then said, "We're very close, I'm sure," he insisted. "Haven't been here for years, but Antonio was here just a couple of weeks ago. He knows the jungle like you do your backyard."

Their guide, Antonio cried out, and they hurried to catch up with the old Indian. He pointed at a makeshift, abandoned camp site in front of a rolling hill piled with brush and stone. To David's practiced eye, the stone and weeds appeared incongruent with the surroundings.

"That's it. We're here," gestured Marcos. He issued orders to his Zapatista soldiers and they commenced moving stone from the hillside. Soon the low, oval outline of an entrance appeared. A cave!

The professor felt his heart pound. Pretty cool, he thought. After all these years I can still get excited about stuff.

When the workers stood aside, Marcos called for another lantern. With Antonio and his torch leading the way, Marcos and David stooped and entered the cave. Light flickered, casting capricious shadows while David's eyes slowly adjusted. Straight ahead in the middle of the cavern lay a stone altar topped with a line of grinning skulls, a few missing jawbones. Empty *posh* bottles, long deteriorated food, and piles of copal incense ash to send prayers into the ether of the supernatural world, were strewn along the altar. People like the curandero Balaam visited this place. Still-colorful Mayan glyphs with flaking, decaying paint lined the walls.

Crap, thought David. *Torches are bad in this enclosed space. They'll smudge, maybe ruin the paint. Need to get better equipment and return.* Leaning on the wall to the right, he saw several stelae - tall, ancient stone tablets with incised writing, commemorating special events: wars, victories, the erection of religious buildings and pyramids, etc. They must have been transported here for safe keeping, perhaps salvaged by the Bone Man in his travels through the jungle the last sixty years. David caught his breath and let it out slowly, trying to calm himself. *What a story this place will tell.*

David felt his legs trembling and realized that he had forgotten to breathe. Some of the glyphs appeared to be proto-Mayan, perhaps Olmec. But they had never come this far south of the gulf coast had they? The archaeologist stood in awe, sensing ancient voices hinting at unknown secrets, teasing him with the gift of knowledge denied others. He felt he had entered another time and place and that he was in a foreign country or different time and era surrounded by an unknown culture. This, he knew, was to be his new home for the next several years. The excitement of finding new treasures energized his mind.

You know, he thought, rather kindly. *Maybe I won't have to strangle Balaam after all.* He wondered what had been in the cavern originally and what the Bone Man had added and deposited over the years. It appeared that the irascible, cranky old man was paying a debt to the professor – or at least that's how David decided he would understand it. Age and Mother Nature were having their way with the old shaman and he believed David was the one who would properly care for this sacred space in the rigors of the modern world. Nonetheless, the Bone Man's parting gift was surprising, substantial, and very, very valuable, and David was grateful.

****

Luis and his family – a daughter, grandson, and the musician impregnating his daughter – had been in Costa Rica for over a week. The first two days in this two-bedroom house near the Pacific Ocean in the coastal town of *Punta Arenas*, Sandpoint, had been full of rancorous arguments with his daughter, over lifestyle and the unnecessary death of her mother, for which she blamed him. The boyfriend spent the first two days searching the town for a bag of marijuana. Then anger and frustration seemed to subside and it all came together. They were doing okay now. The marijuana secured, a couple of six-packs of beer in the fridge, and eating out twice a day had relieved the hard edge of close living arrangements. He was certain that he had seen her smile this morning for the first time in a week. The boyfriend, Emilio, was smiling too. Apparently, the infant grandson and Luis were the only ones not getting laid on vacation, but that was okay. The *sicario* wasn't here to chase women. He was here for his family. Maybe with time, safety, and comfort, Cuca could learn to forgive him?

Luis decided he liked this Costa Rica place a lot. He'd heard about it for years and it seemed to live up to the hype. Could he convince his daughter to move here? He would have to try. The thought of Tapachula and returning to the *sicario* life gave him an extreme case of the heebie jeebies. His nerve was gone. He was done. Better a bullet in the head than a life of a cartel soldier.

Luis stood with a bottle of beer in hand at the fishing docks below the condos. He sipped and enjoyed yet another brilliant sunset of coral and turquoise. He liked watching the boats come and go. He had watched every morning as they loaded nets, buoys, gaffs, and supplies, and then returned at late evening with their catch. Had a nice rhythm to it. Looked like hard work, but uncomplicated. Just you, the ocean, and the fish. No one to kill or cheat, or lie to.

He turned when he heard a voice.

"Pretty nice, eh, amigo?"

"Yeah, a guy could get used to it," Luis agreed, taking a swig from the bottle. He eyed the man who approached. Khaki pants, belt, clean deck shoes, and a Panama hat for the sun. He reeked of prosperity – probably had an education, too.

"You a fisherman, amigo?"

"Nope."

"You a business man?"

Luis turned and gave him a hard stare. Nosy bastard, but said, "Yeah sort of. I'm in the shipping business back home."

The man noticed Luis' forearms. "I see, well…" he began to wander away.

"But I'm retired," said Luis.

"Retired, *señor*?" His new acquaintance smiled. "You must be very successful. You are a young man."

Luis smiled noncommittedly, "I do okay, you know."

The man stepped closer. "Lots of fishing in these waters. You know how to fish, *señor*?"

"Could be. I spent some years fishing with my dad out of a small skiff up in Sinaloa around Culiacan when I was a kid. Maybe you've heard of it?"

"I think most people have heard of Culiacan, *señor*. But you don't fish now?"

"No. I joined the army for three years when I was young. Not a good job, but I learned a lot about discipline and military stuff - you know."

"I think I do, *señor*." The man smiled, glancing again at Luis' forearms.

They conversed at length, Luis attempting to reveal little about himself. He preferred looking at the beautiful sunset and considered how great it would be to see one every single night for the rest of his life. The thought filled him with discontent and melancholy regarding his present situation in Mexico. He would talk to Cuca. She and her boyfriend must agree to live here with him. She could sing here in Punta Arenas. Great town; clean streets, ocean breezes, bustling tourist economy, and no tattoo-faced *Maras*, gangs, on every street corner. Everybody liked Tejano and Bolero music didn't they? He would pass her demo CD's around. The stoner boyfriend, Emilio, could go blow his fucking horn in a local band – probably a hundred of them in a town this size with all these tourists – and Luis would help raise his grandson. They could make it work. Luis wouldn't even go back to Mexico. Very dangerous if someone spotted him. He had plenty of money. His lawyer could sell his house. That was another hundred grand or so that he could use to get into something nice down here. His daughter needed to grow up and see that he was not the same guy he used to be. He wasn't the "Bogey

Man". He *wanted* to be better. He was going to work very hard at being a good person.

"Well, anyway, it was good meeting you, *señor*," offered the businessman to the distracted sicario.

"Yes, you too *señor*, er…I don't think I ever heard your name."

"Bojorquez, *señor*." The man pointed, "Like the name on the fishing boats and restaurant there."

"Oh, I see, yes. Well, nice meeting you, *Señor* Bojorquez." Luis seemed a little surprised. "Good luck."

"Good day!" said the businessman, cheerfully. He removed his hat, inclining slightly toward Luis. He replaced it and turned to walk uphill towards the restaurant, but thought better of it and returned to Luis.

"I'm always looking for a good man, an honest man with experience in the world." He gave a very obvious look at Luis' forearms, then caught his eyes. "You know, someone who's been around a bit, who knows things; someone who has acquired valuable life experiences." The businessman spoke as if his meaning was clear. "If you are *really* retired," he said with emphasis, "maybe we should talk if you are looking for a job. Costa Rica is a country of opportunity you know." He smiled again, proffered a hand, which the surprised Luis accepted. Bojorquez turned and slogged uphill through the sand towards his restaurant.

WTF, thought Luis. A job? Where did that come from? He pondered the interaction a moment, then concluded that something important had just occurred. It wouldn't do him any good to move here if he just laid around and did nothing: no goals, and no hobbies. He had a grandson now. He couldn't be off drinking and whoring all the time when he was feeling low. He needed something constructive in his life – like a real job. Finding a decent woman for a companion wouldn't hurt anything either. He needed a purpose, a reason for being.

Luis recalled *Señor* Bojorquez eyeing his tats a couple of times. He glanced down at his forearms. *La Santa Muerte* and *Jesus Malverde* stared back. Maybe time for these to go if he was going to hang out in society now. He had a friend who left the *sicario* business and had converted his narco saints to dolphins. Luis was surprised at how cool they looked. Unfortunately, he recalled, his friend had foolishly returned to the game after not finding anything that paid like the cartel. He was shot dead at a small landing strip north of Los Mochis, Sinaloa six months later.

Luis felt years of stress flow from him to the magenta horizon. It faded pink, then gray as the sun lost its battle and succumbed, becoming someone else's dawn. This was the best vacation of his life. He hadn't had a Xanax in three days. A magnificent Frigate Bird soared high in the darkening sky and his hopes accompanied it. If he was going to make a stand, this tourist place was as good as any and better than most. He bet they were several nice old churches in this town. Maybe tomorrow he would go check them out. He turned and headed up the sandy beach toward Bojorquez's restaurant. No hurry to get home – no hurry to be anywhere. No hurry to do anything.

Luis entered the palapa-roofed eatery and took a seat at the bar where he could see the television and watch the locals come and go. After a couple of tequila shots, he was bored enough to leave. Nothing much on the news, and the bartender was more interested in talking to the waitress than him. He slipped off the stool, but stopped as the TV grabbed his attention. A video showed the pope's trip to Mexico. *Lucas...wasn't that the name of the old priest at the ruins?* The *sicario* grabbed the edge of the bar and stared as the Pope's picture appeared. *It was him.* Luis knew faces – even those bloody and beaten. Couldn't be, but it was. He was positive. For a moment he could barely breathe, and a ripple of liquid fear seized him. He forced himself to stroke his forearms to calm himself. He took a couple of deep breaths, and a smile tugged at his face. Maybe he had finally done something right? He had saved the pope, even though no one would ever know. Maybe God did have a plan for his life – Luis the *sicario* – the most worthless man on the planet. Maybe he *was* salvageable. God had allowed him to do something good with his life. It was like the story of the bad guy the Jews had chosen to set free instead of Jesus right before the Crucifixion – Barnaby or Badass, or something. Couldn't remember his name. Guy ended up a saint in the Church. The short news reel ended, and Luis tossed money onto the bar, waved to the bartender, and exited into the gentle night and salt air. Lightning bugs flickered and glowed over the grassy knoll above the beach. Sequined sparklers grew strong and numerous in the velvet sky, and a cloud passed over the moon, a glowing halo in search of a holy person.

Luis walked with a spring in his step, and began to hum a melody from his daughter's CD that recalled joy and heartache, love and loss. The *sicario* accepted that he was going to retire from the life. He felt cheerful - an emotion foreign to him - and paused to savor it. Maybe he would stop at a church tonight instead of waiting until tomorrow? He had been taught that God was always available to those seeking the Almighty, and Luis felt the pull tonight. But it was probably too late to go to Reconciliation. Luis hadn't even tried to confess his sins for over 15 years – partly out of guilt, but mostly because he couldn't find a priest that would grant him absolution unless he gave up the *sicario* life. "God has standards," he'd been told. Yeah…well, he guessed that made a lot of sense. But all was different now. Luis could have a new life, with purpose, and hopefully forgiveness – maybe even from his daughter. That was how the system was supposed to work wasn't it? If that Barnaby-Badass, or whomever character 2,000 years ago merited it, so did Luis. With a deep breath and a satisfied sigh, he took a final look at the alabaster moon, then turned and walked toward the steeple of a nearby church he'd spotted earlier.

****

The pope was joyfully humming a song from his youth. It was 9:00 at night in the Domus Sanctae Marthae Hotel, and his Argentine friend, Angelina, not Sor Juana or Sr. Angelina, was scheduled to drop by any time. He knew she wanted to talk about her reasons for deciding to leave her vocation. He didn't disapprove, and knew that such a change would bring her pain, and talking was part of the healing process. She was a dear friend and a person, not just a nun. He loved her as one would a sister and wanted to be there for her.

The pope felt better and stronger than he had in years. He hadn't been taking his insulin. A miracle of healing had happened to him – to him! - in the jungle of Mexico. He had an obligation to not squander this precious gift. Gone was the fog and indecision brought by chronic stress and the fear of making a wrong decision. Maybe it just took longer than he had anticipated to really understand this job, but regardless, he attacked it with new fervor upon his return. Needless to say, things were hopping around the Vatican in just about every department. It was called *'accountability'* he told his staff. We have several million bosses, devoted Catholics all over the planet depending on us to do the right thing, to provide leadership, solace, and occasional joy. *'Don't forget it. This is a good thing. Get to work on it!'*

Politics remained...damnable politics. Cardinal Cardona was dispatched with ceremony and pomp at his Vatican funeral, although he probably hadn't merited it. But the renewed, reinvigorated pope could and did reassign administrative heads that had grown self-indulgent and complacent over the years. He could and did fire two whom Montoya said were stealing money, and had personally taken the keys to Cardinal Parisi's Vatican owned, luxuriously remodeled apartment. The pope sold it, giving the proceeds to the Catholic Charities. Part of Parisi's penance was that he now lived in the Domus Sanctae Marthae hotel with the pope. Of course, if Parisi wanted to use his own money, he was free to secure alternative housing. Regrettably, permanently retired, he chose not to.

A knock at the door announced his friend, Angelina, and Pope Lucas moved with alacrity to open the door and welcome her. He had a surprise for her. But as the door swung open, Pope Lucas saw that his friend appeared tired and sad. She mustered a smile and entered. With the door closed, they embraced as friends and family, not pope and petitioner. There was no ring to kiss.

"Your friend?" Inquired the pontiff.

"His daughter has a cold and, well, we didn't have time to find a babysitter."

"Come in, young lady," the pope's arm swept wide toward his living area. "I think we have many things to talk about."

"I don't know if I can talk about some of it, Lucas...er, Holy Father."

"Lucas, is fine, Angelina. It's just you and me here. Montoya is gone for the evening. The Swiss Guard won't bother us."

"I missed you so badly, and now that you're back I feel like I let my emotions get the best of me while you were gone. I had no idea how much I depended on you to maintain my stability. I'm just a crazy old woman."

Whoa! thought the pontiff. His friend was seriously depressed. With so much to do, he had neglected their friendship since returning. They had seen each other daily, but within a professional framework. They needed a major sit-down to get caught up.

"A crazy old woman?" he repeated. "Crazy maybe, but not old. You're quite young and attractive, Angelina, only thirty years of age."

She smiled. "And so it begins, the pope who wanted to be a comedian but couldn't remember which punchline to use."

"A good description of me. We've all felt failure, Angelina. At least if we are human and honest, we have. Know that I support your decision completely, whatever it is and I will not second-guess you." The pope smiled and took her hand. "Tell me, have you discussed this with the Mother Superior?"

"Several times. I wish I had come to her earlier. She's a very wise woman and has been amazingly supportive. I never expected it. When I described my family and history, she sounded as if she had heard it all before."

"I'm sure she has. The Catholic vocations: the priesthood, convents, and abbeys are all losing adherents and recruits in these times, Angelina. The Church has always relied on them as the Stormtroopers of our faith, but modern times and pressures have put us in a position where we must change or fail."

"You always were a closet heretic," she accused, benignly.

"Perhaps you should review your own writings," he countered.

"I have…and I'm very ashamed of some of them. I don't know how you've tolerated me for so long."

The pope hesitated a moment then said, "Angelina I had planned to offer you something special tonight as a reward for your hard work and diligence, not just as my aide and second conscience, but because of your academic accomplishments."

"What? But I have none. You know, I've never…"

The pope held up his hand for her to stop. "Angelina," he continued, "because I and others think you have such special abilities, I took the liberty of enrolling you in a special course of study here at the Pontifical American University. I have a…er…very good friend there, actually he's the president, who agreed to work with me after reading some of the emails that you sent me over the years. Like me, he believes you are brilliant, possibly a savant, someone who could work in a field of study they don't normally offer."

"What?" She was obviously alarmed, and stood, as if panicked. "Lucas, you're talking nonsense again. What course of study? How could you? Why didn't you tell me? My emails? Those essays will get me burnt at the stake if they're released." She looked aghast.

"No, and no, Angelina. It's time for you to accept that you have a gift and that you must make a contribution to your chosen field of study. You must put yourself out there."

"What chosen field? What have I…you, chosen for me, Lucas? This is nuts. Lucas, you've gone too far this time. Typical male behavior, blazing straight ahead, expecting the female to follow suit."

The pope ignored her. "My friend, you are receiving a Ph.D. from the Pontifical American University this spring with a special Doctorate of Letters in Gender Studies. I've been assured by the president that you have already read more books and written more meaningful essays on the subject in the last five years than most academics do in a lifetime. I have submitted several of your essays for publication and I'm sure they will be accepted. Your qualifications are not an issue. What is not certain, is whether you will accept a position offered in the Department of Social Sciences to teach newly required courses in Gender Studies. From now on, at least as long as I'm pope, all students, especially our priests in training, are required to take at least one course in gender studies. We must do a better job of preparing our religious leaders for the real world at the parish level. I strongly suspect that your classes will be so full that they will overflow into the hallways."

She said nothing for a full minute, then said, "Lucas, I'm so grateful. I'm...I'm so not capable of standing up in front of crowds and talking. I'm not an academic. I'm not deserving..." she protested, flustered.

"You will and you are, young lady." The pope used his *I'm being firm with you* voice. "I expect you to call President Smithson sometime in the next week and make arrangements to meet him, tour the University and converse with the other professors. Your pay will be the same as any other new professor just beginning their career. I believe he mentioned something in the area of 50, 000 Euros a year."

"What! They'll pay me? I get a paycheck?"

"You will no longer be dependent on a male or the Catholic Church for your livelihood or self-respect, Angelina; something I know has always chaffed you. You will pay your own bills, manage your own private affairs, and publish-or-perish with the rest of your academic brethren."

Angelina cried, silently, hand to mouth to stifle any noise. The pope looked away while she recovered, his eyes falling on a painting of the Guadalupe on his wall.

"I...I don't know what to say, Lucas. I just came by because you promised to finally tell me about your trip to Mexico. I had no idea." Angelina sat down and her sniffles subsided. "I just can't believe it."

"It's done then," the pope said with finality. "Let's get your personal life straightened out. Will it include your Gunther? That's up to you, isn't it, my friend? Please continue to meet with the Abbess for counseling."

The pope rose and went to his kitchenette. "Tea?" he asked.

She nodded assent. "Please." Angelina dabbed her eyes, looked at the framed print of the Virgin Guadalupe hanging above his altar and made the sign of the cross.

Lucas called from the kitchenette. "On a different note, Cardinal Nizzi tells me your visits to the archives are fruitful and he's never had a hobbyist such as yourself grasp material so quickly. He says that he is nearly ready to put you to work translating documents or checking the work of others."

"He lies," she joked, then added. "He's a very nice man, Lucas. And so very patient. Reminds me a bit of you." She accepted a cup from him. "I have lots to think about, Lucas. Thank you. Sincerely."

He dismissed her thanks. "You're very deserving, Angelina. Occasionally in life we get what we deserve. It's when we don't that life turns sour and spoils our ability to find joy."

"Lucas," she said.

"Yes, dear friend."

"I didn't come by for me. You've been avoiding me, been avoiding everything except work. Montoya says you've turned into an emotional chameleon. Why? What's going on? With all due respect, Lucas, why do you look so healthy and have so much more energy all of a sudden? I'm starting to hear whispers of miraculous bodies and cups and ancient books and all sorts of ridiculous stuff that can't possibly be true. You need to put the stymies on these rumors, or they will leak out and cause trouble."

He sat and placed his cup and saucer on the coffee table. "Ahhh…yes. Mexico. I wanted to sit with you and explain it all. It's just that, well, I'm still trying to sort out everything myself, Angelina. The trip didn't go at all the way I expected. Frankly, some of it was beyond horrible – beyond belief."

"Horrible? In what way? Please, you're killing me here. Tell me something!" she demanded. "You have spent countless hours with me over the years helping me keep my head screwed on right. Then you disappear for a couple a days and you won't talk about it, don't want to deal with it. I'm not leaving until you tell me. Period."

The pope grimaced. He hesitated, and then sighed and said, "Okay, yeah, well some of it maybe. I can give you a summary."

Lucas took a sip of tea and settled back. His gaze growing distant. "Mexico is the most fascinating place I've ever been," he began, "they have Indian shamans, one of whom tricked me into taking hallucinogenic psilocybin mushrooms. They have lots of bad men in drug cartels, two of whom captured and beat me and tied me to a tree at an isolated old ruin. Then another one found me and cut me down. That person gave me water, but then left me alone in the jungle with crocodiles for company. I almost died of Dengue fever, but was saved, then healed by the Holy Man, Salvador Lopez. He's a renegade priest who ministers to the Mayans, and is the greatest man I've ever known. He had an ancient cup which the Mayan shaman removed along with five ancient scrolls from the sarcophagus of an ancient old Holy Man, who may be our own St. Thomas, and whose body is with Cardinal Nizzi being examined as we speak. Fr. Lopez gave the cup to me!"

Lucas leaped to his feet and began pacing. He pointed to the non-descript, aged ceramic vase on his shelf. "The cup appears to be a regular old chipped ceramic cup from the 1st Century, as are the books. Father Lopez, the Holy Man among the Mayas, was performing miracles and thought it was because of the cup. But later, when he forgot the cup, the healings continued. I told you he healed me, didn't I? From Dengue fever! And I don't need my insulin anymore. He's the real deal, you see. A genuine holy man who performs miracles among some of the poorest people on earth. Truly a saint in every definition of the word."

"Lucas, Lucas, come on! Not good enough. You're doing it again. Denying yourself to spare others. Trying to rationalize your way out of issues you can't move past. You're sidestepping this!"

Angelina stood and went to retrieve her purse. "Here!" she nearly yelled, "Look at this! Explain this!" She removed a file from it and tossed it onto his lap. "Dr. Cabrini would like to know how you got the scar on your face. He wants to understand why you are no longer diabetic and why your endocrine system is operating like that of man half your age, and he *really* wants to know how you grew another kidney! I want the whole story. *We* want the whole story, not some made up, hurry up and get it over with Readers Digest version." She huffed for a bit, and then refilled their cups.

"Montoya isn't talking because you swore him to silence," she accused. "That Professor Wolf character in Chiapas said, he's out. He's not involved anymore. He says you have all the information."

"You know what the abbess said to me last week? *Sometimes we have to talk about very unpleasant things in detail in order to heal and move on.* Sound familiar? I've got all night, and I'm not going anywhere until I hear the whole story." She plunked herself down, gave him a stern look, and said, "Let's try again, Lucas. Start easy. Why don't you begin with San Cristobal just before you left for the Lacandon to meet all those nutty people, okay?"

Pope Lucas sighed. He looked at his watch and saw that he had plenty of time.

"If you're not going to believe me, we shouldn't even start with this, Angelina."

"Start talking, old man," she smiled affectionately. "I'll let you know what I think in good time."

"Well..." he began, wistfully. "Some of this is rough stuff, but, let's start in San Cristobal, okay? You really must see the Tzotzil Indian village of Chamula someday. It's in the highlands above San Cristobal. The church is four hundred years old, pretty well kept up, but doesn't have a single pew in which to sit down. Masses are - how can I say it? Quite a bit different than any Catholic Church in the world. The Indians wouldn't even allow a Catholic priest in the place for nearly fifty years. They ran *"Catholic"* services themselves based on traditional village life and a system of *"cargos,"* ritual obligations performed annually that were assigned to individuals in the community. The floor is covered with pine boughs and needles and the saints enclosed in glass cubicles along the walls look just like the Mayans: large noses, coffee colored skin and such. Hundreds of candles burn during services. The white ones are for blessings, the black ones to avoid and nullify curses. They divine illnesses by sacrificing chickens and do all sorts of things that would horrify your abbess at the convent. When Protestant evangelicals started proselytizing in the late 60's, the Indians forced hundreds of people, some of them relatives and family, to leave Chamula when they converted. We should learn something from these Indians," he joked. "It's really a remarkable place that…"

And so it went, late into the night, the pope speaking in detail, sometimes with animation, occasionally with sadness, conjuring up details he had hoped to forget. Angelina asked questions and held his hand. Two hours later, she sat next to her friend as he shed tears and spoke of how afraid he had been, how badly the kidnappers had hurt him, and how alone he had felt.

He spoke of his savior, the strange man that shot the kidnappers and cut Lucas down from his crucifixion. Even this person had abandoned him, giving him a half-full bottle of water, then left him to fever, pain, and crocodiles. He had somehow managed to drag himself to the edge of the ruin and stairway leading down to the sandbar and river below. A small boat lay beached on the north end, but he saw that it was surrounded with crocodiles – and one was moving toward the steps – and he was too weak to move. In the throes of a raging fever, he lost hope, and then his faith. And then he had done the unthinkable. He cursed God for abandoning him, no longer caring whether he died. Then his life had somehow been redeemed and he lived. He awoke from a surreal, bizarre vision about a cunning snake that glistened and reflected light. The serpent's neck was festooned with brocades of purple and red flowers, and then he became aware that he was conscious and that he lay with his head in the Holy Man's lap. Father Lopez had given him water and was talking of his own life as if they were in the middle of a conversation. And then Lucas started feeling better – much better, and it was all a miracle, he was sure.

Angelina stroked his hand. "A miracle. It's a miracle, Lucas."

"But I am nothing but a bookish, meddling, unhealthy old man. I cursed God, and knew when I was dying on the side of that river that He didn't exist, or if he did, was indifferent and really didn't care that I was sick and dying, beaten and tortured." This scared him most, he said, and scarred him deeply, and had somehow fundamentally changed him. He had avoided thinking of it since returning. Had God tested him and found Lucas wanting? Did God really do stuff like that? Why him and not someone else? Was there a grand plan to life, or do we just make it up day to day?

His health restored by the Holy Man, and imbued with new energy, the pontiff had returned determined to move ahead with his plans to reform the creaking bureaucracy and archaic rules of the Vatican. The attempted coup had failed – primarily because of his friend, Sr. Angelina. He could concentrate on reforming a bureaucracy which, he decided, was the easy part. The difficult issue was his unresolved personal realizations – the need to slay the demons of doubt that raised their heads in Chiapas. If prayer was the fuel, and faith the engine, Pope Lucas was concerned that he had been using a faulty or misunderstood engine his whole life. The events in the Lacandon Jungle had broken his heart and shook him to his foundation. The clarity and conviction of his faith, his belief and core values, were what defined him as a person, and he had rejected them during his great trial. He would never be the same again.

Pope Lucas wept again, and his friend Angelina held him until it passed. Finally, he was done, she gathered; the personal bloodletting and catharsis complete, now he could heal.

"Lucas, if you recall, almost all of the holy people of our church from Aquinas and Augustine, to Mother Theresa report that they questioned their faith, felt abandoned, and blamed God. Really, it just seems to be part of the process in making a really good person into a great one. You accomplished incredible things under impossible conditions, Lucas. Maybe you are Indiana Jones!" she joked. "No one else could have done what you did. And God rewarded you. Why you? Why not you! You brought home the cup, the books and the body of our St. Thomas. You returned whole in body – you even have a brand new kidney! Does God hold a grudge? I don't think so, Lucas. God is a lot of things, but I don't think petty is one of them."

They sat quietly for a while, each in their own thoughts, then Angelina prepared another pot of tea. Upon returning, she poured them both a cup, sipped her own steaming brew carefully, then spoke of her friend, Gunther, and his beautiful daughter. She hoped the possibilities were not mere fantasies, but a path to personal happiness. Did God care about personal happiness? She would see.

Morning broke. She rose, looked at the desk clock and mentioned breakfast. The pope declined, saying he must shower and dress and meet the day, but reached and grasped her hand, fervently thanking her, saying, "God bless you, Angelina. God bless you, my friend."

"God bless, you, Holy Father" she returned a big smile. "It's time for you to get to work reforming this bureaucratic mess. I'll see you later today."

Epilogue

"You promised, Holy Father!" accused Angelina. "You said that if it was real you would act on it, you wouldn't bury it in the archives!"

"We're simply not ready yet, Angelina," protested the pope. "There's a process that cannot be circumvented. It doesn't work like this," he attempted to mollify her. "We have to be patient and involve more people. We must invite experts from other fields; archaeology, ancient history, ancient languages, papyrus paper, chemical analysis, and Jewish scholars: maybe even Protestant theologians to examine what we have. There must be a consensus before releasing it. Be assured its authenticity will be attacked anyway. That's just how things work."

He continued, "We may not be able to release the book as a new gospel without presenting the body of St. Thomas. I can guarantee *that* won't go well. Everyone will want to examine it, test it, poke and prod it - cut it open. When items like this are discovered, they have no validity unless you can prove provenance, where it came from and how."

"You're obfuscating! You're trying to let me down easy. I won't stand for it, Lucas! I won't. You promised. *'Whatever it takes to do the right thing,'* were your exact words. Singing a different song now aren't you? If you and Nizzi try to suppress and bury this new gospel, this *Gospel of Jesus' Wife*, I'll release a copy of it I made for myself. I won't stand for it! I won't!"

"If you do, you'll kill it, Angelina! As I said, you must provide credentials and have wide support, otherwise no one takes it seriously. You will doom it before it has a chance." The pope stood, spread his arms wide in a plea. "It will be just like the *Gospel of St. Thomas* that we have now. We have copies of the text from three years ago sent to us by Father Gregory, but it's worthless as a genuine article from which we might glean new insights of early Christianity because it can't be authenticated. Our Papal Inquisitor told us there were seven cylinders. Then he died three years ago in Chiapas. We recovered five. The chances of finding more are extremely remote, Angelina. Although we can say this is what we have now and that we did had the original at one time, it will never be taken seriously. The worst that can happen is to be accused of promoting a forgery and having nothing material to counter the accusation. That's how scholarship works. With new technologies, scams abound and forgeries proliferate. We want no part of that."

Angelina stood and paced. She stopped and turned. "We have the old saint downstairs. There's already rumors here and in Mexico. You can't deliver something that size into the archives without somebody noticing. That's just the way it works. But you somehow don't seem to be as intrigued, or invested in this as I am. But then I guess that's understandable. Tell me, Lucas, have you actually sat down and read the translation?"

The pontiff hesitated. "Well, er...not really," he admitted. "Cardinal Nizzi sent me a summary by email. Been busy with, uh...all this," his arm swept wide to indicate Vatican City.

"You haven't actually read it?" She widened her eyes in disbelief.

The pope squirmed. "Well...I...I said I hadn't, Angelina. I did read the summary though, you know." The pontiff considered he might be arguing about something that he didn't know as well as he should.

Angelina put her index fingers to her temples, then took a deep breath. "Lucas are you familiar with the apocryphal story of Mary Magdalene, Joseph Arimathea, and Marta fleeing to southern France after Christ's death?"

"Of course. I went there, maybe thirty-forty years ago. Southern France - St. Maximin la Ste-Baume. My sister and I traveled there together. Such a beautiful area; rolling, rocky hills and cultivated fields. We saw the gilded skull of Mary Magdalene on display. The tourist narrative in the Visitor Center says the she spent the last thirty years of her life praying and meditating in that beautiful cave." He hesitated, then said. "But there's little evidence for the story. Mostly an apocryphal tale that has persisted in southern France. The Church has never been able to verify it."

He thought a little more then said: "You know, that area became a fertile ground for a heresy. I can't remember what it was called." The pope's pursed his lips as he searched for the link in his brain.

"Cathar." The ever-knowing Angelina supplied him. "The Cathars with those old Knights of Templar treasure stories probably originated there. It was the Albigensian Heresy, one of the first Christian heresies. The Catholics built a chapel in her cavern and claim to have other relics from Mary Magdalene, including her bones."

"Yes, I recall it as you say it. Yes…"

"Back to the present, Holy Father," Angelina prompted. "Sorry for the tone of my voice earlier. I'll try again." She took a deep breath, "It appears you haven't had time to sit down and read the document." She spread her hands wide. "It's not that long, and you read Aramaic, Italian, Spanish, and English very well. This is a translation. It won't take more than thirty minutes, Lucas." She paused. "Half the population on Earth is female, Lucas. Can I remind you that God may be female? Maybe Her name is Isis, Ishtar, Astarte, Mary, or Mother. Can't you take a few moments to read Mary Magdalene's story and see that she is calling out to us from her cave in southern France?"

"Southern France, where the Cathar Heresy took place?"

"Yes, where her remains and cave were discovered in the 13th Century. The text states that she's living in Gaul and that she can't write. That Joseph of Arimathea has brought her because he was concerned about her and the baby. He wrote the text as she told him to."

"Mary Magdalene and the baby?" he repeated.

"Yes, Holy Father."

"Yes," he tapped his lips. "That does sound important. I suppose I can't put it off any longer." He sighed. "Give me a few moments and I'll take a peek at Nizzi's translation." He reached for and began reading the document while Angelina went to his office window and looked out over the red tiled roofs of Vatican City, the wall surrounding the town, and then further, to distant Roman neighborhoods and villages carpeting the famous seven knolls of the ancient city. The eternal Tiber River snaked through the hills.

Angelina turned to walk toward him once, but he waved her off, impatient. His face was almost frightening as he occasionally reread a line. Although the pope was a lifetime student of ancient languages, he rarely had time to pursue his first love nowadays. He read carefully and thoroughly, then read it again. Finally, he sighed and sat back in his chair.

"This translation was seen and approved by Nizzi?"

"Yes, Holy Father."

"The papyrus and ink have been investigated and found to be sufficiently old and made of the correct materials for that era?"

"Yes, Lucas. The papyrus is almost identical to that used in Egypt for a couple hundred years."

The pope hesitated, then said to no one, "A testament, from St. Thomas about Mary Magdalene with a child, saying her husband was Jesus. This isn't just new, it could change everything for the Church."

"Yes, Lucas," she repeated, hanging on every word, waiting for him to arrive at the critical sentence.

"You know, Salvador Lopez is a walking, talking, living saint. A priest. Healing people." Lucas patted his belly. "Miracles. And, he has a wife and child." Lucas sat in thought and Angelina felt she would expire from anticipation.

"I'll release it, Angelina. I'll talk with Nizzi. He'll need to invite experts from the top schools in England, France and Germany - even the United States." He rubbed his eyes, looked at the documents in front of him, then added.

"It really doesn't make any difference what I think or say, my friend," he reflected. "This '*gospel*,' he used his index fingers for emphasis, "doesn't belong to just us and we will not make the ultimate decision. The overwhelming majority of Christians in the world are Catholic or near Catholic if you include our Orthodox and Anglican families. We're easily the largest denomination, about sixty-five percent, but no one follows our lead. Protestants have little or no tradition of scholarship regarding the beginnings of Christianity. Their history begins with Martin Luther in the 16th Century – God bless his constipated soul. Regardless of what I say and think, or what the Church articulates, people will make up their own minds. This *Gospel of Jesus' Wife*, as you call it, will be hailed by people like you and condemned as fraud by traditionalists. Even here in our very own special city, this document will be polarizing."

"Lucas, will you support it or not?"

"Yes. God has brought it to me, or me to it. We'll put it out there and see what happens. The trite phrase is, *'God works in strange ways,'* but I don't think so. Sometimes I think He's very obvious. I don't think He would have teased me into going into the Lacandon and allowed me to come out alive, carrying ancient, holy treasures if He wasn't planning a revolution. Maybe God has decided it's time."

Then he added, "Be careful what you wish for, Angelina. You've wanted an insurrection for a long time. Looks like you're going to get it. People take their religion very seriously. Good, Lord! Look at the Middle East! Consider the Rohingya and Buddhists in Myanmar. Buddhists are supposed to be the most peaceful people in the world. Humanity has murdered, massacred, raped, and tortured more people over religion than almost anything that humankind does. It may sound extreme, but it's not an exaggeration to say that we could end up with a major heresy, or worse, a schism in the Church."

Fin